WHUPPED

By Jim Stevens

Published by Creative Inc., Hermosa Beach, California

ISBN # 978-0-98492473-8

"Whupped" A Novel by Jim Stevens, First edition

For Bill Muhlenfeld

Invaluable help, invaluable friend.

CHAPTER 1

Alyssa, the Bride

I always put down a towel. No way am I going to ruin one-thousand thread count Millesimo sheets, or sleep around a sticky, wet spot the rest of the night.

I'm on my back. He's on his side, propped up on one elbow. He kisses me twice, moves his head down my body and kisses my nipples. He licks the end of his two fingers before his hand goes exactly where I showed him. That first touch turns on my water-works and I'm wet. He gently massages, exactly how I've taught him. In one minute I'll have my first orgasm of the night. He loves it. Male ego, pride, conquest, whatever floats his boat. I could do this myself just as easily, because I've never had a problem in that area. I moan, sigh, and relax. Half of the foreplay is over.

It's my turn.

I gently push him onto his back. I lean over and kiss his lips, neck, and chest. I reach down and take him into my hand. He's like a rock. Jake can get hard thinking about sex. I stroke him as my head heads south, but before I taste him, I pause.

"Jake…"

"What?"

"You were kidding about the wedding shower, weren't you?"

"No."

I stop. My hand releases his penis. "You weren't?"

"No. I'm not going."

My head comes up out of the sheets. "You have to go."

"Why?"

"Because you're the groom."

Jake squirms. "Do you think we could talk about this later?"

"No."

"Alyssa…"

"What, Jake?"

"Can we finish what we're doing and then discuss it?"

"No."

"I'm really horny."

"So?"

"It's been a week."

"Then a few more minutes won't make that much of a difference, will it?"

Jake props himself up and says, "I'm not going."

"You have to go."

"Farrin is throwing the shower for you, not me."

"She invited you," I remind him.

"Because she's cruel."

Farrin is my stepsister.

Jake plops back down onto his back. His erection makes a bulge in the sheet. "Come on, Alyssa."

"You're going, Jake."

"I don't want to go."

"I don't care."

I lie on my back, matching his posture. I pull the sheets and blankets up to my chin, and fold my arms across my chest. Neither of us moves for a few seconds. We must resemble side-by-side corpses waiting for an embalming session.

"They're your friends, not mine," he says, as if he's going to convince me.

"They're *our* friends."

"Name one I've been to a ballgame with, seen naked, or heard fart?"

This is why I hate to argue. What's the point? It's a stupid waste of time. Jake knows he's going to lose, but he has to put up his version of Custer's last stand.

"Look at it from my standpoint, I'll be the only guy there."

"Riley and Milo are coming."

"They don't count."

"They're guys."

"They're gay."

I stare at the ceiling. "Guests will want to see my future husband."

"Show them a picture."

"No."

Jake moves onto his side to face me.

"I'll be there in spirit."

"That won't cut it."

"I could make a funny video and you could play it for everybody during lunch, then we could put it on *YouTube*."

I'm getting angry. "You should be there because I want you to be there."

"A guy at a wedding shower is like a designer dress at a Walmart."

"I wouldn't know, Jake, I've never been to a Walmart."

"A Cracker Jack ring at Tiffany's?"

His second attempt at humor is as pathetic as his first.

"Alyssa," Jake moves closer, putting his arm across me; but I raise my arms so he doesn't rest his across my chest. "You know we haven't been very close lately."

I don't make a sound.

"Maybe we need to settle back, review the situation from another angle…"

I continue silence.

"… after we finish having sex?"

"No."

"Remember, we're not supposed to go to sleep mad."

"Who's going to sleep?"

Jake smiles.

Only a man would take that comment as an invitation.

Men and sex, *my God*. It's the first thing they want when they meet us, and the last thing they want before passing out at night. Sex may have its purposes, but it is hardly the be-all, end-all of everything in life. Sex doesn't solve problems, and only temporarily alleviates stress. Matter of fact it's probably caused more problems and added more stress than anything I can imagine. But could you ever convince a man of that? No way.

Jake nuzzles his nose into the crook of my neck. "Alyssa, we've had way too much wedding, and not enough *us* lately."

I push him off me. I'm mad. If he thinks he's getting any tonight, after pulling this bullshit, he's smokin' something.

"How the hell would you know? You haven't done shit so

far."

"Because you haven't let me."

"Well, now is your chance. Go to the shower."

"It's the principle, Alyssa."

"Principle, what principle? It'll be two hours out of your Saturday, Jake. Whatever game is on TV, you can record. What the hell is such a big deal here?"

"Oh, come on, I'll sit there with nothing to do around a bunch of yippy women, getting drunk, while you rip open packages like it's Christmas morning."

"You want to help open the gifts?"

"No."

"Why are you fighting me on this, Jake?"

"Because I don't want to go."

"I don't want to do a lot of things I have to do either; but I do them because they are the right things to do."

"Name one."

I'm hard-pressed to come up with one so quickly. I raise my voice instead. "It's not like I'm asking you to clean up after Mister Chips."

Mister Chips is my horse.

"How about if I show up at the beginning, stand at the door, say 'Hello' to everyone, and leave you and your friends to have the time of your lives?"

"When are you going to say 'thanks' for the gifts?"

"Later."

"When?" I ask. "When you write out the thank-you cards?"

"Okay, I'll come at the end and thank everyone on their way out."

"Don't argue with me, Jake. You're coming to our wedding shower."

"I don't want to. I'm not going." Jake sits up against the headboard, folds his arms across his chest, and doesn't speak. He reminds me of an old doll I once had. Petulant Patty.

I wait. He doesn't speak. I wait longer. He still doesn't speak. This is unusual.

I sit up, face him. "Tell you what, Jake."

"What?"

"I'll do for you, if you do for me."

He waits.

I reach under the sheet, grab Little Jake's two buddies and roll them around in my hand like a pair of dice. "I'll give you a choice: You either come to the shower or not come at all."

Little Jake rises to attention, casting his vote.

"You drive a hard bargain, Alyssa."

CHAPTER 2

Gideon, the Best Man

Strip Clubs. Boxy, windowless structures reeking of musty, spilled beer and old cigars, with a side-scent of cheap perfume. They are mostly populated by a clientele of horny losers who aren't getting enough at home, or don't get any at all. Add bad, crackle-loud, dated music, which is chosen by DJs who actually believe they have a talent for picking tunes. And no strip joint would be complete without a couple of out-of-shape, steroidal bouncers who thought they once "coulda been a contenda." Whether it is a skuzzy place off the interstate, a trying-to-be-classy West Hollywood club, or the suburban spot we're now in, the modus operandi remains the same, fuckhead guys ogling naked girls, an entertainment as old as time and timeless in its everlasting appeal.

There is an Oscar-winning movie to be made about a strip club, and I'm going to make it. Nobody knows these places like I do. I've studied them for years—up close and personal. This is my audience, my demo, my people, my milieu. I don't come here for the tits, but the stories behind the boobs. The women, not the men. What brought them here? What keeps 'em here?

Guys come for the women. Up on the stage or in their laps, women contort their bodies in pseudo sexual variations for the delight and money of customers, who can only dream of such an actual experience. These are women at the top of their game, because after this career is over, they will never have another job that will reap them as much coin for so little effort. Few can dance, and even fewer can dance well, as if this would ever be a prerequisite for employment. Large breasts, a tight ass, or the look of a school girl is what gets them hired. Tips, stuffed in their gstrings, are what keeps them employed.

My film will be a documentary. I'll call it *A Day in the Night of a Strip Club*.

"You two look at boobs all day," Jake says as we find three seats at the edge of the stage, "then to unwind, you go to a titty bar?"

"There is motive behind the madness," I tell him, as the dancer frees her breasts from the lacy shackles of a Victoria Secret bra.

Conrad says, "I'm only here for professional purposes."

We-Jake, Conrad, and I-watch a girl with too much cellulite on her thighs, and too many spaces between her teeth. "Plus," I add, "I'm always on the lookout for something interesting."

"So, you consider this part of your job?" Jake asks.

"Yeah," I tell him, "it's a tough job, but somebody has to do it."

The girl squeaks as she slides down the pole.

"I wonder if chafing is a workplace hazard," Conrad muses.

The stripper lands on the floor with a little too much oomph, swings her legs out from under her, and comes up on all fours to do a series of yoga cat-cows to the beat of some awful rap song. Her breasts hang down, reminding me of two, side-by-side ICBM missiles heading for earth.

"Now, take this girl," Conrad says, "you two probably see her as nothing more than a sex object, but my trained eye sees a woman who has made the same mistake that ninety percent of the women who get enhancements make."

"Putting a foreign substance in their bodies that could leak and cause them irreparable harm or even death?" Jake asks and answers.

"No," Conrad calmly replies. "Smorgasbord Syndrome."

Jake says, "Eyes are bigger than their stomach?"

"So to speak."

I smile. This is a typical conversation for the three of us, which we've been having since we were kids.

As the girl crawls around the stage, purring, growling, and licking her chapped lips, Conrad explains, "Girls who have gone their whole lives with a flat chest get this idea that if they are going to get 'em bigger, they might as well err toward the upsize." So they opt for the C or D cup instead of the B cup that fits their body."

Conrad's the expert.

The stripper evidently has been tipped off as to who I am, and ignores the rest of the guys at ringside. She squats right in front of me. Her knees on each side of my head are inches away from my ears. I smell heavy, bad perfume. I'll call it "Eau du French Whore." I hear Conrad continue, "If most women were smart like Alyssa and made it look perfectly natural…"

A surprised Jake is quick to point out, "Alyssa's never had a boob job."

"Yes, she has."

"No, she hasn't."

I look away from the girl to see my two best friends eye-to-eye.

Jake raises his voice. "I think I would know if my fiancée has had work done."

"Not if it was done by someone as good as me," Conrad calmly replies.

"Alyssa would have told me."

"Why?"

"Because that's what you do when you're engaged to be married."

I turn toward Jake, "Did you tell her about our weekend in Acapulco?"

He answers, "That was before we met."

"She still might find it of interest," I say.

"Fine, I'll tell her," Jake says, "but I want to wait for the right moment."

The stripper's left nipple almost pokes me in the eye.

"Alyssa's been enhanced," Conrad says. "Sorry to be the one to break you the news."

"I don't think so." Jake holds his ground.

"Ask her."

I see Jake pull back with a non-reaction and, at the same time, feel the girl's hand rub across the side of my face. She is giving me a not-so-subtle smile. I give her a wave as she moves to a guy with a ten-dollar bill stuck to his forehead.

"What is it with you and slutty women?" Jake asks, fleeing his conversation with Conrad.

"After a hard day at work, I smell like sex," I explain.

"Are you going to go in the back room and do her?" Jake asks.

"I doubt it."

"You don't want to do her," Conrad interrupts, "she's on her period."

"What?"

"The girl is riding a cotton pony, as you two idiots would say."

"And how the hell would you know that?" Jake asks Conrad in more of a statement than a question.

"Skin tone changes," Conrad says. "A woman's oil secretions drop off drastically before she starts her period, causing her skin to get puffy. And, on her first day, less blood circulates in the superficial layers of the epidermis, which turns her skin pale."

"That's probably why she hasn't dropped her drawers," I conclude.

"Look where her make-up starts and stops, and you can tell every time."

"So glad to see you're putting all those years of medical school to good use, Conrad," Jake says.

"I'm only here to help."

The music ends and the stripper walks around, picking up the articles of clothing she recently shed. She pulls the bills out of her short-shorts and stacks them in her hand, getting a quick count and gives me a quick wave before she disappears behind the curtain.

The DJ announces, "All her friends call her the 'little lady' but you can call her Ruby. Ladies and gentlemen give it up for our next little slice of heaven."

Another dancer pops out from behind the curtain, wearing an outfit with enough sequins to blind Elvis.

"How are the wedding plans going?" I ask Jake.

"Great."

"She has you tagging behind her at Neiman Marcus…I mean Needless Mark-up, writing down the wants and don't-wants for the prize registry?" Conrad asks.

"No."

"She will."

"No, she won't."

"There isn't a groom alive who hasn't had to endure that torture," I tell him.

The stripper is prancing around to some eighties song by one of those girl groups, the Bangles, maybe? If this is the extent of her dancing ability, she better start getting undressed soon.

"So, Jake, how is it *really* going?" I keep the topic alive.

Jake says, "I'm surprised more people don't get divorced while planning their weddings."

Conrad asks, "Why do you even bother?"

"It's not like I have a choice."

"You always have a choice," I tell him.

"No, you don't," Jake says. "Women get into this zone before the wedding. They enter this new dimension where all the planets have to revolve around them in order to sustain their pre-planning marital existence."

"You don't say?" Conrad asks, with sarcasm as thick as biscuits and gravy.

"Obviously, you two have never been on your way to the altar," Jake says.

"Maybe we can help break her out of it?" I suggest.

"Please, don't."

Jake Dombrowski, Conrad Blaine, and I, Gideon Batch, have been friends since St. Theresa Grammar School. We grew up Catholic, in a white, middle-class, Los Angeles suburb, where dads went off to work at jobs they didn't like, and moms stayed home to raise their perfectly planned families that never turn out the way they planned. We were the three amigos of fun, frolic, and fooling around. I was the bad-boy troublemaker, Conrad the kid too smart for his own good, and Jake was the dreamer. Jake came up with the schemes, Conrad figured out how best to do them, and I led the way, carrying them out.

One time Jake "mistakenly" kicked the fifth grade girls' kickball onto the roof. Conrad, being the savior, arrived to convince Mister Steve, the school's illegal-alien janitor, to get out his ladder to retrieve the ball. Just as the dimwitted maintenance man gets on top of the roof and disappears, I sneak around and remove the ladder. The recess bell rings. We all march back to class and are soon serenaded with the loud, echoing anguished cries of, "Halp, Seestor, halp."

We were thick as thieves, best of friends, and blood brothers.

There was this priest at St. Theresa, Father Celcius, who loved to inflict pain on prepubescent boys who were not fast enough to outrun him. Someone said he was a professional wrestler before he became a priest; but I suspect he was just a run-of-the-mill pervert. One day this prowling, sadistic pedophile sneaks up behind me and puts me in a hammerlock. "Let's see you get out of this one, sonny-boy."

The bastard was putting on the pressure and, no matter which way I squirmed, I couldn't break the hold. The crowd gathered around to watch the slaughter, but no one came to my aid. I was helpless, tears welled in my eyes, and the last thing I wanted was to let this asshole see me cry.

"Suffer, boy, suffer," Celcius said into my ear.

I remember looking up to see Jake push his way to the front of the crowd. "Let him go," he said

Celcius applied more pressure. Spittle formed at the corners of his mouth. I still remember the sickening stink of tobacco, raw onion and communion wine.

"Let him alone, you horny bastard," Jake said, stepping less than an arm's length away.

"Your turn next, potty mouth," growled Father Celsius.

Jake looked right at me. He knew I couldn't take much more. "I said, *leave him alone!*"

Celcius freed one arm to reach out and swipe at Jake, but missed and fell off balance. I can still see Jake make a fist, wind up, and throw a right uppercut smack dab into Father Celcius' crotch. His family jewels were crushed like fresh walnuts.

The air exploded out of the priest's lungs. His face turned bright red, and his tongue shot out of his mouth. He broke the hold and collapsed into a fold of fetal mush, holding his nuts with both his hands, the priestly steeple pointing downward. A whimper of "goddamnit" could be heard just before the crowd erupted into a cheering frenzy. I stepped back, feeling the blood running again into my arm. Jake is beside me, a bit amazed he actually did what he just did, unable to take his eyes off his prize. Celcius let out a cry of anguished pain. It is music to our ears.

Celcius squirmed on the ground, panting, pleading, praying for God's help. I stepped in front of Jake, reached down, gripped the priest's collar and lifted him up so his red face was only inches from mine. "You ever lay a hand on me or my friends again,

Father Faggot, I will put my foot so far up your ass, you'll be saying mass with a sneaker in your throat."

Someone shouted, "Sister Superior's coming."

I planted my foot down, as hard as humanly possible, in the exact spot Jake had already hit. Celcius' second cry of pain was even sweeter than his first. We ran away before the boss nun arrived.

"I owe you one," I told my friend.

If not the fondest memory of grammar school, it certainly ranks in my Top Ten. We have been watching each other's backs ever since. At this moment, it is my turn.

"Jake, do you really believe Alyssa is the woman you should marry?" I ask, ignoring the bad stripper on stage.

"What the hell kind of question is that?" He looks at me with disbelief in his eyes.

"Maybe I didn't phrase that as well as I should have."

"No, I don't believe so," Conrad says.

"I wonder if you two are compatible."

"Jesus Christ, Gideon."

Conrad and I have previously discussed this topic, and, although he wasn't as convinced about it as me, I'm baffled why he sits there giving me little or no support. Conrad's supposed to be the smart one in our group.

"We've been going out for over a year," Jake says.

"Is that enough time?"

"You ever go out with anyone that long?" Jake asks me.

"I'm a bad example," I tell him.

"Duh."

I press on, "You said yourself, it hasn't been easy."

"Relationships are never easy," Jake says. "You have to work at 'em to make them work."

"Interesting line of reasoning," Conrad says, "but where do you draw the line on working too much?"

"What the fuck are you talking about?" Jake asks with fervor in his voice.

The chick on the stage is down to her high heels, one nipple earring and a gold thong, and I couldn't care less.

"I mean," I say, "have you really sat down and thought about this?"

"Of course, I have."

"Why her, then?"

"I love her."

"Besides that?"

"We got great chemistry."

"*Chemistry* is a fucking chick term."

"Okay. We want the same things. We have the same goals. We're going to make great kids."

"And that's why you're getting married?"

"Yes."

"To have kids?"

"Yes."

"Way to go, Darwin," Conrad adds.

"Shouldn't there be a lot more to consider?" I ask.

"Yes."

"Like what?"

"You want a list?"

"Do you have one?"

"No."

"Maybe you should."

"You just don't like Alyssa," Jake says. "You're still pissed at what happened at the Junior League benefit."

"No," I say, "but do you know why members of the Junior League never participate in orgies?"

Jake gives me a dirty look.

"Too many 'thank you' cards to write."

Conrad laughs, but not Jake.

"What the hell is going on here?" Jake asks.

I am hesitant to answer honestly. This is not the time. He wouldn't take it the right way.

"You know, I think this is pretty shitty, you bringing up this bullshit a couple weeks before I'm getting married," Jake says.

"Sorry," I say and turn to watch the stripper. "I was just trying to watch your back."

CHAPTER 3

Jake, the Groom

I hate this. It is absolute torture. I am the only man in the middle of thirty-seven women.

We're in a big, private room. Flowers are everywhere. Big arrangements, not those cheap fern-laden bouquets. Soft rock music plays in the background. Platters of finger food are laid out for the taking. I'm the only one eating the big nuts wrapped in bacon. The mountain of booty is piled high, laying there, just waiting to be ripped open. Booze is flowing. The color of the martinis clash with some of the wildly inventive fingernail polishes being worn. The women sip cosmos. I nurse a light beer, a domestic, light beer.

The attendees are mostly late twenty-something or early thirties. All hot, not a bow-wow in this bunch. The few forty-somethings are just as attractive, they just have to work harder at it. All dressed to the nines. Everyone wore her best. Women dress to impress other women, although they'd never admit that to a man. And this is the perfect place to do so.

I didn't put on a tie.

I know the women. Seen 'em around, been out with them, talked over the phone. I can't remember each and every name. I just keep smiling as each takes her turn to come over and touch, hug, or run a hand over mine, as clever banter and inconsequential comments are exchanged. Some bump up next to me, rubbing their tight, gym or surgeon-sculpted bodies, against mine. The friction would give any other guy a massive erection, but I have to hold myself back. This is not the time or place for a woody.

Perfect teeth, white sexy smiles—the kind you see on TV that look like they could jump out and bite you. Their makeup is subtle, because few need much. Not only do their flawless coiffed styles

14

fit each face perfectly, but each hair follicle emits its personal pheromone, which intoxicates sexual senses. Along with their looks, they've got brains, or at least college credits. Some graduated with a Mrs. Degree, which will guarantee a rich and prosperous life. They walk, talk, and act with an identical air of superiority, the kind you get from having lots of money. These women were either born, married, or divorced into it. They all have uppity first names: Anastasia, Brooke, Jocelyn. There's not a Moesha or Sue or Rashid in the group. Some are Jewish, but there isn't a Jewish nose to be seen. Some sport ice cube-sized rocks on their ring fingers. If they don't have the left hand, third finger filled, they don a diamond someplace else to alert possible suitors of their level of expectation.

But what really sets these women apart from the regular female hoi polloi are their shoes. What is it with women and shoes? They certainly don't wear them to impress men. Men never look that far down. High-heeled footwear has to be uncomfortable, balancing on three and four inches is a feat in itself, and will cause lumbar problems when they're covering-up their gray. The amount of space given to pumps in a closet is ridiculous. How many shades of black does one really need? If I added up the equivalent values of all the designer shoe leather in this room, I'd probably reach the GNP of Angola.

The women mill around. They've all done this before. It's my first time. I'm a rookie among seasoned vets. They enjoy it. I don't. I'd rather be at a bar, watching the Dodgers with Conrad and Gideon.

The word goes out to be seated. Individuals search place settings until they find the folded piece of cardboard with their names printed in fancy script, then hover over the chair not wanting to be the first to sit. I notice three women flipping the cards and reseating themselves according to their wishes. One, in what she thinks is a subtle and unseen move, exchanges one card from her table for a card at the table behind her.

I'm off to the left, at the farthest table from the guest of honor. I've been seated next to Farrin, my pseudo-punk, future sister-in-law. I wonder whose idea that was? In her black leather pants and studded rhinestone jacket, she stands out more than I do. There are eight other women at the table. They all are chatting, snickering, and giggling, undoubtedly in the middle of the first giddy liquor stop on the road to getting skunk-drunk. The waiters bring on the Pinot Grigio and begin to fill crystal. How anyone could drink this crappy wine is a mystery. The only drink sweeter is Kool-Aid. A couple glasses of Pinot on top of a couple of cosmos are going to produce some head-banging hangovers.

The actions of the waiters break the stream of small talk and I use the opportunity to glance over at the woman who will be my wife.

Alyssa sits at the head of the #1 table, surrounded by a mountain of gifts, chatting aimlessly as compliments and congratulations arrive in unstoppable waves. I am always in awe at the sight of her. A more beautiful woman is hard to imagine. She has long blonde hair, flawless skin, a twenty-two-inch waist, perfectly shaped tush, long, slender legs, and perfectly natural—no matter what Conrad says—breasts. Alyssa's breezy print dress accentuates her curves and puts the other women at the table, in the room, in California, in America, into a lesser category. Women always dress their best to compete with their peers; Alyssa has no peer.

I smile, but she doesn't see me.

I am absolutely infatuated with this woman. Besides her beauty, she has style, quality and substance. As a teen, she worked as a "petting" volunteer at the LA Zoo. Now, she gives autistic kids rides on her horse. She was the Secretary/Treasurer of her Junior League chapter.

Farrin sits, looks at the faux-tuxedo wearing man pouring her wine and says, "You look familiar."

The waiter, no doubt an out-of-work actor (this is LA don't forget), gives her a mischievous smile.

Lunch is served. Salad Nicoise, grilled salmon, vegetable medley. The married women dig in with gusto, single ones nibble. Sweet wine causes sweeter laughter, although I haven't heard a funny line yet. I continue to be cordial, even engaging, making myself available for needless and pointless chitchat. I'm dying for a burger and fries. I don't belong here. When I told Gideon and Conrad where I would be this afternoon, they were on me like a cheap suit. It is amazing how many ways I can be called a "pussy."

"Squeeeeegle."

The shrill, ear-splitting shriek fills the room like an air-raid siren. The magnified wail, a cross between a squeal and a giggle, whips me back into reality.

"Squeeeeegle."

The sound bounces off the walls, echoes into my ear canals. Each time a gift is unwrapped another sqeeeeegle reverberates.

"Oh, potpourri, I love potpourri," Alyssa announces to the assembled, raising the unopened, but pungent present.

Farrin whispers in my ear, "Potpourri is from someone who got potpourri at her own wedding shower."

"It will go perfect in the new bathroom," Alyssa forces a phony smile of thanks and moves onto the next gift, a box of perfumed soaps.

Yet another item *for the both of us*.

And on and on we go. Me, thirty-seven women, and two gay guys.

Glass after glass of Pinot Grigio is refilled and refilled again. The women don't speak to one another; they chatter back-and-forth reminding me of a troop of monkeys on Animal Planet.

We, and I use the term loosely, receive picture frames, sheets, a fondue set, napkin rings, two throw blankets, flutes, a Pilates ball, and perfumed stationery—all the things I've always wanted, but never could afford to buy. I'm as excited as a little kid ripping open a three-pack of pajamas on Christmas morning.

Cherries Jubilee is the dessert. Whoever thought of pouring high octane, flaming brandy over ice cream must have been one sick pastry chef.

Flaming or not, the women dig in, as if they have never met a dessert they didn't like. After a diet-sensitive lunch, a load of fatty calories will help balance out their systems. I faintly hear a couple of ladies promise to "work it off later." The fruity, slushy dessert disappears from plates quicker than peanuts at a ballgame. A sugar-high cacophony of chatter, clinking wine glasses, whoops, guffaws, and the scraping of last bits of burnt cherry off plates fill the room. The high-pitched plethora of female blather stings my eardrums. I am the only human in the room seated quietly, bored, and uncomfortable. Am I having a good time, or what?

The energy level hits a crescendo, and then falls quickly, like a deflating, pin-pricked balloon. It is the crash from the Jubilee sugar-high, like sixty seconds between rounds, the pause before the next thunderclap, the digestive calm after the food storm. If there were guys in the room, they would sit back and release massive burps, farts or other signs of bodily pleasure, and feel much better for it. Instead, the ladies shift in their seats, readjusting whatever needs a bit more room for their now- bloated tummies. Some sigh, a few yawn. Almost all sit back to relish the temporary gastronomical bliss of almost-gluttony.

I am not psychic, but something strange is about to happen. I can feel it. Looking around, there isn't a waiter in sight. The outer doors are closed. The air conditioning is off. The piped-in music is suddenly silent. I wonder if we are the victims of a terrorist plot and gas is about to be released into the vents that will render us unconscious while a group of masked, crazed terrorists burst in to steal all the shoes from the now-anesthetized ladies' feet.

Finally, a minute hum can be heard. I search for its origin. I turn my head to discover the noise emanates from above, in the center of the room where an ancient, antique 1980's disco ball starts to slowly turn and pick up speed. As if on cue, the chandeliers switch off. The room is plunged into darkness. An immediate gasp is heard from the women, not so much of fear, but of surprise. Suddenly, bullets of laser light shoot out of the disco ball spinning out in the frenzied staccato of a 1970's strobe. There is a rustle of activity in the rear of the room as the doors are heard opening then slamming shut. I look over at Alyssa and see through the streaks of light that she has no idea what is going on. The sonic boom hits in the form of a pounding baseline pulsating through the room like a Southern California earthquake. It is an opening musical riff that I have heard before, but can't seem to place immediately. Only when Donna Summer belts out "*Looking for a lover like no other…*" does my "Name That Tune" memory kick in.

Spotlights illuminate two of the waiters, who have traded their kitchen tuxedos for actual formal wear. Every eye in the room focuses on them as they dance their way to the space between the four tables. Their hips gyrate and fists pump like boxers-in-training to the disco beat. They spare no energy or expense as they perform dance moves that are hardly practiced or polished. Less than a minute into the song, they strip off their tuxedo jackets, leaving only Day-Glo bow ties above bare, greased, sculpted chests.

You couldn't shock the women any more than if you hit each with a cattle prod. Their eyes follow the rippling pectorals and six-pack abs bouncing before them as the music increases in volume and tempo. It takes no time whatsoever for the spectators to become part of the show. Some stand for a better view. Some, mesmerized by the writhing, muscled flesh, bounce their shoulders, swing their arms, and toss their heads in primal unison with the performer. Many sing along with Donna who promises *"Gonna get some hot stuff, gonna get some love tonight…"*

Alyssa is the most shocked of all, except for maybe yours truly. She sits, slack-jawed, her back pushed against the chair, eyes darting from one dancer to the other. If she could speak, nobody would hear a word, for the atmosphere is thick with sound and fury. She doesn't like this, it's obvious. I see her glare at Farrin, who stands, whooping it up. Alyssa has, no doubt, accused, tried, and convicted her stepsister of perpetrating this tasteless debauchery upon her and her guests. I can also surmise that Alyssa knows she is powerless to stop the spectacle. By doing so she would not only be depriving her guests of their after-dinner pleasure, but labeling herself a prude. No woman wants to be known as a prude. Just like guys never want to be called a pussy.

The music comes to a sudden halt. The back door opens. Spotlights hit the head waiter, now dressed as a groom. The music segues into the second song: "Get Down Tonight" by KC and his Sunshine Band. Our waiter, the star of the show, dances his way to the front of the room, takes his rightful spot between the lesser entertainers, and begins to flaunt his equipment. One glance and I suspect the guy has either added a cucumber into his too-tight pants, or he is a candidate for the *Guinness Book of World Records*. Unfortunately, we'll all find out soon enough. He bounces his lower torso back and forth with such gusto, that I won't be surprised if he dislocates a hip.

The women love every second. Guilty pleasure knows few bounds. They swing and sway, arms flailing, heads bobbing up and down, whole bodies pulsating with each of KC's notes. I hear Farrin point at the main man's crotch and scream, "Now I remember you."

My initial instinct, lying in the bed that night, arguing with Alyssa, was correct. I should have never come to this party. I have no clue as to what to do. My face feels warm and sweaty. I must be a radiating beacon of embarrassment.

Liquor, sugar, and adrenaline have been shaken, not stirred. The concoction is like a mad, orgiastic blender of abandon. The women scream, wail, laugh, sing, whoop, and holler. We're a long way from a squeeegle.

I stand, back away slowly from the table, trying to sneak away, when suddenly my chair is swept up by one of the dancers, who uses it to climb upon the table, making it his personal stage. I drift backwards toward the outer wall, about to make my escape as the dancing groom approaches my lady-of-the-day at the #1 table.

The spectators squeeze in to form impenetrable walls around each dancer and writhe wildly in anticipation of what is to come next. The performers do not disappoint. At the loudest riff in KC's melody, the three men rip off their tear-away pants, leaving little left to anyone's imagination. Lights change. A black light replaces the white lasers and strobes its purple ink through the disco ball. Spotlights go black and suddenly all that can be seen are the Day-Glo thongs of the three dancers bouncing at the women's eye level. The effect gives a whole new meaning to *follow the bouncing balls*.

The spotlights come back up. The women are bumping and grinding along with the dancers. Some replicate the bad dance moves. The two gay guys, Riley and Milo, must think they have died and gone to heaven. They push the female competition out of their way to stuff dollar bills into crotches, and manage to get close enough to sniff the sweaty, unclad butt cheeks in front of them.

I move to the side, positioning myself to see Alyssa's eyes open wide as a man's crotch pulsates, just inches from her nose. He repeatedly squats, his pelvis riveting back-and-forth in a mindless, sexual frenzy. She seems to be in a state of suspended animation, transfixed by the sights, sounds, and raw, truly raw, energy engulfing her. She hates this. I know she does. I want to stop it, but can't. The song is playing forever; it must be the extended version.

I slink out the back door like the kid who didn't get picked to play in the kickball game. I close the door behind me, trying to at least muffle KC and his Sunshine Band, and am met with a different kind of noise. Raucous, almost hysterical laughter bursts from my two best friends, Gideon and Conrad. They lay on the floor doubled up, clutching their guts, tears in their eyes, laughing so hard they will be sore in the morning.

"You did this."

They can't answer; but they can point, which they do, right at me, and laugh even louder.

Conrad chokes out, "Aren't you glad you came?"

I have nothing better to do than to stand before my two friends and watch as they convulse on the floor. Nobody likes to be left out of the joke, especially if the joke is on you. From inside, there is a loud whoop and holler, followed by rousing cheers and applause. I hear the door open behind me to see three might-as-well-be-naked men come out and give thumbs-up to Gideon.

I want their laughter to stop, but it doesn't.

An unseen power overtakes me and I turn around and see Alyssa. She stops next to me, stands with her hands on her hips, hovering over the two hyenas beneath, and says, "I should have known who'd be responsible for this."

CHAPTER 4

Alyssa, the Bride

I wish one of these bride's magazines would have had an article on "What To Do If Your Shower Gets Hijacked." Was that tacky or what? I could have killed those two idiots.

Mark my words. Nobody is going to screw this up again. Everything will be perfect from this point on. This is my wedding, my time, and I'm going to have it my way. I'm not letting my mother get close, or my ex-stepmother, or my father's halfwit girlfriend. I'll do it all myself. If I have to put shock collars on Gideon and Conrad to keep them away, just watch me. I don't have my job to worry about anymore and I'm sure I can get Dad to go along with just about anything. I've waited for this my entire life and I'm not letting it be anything less than perfect. My wedding would make Princess Di proud.

"Spode or the Revere?"

"Spode sounds like an STD."

"Jake…"

"If you pick the Spode, better put penicillin on the list."

"Could you please be serious?"

"Alyssa, I don't care."

"You should. We don't want to get gifts we have to take back."

"Oh, come on, you're going to take back half the stuff whether it was on our list or not."

I take a deep sigh and move on to the housewares department.

We are in my favorite store, Neiman-Marcus. They know me. I know it. They offered to send a limo over to get us today, but I declined. Overkill makes Jake uncomfortable. Not that he's comfortable now, standing behind me with the clipboard, marking the computer printout like a personal assistant.

"How about if we put down matching snowboards, a pool

table, and season tickets for the Lakers?"

"Jake…"

"I'm serious."

"You ask for gifts you use to start your life together," I say.

"Like the needlepoint Christmas tree skirt?"

I take the printout out of his hands. "Why are you fighting me on this?"

"Because, no matter what I say, it is not going to make a difference."

"That's not true." I spot an interesting crystal salt and pepper set. "You should help to help pick out the glassware." I hold the salt shaker up to the light.

"The six-hundred dollar, crystal beer mugs that no one will give us?"

"You might be surprised." The shakers are only eighty-dollars; forget 'em.

He follows me to Kitchen Appliances.

"Do we want a Cuisinart?" I ask.

"Neither of us cook."

"One of us may have to learn."

"Is that a threat, an order, or a statement of fact?" he asks.

"You pick."

I reread the printout, tapping a fingernail against an incisor, that's what I do when I'm deep in thought. "It might be best if we eliminated all the small appliances until we see what we will have as built-ins, in the new kitchen."

"I had the same thought when I got up this morning."

"Not going to put down any kitchen doodads, either." I cross out a whole section on the list. "I really think we are making great progress here."

"Are we done yet?"

"No."

I didn't come down on Jake after the shower. He didn't know. I wish he didn't have such cretins for friends. He considers them the brothers he never had. I never had any brothers, but you don't hear me complaining.

Conrad is the lesser of the two evils. One on one I can deal with him. He is as sharp as a tack, can talk about anything, best

Trivial Pursuit player in the universe, and wears English custom-made suits. He's tall, with black hair, a rock-hard body, and I'm positive he gets facials. He's the hottest plastic surgeon in Beverly Hills. I have considered setting him up with a few of my friends, but I suspect he has a major commitment problem. Gideon, he's a spawn of the devil. And even if he didn't do what he does for a living, he'd still be wicked. Maybe five-ten, with hair no one could pull a comb through. He lives in jeans, wears Nike's, thinks he's a film auteur. Hollywood wannabe is what he is. After we're married, Jake will be spending a heck of a lot less time doing whatever the three of them do together.

I love Jake. He will make the perfect husband. We have great chemistry. He is an unpolished diamond waiting to be encased in a spectacular setting. Loyal, honest, willing to compromise, fair, and most important of all, he adores me. His sense of humor can be a little much, but I can ignore that; and he is a bit over-sexed, but that will fade in time. He loves women, but would never play around on me. On that point, I would stake my life.

I'm sure some people say I'm marrying down, but I don't care. So, I have a couple of years on him, so what? Jake and I want the same things: kids, house, SUVs, and private schools. We fit. We're compatible. He lets me be me, which, I realize, isn't always easy. Jake has done more to help me though my trust issues than any person on the face of the earth, including a long line of shrinks.

Jake is one of the few guys my dad has actually liked. Daddy hired him, that's how we met. And Dad will turn over the business to him some day, but hardly soon. The only way my dad will ever leave the trash business is to be carried out, no pun intended.

We can handle problems. We even share one: We both have walking embarrassments for mothers. The only difference being his has no clue and mine has no excuse.

I love Jake. Jake loves me. We're going to make the perfect couple.

"Here is a fascinating item," Jake calls out from the nursery section of the store, "a Calder mobile with an iPhone app, which downloads and plays the top fifty nursery rhymes and songs."

"No, dear," I tell him, "we wait for the baby shower to receive those items."

CHAPTER 5

Jake, the Groom

Conrad is supposed to be downstairs, waiting. He's not. It takes four trips around the block to find a spot. Parking is a bitch in Beverly Hills.

Rejuvenature, Inc. is located on the top floor of sleek, steel file cabinet stretching to the sky. The suite resembles more of law office than a medical facility. There is an oak reception desk, with a stunning blonde in a designer outfit, answering phones and greeting the "guests." No smock-wearing, fat, middle-aged assistant behind a sliding glass window in this place. The couches are plush, comfortable and clean; the chairs leather, the coffee table teak. The magazines, all current, are *Vogue, Cosmopolitan*, and *GQ*. There is a small engraved plaque stating, "Wi-Fi Available." The carpet is a warm, subtle shade of gray. The art on the wall looks to me, to be stupid and horribly expensive. Some designer had a very profitable field day with this assignment.

"May I help you?"

"I'm here for Conrad."

"You have an appointment with Doctor Blaine?" Incredulously put.

The other two women in the waiting room, who are young and hardly in need of any re-do work, glance up from their iPhones to get a better listen.

"Actually, he has an appointment with me."

"He does?"

"Tell him Jake's here."

Barbie, at least that's what the nameplate on the desk says, punches a line on her phone console and speaks. "A Mister Jake here for Doctor Blaine." She waits, listens, and relays to me, "He'll be a minute. You can wait over there."

"Tell him to hurry up."

Barbie answers, "No, I don't do that."

I take a seat between the two women, who must think I'm going in for a procedure. I nervously page through a magazine, glance up to see the women trying not to notice me. After five minutes, I return to Barbie, the receptionist on a clothing budget. "Could you call him and tell him to hurry up?"

"Ah, no."

Both women stare as I return to my seat. I make eye contact and say, "If you've waited as long as I have to become a woman, you'd be in a hurry, too."

Each does a poor job of pretending not to have heard what she just heard.

Conrad walks out the door, dressed in a three-thousand-dollar suit and two-hundred-dollar tie, carrying his little black bag with him.

"What are you going to do, shoot some Botox in the car on the way up?"

"You never know when a wrinkle will scream to be filled."

Conrad smiles at the ladies patiently waiting and says, "You look fabulous," and makes his way to the elevator bank. "Gideon called, he's still on set. We'll have to pick him up on the way."

"No."

"He said his star had a meltdown."

"That'll add an hour."

"Quit complaining."

There is a parking ticket on my Volvo's windshield. "If you would have been waiting downstairs like I asked, I wouldn't have gotten this."

"If you would have put two quarters in the meter, you wouldn't have gotten it, either."

"I hate change."

"Give it," Conrad puts out his hand for the ticket, "I'll pay it."

I hold back the citation. "No, you'll take it, forget it, or throw it away. Then someday, years from now, when I'm pulled over for doing something I didn't do, I'll get thrown in jail for non-payment and about a thousand dollars of interest fees on the twenty-dollar fine."

"Yeah, you're right. I wouldn't take that chance, either."

We make it out to Chatsworth in less than an hour. The three-bedroom ranch house is located on a cul-de-sac lined with thorn bushes. The house is painted red. Devil and sin are my only thoughts. It's hell to be a Catholic—even a lapsed one. We park behind the craft services truck.

"Don't forget, we can only use his porn name," Conrad reminds me.

The security goon in hip-hop shorts and the requisite wife-beater t-shirt leads us into the house. "Careful where you step," he warns.

There are cables running every-which-way, unused light poles, sound and video equipment stacked against walls and in corners. We walk by a girl mixing egg whites and sugar in a small bowl with a honey dipper. Gideon is in the den, sitting in a canvas chair with *Dick Snatchly* stenciled on the back. He wears a set of headphones and watches a video monitor. He calls out, "Okay, we're ready. Roll tape."

Conrad and I stand back, far enough not to get any on us.

"Action."

The scene takes place on a pool table. Two girls and three guys are giving a whole new meaning to *sinking one in the side pocket*. The girls are tiny, skinny wisps with oversized chests. The guys are gym rats with six-pack abs. One guy wouldn't need a cue to play a round of snooker.

We remain quiet with the rest of the crew. One girl/actress/slut, sitting alone, bored with the scene, perks up, smiles, and waves at Conrad as if he were a long lost relative.

The performers seem to know exactly what to do and when to do it, as though the whole rigmarole was a choreographed ballet. Three camera guys move around, getting different shots. The boom operator dips his fuzz-covered microphone up and down to pick up the grunts and groans of artificial ecstasy. I wonder if there is a script lying around, specifying Sexy Sindy to say, "Oh, yeah, baby, give me all you got," and Hillary Ho to enunciate, "Fuck me harder."

Nobody has sex like this in real life, except maybe gymnasts, yoga masters, and Adagio dancers.

Director/writer/producer Dick Snatchly, Gideon's porn moniker, verbally orchestrates the performers and crew from his position at the monitor. "Left, right, back, forth, look up, look down, more light, less light, get in the light." All he needs is a baton. He is the puppet master in a human drama of cataclysmic copulating. After about twenty minutes, evidently running out of angles and positions to shoot, he calls out, "Okay, boys and girls, line up on the firing line."

The techs, sound guys, girl with the egg whites, and a few hangers-on/assistants all reposition for the "martini," the last shot of the last shots of the day.

Bang, bang, bang.

The climax is *in the can* ten minutes later. The lights go down, camera guys stop rolling and the performers unravel. Two assistants wearing latex gloves hand large wet wipes to the actors and white towels to the actresses. One guy takes a portable hair dryer to the felt, which is not designed to absorb.

"It's a wrap."

"I love 'em." The girl previously smiling at Conrad is now at his side, thrusting her chest at him. "I just love 'em."

"Nothing could make me happier," Conrad says to her, then makes the introduction, "This is my friend, Jake."

The woman turns toward me, "I'm Missy Prissy," she says and lifts up the bottom of the tee-shirt up to expose herself, "and these are my new breasts."

"Nice to see you."

"Doctor Blaine is a genius with gel packs," she declares, resting the tee-shirt material on top of her boobs.

"You're too kind," Conrad says.

"Touch 'em," she says to me.

"Excuse me?"

"Go ahead. Touch 'em. I dare you to tell the difference."

I'm hesitant.

"Go ahead," Conrad tells me, "it's purely medical."

I reach out and take hold of two boobs, one in each hand, as if I were measuring the weights of two sacks of flour.

"Go ahead, give 'em a squeeze."

My face must be red from embarrassment. Conrad snickers.

Missy's excitement barometers rise before my very eyes.

"What did I tell ya?" she says proudly.

I back off, allowing her boobs to salute unattended. "Quite

impressive," I proclaim.

Conrad reaches into his black bag and takes out what looks like a ruler, but is actually a level. He lays it across her erect nipples, and, as the bubble centers, remarks, "Perfect."

Dick Snatchly comes over. "Let's get out of here."

Conrad hands Missy Prissy a few of his business cards, "Tell all your friends, okay?"

"I will."

On the way to the car, Gideon acts as if he's had one too many double, double lattes, "Right in the middle of a two-on-one this morning, the star of the show goes into this meltdown. I thought I was going to have to call the shrink squad."

"What's a meltdown?" I ask.

Gideon's talking a mile a minute. "I got tape rolling, two guys standing there with wood, a grip hanging upside-down shining a honey light, and this chick can't turn off the tears. Cost me an hour and a half."

"What's a meltdown?" I ask again.

"When the star of the show realizes what she does for a living and starts in on a whole different kind of ballin'."

"Like Alyssa at her wedding shower," Conrad says.

"Very funny."

I've never gotten into porn. It seems dumb. Watching people suck, fuck, and fornicate in every possible position, although I will say some positions are quite inventive, seems pointless to me. If porn is the ultimate male fantasy, I'd hate to see what is last on the list.

A porn movie can't be judged as a film, because there is no plot, no theme, no character development. The only suspense is how long this guy can last. They don't even use film. It is all done on tape or some digital device. There is nothing clever or intriguing about it. A couple of the scenes might give you a boner, but who wants one of those when you're alone or out with the guys?

The fact that Gideon is in porn makes me crazy. Gideon is wasting his talent on a bunch of phony-named, surgically enhanced bimbos, and steroid-filled, Viagra-poled studs. If they weren't actors/actresses, they'd be working at K-Mart. The entire business operates on the edge of fleshy cliff, waiting to fall into a chasm of

AIDS.

In college, Gideon made films about kids, which were clever, inventive, and thought-provoking; and carried a message that stayed with you after the lights came back on. Now he's doing this bullshit. What a shame.

We stop for a twelve-pack before we get on the 5 North.

"You going to tell us where we're going?" a calmer Gideon asks, popping his third beer.

"No."

"This better not be another Jake brain-fart."

"You guys owe me."

"We supply free-of-charge entertainment for your future wife's wedding shower and you say 'we owe you?'"

"Yeah."

"Those Beverly Hills sorority girls were eating it up like half-priced Botox," Conrad says.

"A couple of 'em almost jumped inside Jimmy's jockstrap."

"That was the two gay guys that were there," I correct Gideon.

"The sister, Farrin, was getting into it," Conrad says with a horny lilt in his voice. "I like a chick a little bit off the wall."

"Her tits are a little too small for you, Conrad." I inform him.

"I can fix that."

"Trust me; she's not your type."

"Is she my type?" Gideon asks.

"I'll ask next time I see her," I mockingly add, "excuse me, Farrin, are you a slut?"

"All women are sluts," Gideon says. "It's just a matter of when and where."

We head up the Grapevine, a stretch of California highway separating the LA basin and the mid-state farmlands. It is a beautiful, clear, spring day. The Santa Ana's must be blowing.

"Whatever happened to those road trips we used to go on?" Conrad asks.

"We had to stop."

"Why?"

"You two got successful," I finish my answer.

The San Joaquin Valley stretches out before us in a never-ending green-and-brown checkerboard. No matter how big Los Angeles may be, it pales in comparison with the amount of farmland in the state of California.

"Where the hell are we going?"

"We're almost there."

"Will there be a "there," there, when we get there?" Conrad asks.

"You know," I say, "I don't ask a lot of you guys."

"And we appreciate that."

"All we can say is," Gideon says, "this better be good."

We arrive an hour later.

"Oh my God," Gideon coughs out after his first whiff.

"This is disgusting," Conrad follows.

I park the car on the downwind side of the lot, "This is it, boys, the smell of money."

The stench is unbearable. The odor literally clings to your nostrils as if it has been sprayed on. The dreary cacophony of mindless baying stings your eardrums. On the ground is a layer of shit as far as the eye can see. We stand in the middle of a massive feed lot. There must be ten thousand head of cattle being fattened-up before they become meat on America's big table. They live in huge pens, with computerized feed troughs dispensing corn slush. The animals have nothing to do except eat, fart, and shit.

"I have two words for you guys," I pause for effect, "methane gas."

Gideon and Conrad hold handkerchiefs over their mouths. Their eyes water from the pungent aroma.

"Do either of you know what caused the dinosaurs to become extinct?" I ask.

"What?"

"The prevailing theory is that there were so many dinosaurs, all eating grass, their farting put too much methane gas in the atmosphere, which formed a cloud which blocked out the sun and caused a cataclysmic climate change that ended up killing them."

"Who gives a shit?"

"Now couple that fact with the fact that, in California, forty percent of the methane gas released into the atmosphere comes from animals, the vast majority of which are cattle." I pause. "Can you see where I'm going here?"

"No."

"Methane gas is natural gas, the perfect clean energy source."

"What the hell are you talking about?" Gideon finally has the breath to yell out.

"I'm talking about building airtight, feedlot enclosures and sucking the cow farts and shit smell out, and storing the gas in holding tanks. Then we pipe the stink to a power plant where it can light up Las Vegas. What you're smelling right now is pure, clean, profitable energy."

"You have got to be kidding?"

"No, is this idea genius or what?"

I give them a little time to process.

Conrad sways, "Great, can we go now?"

"Not until you tell me what you think."

"I think you are out of your frickin' mind," Gideon says.

"Why?"

"Because it stinks."

"That's the beauty of it."

I chase them back to the car. "For less than a million, I can build a prototype, prove it works, then go to venture capital guys and get the rest of the money. What we have here is a free, unending supply of clean energy. All we have to do is capture it, condense it, pipe it, and rake in the money. This is the oil business of the twenty-first century."

I'm the last one back in the car. Gideon has turned on the ignition and is bent over, sucking the air out of the a/c vent.

"Drive, hurry up. Drive!"

"Think of it this way," I say before pulling away, "one man's fart is another man's fortune."

CHAPTER 6

Conrad, the Groomsman

So far, this day has been a bad idea, and it is getting worse. Back in town, we stop at a trendy, overpriced, Westside steak house, the kind with polished brass rails, red leather booths, surly waiters, and slabs of meat fit for Paul Bunyan. What do I care? It's all going on my expense account.

"Come on, guys, what do you think of my idea?" Jake asks the minute our butts touch down.

"We already told you," Gideon says.

"It stinks."

"Come on, seriously."

"Seriously," I repeat, "it stinks."

"It's supposed to stink, that's the genius of it." Jake never gives up.

The waiter arrives. Gideon has Chivas, me Maker's Mark, and Jake, a Heineken.

"I want to think about it."

"Is that your way of saying no?"

"Maybe."

"You got a business plan?" Gideon asks unexpectedly.

"I'm still in the preliminary stage. I want to give my best friends the first chance at this once-in-a-lifetime opportunity."

I tell him, "My accountant will want to see financial projections, timetables, cost breakdowns, tax advantages, and government regulations."

"Okay," Jake says, "I'll do all that."

I picture myself asking my financial advisor, *What do you think about bovine flatulence as an investment?*

"Then will you consider it?"

"For you, Jake, we'd consider anything."

The drinks arrive, although Gideon doesn't really need another. He's polished off most of the twelve-pack. When Gideon drinks, he drinks too much. Does this worry me? Yes. Gideon is the type that when he gets onto something, he can't let go. He's either one hundred percent in or one hundred percent out. This is good if he is your doubles partner in tennis, and bad if he gets some wild hair up his ass.

There is a lull in the conversation. Gideon gives me a glance, as if to say it is time to begin. This was all Gideon's idea, but now I'm not so sure it's a good one.

"Alyssa still hates us?" he asks.

"Let's just say, neither of you are being held in high regard."

"Alyssa always that uptight?" he asks.

"What?"

"I thought she might burst an artery."

"Can you blame her?" Jake rhetorically asks. "There was a one-eyed snake in her face."

"I've never seen her laugh, Jake." I'm serious.

"Alyssa laughs all the time."

"With you or at you?" Gideon asks.

Jake pushes back against the booth. "What the fuck are you guys talking about?"

"Alyssa."

"What about Alyssa?"

"She doesn't impress us as being a happy person," I say.

"Who would be, after what you two assholes did? She's been waiting years for payback on all the showers she's had to go to."

"She can't take a joke," Gideon says.

"Jesus Christ..."

"We make her shower the most memorable ever, and she gets mad at us?" Gideon continues.

"It's not how memorable you made it. It's how you made it memorable," Jake snaps back.

"The last time I saw a woman get that ugly, a house fell on her sister."

"Fuck you, Gideon."

Gideon's shitfaced. I'll have to carry the conversational ball. I ask, "Does Alyssa have a sense of humor?"

"Of course she has."

"She sure wasn't letting it out that day," Gideon says.

"Jake, I thought she was going to have an aneurysm," I add.

I doubt if Jake has any idea that this has all been planned. The only reason Gideon and I went on his investment excursion was to get him alone, so we could have this talk.

Gideon and I worry that Jake and Alyssa getting married is nothing more than the first step to their divorce. They are a mismatch from the starting gate. She's *Vogue*, he's *Popular Mechanics*. Rolex/Timex. Mercedes/Ford. DKNY/Levi. Get the picture?

I take a breath and ask, "Does Alyssa ever go into a dark place, show any signs of inward depression?"

"No."

"There's a bomb inside that chick waiting to explode," Gideon says, "and when she does, Katy, bar the door." Gideon is not helping my line of reasoning.

"Bullshit," Jake lashes out.

"Clinical depression can take many forms." I try to keep it medically related and speak as if I'm talking with a patient.

"You think she's clinically depressed?" Jake asks with a sneer on his face.

Gideon slurs, "You don't have any guns in the house, do you?"

"Psychologically speaking, women are much more violent than men." I attempt to bring in reasonable thought.

And Gideon destroys it. "That's why they didn't let them into the Army until Iraq. And they still won't let 'em into the infantry, because not even cockroaches would survive their wrath."

Jake shakes his head side to side. "Where do you guys come up with this bullshit?"

"There are outward signals that point out certain psychological traits which can trigger mood swings or aggression." I stay on course.

"What?"

"Now if Alyssa was an MMA cage fighter or a prison guard, we wouldn't be so worried."

I wish Gideon would shut up.

"I'm worried," I say.

"Worried about what?"

"Alyssa."

"Don't."

"I'm a doctor."

"You're a fucking plastic surgeon."

"I'm just trying to tell you…"

"Tell me what?"

"That Alyssa shows signs of behavior that can become troublesome in a long-term relationship."

I have no clue what I'm talking about here, but when you have MD after your name, people will believe just about anything that comes out of your mouth. Truth be told, psychiatry is the lowest rung on the medical ladder. Doctors who do, practice. Doctors who don't, practice research. And, doctors who don't practice research, become shrinks.

Jake takes a deep breath. "I admit," Jake tries reason, "Alyssa is an extremely controlled person."

"Controlling."

"No."

"Yes."

"She's the most level-headed, even-tempered human being you'll ever meet."

"And that's a good thing?" I question.

"Yes."

"Why, you're not." Gideon says.

"That's why I need somebody who is." Jake tosses back.

"We want you to be happy, Jake."

"I've never been this happy in my entire life."

I don't know where else to go with this. I'm at the end of the discussion, which wasn't my idea to begin with. It was the Gideon's, who's drunk as a frat boy at his first kegger.

The waiter arrives. We order platefuls of cholesterol. I add a hundred dollar bottle of red wine.

"Alyssa thinks we're a bad influence, doesn't she?" I ask.

"You are."

Gideon sucks the ice cubes in his empty cocktail. "You sure she's the one?"

"Yes, I'm sure."

"Why?"

"She's everything I ever wanted in a woman. She's

gorgeous…"

"Would you still love her if she was ugly?" Gideon asks as he starts in on the wine.

"What kind of a dumb question is that?"

"A good one," Gideon says. "Would you still want her if she lost a leg?"

"Are you ever serious?"

"Would you still love her if she wasn't beautiful?" I ask.

"Yes."

Gideon asks, "How about the money? If she wasn't rich would you still marry her?"

"Yes."

"Why?"

"Because you guys are going to give me the money so I can go into business for myself."

"And until then," Gideon says, "your quill stays dipped in the company ink."

"You're not only marrying the girl, you're marrying the business, which puts a whole different pressure on the relationship," I say.

"So?"

"There is an old saying," Gideon says, "you don't slap ass where you bust ass."

"You know someone who makes films titled *Champagne Jizz* and *Butt Buster 14*," Jake says right into Gideon's face, "makes for an odd candidate as a relationship expert."

"And you," Jake says to me, "the only band you've ever given a woman is a lap band."

"Okay," Gideon says, "I'm no Doctor Phil."

"Neither of you have ever had a relationship that lasted past you saying, 'Was it good for you?'"

"At least I'm nice enough to ask."

"You don't like Alyssa."

"No, that's not true," I lie.

Gideon says. "We don't like her, not because she doesn't like us. No, that's not it…"

It must have been six months ago, Alyssa was hosting a Junior League, society, soiree for the eradication of acne or something at the Bel Air Hotel. I bring some cute little ingénue, who chatted me up at the Jonathan Club the previous weekend. Gideon brings this babe with breasts the size of volleyballs. And, not only was she over-endowed, the tiny clasp holding those breasts in check was ready to break at any moment. One glance at this woman and you imagined she could have been A: a porn star. B: a stripper. C: a hooker. D: Any combination of A, B and C. The woman was a walking embarrassment. And Gideon knew it. Alyssa takes one look, shudders and immediately orders security to ask the woman to leave for breaking the dress code. Needless to say, from that point forward, for Gideon and Alyssa, it hasn't been pretty.

Gideon finishes his comment. "...we don't like her, because she can be a real bitch."

I'm thinking to myself, *Gideon, this was your idea and you turn into a fucking idiot.*

"She doesn't seem happy," I say.

"How the hell does anyone seem happy?" Jake asks.

"She never smiles."

"She's guarded," Jake says. "Women like her are always guarded. Guys have been hitting on her since she was eleven."

"And they are going to keep hitting on her, whether she's married or not. Are you ready for that?"

"Alyssa could have married a hundred times before this, but she picked me."

"Why?"

"Because she loves me."

"Forget love, Jake. Ever ask yourself what is it she wants from you?"

"Family."

"Every woman wants a family. What else?"

"Love."

"Get real."

"Lifestyle?" I ask. "She wants *your* lifestyle?"

"Your dowry?" Gideon jumps in.

"Maybe it's because I'm a great guy," Jake says almost out of desperation.

"There's a lot of those available," I say.

"Right at this very table," Gideon adds.

"All we're saying is that you might want to figure all this out before you take the trip down the aisle," I tell him.

"You guys are drunk," Jake says.

"Yeah," Gideon says, "but I'll be sober in the morning, and you'll still be on the way to the altar with a woman who is a flaming bitch."

Gideon has crossed the line.

Jake screams, "You're jealous, that's what it is…of me with a beautiful woman."

"Oh, yeah," Gideon wallows back, as he points at me, "like he doesn't fuck beautiful women?"

"Alyssa's not some porno whore or airheaded idiot," Jake screams louder than before.

"That's our whole point," I say as if I hadn't had a drink all day. "We're trying to get you to look at Alyssa with your brain instead of your testicles."

"If it was me," Gideon says, "I'd expect you to do the same."

"Listen," Jake says, slamming his hand onto the table. "I love this woman. She loves me. We're going to have a family, a great life together. I know what I'm doing, dammit."

The fifteen or twenty other customers in the restaurant pause their conversations to look our way, just in time to hear Gideon belch.

This has been a disaster.

The food arrives, three sizzling hunks of cow meat, fat-juicy and cooked just enough to clog our arteries.

The waiter refills the wine glasses. He motions a bit impatiently for a second bottle and I decline. We attack the end result of the bovine we saw previously in the day with carnivorous abandon.

A few minutes of mastication go by and Gideon breaks the verbal silence. "So, what do you think of them Lakers?"

CHAPTER 7

Alyssa, the Bride

The smartest move I made was quitting my bullshit job at the Endeavor/William Morris Agency. Since the primary duties of the receptionist are to dress well, smile wide, and look sexy, the job could hardly be considered a resume builder. As if I ever wanted a career.

I could never, no way, plan a wedding and work at the same time. Jake complains on having to do too much, but he has no clue of the time, effort, and all the decisions that have to be made. Church, ceremony, vows, food, music, rehearsal, flowers—I could go on and on. I should make him walk a mile in my Jimmy Choos' and see how it really feels.

"Do I look fat in this?"

"Alyssa, you wouldn't look fat in a Santa suit."

I return to the dressing room, take off the DKNY, try on the Cassini and go back out.

"How much is this one?" Farrin asks.

"Eleven grand."

"LaRue know how much these things cost?"

"I haven't told him."

"If I ever get married, it'll probably be at Elvis' Hunka Burnin' Love Chapel in Las Vegas," Farrin says.

I turn in the mirror six or seven times, try three or four different shoes, a different veil. This isn't it. I go through the rack again. I've been at this since before Jake even popped the question. If there is a cure for shopaholics, it would be finding the perfect wedding dress.

"Maybe," Farrin says, "if you narrowed the number down to under twenty, it'd be easier."

"I think I'm going the custom route," I say exasperated. "Your turn."

There are a number of bridesmaid's dresses waiting for her on the rack. "Start with the pink."

"Pink? Me?"

I have brought Farrin along for moral support, not her opinion. An opinion from someone who wears goose-step boots, leather chaps and navel jewelry, I don't need. I have decided to do this all by myself. It is my wedding. They will be my choices.

My mother has called and asked a number of times to be included; but my mother would be no help, and I don't need any more aggravation. Brady and I have been on the outs for years, especially since she married step daddy Simon, who doesn't look at you; he looks through you. The guy gives me the creeps. Why she ever hooked up with him is beyond my comprehension. He was not yet divorced, unemployed, living in a studio, and taking the bus. What a catch. Mom claimed after her previous divorce, she was lonely, bored, and "My heart had been broken twice. I needed someone to love me."

"Get a cat," I told her.

When I was eight, happily living with dad, Mom put up a fuss, got a new lawyer, and threatened to go back to court to gain custody. By that time, I was already daddy's little girl. I wanted no part of any of it. She really put the screws on dad. I found out years later, that to get her to drop the case he agreed to pay support until I was eighteen, even though I was living with him.

I would see Mom on weekends and we'd go shopping with dad's money. She'd show up at school functions or when I was cheerleading, but I couldn't say we were close, then or now. Oftentimes I feel closer to Mr. Chips than my own mother.

"This dress sure doesn't come close to matching any of yours," Farrin says as she previews herself in the three-sided mirror. "I look like a neon flamingo."

"Good," I say. "Sides can't taste better than the main course."

Farrin goes back in and comes out in dress number two: a red, fluffy, off-the-shoulder number.

"This doesn't work either," she says, "unless there's a fire in the church that needs to be put out."

She's correct.

"My mother call you?" I ask.

"Three times this week."

I figured as much. "What did you tell her?"

"Nothing."

"Good."

Farrin turns away from the mirror and kicks off her shoes. "It would be a lot easier if you talked to her."

"Why should I?"

"Because she's your mother."

"You don't talk to your mother," I tell my stepsister. "Why should I talk to mine?"

"Because you're the one getting married."

"What difference does that make?"

"Brady wants to be involved. You're her only daughter. She wants to be a part of your wedding and your life."

"She had her chance."

"Quit being such a hard ass, Alyssa. Lighten up."

"Why should I?"

"She's your mother. You can't keep punishing her for what she did twenty years ago."

I am about to argue with her, but I pause, think, and admit, "It still hurts."

"Hey, it hurts me every time my mother tells me I look like something out of the Rocky Horror Picture Show."

"All you would have to do is dye your hair and take out the metal. It is a little different with Brady and me." I stop for effect and say, "Your mother didn't walk out on you."

"But now she wants to walk back in, so let her."

I don't answer.

This isn't the first time we've had this discussion, but it is ending exactly the same way it always ends. I fold my arms across my chest, stare at my shoes, and sit quietly.

In a minute or two, Farrin says, "I'll try on the green," and walks back into the dressing room with a Peter Pan number.

Farrin's a punk past her prime. Why she's kept the purple streaks in her brunette hair, metal in her nose, and more earrings than

Captain Jack Sparrow is anybody's guess. Maybe it hides the junk in her trunk and her total lack of a bust? A Farrin bra is nothing more than two oversized band aids. Oddly enough, she's cute in the sexy, pseudo-slutty way guys sometimes go for.

We inherited each other when I was sixteen and she was fourteen. About the only thing we could agree on was how much we hated one another. We had to share a room for the first year, which was hell. I'm neat. She's a slob. When she tried to wear my clothes, I'd rip 'em off her back.

"Come on, let's trade," she'd plead.

"I wouldn't wear your clothes to a carwash."

We'd fight about everything. It got so bad, our parents arranged opposite weekends so she would visit her dad when I was home and vice-versa. The happiest day of my life was the day we moved into dad's new house and our rooms were at opposite ends of the hall.

I had to tutor her, chauffer her, and, make-nice to her mother, put up with her disgusting friends, listen to the Ramones, ignore her when she was lying through her teeth, clean her up when she was drunk, breathe her secondhand marijuana smoke, and pretend I cared about her.

When I was at USC, her mom and my dad divorced. Farrin was devastated. It bothered me, too, although I'm not sure why. It was the summer Farrin and I discovered that misery loves company. We've been weirdly close ever since.

Farrin comes out in a green dress, which hangs on her like a rain poncho.

"I think it clashes with my black eye shadow," Farrin remarks as she heads for the mirror. "Can't I wear leather?"

"No."

She turns a few times in the multiple mirrors. She looks absurd in triplicate.

"Are you bringing a date?" I ask her.

"Yes."

"Who?"

"Does it matter? Dinner's gonna be a fucking zoo."

Farrin's right. Jake, his disgusting buddies, Marge, Dad, his two ex-wives and their idiot husbands, and I at one table. Sounds like the cast of a bad reality TV show.

"Put me next to that doctor friend of Jake."

"He's bringing a date."

"I don't care," Farrin says, "I think he's kinda cute." She walks away from the mirror. "Maybe I'll invite the dancer from the shower. He could wear his tux with the tear-away pants."

My stepsister's sense of humor has much to be desired.

"And the Day-Glo jockstrap."

"Try on the blue dress, Farrin."

I wonder if Farrin will ever find a husband. She goes through guys and they go through her, so to speak. She never seems to last more than three dates with any of them. She'd have more men in a month than I'd have in a year. There is always some problem with every guy. "The guy's thirty and already losing his hair," is a typical Farrin critique, one which is always uttered after she sleeps with the guy.

For a while she only dated musicians, until she realized a musician is only a bum who thinks he has talent. She had a construction worker phase, dating twenty-five-year-old workers with rippling pecs. Only when she started seeing forty-year-old lunch-bucket construction Joes with hanging guts instead of six-pack abs, did it occur to her to move on. Lately, she's been doing the Match.com thing, where dating is the equivalent of playing liar's poker.

Farrin comes out of the dressing room in the blue dress, which clashes badly with her purple hair. "What do you think?" I ask her.

"It makes me look flatter than I already am."

It did. The dress had done the impossible.

CHAPTER 8

Jake, the Groom

The morning ritual begins at 7:00 A.M. The trucks have been washed and serviced. The workforce of sixty-eight lines up in a semi-military formation, facing their fearless leader, me.

"Okay, pull 'em out."

Each man removes his documentation and holds it up until I pass by and make my approval. Truth be told, I'm not sure I would even recognize a legal Green Card if one slapped me in the face. The Green Card is the most forged document in California. The small-time crooks, who used to eke out a living doing phony IDs for rich college students, found a bonanza in the illegal immigrant trade. I don't really care if the cards are authentic. As long as each guy has something to show a state inspector, the onus will be on them and not the business. Avoiding a company-wide sting is the most important aspect of my job.

I don't say much as I make my way through the ranks. Few speak any English and my Spanish doesn't go much farther than "taco" and "cerveza." This is the only time during the day their uniforms are clean. After a few hours of work in the hot LA sun, the rank-and-file will be just rank. Ten years ago, I'm told, the workforce was almost one hundred percent African-American. Today they are all Hispanic. They show up on time and work hard. Few complain, or if they are complaining I don't know it, because they do so in Spanish, and I listen in English. I hire only Mexican Mexicans, not Mexican Americans, the ones who are just happy to be here, who don't understand social security taxes, health benefits, or union affiliations. All they care about is how much the guy behind the glass at the check cashing place counts out every other Friday. Although I have worked with some of these guys since I started here, and they seem to be pretty nice people, none will be invited to my wedding.

My title is VP Operations. My job is to have the trucks running in the morning, picking up all day, emptied in the afternoon, and returned before dark. Garbage collection wasn't really what I envisioned myself doing after five years of undergrad business courses and three years in an on-line MBA program, which I still have two courses to finish before getting my degree. I was preparing more for a career in corporate takeovers, high-tech innovation, or web-based marketing; but you have to go where the opportunities present themselves. And after my first four jobs out of college ended in, "We're letting you go," "This isn't working out," "You're fired," and my personal favorite, "We've had a budget cutback and you're it," me, like my fellow workers at the Walworth Recycling Corporation, are just glad to have jobs.

And I'm pretty good at it. The new improvements I've been allowed to make, changing the routes to avoid left turns, hiring a mechanic to service the trucks before they break down, and requiring the men to wear back braces have reduced fuel consumption 11%, decreased truck downtime 19%, and cut down numerous lumbar vertebrae pains. I can only assume the success of the latter by fewer grimaces seen in the morning Green Card lineup. I have lots of other ideas, but present management is a bit slow to move the company into the twenty-first century of garbage.

"Get in here!" LaRue, my boss and future father-in-law, summons me at the end of the day.

His office is three times the size of my cubicle. He has pictures of Alyssa on his desk, on the credenza, and on the wall. "Sit down, something I want to discuss with you."

LaRue never discusses with me, he prefers yelling.

"About what?" I nervously ask.

"Marriage."

"I already signed the pre-nup," I remind him.

"Want a drink?" LaRue keeps a bottle of twelve-year-old scotch in the corner credenza.

"A little early for me."

"That'll change," he says, pouring himself three fingers worth.

He has an odd look on his face. "Wedding's costing me a

fortune. Can't you keep her in line?"

"No."

He doesn't argue. He drinks about a finger's worth.

I fidget.

"Jake Dombrowski," he says. "You like that name?"

"Jake? Yeah, it's tough to misspell."

"No," he says, as if I'm the idiot in the room. "Dombrowski."

"I don't think you have much choice when it comes to last names."

"Yes, you do."

He downs the last finger in the glass.

"I mean, come on, wouldn't you have rather grown up a Smith or a Jones instead of a Polski?"

"I've never given it a lot of thought."

He pours himself three more fingers worth, tastes to be sure it is the same as before, leans back in his big, leather chair, and puts his dirty boots up on the edge of his desk. "I got three sisters, one daughter, no cousins that I know of." He pauses. "The Walworth name dies with me." He pauses again, waiting for me to say what he wants me to say.

"Okay."

That wasn't it.

His feet come off the desk, folds his hands in front of him, leans forward and asks, "You really want your kids growing up Dombrowski? I mean, come on, the abuse they're going to take being called dumb Pollock, sausage squeezers, Krakau krauts. You really want to put your kids through all that?"

"I can't remember ever being called a Krakau kraut," I tell him.

"Wouldn't they be better off as Walworth's?"

"Huh?"

"Doesn't Jake Walworth sound better than Jake Dombrowski?"

"What?"

"What would you say to dropping the Dombrowski?"

I never saw this coming.

"Switch it to Walworth." He takes a big gulp of scotch. "I'll make it worth your while."

I am about to say, "No way," but I quickly figure that I have nothing to lose by hearing what number he has to offer. "What does that mean?"

"Fifty grand."

"Fifty grand to drop my name for yours?"

"Yeah."

A thought comes in my head. "But if I do, the Dombrowski name will die."

"There's plenty of Dombrowskis out there, I don't think anyone will notice one's gone."

"We'll go from the front of the alphabet to the rear."

"What the hell difference will that make?" he raises his hands as he asks.

I am not good in these situations. I've never been fast on my feet. I need time to think things through, see the problem from different angles, get opinions, let my brain process it at its own pace. Gideon told me, "Never make a decision when you're hungry, angry or have to take a crap."

I stall for time. "Have you talked to Alyssa about this?"

"No."

He's lying. I know it and he knows I know it.

"Well," I say slowly, "maybe I should."

He looks at me funny. "Alyssa's keeping her last name."

"She is?"

"Yes."

"We haven't talked about that."

"It'll be a short discussion," he tells me.

He jumps to his next point, "Don't you want everyone's name in the family to be the same?"

"Yes."

"Then it's settled?"

"No."

"Fifty grand is a lot of money for a Pollock name." He puts space between the words "Pollock" and "name."

LaRue waits for me to take the money. If the tables were reversed, he'd have the check already cashed.

"I'd like to think about it."

"Why?"

"My name's been in the family for a long time."

He looks at me, probably thinking that's something a dumb Pollock would say.

"But I appreciate the offer."

LaRue lays his hands flat on his desk. He will not let this die. He hates to lose. "What if you give the children the Walworth name?"

"If they're girls, aren't you right back in the same boat?"

He pauses. A point he obviously has not considered.

"Those ex-wives of mine would have given me a son, we wouldn't be having this conversation."

I could inform him that the man is the one who carries the Y chromosome, which determines the sex of the child, but I don't. "LaRue," I say, getting out of the chair, "I'll think about it. I promise."

I'm lying, but it is not really a lie since LaRue knows I'm lying.

Alyssa is already in bed, reading her chick lit when I climb between the sheets.

"Your dad and I had an interesting discussion this afternoon."

"About what?" Alyssa doesn't look up from her book.

"He wants me to change my name to Walworth."

"He does?"

"You didn't know about this?"

"No."

Alyssa is a lousy liar.

"He says he doesn't want the name to die."

Alyssa puts her book down. "What did you tell him?"

"I told him I'd think about it."

"Are you going to?"

"No."

Alyssa looks at me. "You shouldn't lie to your boss, Jake."

"I didn't. He knew I was just letting him down easy."

I prop myself up against the head board. "He said you were going to keep Walworth."

Alyssa hesitates. "I haven't decided." She hesitates again. "I might hyphenate."

"Alyssa Walworth-Dombrowski?" I say the name slowly. "You'll take up two lines in the phone book."

"Dad wants to keep the business in the family." Alyssa says. "He wants a Walworth in the Walworth Recycling Corporation."

"It's not like our customers come into the yard and ask to speak to Mr. Walworth."

"The employees do…"

"They don't speak English."

Alyssa marks the spot she is reading with her fancy bookmark. "He's beginning to think of his own mortality."

"Your dad?"

"You should know what he's feeling. A man wants to pass his legacy to the next generation."

"That's not going to stop."

"In name it will."

"That's not it." I take a second before saying, "He doesn't want his grandchildren to be Polish."

Alyssa is quiet.

The funny thing is, the only thing Polish about me is the name. I got so many different breeds, I'd give a mutt a bad name. My dad was part Polish, German and Hungarian with a little French thrown in for flavor. My mom is Greek, Italian, and Spanish. She told me once there was some Jewish blood too, from way back when. I've never told Alyssa this and never will.

Alyssa puts her book on her nightstand and turns toward me. "Why don't you just consider it?" She places her hand on my bare chest, leans over, gives me a kiss.

Monday sex, this doesn't happen often.

She flips off the light, lays down, pulls off her night shirt.

I lean on one side, begin the process, and she pushes me away.

"Wait."

"What?"

"Diaphragm."

"Why?" I say as she slides out from beneath me. "We're going to be married in a couple of weeks."

"Because," she says on her way into the bathroom.

"It's not like we don't want kids."

"Because we're going to get pregnant after we're married."

"Who would know?" I say as she flips on the light and fumbles around.

"That's not the point, Jake."

"If we get lucky tonight, we wouldn't have to explain a thing," I call out.

"I'm not walking up the aisle pregnant."

"You wouldn't even know."

"I'd know."

I can hear her making the insertion. I've always wanted to watch her put the thing in, but she won't let me.

Alyssa comes back to bed, lies down, pulls up the covers, and invites me aboard. "Come on, Jake, do me."

I start with a long, tongue-wagging kiss, move to the crook of her neck, lick a diamond-studded lobe and go south to her nipples. I suddenly can't get Conrad's assessment out of my head and I'm all over her breasts. As I touch, taste, feel, and squeeze, I examine for traces of surgery, equal size, shifting matter. Does one fall to the side differently than the other? This is difficult, but fun. I try to make some comparisons as to what I remember of the touch and texture of women in my past who have had their breasts done, but my mammary memories have long since faded. Can I feel a difference? If she had her boob job before I met her, there's no comparison to make. I'd like to turn on the light, get out a magnifying glass to search for an incision scar, but that's not going to happen. All I have is Missy Prissy as a basis for comparison, and considering her size and bulk, I'd be hard pressed to draw any conclusions from that hands-on comparison.

My extra-curricular, above-the-waist, activity seems to put a little more zing into our usually predictable lovemaking: I do this, she does that, I do this, we come, we go.

Alyssa is a quiet lover, little chitchat, but lots of movement. She's shown me what she needs to get what she wants. Her capacity to climax never ceases to amaze me. God was cruel when he decided who gets how many during the act.

She gently pushes me off almost the second I'm done.

We lie on our backs catching breaths. I consider carefully how to phrase my next comment.

"What do you think about women who get their breasts done?"

Alyssa cuts a breath short and answers, "You think I need a boob job?"

"No," I say with defense in my voice. "I merely wonder what you think of the procedure in general?"

"Why?"

"I'm curious." I roll on my side to face her.

"What brings this on?

"I don't know."

She remains on her back. "Your friend Conrad say something?"

"No."

"Sure?"

"Yes." I pause. "I read that breast enhancement became the number-one plastic surgery procedure last year, beating out nose jobs and face lifts."

"Where did you read that?"

"*USA Today.*"

Alyssa is quiet for a few seconds. "For some women it's okay, I guess." Her voice gets a little louder when she continues, "Why not? They have the right to do what they want with their own bodies."

"Do you think it is an honest thing to do?"

"What does honesty have to do with it?" A defensive tone rises in her voice.

"Well, maybe honesty is the wrong term."

"If a woman has a boob job, she should wear a sign around her neck announcing the fact?"

Missy's introductory revelation comes immediately to mind.

"Usually you can tell right away."

"Oh, really," she asks, "how?"

"Most women get them too big."

"Was that in the article, too?"

"No, Conrad told me that."

"So you were talking to Conrad about it." She turns slightly to face me. "That's what you did on your afternoon off? Sat around and discussed the whys and wherefores of breast enhancement surgery?"

"He talks about it all the time, that's his job."

"I bet Gideon had a few choice comments on the subject." She turns to again stare at the ceiling. "He's surrounded by fake boobs every day."

"Just wondered," I say, turn, roll up in a fetal position and pretend to go to sleep.

Alyssa turns on her light, reaches for her chick lit, opens to where she left off, and reads.

CHAPTER 9

Alyssa, the Bride

I love Marilyn Beech.
"How did we do this week?"
"Good," I tell her.

Marilyn kicks off the session the same way each time. Jake doesn't like being here. I think it is wonderful.

"No silent treatments?"

"None," I say.

"Sex?"

"Twice."

"Bet you liked that, Jake."

Jake says, "Yep."

Couples counseling is the best thing we have ever done together. Once a week, Marilyn helps us over the rough spots in our relationship. It forces us to sit down and really talk without cell phones ringing or baseball games heard in the background. It is so easy to open up and talk here. Marilyn Beech-time is the best.

The PhD sits in the comfy chair. Jake and I are on the small couch, which isn't very comfortable. I'll bet the discomfort is by design.

Marilyn asks, "How are we doing with the progressive listening?"

"He's doing much better," I say. "He heard my concerns about the wedding shower."

"They were hard to miss."

"Do you feel differently about what happened at the shower now, than you did just after it happened?"

"No." Marilyn likes it when I'm upfront and forceful, she says it is one of my best qualities.

Jake explains, "My friends are a little bit out there."

"You'd have to be a little out there," Marilyn answers, "to be a pornography director."

"It was the only job he could get after film school."

"That's like an unemployed finance guy saying the only job he could get is robbing a bank." I put things into perspective.

Marilyn interrupts Jake before he speaks. "Now, before you answer Alyssa, think of how she is going to feel and consider it before you respond."

Jake sits, picks at his fingernail, and says to Marilyn. "If I'm always stopping to think, our conversations are going to last for hours."

"Baby talk, remember baby talk," Marilyn reminds Jake. "We take baby steps in the present to be able to walk freely in the future." Marilyn quotes from her own self-help book, which I read twice.

I can't believe it didn't become a best seller. *Baby Talk* is all about reverting back to our simplest forms of communication and using those skills as phonetic building blocks, which you then use as a basis for articulating needs and feelings in your day-to-day existence. Marilyn is a genius.

Jake picks at a different fingernail. "I really don't know what to say here," he says. "I'm going to pass this round."

"Let's move on." Marilyn refers to a notepad, where I've never seen her enter a note. "This is a very big week for the two of you," she says. "What is foremost on your minds?"

"I don't want strippers on the engagement party dinner table."

"Have you voiced this to Jake?"

"He knows."

"I'll talk to them. I told you I'll talk to them. "

"I feel threatened."

"Hear that, Jake? Alyssa feels threatened." Marilyn leans a bit forward in her chair. "Respond to her feelings."

"Don't worry. I won't let 'em do anything crazy. I promise." Jake turns to Marilyn. "What more can I say?"

Marilyn doesn't respond to Jake, she speaks to me. "You have to acknowledge his efforts in your behalf."

"Fine, Jake, I'm counting on you. I want the dinner to be perfect."

"That was good couple-conversation. We are making progress

here." Marilyn pauses. "Let's go back to the sex for a minute."

"Good," Jake says.

Sex is the only topic that perks Jake up during a session. For some reason, he loves to get a third party take on our sex life.

"Is it getting better? Are you two both feeling more of a connection?"

"It was different this week," I say, being honest.

"How?"

I squirm a bit. "Just different."

"Different bad or different good?" Marilyn asks.

"I'm not sure."

This is the first time I can remember I'm the lead in a discussion about sex with Marilyn, usually it is Jake bitching and moaning.

"Jake?" Marilyn asks.

Jake shrugs his shoulders. I don't know why he's not jumping in, this is the perfect opportunity for his favorite topic.

"I didn't think it was all that different, same-old, same-old to me." He hesitates, and then adds, "Except that it was a Monday."

"You don't have sex on Mondays?" Marilyn asks.

"No," Jake answers emphatically.

"That's not true," I say.

"Okay, tell me, when was the last time we had sex on a Monday?" Jake asks me.

"I don't know. I don't mark it on my calendar."

"You mark other sexual stuff on your calendar," he says.

This is way too much information.

Marilyn senses my unease. "How about the after-sex, was it different, too?"

"He launches into this discussion about breast implants."

Jake stares back at his fingers. I can't believe I've embarrassed him.

"What about breast implants, Jake?"

Jake's eyes go to Marilyn's chest, which has been enhanced. "I read this article about implants becoming the number-one plastic surgery procedure."

"And talking to his friend about it," I add.

"Conrad does breast implants for a living, that's his job."

"He should leave his work at the office," I say.

"Why are you being so defensive, Alyssa?" Marilyn asks me.

"I'm not."

"Yes, you are."

"I don't want my husband constantly scoping out other women's breasts. That will make me feel vulnerable."

"She's telling you how she feels, Jake."

"She's making me into some horny, tit-magnet."

"You were the other night."

"With you," Jake says. "I thought you were enjoying it."

I hesitate.

"Were you?" Marilyn asks.

"Yes."

Now I'm embarrassed. I stare at my shoes.

"I'm sensing a conversational impasse here," Marilyn says to me.

I swallow hard. I hate talking about my breasts.

"What's the problem, Alyssa?"

"Jake loves my breasts now, but what happens after I breastfeed a couple of kids and they're not what they are today?"

Jake says. "Conrad will give you a deal if you want them redone."

"Oh, yeah, that's what I'd want, that guy's hands all over me while I'm out cold."

"He'll get one of his partners to do you."

"I don't think so."

Marilyn says, "A lot of women, after having their children, are restoring their bodies and feeling very positive about it."

"Is anyone hearing what I'm saying?" I ask the group.

"Jake?"

"She just figured out I'm a boob man?"

"No," I almost scream.

"Jake?" Marilyn repeats the question.

Jake sits twiddling his thumbs.

"What do you sense Alyssa is feeling right now."

We're waiting...

Jake looks up, he has his *I don't want to be here* look on his face. "I'm thinking my answer over," he says.

Marilyn breaks the impasse. "I believe Alyssa is feeling emotionally afraid."

"Thank you," I say.

"Of what?" Jake asks.

"My body."

"Your breasts are perfect, just like the rest of you."

"Now."

"So, after the kids, get them done. Why the hell worry about it?"

I'm exasperated. I sit, lean back. Marilyn does the same.

Jake stares at the wall for a few seconds then says to Marilyn, "Although it is important that we keep abreast of this problem, let's put the boobs on hold for a while. We can touch upon them later." He looks up and smiles that stupid grin of his, as if waiting for the two of us to bust out laughing; no pun intended.

"Fine," I say, matching his ridiculous cynicism, "I'll hold you to it."

The remainder of the session is boring. Marilyn had us play a word association game, which is designed to help understand the inner feelings of our partners by the words used in everyday discussions.

After forty-five minutes, Marilyn announces, "Our hour's up." She closes her empty notepad. "That will be two-hundred-fifty dollars."

CHAPTER 10

Gideon, the Best Man

I hate the fucking bitch.

The first time I met her was at Jake's apartment; his mother's sixty-fifth birthday. Why Jake would have a birthday party for a woman who didn't know if it was six o'clock or Wednesday, is a total mystery. There are much better ways of celebrating the start of Medicare and Social Security payments.

I've always loved Mrs. Edith Dombrowski, she'd have me over for dinner when she could hardly afford to feed her own family. She never judged me, questioned me, ragged on me, tried to get me to do things I didn't want to do. She accepted me as me, and let me be me; something my parents never let me do. It is very hard to see her now, very hard. Personally, I'd rather be dead than have Alzheimer's.

Alyssa knew who I was before Jake's introduction. She fiddled with a cup of wine and a cheesed-up cracker and used both as a reason not to shake my hand. I tried to be nice, but that lasted about thirty seconds. I know these women. Everything they have ever gotten comes gift wrapped from someone else. They think they have this divine right to the best of all that life has to offer; the only payments they have to make is to stay gorgeous. Start any conversation and watch her steer it in her direction. Take any situation and see her take control. And if she comes to a problem she can't figure out, get somebody else to solve in her favor, or doesn't want to be bothered with, she merely ignores it, until it is no longer pressing upon her. Someday I'll write a screenplay with a spoiled-rotten, selfish, self-centered, conceited, antagonist, and I'll name her Alyssa.

So, we are at this horrible, birthday party. Mrs. Dombrowski is walking aimlessly around with this ridiculous, pointy hat on, and wanders into Jake's bedroom. I watch her go in from the other side of the room. The door closes behind her. Now, I don't know what happened in that room. All I know is that Alyssa comes out of it a few minutes later. There is a ten minute intermission, then someone says, "Where's Edith?" Everyone looks around. The whole party stops. Jake runs out the front door, and then runs back in. Another guest goes into the bedroom and comes right back out, shrugging shoulders. I watch Alyssa, who doesn't move from where she is standing, chomping on a celery stick. Jake starts to panic, asks Conrad to go out and search the parking lot. Jake starts calling out "Mom, Mom," while frantically searching an apartment too small in which to hide. I walk into the bedroom, look first under the bed, and then open the closet door.

"Mrs. Dombrowski what are you doing?"

She stands in the small closet lost among Jake's crummy wardrobe. "Looking for asparagus," she tells me.

I take her by the hand "Come on, I hear it is on sale this week." I take the stupid hat off her head, and lead her back to the party in the front room. Our entrance causes immediate relief and a premature end to the party.

I can assume and imagine, but can't prove Alyssa shoved her in the closet. That is why I've never mentioned it to Jake. All I know is when I explained to the group that she had decided to "go back into the closet, instead of coming out," Alyssa was the only one who didn't at least chuckle.

Fucking Bitch.

Conrad met me at the bar a half-hour early. We sit in a back booth instead of up front by the stage. There is a sticky spot on the phony leather. We must be in a booth where the girls do private lap dances. I cover the spot with a couple napkins.

"We have to try again."

"What?"

"Talk him out of it."

"Gideon?"

"I fucked up the first time."

"I'd say so."

"I'm serious, Conrad, we have to talk him out of it."

"And how are we going to do that, Gideon?"

"I don't know. You're the genius."

Conrad scored an 800 on the math section of his SAT test. He had two years of college courses completed the day he finished high school. He did medical school in three years instead of four. And now he's the most in-demand surgeon in Beverly Hills. But for some reason, he's not smart enough to come up with a plan for talking Jake out of marrying Alyssa.

"I gave it my best shot, but I doubt if you remember," he tells me.

"I remember."

The girl on the stage, dancing, has got lousy tits and acne. I wish they'd turn down the volume on the rap song playing.

"He's going to be fucking miserable if he marries that bitch."

"He's in love with her, Gideon."

I'm starting to get pissed here, "Whose side are you on, Conrad?"

"The invitations have already gone out."

"What difference does that make?"

Conrad loosens his tie. "We've waited too long. The patient's prepped, and ready for surgery."

"That doesn't mean we stop trying."

"Jake's whupped, Gideon."

"Then we got to un-whup him."

I see Jake come in the door. He pays the cover and goes to the stage to look for us. Conrad yells from where we sit, "Jake."

"What are you doing way back here?" Jake says before sliding into the booth, sliding right across the napkins.

"Did you pay the cover?" I ask.

"Yeah."

"If you're in here with me, you don't have to pay. How many times have I told you that?"

"It's okay. I had a five-dollar-off coupon."

Jake is the only person in the world that would use a coupon in a titty bar.

The waitress delivers three beers.

"There's something I got to talk to you about," Jake says.

"There's something we'd like to talk to you about, too," I say.

"My cow manure idea?"

"No."

"Have you thought about that?"

"We're considering it," Conrad says.

"It's about Alyssa," I say.

"That's what I have to talk to you about," Jake says.

"You, first."

Jake twirls the beer bottle around and around. He's nervous. I'm not one to pray, but I say to myself, *Dear God. Please let him tell us he's dumping the bitch.*

"Guys, you can't fuck up the engagement dinner."

God has deserted me once again.

"You think we would do something like that?" Conrad asks.

"Yes." Jake eyes go from Conrad to me. "No male strippers, x-rated cakes, Jagermeister shots, or showing up in a latex suit."

"Her old man might like a shot or two."

"I'm not kidding, guys, from here on out everything has got to be perfect."

"What happens if it isn't?" I ask. "Is she going to dump you?"

"You guys don't know, because you haven't been there, but women go nuts before they get married."

"When did you finally figure that out?"

"The counselor warned me about it a month ago."

"Doesn't it tell you something, Jake," I say with as much sincerity as I can muster, "that if you're seeing a marriage counselor before you're married, something's wrong?"

"Hey, she's helped a lot."

Conrad says, "Let me tell you, the only reason psychologists become psychologists is so that they can talk with people more screwed up than they are."

I ask, "Are you getting laid more often?"

"Yes."

I bet he's lying.

There is a change of scenery on the stage. This chick is much better looking than the last one. The night shift must be coming on.

"We were all drunk the last time we talked about this," Conrad says, "but we're worried about you making a big mistake, Jake."

Good, Conrad's kicking in. Maybe he's got a new idea.

"A bad marriage can be cruel, but a divorce worse."

"How would you know?" Jake starts to get up.

"Jake, just listen."

"No."

"We're your friends."

"Not right now, you're not."

"We're trying to protect you."

"And who the fuck are you? Neither of you have ever been engaged. Neither of you have ever even been close. You're too busy fucking anything that moves to get serious about anybody."

Jake is half right. I haven't had a serious relationship with a woman in over two years and haven't been with a woman in over eleven months; a fact I don't reveal to anyone. For me, being around sex, all day, five days a week, has completely destroyed any sexual desire I had or want to have. Working in porn has rendered me impotent to any desire, feeling, or need for an act of physical love. Ironic, isn't it?

"Jake, listen."

"No, you fucking listen. You've never given Alyssa a chance."

"Bullshit."

"You think she's too good looking and classy for someone like me."

"Jake, calm down."

"No, I'm not going to calm down. You're supposed to be my friends and you can't stop calling my future wife a bitch?"

"Because she treats you like shit."

"No, she doesn't. She loves me."

"She has an odd way of showing it," Conrad says.

"I don't know what you're trying to prove. Maybe you think she's breaking the three of us up, or you're threatened by a beautiful, intelligent woman. Well, I got some news for you, we're not in grammar school any more. We're twenty-eight years old. We're no longer scoping out training bras or stealing *Playboy*s. We're adults and should be doing adult stuff like getting married, having a family, and doing something more with our lives than hanging around strip clubs."

"That's not it, Jake."

"Yes, that is it. It's time to grow up, boys."

"Alyssa's going to make you miserable, Jake," I say. "The chick is going to make you fucking miserable."

"Fuck you, Gideon."

Jake pushes his beer away, slides to the edge of the booth, but before turning away, says, "And if you do one thing to fuck up the rehearsal dinner, I swear I will fucking cross you off my list forever."

Jake jumps up and heads for exit. He doesn't look back.

Conrad and I stare at each other like a couple of sixth graders, caught stealing the weekly milk money.

"Now, what the fuck we gonna do?" I ask.

"I have no clue."

"You're the fucking genius, Conrad."

"Maybe there's nothing we can do."

"Don't say that."

"He's whupped, Gideon. He's fucking whupped."

CHAPTER 11

Jake, the Groom

Alyssa reserved a private room at The Ivy in Beverly Hills. Alyssa doesn't do inexpensive, theme, or chain restaurants. The place is crowded when we arrive at 7:45.

It happens every place we go, but especially in the Hollywood-type restaurants. With her on my arm, every eye comes our way. Alyssa is a beautiful woman, but made-up and dressed to the nines she rivals any starlet, young or old, past or present. People stare, gawk, can't turn their eyes away. Some approach asking for autographs or photos, but she tells them politely she is not in the business. Some want her to pose with them anyway. She smiles with her refusals.

I have been asked a hundred times if this scene bothers me or makes me feel small and insignificant. It did at first, but when I realized that every person who saw Alyssa, saw me, my mood took a one-eighty-degree turn. I was being viewed with envy and respect. Me, being with Alyssa, meant that I had something special. Money, sex, power, breeding, aura; who knows what they saw, assumed, guessed, or hated? The man who has the most beautiful woman in the place on his arm, is the man of the moment.

As we walk into the Ivy tonight, I am that man. And it feels great.

We are the first to arrive. This is by design. Alyssa, the detail-oriented one, has to be sure all is in order.

The room is a bit small, but has a long table with high-back chairs. Alyssa tests the move-ability of one of the chairs, and seems satisfied with the difficulty. From her purse, she takes out a stack of silver-and-gold lined cards. She carefully folds one at a time and places a single one on each place setting. Mom Doris will sit at the far end to my left and mom Brady the far end to my right, they won't even be able to see each other. She puts Farrin between Gideon and Conrad as a safety bumper. We will sit center, with daddy on her right and, for some reason, an empty seat next to him. Shannon, the only bridesmaid able to attend, and her husband will sit next to me.

"Farrin bringing a date?" I ask.

"I hope not."

Alyssa stands back to take one last look at the perfect table. We are ready to rock and roll.

LaRue and Marge, or as Alyssa likes to say, "Daddy's latest gold digger," arrive at 8:00. The rest will be fashionably late. The cleavage on Marge's dress seems more appropriate for a Red Lobster than The Ivy.

"Congratulations, I am so happy for the two of you," Marge says. She air-hugs Alyssa and shakes my hand without her other hand breaking her touch with LaRue. If it were up to Marge, this would be a double wedding.

LaRue doesn't bother shaking my hand, but does say, "Can you believe the valet gets twelve bucks plus tip at this place?"

"Scotch?" I ask.

"Straight up."

I signal our waiter, who stands like a sentry at the back of the room.

Gideon and Conrad arrive together, with dates, saving money on the valet service, no doubt.

Conrad has a delectable piece of eye candy on his arm. Blonde, blue-eyed, great breasts. "This is Tiffany."

"Nice to meet you."

Tiffany doesn't have to utter a word, one look tells all she has a hard time getting both her brain cells to work simultaneously. "Hi, I'm Tiffany."

"I just told them your name, honey," Conrad tells her.

"Oh."

Gideon's date looks young enough to be fronting a high school cheerleading squad, "This is Kay Cameron."

Kay is extremely cordial in greeting Alyssa. "Congratulations, I bet you are thrilled to know the day is only weeks away."

Alyssa is taken aback by the sincerity in Kay's voice. "You have no idea."

"But I wish I did," Kay says.

As the girls converse, I whisper into Gideon's ear, "Where'd you find her, in a Barely Legal video?"

"Believe it or not, she's twenty-six with a kid," he whispers back.

The waiter delivers LaRue's twelve-year-old scotch. Tiffany orders an Appletini, Conrad and Gideon Maker's Mark, Marge a gin and tonic, a beer for me, champagne for Alyssa, and Kay a Diet Sprite.

"Can't drink yet?" LaRue asks bluntly.

"I can, but don't." Kay answers, sensing his concern. "If you'd like to see my ID, I'll be more than happy to show you." She's obviously handled this situation before.

Shannon and her husband Gary arrive a bit flustered. Gary is in jeans with an Ivy-supplied, oversize sport coat. "They almost didn't let us in," Shannon says.

"I thought I'd have to go down the street and buy some overpriced pants," Gary, who works as an engineer in a computer chip plant, says.

If you look up "regular guy" in the dictionary, you'd see Gary's picture.

People would never suspect Shannon of being a close friend of Alyssa's. She's attractive, but hardly stunning; smart, but no Mensa member, and has few, if any, airs about her. Shannon is one of those people who are *just there* and happy to be *just there*. She and Gary, who were married seven years ago, before I knew Alyssa, would be the perfect next-door neighbors. They have one child, Margo, the cutest little five-year-old you have ever seen. I was shocked, but pleased when Alyssa asked Shannon to stand up in her wedding.

Alyssa's face drops the instant Brady enters the room with Simon. She repeats the activity seconds later when Doris enters with Arty. To avoid the couples, she joins LaRue who has backed up like one of his trucks, just to get out of the path of his two ex-wives.

"Nice place you picked."

"Oh, daddy, don't start in on me now. There is always going to be trash out there to pick up."

The group meets, greets, introduces, chits and chats, although Marge, Brady, and Doris do little more than dagger-stare at one another. Tiffany stays close to Conrad. She'd be uncomfortable in any social situation where clothes are required. Arty and Simon chat away, probably comparing ex-wife notes. Gideon seems a bit laid back for Gideon. I pull him aside.

"You doing her?" I ask.

"No," he says, "she's a friend."

Alyssa clinks crystal and announces, "Why don't we all find our seats."

"Farrin's not here yet," Doris says.

"Probably ran into a large magnet and got stuck," LaRue says, pulling out his chair. "Another scotch over here, buddy," he says to the busboy.

Alyssa makes sure that everyone sits in their assigned seat. Simon and Arty order their third round of drinks. Tiffany's smile stays plastered on her face. Brady adjusts her jewelry. Doris rubs red lipstick off her teeth. Kay chats, doing her best to be polite and presentable with everyone who is not.

Conrad says, "I got a box at the races next month if anyone is interested."

Arty and Simon perk up at the thought. "We'll go."

"It's quarter horses, isn't it?" LaRue asks.

"Oh, no," Tiffany says, "they'll be one-hundred percent horses."

This woman would give Marge a run for her money in the stupidity sweepstakes.

Farrin walks in the door with a guy a bit wider and shorter than her. "What, starting without me?"

"If we didn't start without you, Farrin, we'd never start," Brady says.

Farrin checks her watch. "Hey, this is the earliest I've been being late in a long time."

"Have a seat, Farrin," Alyssa says.

"Everybody, this is Fred," Farrin says, smiling at Conrad as she sits.

Fred waves at the assembled. Match.com must have had a computer glitch, because the purple streaks in Farrin's hair are not much of a match for Fred's thinning pate.

Farrin gives Conrad an overly friendly handshake. "Nice to see you."

"Nice to see you, too," Conrad says. "I love what you've done with all the metal on your face."

"You're so kind."

Tiffany gives Farrin a "he's mine" smile. Farrin thumbs her metal-laden nose in return. And our shrink claims men are the more competitive of the species.

One waiter passes out the menus, while another pulls the corks on expensive bottles of red and white wine.

"The specials on the menu tonight are…"

The "special" gastronomical choices described at length, are free-range chicken, scallops in a sauce veloute, and an all-grass-fed filet. All organic, all pricey.

As if on cue, the only question is from LaRue, "How much are they?"

"LaRue!" Marge says.

"Seems to be if they're gonna try to sell us something, they oughta tell us what it's gonna cost."

As the waiter scuttles off to avoid LaRue's abuse, the guests settle into the decadent comfort of plushy chairs. I stand and hold my bottle of beer up. "I'd like to offer a toast, but first I'd like to thank everyone for coming. And thank my future father-in-law…"

Gideon interrupts, "I'm the best man, aren't I supposed to give the toast?"

"Not at the engagement dinner," Alyssa says.

Gideon stands, "Let's break tradition."

I see Alyssa tighten. She's worried Gideon is going to start talking about me and some goat.

Gideon raises his glass, clears his throat, and says, "Please raise your glasses to the bride and groom, for there is nothing more important than their happiness. I am honored to be the best man at the wedding of one of the best men I have ever known." He lifts his glass in salute.

No one is more surprised than Alyssa.

I take a moment to let his words sink in, then raise my drink and offer my own. "To our family who are friends and to our friends who are family."

"Here, here."

The dinner is so far, surprisingly, so good.

LaRue tells the waiter to give him the biggest New Yorker they have, rare. Alyssa orders the appetizer size, wheat pasta with shrimp. Kay asks the waiter, "I need protein, what do you suggest?"

Simon studies the menu like he's about to take a DMV test, then gives the waiter very specific instructions on preparation of his chicken. Oddly enough, Arty does the same. Fred asks Farrin if she is going to order an appetizer, hears her negative response, and orders two, a salad and dinner. Farrin cares more about Conrad than about food. Tiffany says to Conrad after ordering. "I got the ribs, but you gotta tell me if I have anything stuck in my teeth after I'm done."

"This is all going much better than I expected," I whisper into Alyssa's ear.

"Don't get too comfortable, we still have a long way to go."

This is the family I'm inheriting. I don't have a choice. They are a dysfunctional collection, if there ever was one, perfect characters for a TV sitcom. The reality is that all families are dysfunctional in their own particular way. Compared to mine, Alyssa's family is a piece of cake.

Kay asks Alyssa, "Where are you going on your honeymoon?"

"Paris."

"Wow."

"Have you ever been?" Alyssa asks her.

"I remember driving through Paris, Texas, when I was a kid, but hopefully that's not the one you two will be going to."

"Ah, no."

"I'm sure you will have a phenomenal time. I've always wanted to see Notre Dame. I read when you visit the burial chambers, this big old door opens, cold air hits you, and you get this chill that tingles all the way to your spine."

"We'll put that on the list," I say.

"I'm not into graveyards. I'd rather shop." Alyssa makes a joke.

Kay and I chuckle.

The first round of appetizers arrives. Arty, Simon, Fred, and Marge dig in.

I notice Gideon has been nursing his first drink. "You want a refill?"

"No."

Fred tells all that he is one of the few property managers in Los Angeles that owns no property of his own. Oddly, he seems proud of that. Conrad is being physically pulled back by Tiffany each time Farrin leans into him to make a witty comment. Doris bends Gary's ear. Brady nags at Simon, who's eating habits somehow remind me of the Muppets. Marge talks to LaRue who ignores most of what she says.

The drinks keep coming, expensive wine never runs dry, and the service is remarkable. This is going to cost LaRue a bundle.

For me, this is all a big waste of money. I'd be happy at an Olive Garden. Growing up was tough financially, and my college years were downright poverty stricken. If you have ever been poor in your life, the kind of poor where the rent is always late, you eat canned spaghetti five nights a week, and there is no gas for your uninsured car; you never forget it. The memory of living hand-to-mouth is like a tattoo on your financial psyche. To this day, I clip coupons.

Alyssa says to Shannon, "Portia's coming in the week prior, so get a babysitter for the Saturday night before."

Portia, who I have only met once, is Alyssa's roommate from her modeling days in New York. Her significant other is a bond trader at Goldman Sachs.

"Just us girls?" Shannon asks.

"No, Jake will join us."

"What night?" Gideon's question breaks their tête-á-tête.

"Saturday."

"Jake can't. Bachelor party weekend."

"I thought you could do that on Friday night." Alyssa says.

"We are," Gideon says. "Friday, Saturday, and Sunday."

Alyssa pauses. "We haven't talked about this," she says, looking at Gideon, but talking to me.

I shrug my shoulders.

"He'll be back in time for the wedding," Conrad joins the discussion. "We promise."

"I have to be somewhat functional to work on Monday, guys." I say, half-joking.

"Yeah," LaRue adds.

Alyssa sees little humor, "We have a lot to accomplish the weekend before the weekend of the wedding."

Gideon shrugs his shoulders. "So do we."

Alyssa takes a deep breath.

I say, "Don't worry it's not going to be like one of those *Hangover* weekends." I refer to a movie I liked and Alyssa hated.

"How do you know?" Gideon asks.

"We will have to talk this over," Alyssa says.

"No." Gideon is firm.

"I'm sure we can work this out."

Gideon meets Alyssa's stare head on. "Non-negotiable."

This is not good. I know Alyssa's angry because her wrinkle-free forehead now has furrows deep enough to plant peas.

"Oh, come on," LaRue slurs, just in time. "Let 'em have some fun."

Alyssa is outnumbered. Her only ally is Marge who says, "Don't let him do it."

Marge shuts up as soon as LaRue tells her to "Shut up."

"Are you going out of town?" Alyssa asks, not yet ready to give in.

"We might," Conrad says.

"Where?"

"We're open to suggestions." Gideon is having fun at Alyssa's expense.

"How about one of those men-only sweat lodges?" Marge suggests.

"Go to Vegas," Simon shouts from the end of the table.

"What goes on in Vegas, stays in Vegas," Arty adds.

"Can I go?" Gary asks.

"No," Shannon answers.

"Now is not the time to have this discussion," Alyssa says, looking at me, like she looks when she's not speaking to me.

"What's to discuss?" Gideon says, drawing her back to him.

Kay laughs, breaking the tension, and says to Alyssa, "They're just little dogs barking like big ones. I wouldn't worry about it."

"How would you know?" Marge asks Kay. "You're just a kid."

"If there is one thing I know, I know men," Kay answers.

"You don't look old enough to know your multiplication

tables," Marge snaps back.

"Which isn't a bad thing," LaRue tells her.

"Genetics," Kay explains.

"No matter what they come up with for my bachelor party," I say, "I promise I'll be a good boy."

Alyssa looks at Gideon, then right at me. "I'm trusting you."

"When he's good, he's good," Gideon says, "but when he's bad, he's better."

Gideon and Alyssa's stare-down is thankfully interrupted by Tiffany. "I had to go to a bachelor party once and I was the only girl there. It was gross."

The main courses arrive and not a moment too soon.

Tiffany has an interesting way of gnawing on rib bones. I suspect Conrad will receive a similar gnawing later on in the evening. Alyssa picks at her food and talks with Shannon. Fred and Farrin have hardly said two sentences to one another, but neither seems to be too disappointed. Arty and Simon somehow remind me of lion kings at a slaughter. Gideon glances intermittently at Alyssa, but never says a word to her the rest of the evening. Kay savors every bite of food as if it were her last. At least here is someone who knows how to really enjoy a meal.

Coffee is offered, but no one accepts. A number of different desserts are laid out on the table with clean spoons and forks; not a buffet, but share-and-share-alike *fun* time. Simon, Arty, Fred, and LaRue have after-dinner drinks.

The waiter does a subtle lay of the bill between Alyssa and her dad. "Please enjoy your evening," he says in a perfunctory way. He knows his tip is safely tacked onto the bill.

"Don't look," she tells her daddy.

"Why not?"

"You don't want to see."

"I got to sign it, don't I?"

"I gave them your credit card already."

"How about the tip?"

"It's automatic."

"Fifteen percent?"

"Twenty."

"Come on, LaRue," Marge says.

In a way, I feel a bit sorry for LaRue. If he thinks this is expensive, just wait until he gets the tab on the wedding.

Everyone leaves at the same moment. Chairs slide back, barely disguising Simon's loud fart, and the ex-wives help their partners out of their chairs and stumble off toward their cars. Conrad gives Alyssa an air kiss. Tiffany gives her a big hug, neither of which seems appreciated. Fred asks Farrin for three singles so he can get the car. Gideon and Alyssa merely nod, but Kay says, "Thank you very much. I'm sure everything will go exactly as planned and it will be the best day of your life."

"I'm counting on it," Alyssa says to Kay.

"Thanks for having me at your dinner," Kay responds.

My apartment is closer, but Alyssa likes sleeping at her condo. It is an additional five minutes of open freeway time. She hasn't said a word to me since leaving the restaurant.

"I thought it went pretty well," I say.

She doesn't respond.

"The food was great. Hate to know what that all cost."

Her eyes stay on the road ahead.

"I wonder if Farrin will take Fred to the wedding?"

Alyssa can sit so still, her breathing is like a lizard's, imperceptible.

"Don't do this to me, Alyssa."

Silence.

"I didn't do anything wrong."

Not a move.

"This is not the time to go into one of your silent treatments." I pause. "Talk to me."

She sighs.

"Alyssa, you're not going to wait until we are in with that shrink to tell me what's the matter."

Nothing.

"Was it your dad, Marge, Simon, or Gideon?"

Her eyes do not sway from the road ahead.

"You can trust me, so talk to me."

Her head pivots and looks out the window on her side of the car.

"Alyssa, please."

Silence.

Why the hell can't she speak to me like she does when we're in front of Marilyn Beech?

Welcome to the world of Alyssa dealing with a problem. She shuts up, turns off, pulls the switch, quiets down, enters a world of verbal hibernation. Whatever you want to call it, it's awful. She takes refuge in a self-induced mental coma. It can last an hour, a day, a week. Once it went on for thirteen days, six hours, and nine minutes. The average is about three days.

The only time Alyssa is worse is when she is on her period. She becomes a different person: sullen, weepy, and unpredictable. A raw nerve, ready to snap at the slightest annoyance. She's never turned violent, but I wouldn't take the possibility off the table.

I asked LaRue once for advice and he told me when Alyssa was a kid and something happened she didn't like, she'd go into her room, slam the door, and stay in there for indefinite periods of time.

"What would bring her out?"

"Food or pee."

"What should I do now she's got her own bathroom, put a plate at the base of the door so she can smell it?" I asked LaRue.

"Worth a try."

"When she finally did come out, would she talk about the problem?"

"Not that I remember."

Since we took my car, I drop Alyssa off at the front of the six-unit building and I go off to find street parking. I wait until she is safely inside the building.

This late, the Westside is always parking hell. You can drive around for hours without finding a legal spot. Tonight's not so bad, only two blocks away, parking purgatory.

She buzzes me into the building. I take the elevator up. The door is open a crack and I enter. She has left only the hall light on, which tells me she is already in the bedroom. I go into the second bathroom which I use. The secret of a successful marriage, Alyssa believes, is separate bathrooms. I piss, brush, splash water on my face, strip down to my boxers, and make my way down the hall.

My clothes land on the chair, I pull off my boxers and climb in between the sheets. Alyssa comes out of the dressing room wearing sweatpants and a long tee-shirt. She pulls the covers back, lies down, stares at the ceiling.

"You want to talk about this?" I ask.

She reaches over, flips on the light, takes her book off the nightstand, opens to her place and reads lying on her side, facing in the opposite direction.

This is Alyssa being Alyssa.

CHAPTER 12

Alyssa, the Bride

No one really looks at your address, what they see is your zip code; and 90210 shines brightest of all.

The house in Beverly Hills isn't in Beverly Hills, it is in Beverly Hills Post Office, a section adjacent to BH, below Mulholland Drive. Few people, even in Beverly Hills, realize our section is actually in Los Angeles. The residents of BHPO never mention it.

The area was once a brushy hillside waiting for a wild fire until Dean Martin and a bunch of his business cronies bought the land in the 1960s to build a golf course. For some reason the plans fell through, and instead of tees and greens, cheaper, single-family homes sprouted up on hilly streets. Real estate agents sold it as an area to move to before you moved into the real Beverly Hills. In the late eighties and nineties, someone paid someone off and got the Beverly Hills zip code to cover the area. Developers snapped up the properties quicker than an inspector pockets a bribe. Bulldozers were brought in, and five- and six-bedroom mansions rose from the wreckage of many a two-bedroom ranch.

I thank God for the housing crisis because, without it, the one-story three-bedroom on a half-acre never would have fallen into foreclosure. One person's mortgage meltdown is another's rise to prominence.

The view wasn't great, but the lot size was fabulous. We offered the bank five thousand more than their list price, and they accepted the next day. They would have accepted the day we offered, but they had to renege on a bid three grand below the list price, that came in twenty-four hours earlier.

It might be best to explain when I say "we" I'm referring to "me" and daddy's money.

After daddy got over my over-bidding strategy, I showed him Tomas' (the hottest architect in BH) plan to "Preserve the eeenntegrity of zee land with a house fitting of its eeenvironrment." The first floor would be the kitchen, living, great, office, workout, and maid's rooms. The upstairs would be a master suite overlooking the pool, a small den, and three bedrooms with separate baths.

Daddy wasn't as thrilled with the design as me, but that's pretty much par for the course. The only stipulation he insisted on was the deed be in his name until it was decided what percentage would be wedding present and what would be a loan. I couldn't care less.

Before I started looking, I talked to Jake about where we would live. He preferred vintage. "Let's find an old, rambling Queen Anne and redo it with today's amenities and yesterday's charm."

"No," I said. "I'm not living anywhere without granite countertops already installed."

Jake will learn to love the new place. Who could dislike four bedrooms, five baths, a three-car garage, and a media room in Beverly Hills, well, Beverly Hills Post Office?

We, Jake and I, stand around while Tomas and the general contractor argue about the size of PVC, which will need to be reinstalled. It has taken them nine extra weeks to get the second floor under roof. My plan for moving in, upon our return from the honeymoon, was no less a pipe dream.

My cell phone rings. I recognize the number on the screen vaguely.

"Hello."

I hear a familiar voice. A bit shocked and uncomfortable, I move off to the side to speak in private. "I certainly didn't expect to hear from you."

I chuckle at his retort, listen to what he has to say, and respond, "Tomorrow night?"

He repeats his offer.

I glance over at Jake, then answer, "Sure, why not."

"Who was that?" Jake asks as I return.

"Friend," I say. "Do we have plans tomorrow night?"

"Cake designs."

"Would you mind if I rescheduled?"

"Not as long as you reschedule without me," Jake says.

"I'm going to do a dinner with an old friend, talk about the wedding," I say. "You don't mind, do you?"

"I could use a night off."

I've done my future husband a favor. I feel good.

The argument continues about the pipe. I don't listen. All I know is, it will add to the cost, which is already way over budget.

Chez Jay is a Santa Monica institution. It has sat on the same property across from the pier for decades, and hasn't changed a whole hell of a lot. You can walk in a side door. The bar is on the left, populated by soul surfers who used to be real surfers. Signed photos of movie stars, past and really past, fill spaces on smudgy walls, in need of a fresh coat of paint. In the middle are Formica tables with red padded chairs, to the right are red leather booths. My Dolce & Gabbanas crush peanut shells as I enter. There are no windows, and my eyes haven't adjusted from the bright setting sun outside.

"Over here."

From the last booth, Buck slides out, approaches, gives me a hug and a kiss. "You're looking great." He leads me back into his side of the booth.

"You still drinking margaritas?"

"Too much sugar," I say. "I'm into white wine now."

"Too bad, you were always a lot of fun visiting Margaritaville."

Johnny "Buck" Vierra is the guy your mother warns you about, the driver of the van your father won't let you get in.

"Congratulations," he says. "I can't believe you're going through with this."

"I am," I say proudly. "Who told you?"

"Local rag."

"You read the *Beverly Hills Courier*?"

"Somebody reads it for me." Buck sips his drink. "She cut out the picture of the bride." He takes the newspaper clipping out of his breast pocket and points at Jake. "You love this guy?"

"I do."

I was a junior at Marlboro Academy. Buck had already been kicked out of two private schools and was on his way out of the third when we met sneaking outside the temple for a joint at a bar mitzvah for some kid named Jonah or Jacob, but called Jack. Buck had long hair, a scruffy beard, tee-shirt wardrobe, and leather jacket. The 1993 version of James Dean. If there was one person who looked ridiculous in a yarmulke, it was Johnny Buck Vierra.

In high school, I can't say we ever really went together. Buck was hardly prom material. Mostly we hung out, made-out, hot-tubbed, partied, drank, experimented with whatever—all the stuff we didn't see the friends on *Friends* do. At times we were tight, mad-passionate-love close. At other times we hardly spoke. He was the first I ever slept with, but he couldn't say the same about me. Our so-called, on-off-off-on relationship lasted through my four years in college. It also lasted through his dropping out of college twice, numerous affairs, constant unemployment, cocaine addiction, and two stints in rehab. It would be impossible to count the number of times we "broke up." Make-up sex was routine for us. Buck was tough, a wild horse that no one, and especially not me, could ever break.

Buck was one of the few topics my mom, stepmom, and dad agreed upon: they all hated him.

I tried. I worked Buck, worked him every day, until one day, I woke up, walked out to the front of my apartment and found a half-naked Buck passed out on the floor. Next to him, passed out as well, but also totally naked, was a girl with a tattoo of a Banyan tree growing upward from her crotch. It was over, this time totally over. No amount of make-up sex could ever erase the sight of that sapling.

I threw him out, clothes and all. I cut off all ties, mutual friends, places we'd go, parents, things we did. For years I didn't hear a word, although rumor had it that his high-powered entertainment attorney dad plea-bargained a five-year sentence for Buck's drug dealing down to a misdemeanor and time served in the county jail. But I didn't want to believe it. There were always rumors about Buck, usually started by Buck.

A year ago, I'm coming out of Niemen-Marcus on Wilshire and a cherry-red Maserati pulls up, the window rolls down, and the guy driving leans across the leather to ask me, "I'm invited to a bar mitzvah this week, you want to go?"

Johnny Buck Vierra. I couldn't believe my eyes. Just like tonight.

Buck orders another Coke. "What's the lucky guy's name?"

"Jake."

"What does he do?"

"Works for my dad. He'll take over the business someday."

"Everyone's trash is your daddy's treasure," Buck says. He always thought my dad being in the trash business was funny.

My white wine arrives along with one-page menus stained with tartar sauce.

"Still agenting?"

A few years back, Buck's dad got him set up at UTA as a junior agent handling teen actors. Surprisingly, he took to the business.

"All those years I spent lying to you, my parents, teachers, police, and judges are finally paying off," he says proudly. "Only problem is sometimes I can't remember what lie I just told."

I laugh at a man who has found the perfect position for his unique talents.

Buck was looking good, his hair shaggy, but now a styled shaggy. His three-day beard replaced by smooth, moisturized skin. Shirt silk, pants fine wool, the leather jacket morphed to alpaca from Rodeo Drive.

"So, why'd you pick him?"

"I told you, I fell in love."

"Shit, I do that twice a day," he says. "You don't get married because you're in love, you get married because you want something."

He's right.

"I want all the stuff you used to refer to as bullshit, Buck."

Buck imitates a fortuneteller. "I am not seeing the beautiful Alyssa behind some white picket fence."

"No, it's a decorative, six-foot, wrought-iron fence with a remote-controlled, retractable gate. Where have you been?"

"I come, I go, and sometimes I come back," he says.

The waiter brings celery, carrots, and oyster crackers.

"What's this guy going to give you that I couldn't give you?"

he asks as he squirms a bit on the leather.

"What I deserve," I say, and then add, "without the hassle."

"Oh, come on," he says, "I wasn't that bad."

"Yes, you were."

"I was the only one who wouldn't put up with your bullshit, Alyssa."

"Instead, you made me put up with yours."

Buck sits back, takes a long look at me, smiles. "Ah, Alyssa," he states, "the little girl sitting on the edge of a fortune is finally getting what money can't buy."

"And why shouldn't I?"

"Because it's too easy."

"Like you would know?" I question.

He laughs.

"And what is young Jake bringing to the party?"

"Family, stability, and fidelity."

"Ouch."

I sit back in the booth. "You haven't changed much, Buck."

"Likewise, my love, likewise."

We glance at the menus.

"Where'd you say you were getting married?" he asks.

"Beverly Hills Congregational."

"Am I invited?"

"No."

"I'll stand in the back."

"Not cool."

"I'll sneak in."

"Totally not cool."

"Oh, come on, I know you want me to be there."

"Why would you ever think that?" I ask.

"You showed up here, didn't you?"

CHAPTER 13

Jake, the Groom

Night off. What a relief. No cakes, registry, vows, gowns, tuxedo, Kettle One or Grey Goose decision to muddle my brain. Even better, it's LaRue's poker night, so he blows out of work before five. The minute the last truck comes in for the day, the gates slide shut and I'm gone.

In traffic, it takes me about an hour to get to Sunset City.

She didn't mention I missed her birthday. Nobody at Sunset mentioned it either. Obviously, there was no cake. Mom lives in an assisted living facility "with a special section" for the memory impaired, which to me sounds like a roped-off area rather than a special care unit.

Sunset City is not a bad place, nor is it a good place. It's a place where, when combining her Social Security with what I can afford monthly, Mom can exist until her body catches up with her mind and ceases to function. Alyssa, for my wedding present, wants to move her to a 4-star facility near Santa Barbara. Mom would get a much better level of care there than Sunset City. It is exactly what she needs, and I really appreciate the offer; but for some unknown reason I'm hesitant about the idea. I've got to think about it some more.

I used to tell Sunset City when I'm coming, but no longer. The first time I popped in unannounced she was strapped in a wheelchair, mismatched shoes on her feet, hair uncombed, wearing a stained bathrobe and a leaking Depend. They explained she was having a bad day. "Excuse me? But who wouldn't have a bad day tied down, sitting in a puddle of her own urine? The only thing worse would be sitting in a puddle of someone else's urine."

Tonight mom looks pretty good, dressed in one of the sweat suits I bought for her, the most versatile clothing choice I could find. She doesn't recognize me. No big surprise there, but my voice does seem to calm her. "I'm getting married pretty soon, Mom."

"Why?"

"Want to give you grandchildren."

"What am I going to do with grandchildren?"

"Anything you want, Mom, anything you want."

Mom gets to leave the facility twice a week. Mondays and Thursdays they corral all "Al's Patients," as they are referred to by the crack staff, and load them onto the Sunset Happy Bus for a fun-filled, exciting few hours. The bus pulls out of the parking lot and for the next few hours rides around in no particular direction and returns to the facility. What fun.

When I visit, which I try to do once a week, I always get her the hell out of there. Usually, we go on a tour of our old stomping grounds. She seems to like it. First stop, I pick up five bucks worth of daisies at the florist. Second stop, the cemetery. Tonight, we arrive ten minutes before they lock the gates for the night.

Compared to the other monuments and stones, Dad's plaque is small. I always have to pull grass away from the edges to read his name. It seems inconceivable that he has been here more than two decades. Dad telling me, "I got cancer, Jake. I'm gonna die," seems only yesterday.

I don't remember much about my father, except the yelling. He yelled at Mom, me, the cancer, the neighbors, my goldfish, empty liquor bottles, the Dodgers; he wasn't picky. My dad taught me every swear word in the book and numerous swear word combinations, his favorite being "Jesus fucking the Christ child."

Mom seldom talked about him after he was gone. When I asked, she deflected the questions, and soon I quit asking. I don't believe they had much of a marriage. The only thing I wish my dad would have done while he was alive was to buy a bigger and better life insurance policy, which would have made Mom's and my life a lot easier.

All the cemetery plots have built-in cups to stand flowers upright as if they are growing; but the grass has grown over his and I don't have the time to dig around for it. I lay the daisies below his name, and stand still for a few moments with Mom, who for some reason seems to like it here. Maybe she thinks she's not visiting him, but visiting her next residence.

A truck horn blares. It is the caretaker making final rounds before he goes home for the night. I wave, we walk back to the Volvo and drive out of the grounds.

One time, I brought Alyssa along for my Mommy sojourn. Big mistake. Two seconds after the introduction, mom tells Alyssa that women should not be allowed to wear pants to work. I have no clue where this came from, nor do I know why Alyssa would ever respond with an opposite viewpoint. They argue. Mom calls her a "rotten feminist." Alyssa says mom is "stuck in a 1950's Leave It to Beaver time warp." I can't believe it. The whole conversation is absurd. They get to the point of screaming at one another and I have to step in and physically separate the two. On the way home, I tell Alyssa that unless you've had someone very close to you be stricken with the Big A, it is difficult to comprehend. Alyssa had no comment. She just sat and stared out the window.

There was plenty of sunlight left, so I drive over to the crummy house we used to rent. It remains crummy. The only difference was a half-moon arch had been added over the front door. Asians must have bought the place, which faces east, a big plus for those folks.

I next drive past the park where I played Little League baseball, Ellie Sinclair's house where I got my first feel, and the corner market where Gideon, Conrad, and I got busted shoplifting Abba Zabbas. Passing by St. Theresa's Grammar School, I notice a pile of stacked newspapers in a dumpster and start to laugh so hard I pull the car over and park. Mom, if she could think straight, would think I was nuts.

It happened in the seventh grade, when swearwords became everyday language, girls grew breasts, and erections happened at the most inopportune times. It was in that school year the one life-changing, turning point in my life, and the lives of my best friends went down. It was called the parish paper drive.

In order to pay for the flat, round, dried, stale pizza dough they passed out at mass every Sunday, the church requested that the parishioners bundle up their old newspapers and periodicals and bring them down to the cordoned-off area of the parking lot aka school playground. When the stack reached a height beyond Mr. Steve's janitorial reach, a truck came and hauled it all away for about a penny a pound. For years I looked at that stack and said to myself that there had to be more there than just a pile of discarded newsprint. One afternoon, daydreaming through arithmetic, I allowed myself to wildly assume that most of the men in the parish were either horny old geezers or young, sexually repressed future geezers who weren't getting any at home. Taking the assumption a step further, each group had to have some mode of release, and since this was before the internet, there were only a few releases available.

I told my buddies my plan.

"I'm not digging in a pile of newspapers." Gideon was adamant.

"But there's gold in that there hill."

"This sounds like another one of your brain farts, Jake," Gideon continued.

"I got a feeling there's something in there."

"Yeah," Conrad says, "the Ebola virus."

"I'm telling you, the boys and men in this parish got to get rid of their stuff somewhere."

"We're talking good Catholics," Conrad argued.

"Yeah, and that's why they're so horny," I came back at him.

"The pages will be stuck together," Gideon said.

"Trust me guys, one man's trash is another man's treasure."

We waited until after six, when it was dark. Mr. Steve had gone home, the nuns went into their vespers to pray for sinners like us, and the priests were in the middle of cocktail hour. We climbed up and into the middle of the stack. I passed out steak knives I brought from home, and told the boys to first cut open the stacks where, from a side view, magazines could be seen stuffed alongside the *LA Times* and *Pennysavers*. They voiced their objections punctuated by swearwords, showing their displeasure. I knew it was uncomfortable balancing on the pile and the filthy newsprint rubbed off on everything, but I couldn't be swayed. I had a feeling.

"You have to have faith, guys."

Gideon was the first to hit pay dirt. "Oh my," he said. "There is a God."

From that instant, we tore through the stack like thieves at King Tut's tomb.

It was a bonanza past my wildest expectations. *Playboy,*

Penthouse, Hustler, Gent, and Conrad's personal favorite, *Juggs*, sprouted from the pile. Loose papers flew in every direction as we tore through stack after stack in search of centerfolds, ass shots, and girl-on-girl action. We'd barely make it through one photo spread when another treasure trove of tits and ass popped out of the pile. A cornucopia of smut, right under the church steeple, was there for our personal viewing pleasure, an education you can't find in any schoolroom.

After darkness fell, we trudged the three blocks to my house, hiding our porn-gold in the attic of my garage where mom would never venture. The amount of time we spent in that garage over the next three months was equal to years spent in school. We learned more about anatomy, biology, sociology, psychology, physiology, and photographic technique than we could have ever learned in a classroom. And literature! We all became avid readers. Who could resist stories with titles like "Nude Garden Party," "The Horny Housewife Next Door," and "My Breasts Need Air."

We'd lay out the centerfolds to cover the floor, then stand in the middle and discuss the merits of the "three B's" breast, butt, and bush. No longer were we merely dreaming of naked women. They were all here, right in front of us, the real thing. Well, almost.

We had fun. One of us would read "Penthouse Letters" while the others perused "Girls of the Big Ten." Or someone would come up with a scenario for "Baking the Field of Miss Bakersfield." Or we'd become artistic, arranging the photos so Miss April was humping Miss August, or the Pet-of-the-Month was staring into the honey pot of the *Hustler* Ho.

Little did we realize we were defining, even refining our tastes in intricacies of the female anatomy.

Conrad loved breasts. He became a self-proclaimed aficionado. He commented on the roundness, nipple placement, color, tan line, firmness, droop factor, and claimed he could spot "store bought" ninety-nine percent of the time. Gideon preferred the bad girls, the dirtier, raunchier, kinkier, the better. I, of course, rose above their base anatomical perversions, appreciating the shots of the proverbial "good girls." My interests were the cheerleaders, ingénues, and especially the naked coeds who were "taking a break from their pre-med studies." It was the full package that intrigued me—the hair, eyes, shape, tan, the smile so serene and inviting.

These women seemed richer, smarter, more educated, and from families in the better parts of town. They attended private schools, took riding lessons, played the cello. I know because it said so in the written captions under their photos. These were the women I wanted, but knew I'd never have. The ones out of my league, girls I would dream about the rest of my days.

It was the best three months of our lives.

Unfortunately, it all came crashing down when Gideon got caught selling the less-desirable issues to a group of sixth graders. I remember telling him, "Only seventh and eighth graders!" But Gideon didn't listen, profit was profit.

The nuns went godly ballistic, called our parents, forced us into counseling with Father Celcius of all people. "Don't you think it a bit incongruous having us talk about sex with a pervert?" Conrad asked Sister Superior with a straight face.

In the end, my mom had to beg, literally beg, for us not to be expelled.

I find it amazing how something as simple and well-meaning as the parish paper drive could have such a profound impact on Gideon Batch, Conrad Blaine, and Jake Dombrowski.

We were three musketeers. Gideon the bad boy, Conrad the brain, and me, the daydreaming wiseass. We were always in trouble, after school more than in school. If I heard it once, I heard it a thousand times, "You're going to hell, Jake Dombrowski. You keep this up, you're going to hell."

"Oh, come on, Sister, you really think I'm going to end up next to Hitler, shoveling brimstone, for pulling Mary Jane O'Brien's pigtails?"

Her answer was to slap me upside my head.

Conrad never got whacked. His comments and questions were so clever, the nuns never knew when he was putting them on or being serious. "Sister," he once asked with a straight face, "why didn't God have more children? I mean, come on, only one son? It's not like he couldn't afford college."

Gideon got into so much trouble, Sister Superior had his parents' number on speed-dial. And since his parents were religious fanatics to begin with (they named him Gideon, after all), his transgressions were punished at both school and home.

Tonight, I sit in the car laughing, amazed at what I remember. I wish Mom could do the same.

"Want to go back to Sunset, Mom?"

"I want to go on a roller coaster."

"Maybe when I come next week."

"You know, I never pay more than one-fifty-nine for asparagus."

"Good for you, Mom, good for you."

On the way home, freeway traffic is bad going through the interchange. While riding the brakes I pick up my cell and call Alyssa. She's not home. I call her cell. She doesn't pick up. I leave a message. "Alyssa, it's after nine. I figured you'd be done with your dinner by now. I'm not sure if I should go to your place, so call me and tell me what's going on."

Ten minutes later I'm on the 110, and she still hasn't called. I'm not sure if I should get off at my apartment exit, or take the 405 to Sunset. One second after I pass my off ramp, "Don't Stop Believing" rings out of my phone.

"Where are ya?" I say, a bit too loudly.

"Brentwood."

I can barely hear her. "Are you still in the restaurant?"

"No."

"How was dinner?"

"Good."

"This is a lousy connection. Want me to call you back?"

"No."

"I'm on the freeway; want me to come to your place?"

"No."

I wait.

I pass by the "Welcome to Santa Monica" sign and move over two lanes.

"You want to come over to mine?"

"No," she pauses. "We're going to have another drink. I'll talk to you tomorrow."

"Fine."

She sounded funny, peculiar, not "ha-ha-funny." Maybe she had a strange night, although it would be difficult to out-strange mine.

The connection breaks from her end.

I get off the freeway, double back three off ramps and go home. It will be nice to sleep in my own bed for a change.

CHAPTER 14

Conrad, the Groomsman

She's standing at the entrance to the old Venice Pier.
"How are you?"

"I'm hanging in there," she says.

She leans over for a full arm hug and an air kiss, very LA.

"Sorry I'm late, but I miscalculated the amount of suction in my third liposuction of the day."

"Too much or too little?"

"'Very little's' are few and far between when it comes to liposuction."

She smiles.

I turn to my right, "Ready?"

"Let's go."

My date is a walking oxymoron. The purple streaks of hair, nose piercings, dark eye shadow, tattoo on the back of her neck, and enough rings in her earlobes to fill a display case, contrast with her wearing a flowered sundress right out of a *J Crew* catalog. A little big in the rear and flat in front, but she looks good. I point to her flip-flop sandals. "You can walk in those?"

"You're a part-time podiatrist, too?" she asks.

"No, but I can recommend one after your feet sue you for non-support."

"I chose fashion over function just for you."

"Thank you."

I set the pace. "If I'm walking too fast, all you have to do is stop me and I can reset to any speed."

"Does that pertain only to walking?"

"For now."

This is going to be fun. A whacked-out woman once in a while is a good change of pace.

We proceed north past a stretch of oceanfront condos and homes. It is a beautiful late afternoon. The trade winds are blowing in, and not a cloud in the sky.

"You don't impress me as being a Venice kind of a guy," she says.

"Every so often you need a blast of actual humanity to bring you back to reality."

"That's why they invented the Discovery Channel."

She doesn't have bad wheels, and the dress is fluffy enough to cover up what she's carrying on her hips. I could suck those cells out in ten minutes and give her a great ass. "I hope I'm not taking you away from Fred this evening."

"No, Fred's been zapped back into cyberspace."

"Didn't work out?"

She pushes her thumb against the tip of her pinkie finger as if sizing up Fred's prowess.

"Too bad," I say, "a good property manager who owns no property is hard to find."

"He's on Match.com, under the title *Big Sugar Cane 14*, if you want to chat him up."

On our left is a parking lot where a number of dilapidated RVs and Airstream trailers have been parked since Jimmy Carter was president. "How did you ever get the name Farrin, anyway?"

"My mother's father's sister. Mom thought she'd get a big chunk of her inheritance if she named me after her."

"Did she?"

"The old bitch died giving it all to some TV preacher."

"That doesn't seem fair."

"Nobody ever said it has to be fair."

Three black kids, gangbangers or gangbanger wannabes, approach from the opposite direction. They rap out some unintelligible language, "Ain't no motha-fucka no nigga ho, bro."

Farrin grabs my hand, pulls me slightly to the side until the brothers pass by. "I'm scared of black people who don't talk like white people."

I laugh. She doesn't let go of my hand.

We enter the area of Muscle Beach, which is nothing more than an outdoor gym. There are about ten greased, over-cut muscle-heads in skimpy spandex thongs and wife-beater tee-shirts pumping iron, spotting each other, or posing for the people on the sidewalk like us.

My review is simple, "Grotesque."

"Coming from a guy who sculpts women's bodies to perfection, that says a lot."

I point out the one muscle-woman in the group. "Those thighs should be registered as lethal weapons."

Farrin stops, gets my attention directed back to her. "You want to do me?"

"In what sense?"

"New rack, tighten the butt, get rid of these flappy janes," she pulls the flesh down from the underside of her bicep.

"Would that make you happy?"

"It'd help."

"I'll tell you what I tell all my first-time patients." I pause for affect. "Happiness comes from within, not without."

"Oh, yeah, right," she mocks me, "being a miserable, hot babe is exactly the same as a miserable, pudgy troll."

"You're not a troll."

She looks at me funny. I forgot a word in my last sentence.

At the bizarre, beach bazaar at the end of Windward Avenue, we stop at one of the many tee-shirt shops. "You wouldn't think that there would be that much demand for tee-shirts with the word 'Fuck' on the front," I say, pointing out a large display.

Farrin takes one off the rack, "Fuck me, Pay me, and Go Away," and models it. "Do you think this makes me look slutty?"

"Oh, no," I say, "not you."

"I'd buy it," she says, replacing it back on the rack, "but I don't have any sandals to go with it."

From Windward Street north, there are booths and tables of untalented local artisans hocking their creations, and break dancers spinning on their spines for tips. We pause to watch a cross between the Oz Tin Man and Old Man River in a tuxedo doing a Devo-like pantomime. Unique, to say the least. But my personal favorite is the guy with no arms or legs, playing the guitar. I pull out two dollars, stuff them in the limbless guy's hat, and request "Freebird."

"I love that song," Farrin tells me.

Next, I offer to buy Farrin a grain of rice with her name carved into it; but she declines, saying, "I just wouldn't have any place to put it."

There are five different merchants in the *grain-of-rice-labeling* business. It doesn't seem possible that there could me that much demand for personalized starch.

We stop for dinner at one of the many sidewalk cafés, and sit outside where it is still warm and sunny.

"Getting excited about the wedding?"

"Not really," she says. "Girls only get excited when it is their wedding."

"You ever been married?" I ask.

"Close, but no cigar."

"Close, as in take-the-dress-back close?"

"Not that close."

"Disappointed?"

"Yeah."

"Wasn't the right guy, huh?"

"I wasn't the right girl." Farrin looks at her menu.

"You think Alyssa and Jake are right for each other?"

Surprised, she puts the menu down. "You don't?"

"Sorry, but you can't answer a question with a question."

"Why not?"

"Because we'd keep going round and round and round and never get anywhere."

"That the only rule you have?"

"No."

"Give me another."

"I'll let you know as we go along."

She folds her hands as if in church. Her shiny, black nail polish reflects the sun. "Well, to answer your original question," she says, "my sister is used to getting everything she wants. So, if Jake wants what she wants, they'll have a great marriage."

"That's hardly a ringing endorsement."

"You asked."

"There is a theory that a girl usually marries a facsimile of her father. You believe that?"

"Does a guy marry a carbon copy of his mother?"

"Can't do that," I remind her. "Question-question."

"Sorry, I've never been much for rules," she says, then pauses.

Farrin chooses her words carefully. "Jake's probably a lot like LaRue, when LaRue was poor."

"Rich dad, poor dad, which one is better?"

"You ask a lot of questions," she tells me.

"It's a part of my charm."

"What part?"

We are back to sexual innuendo. I love sexual innuendo. "Parts is parts."

She smiles, repeats the thumb against the tip of her little finger routine, and gives me a questioning look.

"I understand your concern," I say seriously.

"You never know the fortune until you crack open the cookie," she says.

"What do you think the odds are of getting two Freds in a row?"

"It can happen."

"Maybe the best road to take is to make a test run," I say, "to be sure all parts are operational, sized right, and can perform at maximum capacity?"

"There's a good idea," she says, playing along.

"Thank you."

"I'll have to put it on my list of important things to do."

"What position?"

Farrin takes out her iPhone, scrolls to a page, and reads. "Let's see. I'll put 'Doctor Conrad's sexual run-thru' above 'Get dress fitted for wedding,' but below 'Buy tampons.'"

Farrin doesn't back down from mental challenges. I like that.

It's dark by the time we walk back to the street where she parked her old BMW. "This was a kick," I say.

"Yes, it was."

"Would you like to follow me back to my place?"

If she says "Yes," I get laid. If she says "No," I'm in the exact same place I was in before I asked.

She unlocks the car and stands with door separating us. "I'd be a slut if I slept with you on the first date."

"I'll go back and buy you the tee-shirt if that's what it'll take."

"What a gentleman." She gives me an awe-shucks shrug and says, "But I have things before you on my list, remember?"

I inch a bit closer to her, check out her skin tone. She's not lying. "But it would probably be best if we schedule our test run before we walk down the aisle together."

"Get a lot of those strange, antsy feelings out of the way?"

"Precisely."

"You know my number."

"Almost."

She places her hand on the back of my neck and pulls my face toward her. She gives me a warm, wet, kiss. Farrin knows exactly what she's doing.

CHAPTER 15

Alyssa, the Bride

So much to do, so little time.

On Monday I take a disinterested and uncooperative Jake to meet with Bitzy, our wedding planner. There is a problem.

"Why are we paying for a wedding planner, when you quit your job?" he asks the same question he asked a month ago when I was lucky enough to hire her.

"Because she'll save money in the long run."

"At two hundred dollars an hour."

"She saved four hundred dollars off the cost of the band."

"Which took her three hours to find."

Jake won't let go.

"Your dad know?"

"Bitzy will put it all into one bill, with a final price, and Dad won't even notice."

"You hope."

Bitzy Schwartz is a woman you don't like, but love having on your side. She's never been married, and I'll bet she's never been a bridesmaid; but she can haggle down a caterer with the best of them. I'm told she'll be as nervous as me on the big day.

Bitzy knew exactly where to go to get the setting I wanted for my ring, the florist with the freshest flowers, the wholesaler for the imported champagne, a clean, pressed, red carpet runner for the church and, of course, the photographers. Bitzy thinks of everything I wouldn't think of thinking of. Bitzy's the best.

"Change of plans," Bitzy announces the moment we sit down in her den-office-second bedroom.

"What?" I ask, adding some absolute terror to my reaction.

"They need the church Friday evening."

"What for?"

"Some Christian saint thing."

"They can't do this to me."

"They already have," she says. "We have to move the rehearsal to this Saturday and the dinner right after."

Jake asks, "This Saturday?"

"I've already cleared it with the minister," Bitzy tells Jake.

"No can do."

"Jake," I interrupt.

"Bachelor party," he interrupts my interruption.

"You can move that," Bitzy brushes the topic off.

"It's not mine to move," Jakes tells her.

"You can always find time for that silliness."

"I don't think so."

I am about to join in, but Bitzy informed me she has had experience dealing with these types of problems. It is best if I let her go it alone.

"Are you going out of town?" she asks.

"I'm not sure," Jake says.

"So, you don't really know if this is a problem?"

"Gideon has plans."

"Is that the porn person?" Bitzy asks Jake.

Jake looks toward me, but speaks to Bitzy. "He's a filmmaker."

"So was OJ Simpson."

I actually see the hair rise up on the back of Jake's neck.

"Listen," Jake says, his anger barely controlled, "they've been planning this for months."

Bitzy is adamant. "Well, they're just going to have to move it."

"No way."

"Want me to put in a call and explain the situation?"

"No. Forget it."

"You only have to push back your shing-a-ling a day."

"No. It ain't gonna happen."

Jake is sitting straight up in his chair. Bitzy edges forward, pushing her oddly pointy bust, as if a weapon, at my future husband.

"It seems to me that the only thing we're arguing about is the timing of your inebriation."

"What?"

"You know they are going to get you drunk and keep you

drunk," Bitzy argues, "so what's the big deal if you're drunk for two days or three? You won't remember anything anyway." She pauses. "I saw that disgusting movie, too."

Jake seems ready to jump across the desk at Bitzy. I put my hand on his knee to settle him down.

"Until we find out what your friends have planned, it's pointless to argue about this," I say.

"I've already had to beg the restaurant to make room for us on the new night." Bitzy has moved to round two, still punching.

"That's not my problem," Jake says.

I tighten my grip on Jake's knee.

"And the flowers, the invites, the table decorations, music, waiters, special dessert have already been rearranged." Bitzy is a bitch-on-wheels. No wonder she's in such demand.

"I don't care."

"You want me to do that all again?" Bitzy snaps back.

I'm surprised she doesn't add "at two hundred dollars an hour."

"I don't give a shit." Jake won't give in.

"May I remind you that you have run out of weekends before the ceremony."

"No, you've run out of weekends."

"Stop!" I take control. "Both of you, stop."

I face Jake. "We haven't even discussed the bachelor party."

"What's to discuss?"

"Plenty," Bitzy chimes in, which I wish she hadn't.

Jake is about to explode. I pull my hand up from his knee to his inner thigh. "Can we have a time-out please?"

The two stare at each other like those UFC fighters I was forced to watch the night Gideon decided to drop by unannounced.

"I promise," I say, "I'll work it out. I'll call Conrad. Maybe you can do it a night during the week. Whatever. It'll work out."

This is not good. I don't need this aggravation. The bachelor party is going to have to move to Sunday night. What's the big deal? This is not 1950 and it's hardly like Jake has never been drunk. My God, the whole idea of the boys going out for one last "big night" is such a stupid, outmoded custom anyway.

Bitzy is about to speak, but my head-wag shuts her up. I rub Jake's thigh, making sure my hand pats his boys. I've got his attention. We all pause as I take control and change the subject.

"Now, can we please move on and discuss the centerpieces?"

On Tuesday I taste six cake recipes and over a dozen wines. Shannon is thrilled to tag along. I feel like a beached whale by mid-afternoon. I drop her off at her kids' sitter and visit the florist to go over the floral arrangements for the church. This part isn't easy. I should have taken Riley or Milo with me to translate. Except for my two gay friends, I'm not really wild about homosexuals. It creeps me out to think what they do with each other.

On Wednesday, I'm back at Neiman's with a photograph of a dress, which will give my team an exact idea of what I want. The designer promises sketches by Friday, and the seamstress will order the material. I don't care what it will cost, what it will take, what they have to do. I've made my decision. This is what I want. My dress will be perfect.

While I'm in the store I decide to finish up the bridesmaids, and choose their shoes —a little more than they probably expect to spend, but they'll get over it. From the salon, I go to the tuxedo store and cancel the frumpy, sweat-stained rentals. I should have been able to trust Jake with this, but who am I kidding? I will not be married to someone in a tuxedo previously worn by some testosterone-leaking nineteen-year-old. At 6:00, I arrive at the caterers to meet the waiters who will be working the reception. This probably isn't necessary, but after the debacle at the shower, I have to be sure there are no wolves in waiters' clothing. I cancel our appointment with Marilyn Beech. She tries to talk me back into it, "this is a critical time," but there are just not enough hours. Jake was pleased when I told him. I make him happy again.

Thursday, I'm with Bitzy all day: hotel to check on the out-of-town reservations, rehearsal restaurant, because they want a credit card in advance; meet, listen, and hire a trumpeter to play at the ceremony, and then back to the bakery to finalize a rum-based chocolate cake with low-cal, butter-cream frosting topped-off in a pink-and-white rosette design.

Thursday night, Jake and I are at the church to meet the minister.

"I'm Reverend Francis O'Grady." He shook hands with a firm, strong grip.

"Shouldn't you be Catholic?" Jake asked.

"Not necessarily."

"O'Grady sounds like you just got off the boat from County Cork." Jake adds a lousy leprechaun lilt to his comment. If he thinks he is being funny and charming, he's not.

"Both my parents were Presbyterian, as were both their parents."

"Sorry," Jake says. "Eight years of Catholic school."

"Evidently."

Minister O'Grady ushers us into his very well-appointed office, all dark wood and stained glass. There is a faint smell of incense. Our file is on his desk. "So, I see that you are not members of our congregation?"

"No," I say, "but we're looking for a church to attend on a regular basis."

O'Grady asks Jake, "Are you thinking of converting?"

"Converting to what?"

There is a very uncomfortable pause.

"Evidently not."

The minister sits, opens the file, and removes one page. "I see you have written your own vows."

Actually, I wrote them. "Yes, we did," I say proudly.

"I've made some minor changes," he says, pushing the page towards me.

I read quickly. He has only corrected my grammar. "Fine."

"I have some issues I would like to discuss with a few of the musical choices," the minister says, putting on a pair of reading glasses and lifting the following page. "I'm not familiar with 'Through the Eyes of Love.'"

"It's the theme from the movie *Ice Castles*."

"I'm still not familiar with it."

"I wanted 'Send in the Clowns.'" Jake's first attempt at humor fell flat. Why he tries again confounds me.

Minister O'Grady takes off his eye-cheaters, leans back. "Making the marriage ceremony personal is one thing, but the inclusion of top-forty hits doesn't keep with our church's standards or recommendations. Solemnity is important."

"I've hired a trumpeter to play 'The Trumpet Volunteer,'" I tell him.

"That I can live with."

"And Pachelbel's 'Canon in D,'" I say, adding, "That was the theme from Ordinary People."

"I will need to hear that."

Like I have the time…

Jake asks, "Do you have iTunes?"

"What's an I tune?"

"I'll find it for you," I say.

O'Grady folds his hands and rests them on his desk blotter. Not the most humorous of men to begin with, he gives us a very serious stare and asks, "What is the foremost reason you have decided to take the vows of marriage."

The question comes out of the blue. I'm stumped.

"Kids," Jake answers without hesitation.

"Children," O'Grady says, "you desire a family?"

"Big one," Jake answers.

"Not that big," I qualify.

"The reasons for the union of two people should be spiritual and emotional, as well as familial."

I really don't have time to listen to this.

He continues, "Marriage is a contract between two people not only to achieve certain goals, but to share equally in every aspect of their lives."

I think about mentioning that this discussion may be a little late in coming.

He pauses, then asks, "Do you fight?"

"Fight?" Jake asks.

"No," I answer, wanting this to be over.

"You should." O'Grady leans back in his chair.

"Fight?" Jake repeats.

"I have a theory. The divorce rate is high because couples have not learned how to fight," he says. "Couples just don't know how important it is to confront one another."

"Really," Jake says.

I want this to end, now.

"If couples would fight, resolve their differences and move on, their lives together would be on a more solid footing. Instead they avoid confrontation and allow bad feelings and thoughts to fester like a cancer."

"Wouldn't jumping from the fight, right to the make-up sex achieve the same goal?"

"No, I think not."

Strike three on Jake's third attempt at humor.

"After you both become active parishioners, we have a six-week course: 'How to be Married in Today's World.'" He pulls a small brochure out of the desk drawer and hands it to me.

All this has been a commercial for an in-church infomercial.

"We already go to a marriage counselor," Jake confesses what he doesn't need to confess.

Minister O'Grady gives him an odd look, probably wondering if Jake is joking.

"We will definitely consider the program," I say. "It sounds wonderful."

O'Grady gives me a slight smile. He closes the file and says to Jake, "The church requires payment in advance."

"Do you take American Express?" I ask.

"Of course."

I find my copy of Dad's AmEx card and hand it over. O'Grady swipes the card through the electronic reader on the desk, punches in the codes, waits for the bill to print, then hands the card back to me with a pen to sign.

As he hands me my receipt, I tell him, "We'd like you to be a part of as many aspects of our wedding as possible."

"That is very kind of you."

"I'll get back to you on the schedule and the music."

"Please do." He ushers us out the door, past the baptismal font and a statue of some saint with a finger in the air. It looks like he's scolding me.

Neither of us say a word until we are in the parking lot.

"Where'd you find that guy?" Jake asks.

"I wanted the other minister here, but he was booked."

Jake chuckles, "Talk about a load of laughs."

The way back to the condo is a quiet ride. There is no good time to have any discussion, which I don't want to have, but this one can't be avoided. I might as well get it over with.

"Jake, about the bachelor party."

"What about it?"

"Well, we seem to have a scheduling conflict."

"You know, Alyssa, I've haven't asked for much in this whole, entire wedding…"

"I know."

"The boys' weekend has been planned for months."

"You're not positive of that."

"Believe me, they've got plans."

"Jake, I don't want you going off and coming back with some weird disease."

"You really think I'd do something like that?"

"One of your friends works in an AIDS incubator. I worry."

"Don't."

I take a little time before asking, "You really want to spend the whole weekend drunk and stoned, lying in some gutter?"

"That's not going to happen."

"Do you know what you're going to do?"

"No."

I consider the best line of reasoning and try a new tactic. "Jake, it's not like I'm telling you that you can't go, but I'd rather you..."

"I'm not going to miss my own bachelor party, Alyssa."

"It wasn't my fault the church screwed up."

"Mine, either."

"But we still have to deal with it."

I touch my hand to his shoulder, then rub his neck. We need calm. I don't want this to be a continuation of his fight with Bitzy.

"Can you do it Friday?" I ask.

"Fly out Friday and come back Saturday afternoon? No."

"What's the matter with Sunday?"

"I have to work the next day."

"I could talk to my dad about that."

"He hates the morning roll call."

I pause. This is not going well.

"How about if we move the rehearsal dinner to Wednesday?" Jake surprises me with the suggestion.

"We'd miss our last counseling session before the wedding."

"We missed this week."

"You know it gets difficult when we miss two weeks in a row."

"Tuesday, then?"

"Bitzy can't rearrange everything again."

"Why not?"

"Because she already told me she couldn't do it."

Bitzy didn't say this, but I assume that is what she'd say.

"How about if you leave right after the rehearsal dinner?"

"We'll never get a flight out that late."

"Maybe you're driving."

"Driving and bachelor parties don't mix."

We are getting close to my condo.

"How about if you do the party after the ceremony?" I say, running out of options.

"We'll be in Paris."

I've been so busy with the wedding I've totally forgotten about the honeymoon.

"I mean," Jake says, "people will understand if we don't make the dinner."

"Jake..."

"We just had the engagement dinner, this is a rerun."

"The wedding party has to be at the church, to practice."

"We could do that anytime."

"No, you can't."

"Maybe we all go to the church, rehearse, then the three of us leave?" Jake tries again.

"That'll never work."

Jake stops my Mercedes in front of the condo's underground parking, inserts the pass key. We wait for the iron gate to slide open. "Maybe we should cancel the restaurant and do a barbeque late Sunday after the three of us get back?"

"You don't do a rehearsal barbeque," I say. "Plus, I'm sure you'll be in great shape after your weekend of debauchery."

Jake parks the car. We get out and walk to the garage elevator, hit the button, go to the top floor, and walk into my unit. "I've done everything you've asked, Alyssa. Lost every argument, gone where you wanted me to go, and made every concession, I'm not backing down from this one."

Jake has got his heels dug in so deep, it is pointless to continue. I don't say a word. I turn on the lights, toss my purse on the end table and go straight to the bathroom. A few minutes later I come out, find Jake in the kitchen, eating pretzels out of the box. I make a beeline to him, throw my arms around his neck, pull him toward me, and kiss him full on the lips. I taste the salty snack. I hoist my butt up onto the edge of the granite countertop, wiggle out of my underwear, spread my legs, wrapping them around his waist. My skirt rides up. I kiss him again, feel him harden. I undo his belt, let his pants drop, reach in and pull his penis upward. I stroke him a few times. My tongue is down his throat. I push my torso closer and maneuver the tip of his dick inside me. I thrust to make the union deeper. We're now locked, thrusting in unison. I go from panting, to moaning, to loud groans of pleasure. Jake takes over the pace, faster and faster, as I get wetter and wetter. I come with a shout he knows well, but don't stop fucking. The pressure inside me increases as his penis swells to its maximum. His red face contorts in a final squint. His breath stops. He explodes inside me. A few more thrusts, and he's empty.

We both catch our breath… relax. He softens, we uncouple. Holding each other in an embrace, we kiss. I help pull his pants back up to his waist, unlock my legs, lean back on my hands.

"Right to the make-up sex," I say.

Jake laughs.

I pat him on the butt as he walks off to the bathroom. I climb down, smooth out my skirt, go into the cupboard, find the Formula 409, spray the counter, and wipe it clean.

CHAPTER 16

Conrad, the Groomsman

As soon as I'm out of the surgical unit, I turn my phone on and it rings immediately. Unknown Caller is on the small screen.

"Hello."

"It's Alyssa."

"Hey."

"What are you doing?"

"Walking out of surgery."

"There's been a change in plans."

I wait, secretly hoping the wedding's been called off. "And?"

"It's really no big deal," she says and goes on to explain the situation.

I am a bit shocked, but hardly surprised. "Jake hasn't said anything to us about this," I tell her.

"Well, whatever," Alyssa hurries. "I have another call coming in I have to take."

She breaks the connection.

I call Gideon.

"Hey, what are you doing?"

"Lunchtime three-way."

"Bon appétit."

"What's up?"

"Alyssa called."

"Lucky you."

"Rehearsal's been changed, can't do the bachelor party until Sunday."

"What did you say?"

"Rehearsal's been…"

"I heard that. What did you say to her?"

"Nothing."

"Conrad…"

"The church booked Saint Stigmata Night or something, so the dinner's been moved up a week."

"I already made the fucking plane and hotel reservations."

"Don't yell at me."

"This is Alyssa bullshit, Conrad."

I imagine Gideon's face, his nostrils widening as he puffs away like an old steam locomotive. "I bet the bitch had it all planned. Just like her to pull something like this at the last minute."

Gideon is pissed. Me, I seldom get rattled, I could do a nose job during Hurricane Katrina.

"So what are we gonna do?"

"Hell if I know," Gideon says.

"I never heard of a bachelor party on a Sunday night."

A lot of useless breathing vents through the phones.

"How about if we leave Sunday, stay Monday, and come back Tuesday?" he asks.

"Can't, I'm cutting Monday and Tuesday."

"Move them."

"Can't."

"It's not like you're doing heart transplants, Conrad."

"It is to these women."

"Well, we're not going to Vegas for one night."

"Get a couple of those starlets of yours. We can film Jake in a three-way and provide him with a nice keepsake for the hope chest," I suggest. "It would probably kick-start the divorce."

Gideon says, "This is fucking bullshit."

There is a pause as the two of us contemplate the problem. Or, at least, he contemplates the problem. I've got four gel packs waiting for installation, and a tummy-tuck to end my day.

"So what are we going to do?" I ask.

"Alyssa is a bitch. Everything about her spells bitch with a capital B. I don't care how much money she has or how good looking she is or that her father gave Jake a cushy job; the woman is fucking evil. I know girls who suck cocks for a living that are nicer than that fucking bitch." Gideon takes a breath. "What we should do is stop Jake from marrying that cunt."

"Calm down, Gideon."

"You know it just as well as I do."

"That horse has already left the gate."

"Not if I can help it."

I can hear a person in the background tell Gideon, "Your orgy is waiting."

"This story was fucked up to begin with, and more fucked up as it goes on." Gideon calms a bit.

"Duh."

I take a few seconds before I tell him, "We have to be at the church at six on Saturday, dinner's at seven."

"You want a ride?" he asks.

"Not really."

"What the fuck does 'Not really' mean Conrad?"

"I'll meet you there."

Before he hangs up, I ask, "So what about the bachelor party?"

"Fuck if I know."

"As the best man, the bachelor party is your responsibility," I remind him.

"You're not going to help?"

"I'll gladly defer to an expert in this particular area."

"What makes me the expert on bachelor parties?"

"Take a look around you."

CHAPTER 17

Gideon, the Best Man

I'm at the church one minute before six. I'm the only one here. The door's locked. If Conrad got the date wrong, I'll fucking kill him.

Conrad shows up five minutes late.

"I thought you said six?"

"I did."

We stand around. A short, pudgy woman, resembling a bowling pin, saunters over to us in a noxious wave of gardenia and hair spray. I smell her before I see her. "Are you here for the Walworth wedding?" she asks looking up at us, her pearls bouncing into her cleavage like pinballs looking for a way out.

Conrad says, "Isn't it the Dombrowski wedding?"

"Whatever. They're on their way," she says.

She then pivots on her clunky black shoes and disappears around the side of the church.

"You think she plays the organ?" I say.

"Not the one you play," Conrad says. He leans against the door and starts to hum "Bohemian Rhapsody." It's the only Queen song I ever liked.

Another five minutes elapse. These are the times I wish I still smoked, at least I'd have something to do with myself. Conrad, of course, is his usual unflappable self. His demeanor is the same whether he's at a funeral or prizefight. Me? I don't want to be here. I want to be in Vegas.

A Volvo and a Mercedes drive up and park in front of the church in the spaces marked "Reserved for Ceremony." Alyssa, some skinny chick with sunken eyes, Shannon, and Farrin exit the Mercedes. Gary and some slick-looking dude climb out of Jake's car. They come up the stairs in a small stampede, when suddenly the ten-foot, carved, wooden door of the church is opened by our mystery woman.

"Did you two meet Bitzy?" Alyssa asks.

"In a manner of speaking," Conrad says.

Bitzy puts out her plump, diamond-crusted, hand to shake, then asks, "Which one of you is the porn person?"

"Why do you want to know?" I answer, shaking her limp limb. "You want an audition?"

"Just wondered," she says, applying hand sanitizer.

We enter the church bunched like a rugby scrum. I pull Jake aside. "Who the hell is the troll?"

"Wedding planner."

The church is dark, cold and dreary. It reminds me of being forced to say the rosary on the days the nuns were too lazy to teach.

"Been a while since I've been in one of these," Conrad says to Farrin who stands close to his side.

"Me, too," she says.

I've done more time in church than a three-strike criminal does in the joint. My parents would lead me up the aisle five days a week plus Sundays until I was old enough to outrun my mother. I hated it then and I hate it now. I'm here for Jake and no other reason.

I follow the group to the center aisle and hear Bitzy yell out, "Minister O'Grady, lights, please."

The overhead altar lights illuminate on cue, and spread enough light for even the darkest corners of the church. A fifty-something guy in minister togs comes walking out of the sacristy, or whatever they call it in a Congregational church, and spreads his hands to welcome our motley flock. Give this guy a staff and two stone tablets and he'd be perfect for a remake of *The Ten Commandments*.

"Good evening."

Jake says, "Hello, Father."

"No, I'm not a priest," he says to the future groom.

"There are those years of Catholic school again," Jake says, as if trying out a punch line.

Conrad and I laugh.

Bitzy takes count. "Where is the father of the bride?"

"He couldn't be here," Alyssa says.

"Why not?" I ask.

"I really couldn't say," Alyssa says.

"What kind of a frickin' answer is that?"

"You're not supposed to swear in church," Jake tells me.

"He's the porn person," Bitzy tells the minister.

"I said 'frickin' not 'fucking.'" I make it official for all to hear.

The guy who is with the anorexic babe seems to get quite a kick out of my comment.

"Let's get started," Bitzy says, taking back control. "Groom at the altar rail waiting. Bride, bridesmaids, and groomsmen in the vestibule, maid of honor at the outer door."

We all go our separate ways, except the slimy guy who sits down in a pew, takes out his Blackberry and finger-smudges its screen.

I stand at attention and listen to drill sergeant Bitzy.

"Music will come up, flower girl released, first groomsman and bridesmaid…"

Conrad puts out his arms like wings. Shannon takes hold and they prance up the aisle like Fred and Ginger before their big dance.

"Next," Bitzy yells out, "Portia and best man."

The girl has a twig for an arm, her eyes are sunken and her skin white. I see a lot of druggies in my line of work and she's definitely a charter member of the society. She latches onto me and we go up the aisle.

"Maid of honor…"

Farrin walks forward. She's wearing a nose ring big enough to slide your index finger through. If I had a clothesline, I could tie it on and pull her up the aisle.

"Now when the maid of honor reaches about here," Bitzy calls out, stepping on a spot in the aisle, "the groom and best man will meet the minister…"

Bitzy is interrupted by the slimy guy who shrieks into his phone, "Can ya hear me now?"

"Excuse me," Bitzy screams, "could we have some reverence within this house of God?"

"I'm having a hard time getting a signal in here," the guy continues even louder than before.

Bitzy hurries down the center aisle, goes up to the idiot and snaps her index finger right between the guy's eyes.

"Ouch, that hurt, bitch," slimy jerk blurts out as he swipes his forehead checking for blood.

"Have some respect, asshole," Bitzy says.

"Screw you, Sergeant Slaughter." Slimy dude slides to the other end of the pew where Bitzy can't get at him easily and re-fingers his cell screen.

The Bitzy Show goes on. "So when the groom reaches center aisle, bride and dad come forward."

Alyssa comes up the aisle and meets Jake, who pretends to shake LaRue's hand and turns back to the minister.

"A few well-chosen words from the minister…"

Bitzy is abruptly cut off by O'Grady, who is checking his watch. "I have some things to do before the dinner this evening. You'll have to excuse me."

The minister walks off, disappears behind the altar. That's two down.

Bitzy continues, clapping in time with the words, "Ceremony, ceremony, rings, more ceremony, kiss, applause, music, leave."

The lights go off in the church. We're left in the dark.

Bitzy pauses, then says, "Well, I guess we're done."

I can't believe this. "What?" I ask, "We came all the way out here to do this?"

Conrad gives me a look that says "Don't start."

I stare at Alyssa and speak loud enough for all to hear. "So I can learn to walk from there to here?"

Alyssa avoids my stare.

"You made me waste three hundred dollars in reservation fees, and blowout my plans for the weekend to practice putting one foot in front of the other?"

"Practice makes perfect," Alyssa says.

"Why don't we try walking and chewing gum at the same time?" I'm hot and getting hotter. "I do more rehearsal for a blow job than we've done here tonight."

Jake steps forward and puts his hand on my chest. "Calm down, Gideon."

"This is bullshit, Jake. We could be in Vegas right now."

"There's always a church rehearsal," Alyssa says.

"It's tradition," Bitzy adds.

"And you're going to break into *Fiddler on the Roof* for us next?"

"I could," she answers.

I say emphatically. "We could have done this over the damn phone."

"I disagree," Alyssa responds.

I give the bitch the coldest stare I can, and say, "Practicing for this wedding is like practicing to take a shit."

And the rehearsal is officially over.

"Reservations are at seven at Wolfgang Puck's." Alyssa announces, turns and exits the church with bridesmaids in tow.

Jake says, "You're in church, Gideon," and leaves with the rest of the attendees and the slimy guy who has enjoyed the scene immensely.

Conrad, Farrin, and I are left at the altar.

"Well," Farrin says to me, "you certainly have a way of making events memorable."

CHAPTER 18

Farrin, Stepsister and Maid of Honor

I've decided to fuck Conrad after dinner. Might as well find out if he is any good before the ceremony, because if he isn't, a wedding is a great place to meet men. He talked a real good game on our walk, but you never know until you're under the sheets.

Gideon, Conrad, and I drive to the restaurant in Conrad's Jaguar. Nice car.

"Enough, Gideon, enough," Conrad tells him.

Gideon sits in the backseat, fingers contorted and fidgety, squeezing the blood right out of them. It is amusing to watch a guy stew in his own testosterone juice.

"There is nothing you can do about it now. It's over, move on."

"We'd be checking into the Bellagio right at this very instant, Conrad."

"Enough."

We meet Jake at the bar.

As Gideon and Jake stand toe-to-toe, I watch Conrad. He's laid back, relaxed, has that air of success about him, primped by some personal shopper, I bet. He looks great. Hard to believe anyone as smooth as this guy could be lousy in the sack, but you never know.

"You let her fuck you out of a bachelor party. Admit it, Jake." Gideon points a finger into Jake's face.

"It wasn't her fault."

"Bullshit."

"The church changed the schedule."

"Yeah, right."

"What do you want me to do, Gideon?"

"I want you to grow some fucking balls. You let her blow off your bachelor party for some dumb-fuck church rehearsal, where half the people didn't even show up." Gideon does get hot when he's mad. "I booked the flights a month ago with no cancellation."

"We'll go during the week?" Jake says.

"Can't," Conrad says calmly as if this isn't a fight at all, "Monday and Tuesday, I got two liposuctions, three nose jobs, and a labia reconstruction."

I interrupt. "Labia reconstruction?"

"It's the new, hot, post-pregnancy op thing."

"Can't wait," I tell him.

"I had every second of the weekend planned," Gideon tells Jake.

"Then why didn't you talk to the minister?" Jake says, pointing to Minister O'Grady entering Wolfgang Puck's. "He's the one who screwed up."

"Nobody gave me a chance," Gideon says.

Conrad says quietly to me, "This is like watching the *Fox News Channel*, vile, angry rhetoric with no possible resolution."

Conrad's not just funny, he's brainy.

Gideon downs the rest of his drink in one gulp. "Fuck it," he says.

Portia, who I have met a number of times over the years, stays close to her Goldman Sachs boyfriend, Sly. They make the perfect New York couple. He's short, with beady little eyes, enough mousse in his hair to be fined for an oil spill, and a shiny suit that screams "Bernie Madoff's my kinda guy." Portia is a rail-thin, lingerie model. Her pale, anorexic, heroin-addict skin color makes her especially appealing during the current vampire craze. I don't know why anyone would waste good money buying her dinner, a Tic-Tac would probably fill her up. Brady told me she and Alyssa went to the spa on Friday and got a manicure, pedicure, facial, massage, leg wax, and matching Brazilians. The only time your body will get more plucking, picking, and probing is during an autopsy.

LaRue arrives with Marge. This woman is dumber than dogshit. She must give great head, because there could be no other logical reason ex-stepdaddy would put up with this moron. I'll never forget the time LaRue was scheduled to get a good-guy citizen award from the Optimist Club and Marge tells him, "Be sure to wear your glasses."

What an idiot.

I glance over at the table. Alyssa is putting down place cards. I'm sitting next to Conrad, no matter what the place settings say.

Jake's drinking beer, Conrad and Gideon bourbon, and I, a kumquat martini. Gideon orders his second.

"We'll go to Vegas another time," Jake says to Gideon.

"Yeah, right."

"We will."

"You actually think she'll let you go after you're wearing a pair of marriage handcuffs?"

"Yes."

"Jake, a sex offender getting a weekend pass to a Girl Scout camp has better odds than the three of us ever going to Vegas again."

Conrad merely sits back, takes it all in and looks really great, better all the time, actually.

At the table, Alyssa has her hand on dad's shoulder, so they must be talking money. Every few moments she glances at her mother, Brady. I wonder what Alyssa is thinking. She never saw it coming when her mom walked out the door when she was in first grade. It must have been awful. Brady said she found the man of her dreams and was so "madly in love" she had no other option than to "follow her heart." This is not what a six-year-old needs to hear from Mommy Dearest. LaRue did everything humanly possible to ease her pain, and if that translated to giving Alyssa everything she ever wanted to make her feel better, I can't fault him for it.

Maybe once you get used to getting anything and everything you want, it isn't easy to change. And Alyssa having the whole package-gorgeous, smart, clever, cunning, and incredibly manipulative doesn't hurt either. Alyssa's always going to be rich. When LaRue retires and hands over the business putting Jake in charge; what's changed? Alyssa will never worry about making the rent and will never go into Saks and wonder, *Can I afford this*? The roof over her head will always cover at least four bedrooms. And a Mercedes to Alyssa isn't a car, it's a birthright.

This wedding is the perfect time and place for Alyssa to be Alyssa.

I'm not sure if Simon is Brady's fifth or sixth "love of her life."

It is hard to keep track without a scorecard. If I were to put all Brady's men on a graph, the chart would clearly reveal the slime factor line making a consistent, upward trajectory, intersecting with the downward line, which pinpoints the personal worth of her suitors. I am sure Brady has kicked herself in the ass more than once for leaving LaRue before he hit it big in the garbage business. Having a real trash-bag like Simon by her side, and into her checkbook, is ironic, to say the least.

Shannon and her husband Gary are talking with Portia and Sly. Bet that's a deep conversation. These four have about as much in common as Joey Ramone and George Bush.

Alyssa signals me to bring everyone to the table.

"Chow, boys."

Gideon has a final comment to Jake before leaving the bar. "Dinner's at six at Ruth Chris'. Be there on time and don't drive."

"Yes, master."

Alyssa sticks Brady, Simon, and Gideon at the left end of the table. Shannon and Gary are across from one another, acting as the buffer. Minister O'Grady is dead center. Conrad and I are across from Portia and Sly, with the remaining four on the right end. With Jake, that makes twelve. If Jesus shows up we can have our own "last supper."

Sly asks Conrad, "Who handles your financial services?"

"Merrill."

"I can do better." Sly says, leans towards him and half-whispers, "Don't believe what you hear about derivatives."

"How would you know what he's heard?" I ask as impolitely as possible.

Sly ignores my question. "Let's talk later," he tells Conrad, flipping him his business card.

I glance down the table to see Marge with her usual "I'm stupid" look on her face. LaRue shudders a bit as he peruses the menu, or should I say the menu prices. Shannon and Gary seem actually excited in being able to order the pricey "frou-frou" food. Simon bends Gideon's ear and, I suspect, talks about porn, since Gideon is doing his best to ignore him. Brady can't read the menu without her cheater glasses, but refuses to put them on and put a dent in the deep crust of makeup she has on her face. I bet she applied the batch with a trowel. I whisper in Conrad's ear, "Are we having fun yet?"

"You make your own good time," he replies.

I reach under the tablecloth and run my hand along the inside of his leg. "Good times are always better when shared."

He knows he's going to get lucky tonight.

The wine is served. The minister says grace. Orders are taken. Appetizers arrive.

The dinner is surprisingly a quiet, chitchat affair. Being in the middle of a loud, crowded restaurant doesn't lend itself to outbursts of verbal venom, which would be the norm for this group.

Jake is his usual good-guy self. Alyssa's lucky to have him. He's no dreamboat, like Conrad, but a real dreamer, the consummate optimist. Jake sees things as he wants to see them, not as they truly are. The three of us were once stuck in freeway construction traffic and Jake noticed a row of cement columns being built and said, "If I were in charge, I'd give one column each to a different artist and let them go nuts." I could see him drift into his own world, imagining multicolored murals lining the highway.

I worry about Jake. He has a naive purity about him, I'd hate to see it destroyed. It is not like he's some goody-two-shoes, but he either refuses to see negatives, or refuses to accept them. It's no picnic working at Walworth, ordering around a bunch of illegal Mexicans, wading through oceans of filthy trash, separating recyclables from the landfill, not to mention putting up with LaRue's ranting and raving. I know. I tried working in the billing department one summer and I lasted three days, one of which I used to call in sick. Jake puts up with all of it, and since he's always smiling, he must have found some way of enjoying his work. But I worry about my future stepbrother-in-law. What if it all comes crashing down and he sees life isn't as rosy as his glasses have tinted it? Reality is the best instructor in life, but also the cruelest.

Jake is totally, absolutely, unequivocally in love with Alyssa. He adores her. He wants a family in the worst way. I want to be in love like that.

At the other end of the table, Gideon is miserable. It is hard to feel sorry for someone who spends his days directing people fucking and sucking, but watching him suffer the inanity of Brady and Simon, I pity the poor bastard. Gideon did get screwed when the rehearsal dinner was moved. No doubt he had an incredible weekend planned: golf, tennis, gambling, liquor and a string of Las Vegas hookers, longer than a line at the DMV, even though I know that Jake would never dip his pen in that ink. Conrad I'm not sure about, and Gideon? I bet his dick has landed in more holes than Tiger Wood's golf balls.

Jake tells great stories about Gideon—the way the nuns would crack his knuckles, whip him with pointers, make him wear his shoes on the wrong feet; but they could never break him. Gideon would finish one punishment and, the next day, come back for more. In the eighth grade he did a month of detention for "taking liberties" with Nancy Jane Bonds. Not only did he admit to his indiscretion, but boasted he had Nancy Jane "moaning like a French whore." In high school, Gideon did his own driver training by taking a joy ride in a yellow school bus. He broke into the girl's locker room during gym, threw all their clothes into one pile, and forced them to mix and match in a before-the-bell-rings free-for-all. And although Jake claimed it was his idea, Gideon was the one who pulled off a Sunday theft of an entire supply of communion wafers and wine, leaving the entire congregation hungry for the body of Jesus and thirsting for blood.

Conrad let on that Gideon's parents are ultra-fanatic Catholics. Daddy is a church deacon and mommy sells burial plots and engraved cremation urns at the Catholic cemetery. His older brother is a priest. I can only guess that the family doesn't have a lot to do with their porn director son, except to pray for the prodigal to return to the fold. He also told me that Gideon is an X-rated auteur. His camera moves, editing, style, and lighting techniques have made him the Stephen Spielberg of smut. He's done his own version of *Jaws*.

Gideon keeps to himself except for his good buddies Jake and Conrad. I'm not sure he has a lot of other friends. As far as I know, he's never had a long-term relationship. Jake says if he were ever in trouble, Gideon would be the first person he would call. There is definitely something intriguing underneath Gideon's rough exterior. He never talks about himself. We were at a party once and I asked him, "If there was one subject you'd like to make a movie about, what would it be?" I couldn't wait to hear what kinky, disgusting, brand of perversion he'd come up with.

He answered without a second of hesitation, "The difficulty of being a kid with crappy parents."

Minister O'Grady, Simon, and Gary have a race to be the winner of the Clean Plate Club Award. It's a photo finish, but I have to give the nod to O'Grady who mops up every last drop of Béarnaise sauce with a hunk of table bread. Give second place to Simon who, after devouring what appeared to be a brontosaurus steak, repeatedly reaches over to Portia's almost-untouched plate to spear the catch of the day.

The busboys clear the table. Alyssa excuses herself and heads for the ladies' room. Gideon gets up and follows her. I follow Gideon.

In the hallway, past the reception area, I see Gideon intercept Alyssa. They stand between the Men's and Women's restrooms. I listen before deciding whether to referee.

"That was really bullshit, Alyssa."

"What?"

"Screwing him out of a trip to Vegas."

"I didn't know he was going to Vegas."

"You knew he was going somewhere."

Alyssa puts her hands on her hips. "What's your problem?"

"I don't like the way you treat my friend."

"You're jealous is what you are."

"Of him?"

"Of me. You don't like having your little playmate taken away."

"You've got to be kidding."

"You don't like seeing Jake grow up, get married, have a family, become an adult."

"No," Gideon says, "I hate seeing him do it with you."

"What—would one of your little whores from one of your dirty movies make a better choice?"

I should break this up before it comes to blows, but I'm a coward.

"He's so in love with you, he doesn't know what he's doing, and you take advantage of him every chance you get."

"We're both in love, but you can't see that because you're incapable of it, Gideon."

"I am not."

"You don't think I've seen guys like you?" Alyssa says. "You go through women like water. What bothers you is Jake's not like you. He wants something more."

"And you've got him convinced it's you."

"It's called love."

"Let me tell you, he's going to wake up one morning and realize it's your idea of love and not his."

"Give it up, Gideon. Go back into your sexual playpen. This game is over. Jake loves me more than he loves you." She hesitates. "You lose."

Alyssa turns and enters the ladies' room.

Gideon starts to go after her, but stops as another woman comes out the door.

I must have moved into the opening of the hallway to better hear their exchange, because when he turns, our eyes meet. He's embarrassed and so am I.

"I'll catch a cab back to my car," he says, rushing past me. "Make up an excuse for me."

"Sure, no problem."

Gideon walks out the front door.

I do not want to be where I'm standing when Alyssa comes out, so I hustle back to the group.

Alyssa returns to the table, as if she hasn't a care in the world. She leans over and gives Jake a kiss, then her dad.

Alyssa clangs the crystal. The table quiets. Jake rises.

"We've lost one?" Jake questions.

"He had to leave," I pipe up, "said something about auditioning talent for tomorrow night."

"Did he say if he needed any help?" Simon asks.

"Certainly not you, dear," Brady answers.

Alyssa pulls at Jake's sleeve. "Just go ahead."

Jake raises his glass of beer, prompting the rest to do the same. "There are now only seven days that separate two people from becoming one. May the time pass swiftly, and may we all arrive at next week's wedding; ready, willing, and able."

The guests reach across to clink glassware.

Alyssa stands and says, "I'd like to make a toast." She raises her wine glass, faces Jake and says, "To my future husband. May we share the benefits and challenges of our new life together, and make the best of both. May we prosper as a couple and create a wonderful family. May our lives be rich in happiness, pure in health, and successful in our pursuits."

"Here, here."

As I expected, Conrad has a great dick and knows how to use it; but for some reason, I do not enjoy the sex as much as I should. I can't get my head around what went down tonight. I can feel the breeze of an ill wind blowing us all into next week.

CHAPTER 19

Conrad, the Groomsman

I was in med school at Northwestern in the middle of a cadaver, slicing up a liver, and this guy I barely know asks, "Wanna go to a bachelor party?"

"When?"

"Tonight."

"Sure, why not?"

"Here's the address, bring two hundred bucks."

"You getting married?"

"No," he says. "Sid is."

"Who's Sid?"

"Who cares?"

I take the el train north to Andersonville, a Chicago neighborhood founded a few generations back by Swedish and Norwegian immigrants. Since the majority of people I saw roaming around Lincoln Avenue were Hispanic or gay, I suspected that the Olafs and Svens had long since moved to the suburbs.

The address on the paper my fellow student gave me was once Louie's Hardware, but now it's an empty storefront. Scrawled on the window were the words, "Home Depot put me outta bisness." At this point I am glad I did not pay any money up front. I walk south, one door down, and see a neon sign over a nondescript door, flashing "Lester's Bowling Second Floor." Scotch-taped to the inside of the glass is a page reading, "Close for Private Party." Lester and Louie must have been classmates in the Chicago Public School System. The door is unlocked. I enter, walk up the creaky stairs, and am transported back in time.

A four-lane bowling alley, circa 1952. No overhead score projectors, no AMF automatic pin spotters, air vents, or fancy ball-return device. The place is charming in a dilapidated, out-of-touch, out-of-time kind of way. There is a cage where they keep the rental shoes, racks of balls for the amateurs, a bar and lounge where about twenty guys are standing around drinking and joking.

A woman, who has probably been here since 1952 meets me on her way out. "Don't spill nothin' on the lanes," she says.

"This your place?" I ask.

"Yeah, so don't spill nothin' on the lanes."

I know no one, so I look for my cadaver buddy. He's not around. A guy in a tee-shirt with the sleeves cut off comes up to me. "You here for Sid?"

"Guess so."

"Got your money?"

I pull out my wallet, take out four fifties and hand the bills over.

"Only tap beer and no name brands, if ya want hard stuff." He counts my money twice, adds it to his wad and reminds me. "And don't spill nothing on the lanes."

"I'm Conrad."

"I'm Guido."

"Where's Sid?"

"Shitfaced, somewhere."

The dirty movies playing on the retractable white screen are as old as the barstools. I've seen sexier women in medical films on venereal disease. The group of guys watching the smut have two things in common: they're captivated by what's playing, and they wear wedding rings. Beer is flowing from the taps and shots of cheap booze are lined up on the bar. One guy is drinking more than the others, must be Sid. He's about my age (twenty-three at the time) or a few years older, starting to get a gut and beginning to establish his male pattern of baldness. Seems like a nice enough guy. He's obviously been looking forward to this night for some time.

I'm standing near where I walked in, when a girl holding a boom box in one hand and three or four full, plastic grocery bags in the other, comes up the stairs, and asks, "You Guido?"

I want to say, "Do I look like a Guido?" but don't. "He's the guy with no sleeves."

She's short, a bit on the stocky side, okay-looking. She chews a large wad of gum, and walks with a rolling, knuckle-dragger gait.

She finds Guido, takes his money, counts it, and heads off to the ladies' room.

Guido flips off the flickering projector and says, "Time for da real deal."

The boys make a circle of the chairs in the lounge and place Sid in the premier, center position.

"Numero uno is da lovalee Miss Zazu," Guido announces as if a Spanish-speaking, Italian David Letterman.

Zazu comes out of the ladies' room door in an outfit that would make Gypsy Rose Lee roll over in her grave: a neon-pink feather-boa around her neck, a silver-glitz cocktail dress, white gloves that run up past her elbows, fake diamond necklaces, and a glass-jewel tiara on her head. She must have raided her grandmother's attic for this outfit. Zazu plugs the cassette into the boom box, waits for David Rose's 1960-something "The Stripper" to play, and enters the circle to perform one of the worst stripteases in the history of burlesque. After the first clothing layer drops to the floor, she reveals a bustier, fishnet stockings and four-inch heels—supposedly to add a rougher sexual element to the act, which doesn't succeed. Uncovered next is a suit of slinky ruffles meant to accentuate her more prominent female assets. It fails miserably. When she finally, and I do mean finally, gets down to her sequined bra and bright pink panties, she stops the music, paces over to Sid, and buries his nose into her sorry case for cleavage. This elicits a "whoop" from the assembled, and a muffled, drunken "whoop" from Sid. The performer pulls back, faces the crowd and announces, "If ya wanna see more, betta start throwin' some dolla bills."

The crowd boos in unison, but Guido tosses a handful of ones and the bra comes off. The whoops return. Another ten or so bills flutter onto the floor and the pink panties are history. She struts around naked until "Eye of the Tiger" mercifully ends.

"Don't quit your day job, girl," I want to tell her.

I have to hand it to Guido. He does an excellent job of improving on the quality of the performers. For the next three strippers, who arrive at forty-minute intervals, are increasingly better looking, especially in the all-important tit-and-ass sense. Each girl strips around a thoroughly stupefied Sid, rubbing, teasing and tickling every-which-way. Sid's face hasn't felt this much skin since he was breastfed. And if enough green is displayed by one of the getting drunker-and-drunker spectators, the girl does an impromptu performance for, make that "on," the big spender, on a cash-and-hump basis.

The *piece d'resistance* arrives a little past midnight. Her face would never make the cover of *Vogue*, but her body is centerfold worthy. From the neck down, she is gorgeous. Accompanied by her manager, a slim, swarthy fellow, the girl, Shiloh, waits for management negotiations with Guido to end before taking her instructions. With the crowd as drunk and rowdy as Wrigley Field bleacher bums during a Saturday double-header, Shiloh exits the ladies' room stark naked, heads right for Sid, and strips him down to his tighty-whiteys. She begins a full body rub-and-tug that drives not only Sid wild, but the rest of the crowd as well.

I won't go into a lot of particulars but, suffice to say that she was a true professional in every sense of the word, because getting Sid to perform in front of the ravenous crowd, after the amount of liquor he consumed in the previous hours, was a feat in itself. To the medley of "I Wanna Kiss You All Over" mashed up with "Bang-a-Gong," Sid and Shiloh bumped and grinded out a performance worthy of one of those X-rated Oscars Gideon always wins.

I happen to be standing next to her manager as all this is going on. "She's great, isn't she?" he says proudly of his chattel.

"She's not shy, I'll say that much for her."

"After Sid blows his wad," he tells me, "I'm raffling her off, fifty bucks a ticket. We got six-hundred at the last stop."

"Bet you really look forward to wedding season," I say.

"Naw, business is always good. She's takin' on fifteen Marines tomorrow."

"How'd you find her?" I have to ask.

"She's my sister."

I left the party without congratulating Sid or waving goodbye to Guido.

I tell this story, because in the four of five subsequent bachelor parties I have attended over the years, the template is pretty much the same; except for the "sister" part. Tonight, I'm wondering if history will repeat itself. All I was told was to be ready with a grand in cash, hire a limo with a fully stocked bar, get a prescription filled for medical marijuana, and bring my medical bag.

"We don't want any accidents if things get out of hand."

"What do you have planned, Gideon?"

"Plenty."

Gideon is uncommunicative in the stretch on our ride to the restaurant. He won't let on, give me a preview, even a hint, of things to come. He asks me to pick up the tab at Ruth Chris.' When I complain of being the banker left in the dark, he says. "Hey, you had your chance, but left it up to me. So, I lead, you follow, with your credit card."

We are about ten feet into the restaurant when Gideon blurts out, "What the fuck are they doing here?"

Jake sits at a back table flanked by Simon, Arty, and Minister O'Grady.

I speak first when we reach the table. "This is certainly a surprise."

Gideon gives Jake a stare that could melt an iceberg.

Jake shrugs his shoulders.

"Bitzy told us to be here," Simon says.

"Why?" I ask.

"Said it would be fun."

"Really?"

"We're looking forward to it," Arty says.

"You know about this guest list, Jake?" I continue.

"Nope."

I see some relief come to Gideon. Some, but not much.

We sit. I call over the waitress and order Maker's Mark. Gideon needs an immediate calming influence.

After the bourbon arrives, Simon signals the waiter for another round for the rest of the table and asks, "So, what's goin' down?"

The three party crashers look to Gideon, who may just gnaw his teeth down to nubs, he's grinding so hard. "Didn't Bitzy tell you?" he says, with a scowl he just can't help.

"No."

Jake says to Gideon, "She didn't tell me anything, either."

"Well, I guess you'll just have to wait to find out." Gideon picks up his menu, places it in front of his face, and reads.

Not a word is spoken. The three Bitzy guests have no idea what to say.

So far, this bachelor party is about as much fun as a barium enema.

Arty attempts to break the tension. "You know what I always say, 'What lays at the bachelor party, stays at the bachelor party.'"

Twenty or thirty more seconds of silence ensue before Gideon finally speaks. "Let's order."

"What are you having there, Padre?" Jake asks O'Grady. "Fish on Friday?"

"It's not Friday," O'Grady informs him.

Gideon remains quiet. I lean over to him. "Gideon, lighten up. Jake didn't know."

I hear words from Gideon as if he is thinking out loud, "That fucking bitch."

"Gideon..."

"Fucking bitch," he repeats. I'm thankful that only I can hear.

"This going to screw things up?"

"No fucking way."

Dinner is low-key. The minister likes his steak rare, his scotch old and plentiful. Arty and Simon do most of the talking, attempting to out-regale each other with one-up lies about their past financial conquests and hot female companionship. They also do most of the drinking. Jake is cordial to the three, as am I. Gideon quietly sulks.

Simon is first to get tipsy and bravely poses a question for Gideon. "Can I ask you something?"

"You just did," I tell him.

Simon leans toward Gideon. "Do you get horny watching all those people going at it?"

"I really don't think that is appropriate conversation with a man of the cloth at the table," Jake says.

"Don't make any exceptions on my account," O'Grady says, with a short burp.

"You get horny watching your wife in the shower?" Gideon answers Simon's question with a question, a no-no in my book.

"Of course not."

"Same principle."

"Oh, come on, a couple of hot chicks banging away on some

stud is hardly the same as my wife's fat ass."

"It's just a job," Gideon responds.

Arty asks, "Ever get a guy with a Louisville Slugger dick and the chick says 'you ain't bangin' me with that thing.'"

"Ever see a baby getting born?" Gideon asks.

Jake, evidently feeling some compulsion to raise the level of the conversation, asks the minister, "So what is the church's stand on adult entertainment?"

O'Grady peers at Jake as if he was a melanoma specimen. "I'm not aware of any scripture or doctrine relating to the topic."

"So, there's no Papal decree on pornography?" Jake asks.

So far this is the worst bachelor party in history.

Arty and Simon order after-dinner drinks. I pay the check. Gideon rises before the boys have had a chance to enjoy their brandies. "Let's go."

"Where are we off to?" Simon slurs.

"Pussy," Gideon answers.

"Now you're talking," Arty says, downing his drink in one gulp.

Everyone is up out of their seats except for O'Grady. Jake says to him. "Well, thanks for joining us Minister O'Grady."

"What," Simon asks, "you're not coming?"

"Ah, come on," Arty says, "this'll be fun."

"Not like you're gonna be seein' a naked Virgin Mary," Simon adds.

O'Grady rises from his chair slowly, "Well, if you insist."

CHAPTER 20

Gideon, the Best Man

Fucking bitch thinks she can ruin Jake's bachelor party by stringing these three idiots along? No fucking way.

"You got sedatives in that bag?" I ask Conrad while the others pile into the limo.

"Gideon…"

"I just want to put 'em to sleep for a few hours."

"You want me to shoot them with a tranquilizer gun?"

"You got one?"

"Don't answer my question with another question."

Conrad can be a wimp, but I don't care. I'm prepared. A good director is always prepared.

"I'm not dosing anyone, Gideon."

"Yeah," I say. "I didn't think you would."

Conrad breathes a sigh of relief.

"Get in the limo."

Jake, Conrad and I sit on the far backseat while the stepdads-in-law and the preacher sit toward the front. The driver pulls out of the restaurant parking lot, heads west, and in a few minutes gets on the freeway. He knows where to go.

"Pour us a few shots there, Arty," I tell the fool, "important to keep the buzz on."

Arty opens the bar, checks out the selections, lifts bourbon for a quick vote, and passes out glasses.

The minister waves Arty off. "Not for me, right now."

"Sorry," I say. "If I would have known you'd be coming, I would have stocked a bottle or two of altar wine."

Drinks in hand, I toast, "To friendship, a responsibility to be taken seriously."

This will be my last drink of the night.

The limo is on the 405 North going up over the hill and I can tell the boys are wondering where we are headed. When we approach the interchange to the 101, Simon asks, "We going to Bare Elegance in Van Nuys?"

"One of your favorites?" I ask.

"I've been there once," Simon lies.

The limo takes the 101 towards Sacramento.

"Anybody want a joint?" I ask.

"Sure," O'Grady says.

I toss him the baggie and rolling papers

"This the way to Chatsworth?" Jake asks.

The driver exits the freeway past Encino, crosses Ventura Blvd. and drives east into a neighborhood of two-bedroom, two-bath ranch houses. He pulls up at a house in the middle of the block and turns off the engine.

"This looks nice," Conrad says.

The minister is the only one who doesn't pause to see where we are. He's sucking on the joint like a reverse chimney.

"You rent this place for the night?" Simon asks.

"Is it one of those secret, private clubs?" Arty asks.

I don't answer. I sit back, relax, and contemplate the faces before me. What a bunch of Bozos.

"Are we getting out?"

"No."

Four or five minutes go by.

"What are we doing here?" Simon asks.

"Waiting," I answer. "Patience is a virtue. Isn't that right Minister O'Grady?"

"It certainly is," he says before burning his fingertips on the roach.

A few more seconds tick off the clock.

"Conrad, get up," I order. "Move to the side."

Conrad does as told. I also move, leaving Jake by himself in the middle of the rear seat.

Perfectly timed, the limo doors open.

"Hi, boys."

Two babes, dressed in matching, plaid, micro-miniskirts and tall white socks, which make a mockery of Catholic school uniforms, climb into the limo.

The minister's eyes almost pop out of his sockets.

"This is Ronnie and Bonnie. They are going to join us this evening as chaperones." I pause. "Does anyone have a problem with that?"

Arty and Simon's mouths hang open wider than an IMAX movie screen.

"You must be Jake," Bonnie says, sitting down on Jake's left side.

"Congratulations," Ronnie adds, sitting down on his right.

The girls drip sexuality. Their blouses are sheer and a size or two too small, legs go all the way to their necks and their tight, little butt cheeks peek out from under their skirts.

Jake doesn't know what to do. He can't keep his eyes off the girls, but he folds his arms across his chest and pushes himself back into the seat as if protecting himself.

"Gideon," he says with trepidation in his voice.

"Jake," I tell him, "it is your night, you can do or not do anything you want. All I ask you to do is have a good time."

"Thanks, Gideon." Jake is relieved.

"Ladies, this is Conrad, Arty, Simon and," I look to the minister, "what was your first name, again?"

"Francis," the minister answers, swallowing hard, his eyes laser-fixed on the girls.

"Frankie, call him Frankie."

"Hi, Frankie."

It is geometrically impossible for the two girls with skirts so short to sit and not flash a cooter. The six oldest eyes in the car stare down their tunnels of love, as if expecting to play *Where's Waldo?* Ronnie, whose real name is Constance, unbuttons the top two buttons on her beige blouse and lets her fake boobs bob to the surface. Bonnie, whose real name is Patrice, untucks her shirttails and ties the ends tight beneath the bottom of her breasts, which pushes puppies up, out, and to attention. It makes me want to salute. These girls could turn on a eunuch.

"So nice of you to join us," Simon says.

Conrad gives me a wink that says, "Nice job."

I signal the driver and off we go.

We arrive at a club outside of Thousand Oaks. It is going to be one expensive cab ride back to the restaurant, but do I care? No.

The bouncer opens the limo door, escorts us past the rabble and welcomes us inside, where we are escorted to a cordoned section of the dancers' stage. Simon, Arty, and Frankie the minister grab the three premier seats at the edge of the raised platform, which I had reserved for Jake and the girls. But that's okay, this will work.

The girl on the stage, a part-time performer in a few of my videos, dances over, points at Jake and asks, "He, the man?"

"He, the man," I answer.

Conrad lays back, takes it all in with a slight grin on his face. Typical Conrad.

Girls stop by, one by one, to congratulate the future groom with slight snuggles, teases, and cheek kisses. Jake is getting more and more embarrassed. He's redder than a strawberry Twizzler. The manager comes over to meet the guest of honor and points him out to the DJ in the sound booth. I grease his palm with a number of large bills and whisper instructions. He smiles. I've made his Sunday night.

Drinks arrive at the table. I exchange Jake's Jaggermeister shot, which Arty ordered for the group, for a light beer. "Pace yourself, big boy," I tell Jake. "There's a lot more going to go down before this night is over."

"Thanks, Gideon, I really appreciate this."

"I owe you."

"Go ahead, try one," Arty pushes Frankie to shoot the shot. After all the dope he smoked, a couple of shots could explode the preacher's skull. But to my surprise, the minister knocks it down quicker than a thirsty cowboy in a B western.

Simon and Arty are feeling no pain. "Having a good time there boys?" I ask.

"This is great."

Perfect time to put the hurt on them. "Don't you think it about time you two kicked into the kitty?"

Both their faces drop lower than a hangman's noose.

"I don't carry a lot of cash," Simon says.

"There's an ATM in the lobby."

Before they have an opportunity to argue, I lead them to the cash machine. "I want to assure you two that whatever you put into the proceedings this evening, it will be more than worth your while."

"What is that supposed to mean?" Arty asks.

"You brought Viagra, didn't you?"

"Of course."

The first credit card Arty inserts is rejected. I make him try another. It works. "Five hundred."

"Five hundred?" he protests.

I punch in the numbers on the screen for him. When the fifties pop out below, I take them in hand. "Your turn, Simon."

"Wife's got me on a budget."

"Budgets are made to be broken," I tell him as I take his card and insert it into the machine. "Put in your pin."

Simon hesitates.

"Arty has brought enough Viagra for the two of you," I tell him.

A few seconds later, I pull Simon's money out of the slot. "Boys, you're not going to believe what's going to happen next."

Back in our little area, Jake sits back to watch Frankie spend some quality time with Bonnie and Ronnie. With his hands running over their bust lines, it doesn't seem probable that he is lecturing them on their evil ways. Maybe it's some new kind of blessing.

"And what do we have down here?" Bonnie asks, as she pats the steeple rising in the minister's lap.

"That, my dear, is God's way of saying, 'Rise up and rejoice.'"

I pull Ronnie aside and whisper directions. A few seconds later she hands me Frankie's wallet.

Six-hundred cash. Some vow of poverty. I clean him out.

Conrad has watched the cash transfer take place, smiles and says, "Nice move."

I order a couple bottles of the cheapest champagne available and make sure Arty, Simon, and Frankie are the only ones who get glasses. Nothing is worse than a champagne hangover and these boys are going to have an award winner. They all chug the first round.

It is getting close to midnight and the thinning crowd is drunk, loud and obnoxious. They are led by the three hangers-on in our group, who flounder about like sailors on leave, screaming, singing and howling, though it all sounds the same from my place of sobriety. Arty and Simon are sloppy drunks, spilling more champagne than they're drinking. Frankie is in the worst shape of the three. With his red nose, cauliflower ears, and a slur like he has a mouthful of swizzle sticks, he reminds me of W. C. Fields. If he had to give a sermon tomorrow morning, he'd probably pass out on the pulpit.

The tacky spotlight hits Jake and the DJ announces, "We have a special guest in attendance this evening. His name is Jake and in one week, he's going to be walking down the aisle. So, let's get him up and give him a proper send off into matrimony."

Jake gives a friendly wave to the dwindling, sloshed, adoring crowd, but doesn't rise from his chair.

"Would you like to come up on stage?" the DJ asks.

Jake waves him off, as I knew he would.

The DJ doesn't miss a beat. "Well, no wedding would be complete without introducing the wedding party... Can we have Arty, Simon, and Frankie on stage, please?"

Ronnie and Bonnie help the three boneheads, who stumblebum onto the stage with the mindless enthusiasm of third graders running to recess. The small crowd's applause ripples from every dark corner of the club, urging on our very own Marx Brothers.

Three strippers, who wear wedding veils and little else, set them in chairs and begin a three-way table dance. Crotch level meets eye level as their hips swing and swivel, the sway having a hypnotic effect on the stupefied partiers. Their hands fumble and grope, but the girls are too quick to get petted. The bustiest of the girls (and this is saying something because all three further prove Conrad's *too much for too little body* theorem), positions herself behind Simon, leans over and drops her tits directly over his forehead. He now has nipples for eyeballs.

"Look my way," Arty begs.

I call the driver of the limo, wake him up, and tell him to be ready the minute he sees us come outside.

The crowd loves Jake's sendoff and nobody is more appreciative than the three manly musketeers, now disgusting sots, who Alyssa and Bitzy were so kind to invite. I certainly hope these three have the decency to send thank-you notes.

To the tune of "Build Me Up Buttercup" faces are nipple-tweaked, hair tousled by designer nails, ears tickled by tongues, and the boys' noses are planted in places I hadn't thought possible.

Very creative, these girls.

I pull Conrad aside to where Jake can't hear us.

"We have to stop it."

"Why?" Conrad says, "This is a hoot."

"We have to stop him from getting married."

"Gideon…"

"We can't let him marry that bitch."

"Enough, Gideon."

"I owe him."

"For what?"

"Remember when he saved my ass by punching Father Celcius in the nuts?"

"That was twenty years ago."

"It's our duty to talk him out of it." I'm pleading with him. "He'll be miserable. You know it and I know it."

"So, they end up divorced like the rest of the world."

"What we have to do is put Jake in a position where he sees the reality of the situation."

"We tried, remember?"

"I have a plan."

"No."

"Conrad, you have to hang with me for one last shot."

"Gideon, are you taking some brain-altering medication?"

"One more chance, that's all I ask."

Conrad takes a breath, faces me. "What do you have planned?"

"Ever see the movie the *Parallax View*?

"No."

"Good."

On stage, the girls remove long silk scarves, clasp the boy's hands together, stand them against three stripper poles and tie their wrists onto the metal. Each of the boy's belts is removed, hooks unfastened, zippers opened, and pants go down to their ankles. Two sets of boxers, one pair of butt-hugger briefs. The boys are so drunk, their heads must be spinning like a camera doing a fisheye 360 shot. It doesn't take long for them to collapse into a small pile of human disgrace. They are completely wiped out.

Jake sits in awe of the spectacle, enjoying every second.

Simon, Arty, and Frankie are on the floor, heads pointing in the same direction, hands bound and white pasty legs exposed. The cobra-girls straddle their victims and move rhythmically. They shimmy forward until they stand above in a position only an auteur porn director or perverted gynecologist could fully appreciate. Arty's tongue darts in and out of his mouth like a lizard catching flies. Simon's open-mouthed head pulses up and down, as if he is trying to catch falling drops of rain. And, to his credit, Frankie has a pole inside his Calvin's which would hold up a revival tent. Minister, the Lord is with you tonight.

"Let's go," I tell Jake and the chaperones. "We're out of here."

"Aren't we forgetting someone?" Conrad asks.

"No," I answer.

I doubt if Arty, Simon, or Frankie saw us make our exit. At the time, the girls were on their knees, butts on chests, snatches over noses, shaking their boobies to the raps of Notorious Big, giving the three boys a new appreciation of rap music.

"How are they going to get back?" Jake asks as the limo pulls out of the club's lot.

"Get back?" I say. "Let them crawl."

"Where to next?" Jake asks, still giddy from the show.

"Yeah," Conrad says. "Where to next?"

"You'll see."

Thirty minutes later we pull into the parking lot of the circular Luxe Hotel, the one off the 405 Freeway in West LA. How they ever got the permits to build a giant stone phallus in some of the priciest real estate in Los Angeles, I'll never know. The boner rises in Brentwood, south of the Getty and north of Westwood. In the past years it has become a destination spot for rich guys after getting kicked out of the house, tourists who have been told they will see celebrities walking the halls, and a popular pickup spot for guys with money and girls who want guys with money. No need to check in, the five of us go straight to the elevator and rise to the penthouse level. The two-bedroom suite I reserved awaits us.

Inside the suite the carpets are thick, tasteful art is on the walls. There is comfortable calf-leather furniture and a spectacular view south. It's crystal clear, and we step out onto the balcony to see a plane coming in for a landing at LAX, fifteen miles or so down the road. The lights of Los Angeles twinkle by the thousands for Jake's benefit.

"We're a long way from St. Theresa's," Jake, says, his mind

adrift in a flashback.

Ronnie brings the glasses and Bonnie pops open the bottle of Crystal.

"You guys are the best friends anyone could ever have," Jake says, raising his glass.

"I certainly hope you still believe that tomorrow morning," I tell him.

We sip instead of drink, taking in the cool night air. All is calm for a few moments. "Jake. Whatever you want to do, it is yours to do," I tell him as I glance at the girls.

Jake swallows hard, takes a long look at Ronnie and Bonnie, who smile at him with enough sexuality to jump-start a loveless marriage. "It's not that I don't want to have sex with the two of you, but if I did I might not like myself in the morning."

Jake's hands go into his pockets and his chin rests on his chest. He resembles the shyest kid in the sixth grade who is about to ask a girl to dance for the first time.

Ronnie and Bonnie each place a hand on Jake's shoulder. Ronnie says, "The woman who is getting you is a very lucky woman."

I peel off a number of hundreds and hand them to the girls. "The driver will take you home. Thanks."

"You're welcome. It was fun."

Ronnie and Bonnie turn to Conrad, "Nice meeting you."

"Likewise," Conrad says, "and may I compliment both of you on your very pretty breasts."

"Thank you," both say in harmony, stashing the cash in their purses.

I usher the girls out the door, whisper my thanks and return to Conrad. "By the way, I need that grand I told you to bring."

Conrad pulls out his wallet slowly, very slowly.

"Come on, you got more money than God."

Conrad reluctantly hands over the hundreds.

"Consider this an investment in your best friend's future."

"I'm not so sure."

The three of us move into the front room of the suite and sit.

We finish off the champagne.

"You sure you still want to get married?" I ask.

"Yep."

"Why?"

"Cause it's time."

"Couldn't you just live together?"

"Nope."

"Who needs a ceremony?" I ask.

"We do. We all do."

I peer over to Conrad. He has an "I told you so" look on his face. Asshole.

"It is the biggest decision in your life, Jake. You have to see it from every perspective, consider every possibility, weigh the positives and negatives. Are you sure you've done all that?"

"It's time, Gideon," Jake says. "Someday it will be your time and you'll be just like me."

As I suspected, I am getting nowhere. I could give him a Powerpoint presentation with all the bells and whistles, but he still wouldn't listen.

I get up, march to the minibar and pull three beers out of the small fridge. I also take out of my pocket a small packet of powder and rip off the edge. I was promised by Pepper, this stuff will do the trick.

Every porn set has a "pharmacist" on hand and Pepper was on our set last week with everything from AZT to Viagra. I tap the powder into one of the beer bottles, wipe off the residue and return to my friends.

Jake gets the special brew. "Cheers."

We take some time to drink.

Jake's head suddenly falls forward, as if someone clunked him on his skull with an iron skillet.

"Just make sure nothing bad happens to him, Conrad."

"What the hell?" Conrad rushes to him, takes his head into his hands and begins to examine. "What did you do?"

"Ever hear of Ambien?"

"Yes."

"Well, this stuff works faster."

Conrad lets go and Jake folds over like Gumby on a bender.

"Help me get him up."

"Are you out of your mind?"

"I wasn't kidding, Conrad. We're going to take him somewhere where he will have the time to realize getting married to Alyssa will be the biggest mistake of his life."

"I won't do it."

"Sure, you will. You're not going to leave him now. Something could happen and then you'd feel responsible."

"No, you'd be the one responsible."

"You're the doctor."

"Gideon, you're sick, deranged, and medically unstable. Even I'm beginning to think you're an asshole."

"Conrad, if you were about to get married to some evil bitch, I'd do the same thing for you. Now we got to get him loaded back into the limo."

"I don't believe this."

"Come on," I tell him. "He's our friend."

We load Jake onto a wheeled room service cart for easier transport. He looks like a corpse. The only hitch on the way out was another couple joining us in the elevator. Thankfully they were also inebriated.

"Bachelor party," was my explanation.

"Sorry I missed it," the guy said.

His date slaps him across his arm.

We lay Jake in the middle of the limo, cover him with a blanket, and watch him sleep like a baby.

Conrad mellows a bit on our trip to the Valley. "Promise me something, Gideon," he says.

"What?"

"If I'm ever getting married, promise me you won't be in charge of my bachelor party."

I smile, place my hand upon his shoulder and say, "No."

CHAPTER 21

Jake, the Groom

Where the hell am I?
My head is ready to burst. It feels like there are two ballplayers with giant baseball bats, pounding the crap out of each other, while the home crowd screams *Hit 'em* at the decibel level of a punk rock concert.

I'm dry, parched. I might as well be in the desert, locked inside a black car with no AC and the windows rolled up, or maybe someone just shoved me into a sauna, and it sucked out all my bodily fluids, Ronnie and Bonnie? I can barely move. Every muscle in my body aches, just like when you haven't done anything athletic in months, then you go out and play touch football. The next day you are so sore it hurts to breathe.

I'm in a room and the room is spinning like a kid's merry-go-round. The couch I'm on is too short, I can't stretch out. In the corner there is an old TV flickering. I can barely make it out, but it must be a horror movie playing. There's this yellowish square glob of something on the screen, jumping around, freaky-scary, making my headache even worse. I shift to my side, but my left leg gets caught on something. I look down and see I'm wearing some kind of ankle bracelet. It's tight. It chafes. *What the fuck?* I try to focus my eyes on an object in the room, any object, to center myself, to establish some equilibrium, stop the spinning. My eyes are so dry, it feels like sandpaper every time I blink. The noise in the room is shrill, the voices too high. I try to make out words, but nothing is making sense. I am halfway-in and halfway-out of some strange Ewok netherworld in the land of Luke Skywalker.

I put my hands over my eyes for a few seconds to dull the pain; and when I open them I see a troll-like creature coming at me. It may be a miniature Bigfoot, a gnome or a pissed-off mini-me. It's hard to tell. My eyes won't focus and my brain can't comprehend what kind of brute might be stumbling towards me. Maybe it's a dream. No, a nightmare. My best guess is that I've been drugged and the creature is only an image in my head. I close my eyes, hoping it will go away, but it doesn't. It's here, right up against me, reaching out, putting its wet, squirmy fingers to my face. It finds my nose, sticks a finger inside a nostril and pulls upward.

"Ahhhhh."

The imp jumps back and releases a banshee wail, which attacks my already tender ear drums with a fury and a vengeance second to none. It screams, I scream, somebody else screams.

"Kevin!"

A voice, even louder, more shrill, pounds my senses senseless, if that's at all possible.

"I'm sorry. I told him not to bother you."

It's a woman's voice, coming towards me. Her face is a blur.

"How are you feeling?"

"Terrible."

"You don't look too good," she says.

"Water."

She leaves the room and returns with a plastic tumbler of water and hands it to me. "Sorry, ice maker is on the blink."

I lift my head, place the rim of the glass on my bottom lip, and drink like a camel coming off a Saharan trek.

"More?" She takes the empty glass out of my hand and once again exits.

My faculties are returning. I sit up. Across from me is a little boy, maybe two, three, four, five... how would I know? He picks his nose with the same finger that picked my nose.

"Here," the second glass is placed in my hands.

"Thank you."

"You were really out," she tells me.

"What time is it?"

"Six."

"Six what?"

"Six o'clock."

"AM or PM?"

"Dinnertime."

I'm leaning against the armrest of the couch. I brush my hair back. I look over at the child, then back at the woman. She looks familiar.

"Do you like mac and cheese?"

"What?"

"Mac and cheese is all he'll eat lately."

"Who?"

"Kevin."

I look again at the little boy. "He's eating right now."

"Kevin, get your fingers out of your nose." She pulls his hand away from his face. "How many times do I have to tell you?"

The fingers go right back into his nostril after a short stop at his mouth.

There is one other chair in the room, in worse shape than the couch. There are toys pushed into one corner, mostly wheeled vehicles, trucks, cars; some are broken. On the TV is SpongeBob Squarepants. It wasn't a yellow monster I was seeing, but a talking, flamboyant spongiform. Each is frightening in its own way. A coffee table has been pushed out of the way. It used to be up next to the couch. I can tell by the scratches on the floor. God my head hurts!

"Where the hell am I?"

"My apartment," Kay says, in what sounds like a whimper. I think I've scared the hell out of her.

"And where would that be?"

"Van Nuys." She sits on the opposite side of the couch and moves as far down as she can get. Kevin cowers at the edge of the sofa's arm. "I didn't have a lot of time to clean before you got here. Sorry."

I pull my bare feet around to sit normally. "Ouch. Goddamit!" There is a heavy chain attached to my ankle with a Master combination lock. "Why do I have a chain around my freakin' leg?"

"I'm not sure, but I could probably give it a pretty good guess."

I stare at her. "Don't I know you?"

"We met at your engagement dinner."

"Gideon's date?"

"It wasn't really a date," she says meekly. "We're just friends." She puts out her hand to shake. "Kay."

"And how did I get to your apartment?" I ignore her hand.

"Limo."

"Gideon and Conrad had to carry you up here. I hope my neighbors didn't see. They're not too wild about us already."

"Why not?" I can barely speak, I'm in so much pain.

She looks away. "They don't like me here. My only friend in the complex is a plumber named Arnold." Her eyes meet mine. "I would really appreciate it if you didn't make a lot of noise. If I get kicked out of this apartment, I don't know where we'd go."

"Gideon and Conrad, huh?" I say, trying to maintain some semblance of calm.

"He didn't tell me what they were going to do."

"Who?"

"Gideon."

"I'm going to grind that son-of-a-bitch into ashes."

Kay gives me an odd look, as if to say *Did you have to say that?*

"What's the matter?" I ask.

"Don't get mad at me. I didn't do anything."

"What? I'm in your apartment, chained up like an elephant at the zoo." My voice is rising, but I can't help it. I'm pissed.

"They just said 'a buddy needed a place to stay.' I didn't know it was you."

"Well, now that you know, unchain me, and get me the hell out of here."

"Sorry, but I can't."

Kay gives me this forlorn look, as if she is merely a pawn in a much bigger game. I'm about to scream again, but I get this pain in my side that feels worse than when my appendix burst. "Ouch."

"Are you okay?" she asks, kneeling down to help me.

I get to a seated position. I'm holding my aching side. The chain around my ankle is cutting into me like a razor blade. "Do you have any idea what this feels like?"

She takes a second to think. "Yeah, Kevin was a nine-pounder."

I sit, head resting in my hands, and wait for the pain to subside.

Kevin comes over, sits on his mom's lap. "This is Jake, Kevin." She points to me. "You don't mind if he calls you Jake, do you?"

"Kevin, call me anything you want as long as you call me for dinner."

"Dinner!" She pops off the couch and runs into the kitchen, where I hear pots rattling off the stove. She returns with two bowls of gooey noodles.

I wait for Kevin to begin, then sample the cholesterol. One bite and I know I won't keep it down.

"Gideon told me to call him when you got up."

"He did, did he?"

"I have Conrad's number, too, in case you stopped breathing or something."

"Why? So he could hop in his car, drive all the way to Van Nuys to give me artificial respiration?"

"Guess so."

"They drugged me, didn't they?"

"I guess."

"You only get three guesses," I tell her.

I can feel my body literally sag into the couch, contracting inward, as if it is on its way to returning to an amoebic state. I haven't hurt this much since my old man beat the crap out of me when he ran out of booze during one of his more active binges.

Kay stands up, finds a cell phone in her purse, but before dialing says, "The guys measured the chain, so you could go to the bathroom if you want."

"They thought of everything, didn't they?" I watch as Kay waits for her call to be answered.

"Hi, Gideon, it's Kay... Yeah, he's awake... He looks a little pale, actually..." Kay covers the mouthpiece and speaks to me, "Gideon says, 'hello.'"

"Oh, please," I say, "give him my best."

She again talks into the receiver. "Jake says 'hello'...Well, since you mentioned it, could you stop and pick up some milk and Fruit Loops?"

Kay breaks the connection. "Gideon's coming over."

"Can't wait."

My knee buckles when I stand. I fall. Kay rushes to me.

"Are you okay?"

"No." I get to my feet. There is a door to my left into a hallway and a door a few feet in. One step and I wince in pain. They weren't fooling around when they chained me up. Samson, even with a ponytail, couldn't break these links. I follow the length of the chain to see I'm attached to a radiator with a padlock.

"I'll help you if you want," Kay offers.

"No thanks, longest journey starts with the first step."

"I really don't think you're going to go too far."

Picking up the chain, I slowly cross the room, but have to hold onto the hallway door frame to rebalance myself before making the turn. Three more steps and I'm into the bathroom.

The person in the mirror can't be me. Grotesque. I've never had eyes this bloodshot, or seen face-splotches this red. One ear is purplish, my hair is greasy, face unshaven and dried slobber stains my shirt. My mind must be playing tricks.

"I forgot to put in clean towels," Kay says coming to the door. "We don't have a lot of company."

"Don't worry about it." I try to shut the door, but the chain is in the way. "The door won't close."

The two of us stand in the small room.

"That's no big deal," she says. "We're pretty informal around here."

"Good to know."

I splash some water on my face, place my shaking hands on the sink, lean forward and rest for a few seconds. I try a few deep breaths.

"Do you want to take a shower?" she asks.

"Good idea. I should be presentable when I'm arrested after strangling Gideon to death."

She helps me off with my shirt, since I can still barely move. "Ah, I think we're going to have a problem here."

"What?"

"There's no place for your pants to go."

She's right. With the chain on, the pants can't come off.

"We could just pull them all the way off and down the length of the chain so they won't get wet," she suggests.

"Whatever."

Kay unbuckles my belt.

I push back against the sink and feel something hard bump my back pocket. "Ah, excuse me," I say, interrupting her.

"Don't you want some help?"

"No."

I position myself so she can't see the bulge the phone makes in my pocket. I try to stay cool, but I'm thrilled that I've found the flaw in my kidnapper's plan.

"You could fall again and hurt yourself."

"I'll manage."

"It's no big deal. I've probably seen more of those than you have."

"I'm shy."

I give Kay a slight push out of the room and close the door as much as possible. I can still see her through the crack in the door. I take the phone in one hand and slowly remove my pants and boxers with the other. I slide the pants over the chain and out the door to her.

"I wish I could wash these."

I'm turning on the phone as I speak. "That's okay, don't worry about it."

"It's important to always be neat and clean," she says.

The phone isn't lighting up. Something is the matter. Out of juice? I shake it. Nothing.

"Turn on the shower and let it get hot," she calls from the hallway.

It hurts to move, really hurts. I stand naked, except for a very unattractive chain around my ankle. I punch every button on the dial and nothing happens. Damn.

"Feel free to use any of my hair stuff."

"I can't wait to try your cream rinse," I answer while I turn the phone over, slide off the removable panel and see the SIM card has been removed. *Goddamn you, Gideon.*

"Here."

My arm goes out the crack in the door and hand her my Blackberry.

"Wow," she says, "this is a nice phone. Can you get the Internet on it?"

"Not now."

"Yeah, I can't either. Those monthly plans are way too expensive."

I turn on the water, let it flow, climb slowly into the tub, close the curtain and pull the faucet diverter up. A splash of cold water hits me, followed immediately by a hot scalding. As I hop around to avoid the stream and adjust the knob, the chain rattles on the old porcelain tub, leaving scrapes that even Comet won't remove. The water temp subsides and the shower cascades over me, washing away sweat, grime, grease, and unknown dried substances only a crime lab could label. My humanity is returning. I soap up, shampoo, wash off, and stand until the water begins to cool. Stepping outside the tub, I dry off, leaving the towel wrapped around my lower torso.

My next look in the mirror is a major improvement from the last, but what wouldn't be?

Through the door crack I see Kevin standing in the hallway. "Waiting to pick my nose again?" I ask.

He doesn't answer.

"You know," I tell him, "you can pick your friends, and you can pick your nose, but you're not supposed to pick your friend's nose."

I hear the front door of the apartment open. "Hello."

It's him, the Gideon-bastard.

Sprinting out of the bathroom, I make a beeline for my enemy, my hands out to grip his neck and lock into an unbreakable stranglehold.

Gideon calmly hands off the shopping bag to Kay and takes one step back.

I am inches away from committing manslaughter, when the chain goes taut, my leg snaps tight and I am ricocheted back from whence I came, landing on my ass. The towel unravels, leaving me a naked, crumpled heap on the floor, in a world of pain.

I writhe in absolute agony. Kevin leans over, staring at my exposed privates. His jaw drops and he gasps, wide-eyed but thoroughly intrigued.

Kay says, "That's going be you some day, Kevin."

"Ewe."

"That chain works pretty well, doesn't it?" Gideon says.

"You son-of-a-bitch, Gideon."

"Jake, nice to see you, too. You're looking well."

"Bastard. What the hell are you doing to me?"

"Excuse me," Kay says. "Could you watch your language? I don't like Kevin to hear that kind of talk."

"You hear the nice lady, Jake?"

"Gideon…" I'm trying to get up.

"It's her house. You have to respect her rules."

I get to my feet. If he was one step closer I swear I would crush his skull. "Untie me."

"No can do."

"Why not?"

"You're not ready."

"For what?"

"To be untied."

"This isn't funny."

"Oh, come on," he says. "This is classic French cinema farce."

"Unlock me."

"No."

"Then tell me what the hell this all about?"

"Tsk, tsk," he says, wagging his finger. What did she just say about swearing?"

"Sorry," I look at Kay, "but after being drugged, kidnapped, and chained up like a galley slave, I'm a little bit on edge."

"I agree," Gideon says, clearly enjoying the hell out of this. "You're hardly being your usual fun-kind-of-guy self."

I rewrap the towel around me and collapse onto the couch. "OK, Gideon, what is this all about?"

"I thought we needed some quality time together before you got married."

"Why?"

"Because we don't want you to marry Alyssa. It's a mistake, trust me."

"This is about Alyssa?"

"Yep."

"You really are insane."

"No, no. I'm the sanest one in the story, the one who initiates the action of the plot."

"You're crazy, a lunatic."

"Jake, Alyssa is the wrong woman for you. If you marry her, you'll be miserable."

"More miserable than I am right now? I doubt it."

"Oh, you think this chain is heavy? Marry her and you'll feel like Kunta Kinte in *Roots*."

"Gideon, take this off my leg. NOW!"

"As soon as we unchain your heart, your leg will be next."

I want to kill one of my best friends.

Kay has stood to the side, holding Kevin, listening to the ongoing absurdity.

"Oh, I hope you don't mind, I invited Conrad. He's coming over with a pizza," Gideon tells her.

"Pizza," Kevin says.

"Hope you like Canadian bacon and pineapple."

"Ewe."

"He only likes cheese," Kay says. "Mommy will take off the stuff you don't like, hon."

"Cheese."

The kid eats too much cheese, but that's not my problem. "What am I supposed to do for clothes?"

Kay explains to Gideon, "We couldn't get the pants off the chain."

Gideon sees the problem. "Do you have a robe or something he could wear?"

"I do," she says, "but I don't know if it will fit him."

"Oh, let's give it a go."

The first thing Conrad sees, walking in the door, carrying two extra-large pizza boxes, is me seated on the couch dressed in a colorful, Japanese, silk robe, nine or ten sizes too small, with a pair of matching furry slippers. "I love your loungewear," is his initial comment.

"Very funny, Conrad."

"The ensemble gives off a real 'I'm not gay, but if I was, I'd wear this' kind of a vibe."

Everybody laughs except Kevin and me.

"Conrad, if you are truly my friend, you will get this chain off of my leg."

"Jake," Conrad says, "I did try to talk him out of this, but, you know, he does have some very valid points concerning your upcoming nuptials."

"Goddammit, Conrad."

Gideon tsks and wags his finger at me.

"Instead of talking him out of it, he talked me into it. Trust me, Jake, you owe it to yourself to think this through."

The water I drank a few minutes ago somehow converted to steam which now seems to be rising out of my ears.

"Plus, it's his lock. I don't have the combination."

"Who wants pizza?" Kay says, breaking the tension.

"Me," Kevin is the first to respond.

Kay passes out cheap, plastic plates, napkins, and mismatched forks. She removes the meat and fruit from the top of Kevin's slice, making him the happiest man in the room.

I eat. I'm famished. I will need my strength to rip that chain apart with my bare hands.

"So, Jake," Gideon asks, "did you enjoy your bachelor party?'

"It was great until you drugged and kidnapped me."

"That Ronnie and Bonnie were really something, uh?"

"Ronnie and Bonnie were there?" Kay interrupts. "Those two do everything together."

"What illegal drug did you give me, Gideon?"

"I forget the name of the stuff. Sure was effective though, wasn't it?"

"I could have overdosed and died. My blood would have been on your hands."

"Doctor Conrad was right there, nothing bad was going to happen to you," Gideon says. "Let's not be getting too overly dramatic."

"You can't do this to me."

"We already have."

There is a short pause while everyone eats.

"This pizza is delicious," Kay says. "I would have never thought bacon and pineapple would go together so well. Kevin you have to try this."

"Ewe."

"So, what's going to happen next?" I ask.

"We're going to take some time, talk things through, make you see the error of your ways," Gideon says.

"And if that doesn't work, what's after that, electroshock therapy?"

"Conrad," Gideon asks, "you know how to do that?"

"No," Conrad says.

"I'll rent *One Flew Over the Cuckoo's Nest*, and that will give you some idea," Gideon says, laughing.

"I certainly hope you two idiots are enjoying yourselves, because once I get free, I'm going to be putting a hurt on the both of you that you'll never recover from."

"We're only doing this because we love you, Jake."

CHAPTER 22

Gideon, the Best Man

Kevin went off to bed after the pizza. Conrad had surgery the next day, so he left. Kay was tired.

"I'll leave you guys alone so you can chat," she said thankfully. "Good night."

I sit in the chair on the other side of the room. I'm out of his reach if he tries to make a run at me. I don't want to laugh, but he does look pretty silly dressed in a kimono, sitting on that old couch. A costume designer couldn't have picked a better outfit for the scene.

"Kay's great, isn't she?"

Jake doesn't respond.

"I don't get to meet a lot of nice girls in my business, but Kay is such a breath of fresh air. The kind of girl I'd like to see you with."

Jake is giving me the silent treatment. He learned it from Alyssa, I'll bet.

"She's nice, friendly, a good mom, youthful, attractive. I bet your mother would really like Kay."

"Didn't you tell me she was a porn star?" Jake breaks his silent treatment as I knew he would.

"Yeah, but I'm sure your mom could see past that."

Jake puts his hands on his bare knees, takes a few seconds, then says, "Okay, asshole, this has been cute and funny, but it has gone far enough. Come over here, unlock this thing or give me the combination."

"Jake, let me ask you something?"

"What?"

"Does Alyssa laugh at your jokes?"

"What does that have to do with anything?"

153

"A lot. Does she laugh at your jokes?"

"No."

"And you don't see that as a problem?"

"You don't laugh at my jokes, Gideon."

"Because you're not funny; but if I was married to you, knew how much you wanted your humor appreciated and wanted to make you a happy man, I believe I would guffaw endlessly."

"Gideon, you are so full of shit, you sneeze diarrhea."

I break into a fit of hysterical laughter. "Jake, you're killing me."

He stares at me like I'm the Creature from the Black Lagoon.

"See my point?"

"No, I don't see your point. What I see is me sitting here, a one-man chain gang."

I notice the pizza box. "Doesn't Alyssa always order pizza with anchovies?"

"What are you talking about?"

"Anchovies, those little fish you hate and have to pick off when she orders the pizza."

"Gideon, this is nuts. Release me."

"She's got two years on you. She'll age quicker, and twenty years from now, you'll be hanging around with an old bag. You don't want that." I pause to let the point sink in. "Maybe Alyssa's a cougar."

"Gideon, you are out of your fucking mind."

"Let's move on to another topic," I say. "Does Alyssa fuck you every time you get horny?"

"Fuck you, Gideon." Jake comes out of the chair with venom in his eyes. He's at full speed, about to reach me when the chain tightens, his leg retracts, his upper body goes forward, his lower torso backward, not good for keeping vertebrae healthy.

"Gideon!"

Lying face down on the floor, moaning in pain, he looks up to see I haven't moved an inch.

"Don't forget who measured the length of the chain."

Jake crawls back to the couch, a defeated man, hopefully more ready to listen to my line of reasoning.

"Sorry, I'll rephrase the question. That may have been a little harsh." I take a beat. "So let's say in the middle of the night or when you get home from work or when you're lying around watching a *Seinfeld* rerun on TV, you feel that added pressure in your nuts and your dick starts giving you 'I need attention' signals; could you go over to Alyssa, slide up next to her, give her a little nuts nudge and be confident that she's going to respond in the biblical sense?"

"No woman does that."

"All the women I know do."

"The women you know suck cocks for a living."

"Yeah, you're right. I'm a bad example for that question. But take Conrad, I bet all his women do him at the drop of a hat."

"Because Conrad's a surgeon, Conrad's rich, Conrad drives a new Jag, Conrad is a catch."

"And you're not?"

"Not like Conrad, no."

"But you consider Alyssa quite a catch?"

"Yes."

"Maybe Conrad and Alyssa should hook up?"

"Allow me to repeat a phrase I used before in this insipid conversation," Jake says slowly. "Fuck you, Gideon."

"Don't worry. Conrad wouldn't go out with Alyssa because he knows she's sick."

"Sick?"

"Diseased," I tell him.

Jake waits.

"She has a terminal case of pretty girl syndrome."

"Christ, where the hell do you come up with this shit?"

"Think about it, Jake. Her whole life men have been chasing after her. What she wants, she gets, because she's never had to do anything except be beautiful. There's always been a guy hanging around willing to buy her this, take her there, do this, do that. All she ever had to do is sit back and enjoy. She's so used to having everything come her way, she has no concept of having to put out. And I mean "put out" in every sense of the word."

"That's not true."

"Yes, it is. Alyssa's never had to work for anything in her life."

"She worked as a model."

"That's not work."

"She worked at William Morris."

"She sat at the front desk. She was eye candy." I pause, knowing he has no comeback. "Consider her relationship with her father."

"She loves her dad."

"She's probably got the guy teetering on the brink of bankruptcy with this wedding."

"All women get a little wacky before their marriage, especially if they have to do it all by themselves."

"Admit it, Jake, Alyssa's got her old man eating out of her hand. He gobbles up every request, even better than that horse of hers."

"That's because her mother walked out on her when she was a little kid and the only way he knew how to deal with it was to give her everything she wanted."

"Are you willing to do that?"

"Yes."

"Why?"

"Because we want the same things, Gideon, which is where your absurd line of reasoning falls apart."

"Ask your shrink. She'll tell you the way a woman treats her father is exactly the way she's going to treat her husband."

"Thought you said all psychologists are whacked."

"I did. The only reason they become shrinks is so they can talk to people more screwed up than they are, and get paid for it."

"Would you please untie me now?"

"No."

"Why not?"

"Because I'm not done."

"Jesus Christ, Gideon, this thing on my leg hurts."

"How about her friends, do you like her friends?"

"Yes."

"That Portia bitch?"

"She's very nice."

"All twelve pounds of her? The chick is the poster girl for anorexia."

"Look at all the women who showed up at the shower."

"Oh, come on. Other women hang around Alyssa to meet the guys she blows off."

"Not Shannon."

"I will admit," I confess, "I certainly don't see those two as buddies, but I don't think you do, either."

Jake pauses. That's an admission in my book.

"How about money?" I ask.

"What about money?"

"She's got a ton of it. You got none."

"So?"

"Is she making you sign a pre-nup?"

Jake doesn't answer. Another confession.

"Is the house in your name?"

He's silent.

"Didn't know I knew that, did ya?"

"LaRue's keeping it in his name for tax purposes."

"Is that what he told you or she told you?"

"It's none of your fucking business, Gideon."

Jake sits back, rubs his eyes with the butts of his hands. All I have to give him is time. The points I've made will take root in his mind, grow shoots, and his brain will branch into reality. In no time he'll be convinced that getting married to Alyssa is a dumb thing to do. I've seen this done in a number of movies. If it worked then, it'll work now.

"I got to go, busy day tomorrow."

"What, you got a big orgy scene you got to orchestrate?"

"Actually, I'm editing a compilation DVD of last year's Best New Comers."

"And that makes you qualified to give me advice?"

"Can't hurt." I get up out of the chair. "Can I get you anything before I leave?"

"The combination to this damn lock might be nice."

"All you have to do is call off the wedding and you're a free man."

CHAPTER 23

Alyssa, the Bride

"Is he there?"

The idiot receptionist says, "I haven't seen him, but that doesn't mean he's not here."

"Page him."

"Jake Dombrowski line one, Jake Dombrowski line one."

Like she has to use his first name? How many other Dombrowski's work there? What a jerk.

"He's not answering his page."

"Let me talk to my dad."

She cuts me off. I have to call back. Finally, dad's on the line. "Is he there?"

"No, and I got thirty Mexicans standing in the driveway, waving Green Cards like they're celebrating Mexican Saint Patty's day.

"Did he call in?"

"No. Did he call you?"

"No."

I wait for Dad to tell me what to do, but he doesn't speak. I'm angry. No, pissed. "If Jake is lying in the gutter of some brothel, I will personally rip the balls off that asshole Gideon."

"Alyssa, it's just boys being boys."

"What should I do?"

"Call him."

"I've been doing that all morning."

"Well?"

"Phone's not on."

"Call his friends."

"Conrad's in the middle of a liposuction. Gideon doesn't answer, won't answer."

"Anybody else go with them?"

"Mom said Simon came home so drunk he couldn't see. She had to pay the eighty-dollar cab fare. The only thing she could get out of him was that they got left at the strip club with no money and no way home. He was missing his socks and one shoe."

"Simon's full of shit. How about that idiot, Arty?"

"Arty was still hung over when I called. Doris said he slept in his car. I don't know what happened to the minister."

"The minister? What the hell was he doing at the bachelor party?"

"Bitzy thought it would be a nice touch."

Dad waits for me to explain, but I'm not going to.

"Let me call. Give me Gideon's number."

I give dad Gideon's cell number and hang up. Portia is still asleep in the other bedroom. We are scheduled to go for a mud bath and massage. I wait a few minutes and call dad back.

"Did you get hold of him?"

"I left a message," he says.

"What did you say?"

"I told him if he knows where Jake is to call him and tell him to get his lazy, late ass into work so I can shove some tortillas where the sun don't shine."

"I'm sure he'll respond to that."

"Hey, I'm the one who now has got to go out there and deal with a pack of illegal aliens, who all want to make *mucho dinero*."

Dad has been no help. I'm more angry than worried. Why the hell did they have to have a bachelor party? We're getting married in less than six days, there are things to do, people to see, places to go, and I can't find my fiancé because he's shitfaced, God knows where, from the goddamn bachelor party. This is awful. This is bullshit.

"You wouldn't happen to have a diuretic laying around, would you?" Portia asks, standing naked in the guest bedroom doorway.

"Sorry, no."

"Aw, piss on it."

Portia goes back into the bedroom.

I try Jake's phone again and get the recording. This is getting real old, real quick. I sip coffee. I've had about a gallon of it this morning, and I'm wired as tight as a bad perm.

Portia, wearing my terrycloth robe, comes into the kitchen where I'm sitting. "Find him yet?"

"No."

She opens the refrigerator, pulls out eggs, milk, and bread, and lays it all on the counter work space. "I wouldn't worry about it," she says. "Sly disappears for a few days at a time too. He always comes back."

"Where does he go?"

"Who?"

"Sly?"

"Oh, I'm not sure."

"Did you ask him?"

"I did once."

"And?"

"He said something, I forget."

Portia cracks three eggs into a bowl, and places two pieces of bread in the toaster oven. She finds the Teflon pan I seldom use, places it on a burner and plops in a hunk of butter. A few minutes later she is devouring a huge plate of over-easy eggs and toast. As she eats, her stomach swells from barren to four months pregnant. Using the bread crust to swab-up the last of the drippy yolk, she asks, "What time is it?"

"Ten."

"Tell me when it's ten-fifty-five."

Portia gets up and makes her way to the couch where she lays down. She's back asleep in under three minutes.

I haven't moved. I stare at the unlighted dial of my cell and hope it rings. It doesn't. I pick it up, go to the address book, find Conrad's office number and push the call button.

I get the receptionist.

"I know he's in surgery, but could you make sure he gets the message that I called and to call me right away."

I repeat my number, but don't have a lot of faith in Conrad's receptionist. She's probably just another hot-looking bimbo, paid to look good at the front desk.

At eleven, I wake Portia.

She rises from the couch slowly. "I have to use the bathroom."

Portia goes into the bath that Jake uses, and closes the door behind her.

I hear her purge. "Portia are you okay in there?"

The toilet flushes, the water runs, she comes out the door. "It's a bitch being a model."

Her stomach is back to flat. She has a bit of yellow spittle dripping off the edge of her mouth. "You didn't get any on my robe, did you?"

"No, I have a pretty good aim. I've had plenty of practice."

She turns back around and starts the shower, takes off my robe, and tosses it on the floor. "You know," she says, "I wouldn't worry about him. He'll come back when he gets horny. They all do, they're men."

CHAPTER 24

Kay, the Porn Star Mom

"**O**h, jeesh." I shake him again. "Come on."

What happens if he doesn't wake up, has an aneurysm or a heart attack, and I can't get him unchained and he dies? What am I going to do? I'll be an accessory to murder.

Kevin comes over and puts his finger in Jake's nose.

"Ouch." Jake pops up like Kevin's jack-in-the-box used to before I stepped on it.

"Sorry."

"Jesus, what time is it?"

"Please don't swear."

"Sorry, what time is it?"

"Eleven."

"I'm supposed to be at work."

"I don't think you're going to be able to go. Want me to call and tell them you're all tied up?" I chuckle at my own cleverness. I can be pretty funny.

Jake leans back on the couch, rubs his ankle where the chain is attached. It is getting pretty red and raw.

"If you put a towel around where the chain is, it would probably keep from rubbing so much." I leave and bring back a dry washcloth, which I push between the links and his skin.

"Thank you."

"You're welcome. Would you like some Fruit Loops?"

"If Kevin doesn't mind."

"I'll get you some in a minute." I pause, I'm a little leery of asking, but I don't have much choice. "Can I ask you a favor?"

"Oh sure, why not?"

"My agent called and said Sexy Sindy Sophomore came down with a herpes breakout this morning and won't be able to work, so

I got a chance to make some money, but I got to hustle, so to speak."

"Okay."

"I'm going to have to get my bush done this morning and on set this afternoon, but I don't have anyone to watch Kevin." I'm talking faster, when I get nervous I talk fast. "I could take him with me this morning, but seeing a wax job could be worse than the swearing thing." I stop, catch my breath. "Could you babysit?"

"Babysit?"

"Kevin."

"I figured who."

"Could you?"

"I'll have to see if I'm free."

I'm not sure if he's being funny or not. I wait for Jake to say, "Yes," but he doesn't.

"He's really no trouble. He'll sit and watch TV."

Kevin is in front of the set watching *Sesame Street*.

"Are you sure that's a good idea?" Jake asks. "You know a lot of people think Bert and Ernie are gay."

I have never considered this possibility. I wonder if this makes me a bad mother.

"Mister Rogers, too," Jake adds.

I get it. He's playing with my mind. "I know a lot of gay people and none of them would ever be caught dead in one of those sweaters."

"I wouldn't be too sure."

I place my hands over Kevin's ears so he can't hear me whisper to Jake. "Mister Rogers is dead, anyway."

"Did he die of AIDS?"

"No." I release my son.

Jake laces his fingers and puts his hands behind his head. "You know, I don't know why I should be nice to you. You're the bad guy, holding me against my will, chained up, feeding me sugar-laden Fruit Loops. Why should I help you out?"

"Because I really need the money. I haven't worked much in the past year."

"Why not?"

"It's tougher to play a sixteen-year-old at twenty-six than it was at eighteen."

"Oh."

"Plus, I won't do certain positions."

"Why not?"

"The body has exit points and entry points, I like to keep mine separate." I'm honest, but still embarrassed.

Jake laughs. I'm not sure why he would consider this funny. It's not funny to me.

"How much is Gideon paying you?"

"Hundred bucks a night."

"I'll pay you five-hundred to let me go."

I hesitate.

"A thousand." Jake ups the ante.

I bite my bottom lip.

"And babysit," he adds.

I hesitate even longer.

"Let me use your phone. I'll call someone to come over and unlock me and bring you cash." Jake says it with such sincerity. It's cute.

"I'm really in a hurry right now."

Jake hustles to his pants on the floor and removes the wallet from the back pocket, opens it up and removes all the bills. "I'll pay you eleven dollars now, and nine-hundred-eighty-nine later."

"No."

He finds a credit card. "Do you take Visa?"

"No."

"Make it fifteen-hundred."

"I can't. It wouldn't be right."

"What? Releasing a kidnapped man wouldn't be right?"

"No. I promised Gideon."

"Promised him you'd be an accessory to his crime?" Jake says and adds, "You could do time for something like this. The longer it goes on, the worse it'll be for you."

"I can't. I'm sorry, but I just can't." I'm starting to get emotional.

"Why not, you'd be freeing an innocent man?"

Tears are forming in my eyes. "When Kevin was born, there were complications. He almost died. My insurance only covered so much. I couldn't work. No one helped, not even my parents. And Gideon paid for everything. He was the only one who came to my rescue."

My tear ducts go on full blast. I'm like one of those lawn sprinklers that throw drops of water in every direction.

Kevin turns to me wondering why I'm crying. He runs to sit in my lap.

"Mommy's okay, honey."

Jake's face, rosy red a few minutes ago, is turning a shade of pale gray. Crying makes men uncomfortable. They don't know how to deal with it.

I sniffle as I weep. "I don't have any Kleenex."

Jake sits closer to me and lifts his arm so I can use the kimono's sleeve to wipe my eyes.

"Go ahead," Jake says.

I blow my nose into the silky material.

"Fine, I'll babysit."

I give him the best smile I can manage.

The three of us sit on the couch for a few moments, as I pull myself somewhat together.

"Thank you."

"You're welcome."

Off the couch, I retrieve my purse, pull out Kevin's inhaler and hand it to Jake.

"If he starts to wheeze, all you have to do is put this in his mouth and give him one puff."

"Asthma?"

"Yeah."

"Bad?"

"Not as bad as some. They say he'll outgrow it."

"What happens if he keeps wheezing?"

"Give him another puff."

"And if he still keeps wheezing?"

"That's never happened."

"You better leave your number so I can call you if anything happens," he says.

"That won't work."

"Why not, all babysitters have emergency numbers."

"How are you going to call me?"

"On the phone."

"But if I give you my phone, then I won't have a phone to

answer your call."

"Don't you have a land line?"

"No. Why would I want one of those?"

"Damn," he says.

I lift Kevin, give him a kiss and deposit him back in front of Big Bird. "Kevin, you and Jake are going to have a great time together. You be a good boy and keep your fingers out of your nose."

"And out of my nose, too," Jake adds.

I pick up the car keys and make for the front door. "I can't tell you how much I appreciate this."

"Oh, think nothing of it. I'm only here to help."

"One last thing…can I borrow eleven dollars?"

CHAPTER 25

Jake, the Groom

The chain won't reach into the kitchen, so Kevin has to fetch Fruit Loops, milk and bowl. "I need a spoon."

"Here."

I've fallen to yet another low, eating with Cookie Monster on the end of my spoon.

After the nutritious breakfast, I go into the bathroom.

Kevin toddles in. "Stinky," is his initial comment.

"This should be a good lesson on the results of too much cheese."

"Broke," he says, holding a toy truck with a busted wheel.

"Can it wait until I'm done?"

"No." He hands me the vehicle and repeats, "Stinky."

"You know," I tell him, "my mom used to say all that stink is bad stuff leaving your body so good stuff can get in."

"Stinky."

"I bet you're no Chanel Number 5 either, kid."

I finish, wash, and go out and sit on the floor next to him. The truck has a bent axle. "Got any tools?"

Kevin goes into the corner pile of toys and returns wearing a loaded tool belt, like an animated "Bob the Builder." He hands me the plastic hammer.

"You wouldn't happen to have a hack saw on that belt, would you?"

"Fix, please."

I'm able to bend the rod holding the wheel and allow it to spin. It's not aligned with the other wheels, and when it rolls it looks like a three-legged cat running from a Rottweiler. Kevin doesn't care. He takes the truck, sits across the floor from me and rolls it my way, although it doesn't roll very straight. I make some minor adjustments and roll the truck back to him. He laughs. Back and forth the truck goes, over and over, sometimes fast, and sometimes slow. This is fun.

"Get another truck," I tell him.

Kevin grabs a pickup truck, goes back to where he was sitting.

"Now when I roll this one, you roll that one and we'll have traffic."

The trucks pass as if on a city street. I catch his, he catches mine. Kevin is amazed. I'm amazed, too, that a person can be so thrilled with such a simple, mundane action.

"Do it again."

Perfect a second time. Kevin is laughing, so am I.

We must flip-flop those trucks twenty or thirty times. I put in sound effects, change speeds, roll from different angles. Kevin remains precise, taking deliberate aim and rolling his vehicle cautiously back to me. When the inevitable happens, and the trucks crash, Kevin, instead of laughing and being excited at the mayhem, yells out, "No!"

"What's the matter, don't you like a good smash-up?"

"That hurts."

We return to safe driving.

We're still rolling when Kay comes home. She's speechless seeing the two of us.

"Everything come off all right?" I ask to break her mood.

She scowls. "You try getting your privates plucked and see how you like it."

"Trucks, Mom."

"I can see that. Want bologna for lunch?"

"We should really have a talk about his diet," I say.

"I don't have time. I'm late already."

Kay goes into the small kitchen. She brings back a loaf of bread, pre-packaged meat, table knife, and mustard. "Kevin likes it plain, but I thought you may want a little more flavor."

"To match my personality?"

She doesn't respond, she's in too much of a rush. "I don't know what time I'll be back, but I'll get dinner from the set and bring some home."

"Boner *appétit*."

Kay gives Kevin another kiss, leaves, closes and locks the door behind her.

Kevin, Dora the Explorer, and I are left alone. After yet another delicious and nutritious lunch, I tell him to turn off the TV.

Kevin is incredulous at the idea. "Why?"

"Kids watch too much TV."

Kevin stands his ground.

"If you got crayons, we could color," I suggest.

The boy beams a quick smile, runs into the bedroom and emerges carrying the Binney & and Smith's boxed set of forty-eight Crayolas. Truly, some things in life never change. He opens the box for me to choose.

"Not until you turn off the TV."

Kevin sidles over to the TV, turns off the cartoon, and sits by my side.

"What are we missing?" I ask.

He looks up at me.

"Think."

He looks around where we sit. "Coloring book."

"Bingo." As he gets up, I tell him, "Bring back some white paper."

He's off to the bedroom and back in a flash.

"Know how to play Squiggle?"

"Squ-a-wha?"

I take a blank piece of paper, make a short, loop design with a crayon and explain. "I draw, you draw, one squiggle after another until we make a picture. "You first."

It takes him about three or four pages to get the concept, but once he does, it's off to the crayon races. Our little, shared designs become faces, cars, animals and buildings in every Crayola color of the forty-eight-box rainbow. This kid's got some real talent. After about two hours he gathers up the finished art and stacks it neatly in a pile. "Show Mom," he says.

"Your first private exhibition," I tell him.

Kevin doesn't get the joke, yawns instead. He cuddles under my arm and falls asleep leaning against me. I wish I could fall asleep that quickly.

I sit, consider continuing to color on my own, but I was never one to stay within the lines. When I was a kid, I colored with my mother. She was the one who taught me Squiggling. I'll do the same for my kids.

With nothing to do, no one to talk to, no place to go; and since the TV is the only one in Los Angeles without a remote, there is nothing to watch. If I get up, I would disturb his naptime, so I use the time to consider my options. A minute later I conclude, I have none.

I sit bored out of my mind for a few minutes, and then decide to make good use of the time planning revenge scenarios. If nothing else, it will be therapeutic.

For Gideon: His shoes are on the wrong feet, pants worn inside-out and backwards, mouth taped shut. He's at the blackboard writing *I shall not kidnap* over and over, as a penguin-posse of nuns whip him with pointers and rulers from every conceivable angle. Father Celcius sits in the classroom's front row, watching the spectacle, with a massive hard-on, waiting his turn.

For Conrad: He's tied to a chair in the bedroom of his penthouse condo, forced to watch me remove every piece of clothing from his walk-in closet, and cut each up with a huge scissors. The tears flow down his face as he pleads, "Not the Saville Row."

I feel better already.

A knock comes from the front door, awakening Kevin.

"Expecting someone?" I ask my sleepy-eyed friend.

The knocks keep coming.

"Who is it?"

"Jake, it's Conrad."

"Nice of you to drop by," I yell. "Just happen to be in the neighborhood?"

"Let me in."

"Is this a social or professional call?"

"Come on, let me in." He's standing up against the front door.

"The chain's not long enough to get me to the door."

"That's right. I forgot."

"Poor planning, Conrad, now you're at the mercy of your own mistake."

"Where's Kay?"

"She went to work."

"Who is that?" Kevin asks me.

Conrad continues to yell through the door. "Someone in there with you?"

"Yeah," said loud enough for Conrad to hear. "He's a hit man and we're in the middle of plotting the ultimate revenge on my captors."

"Have him let me in. I feel like an idiot out here."

"We finally have something in common."

"Open up, the beer's getting warm."

"Kevin," I take him gently by the arm, "do you know how to unlock the door?"

"Yeah."

"Good."

"But I'm not s'pose to."

"And I can understand that, but we're going to make an exception. The guy out there is named Conrad and he's my friend." I raise my voice. "Or he used to be my friend. He can come in."

Kevin pushes a kitchen chair to the door, climbs up, twists the dead bolt, climbs down, pushes the chair out of the way, and returns to my side. Obviously, he's broken the rule before.

"Ollie-ollie-oxen free," I call out.

Conrad enters the apartment. He's got a beer in his hand and a bag in the other. "I brought you a six-pack," he says, then notices his open beer. "Well, a five-pack."

"Say hello to Kevin."

"Hello, Kevin."

"Hello."

The two shake hands.

Conrad looks my way. "How are you doing?"

"My leg feels like it is going to fall off any minute."

Conrad sees the washcloth wrapped around my ankle. "That your idea to put that there?"

"No."

"Well, whoever thought it up was smart, because if you break the skin and it gets infected, gangrene could set in."

"Thank you, Doctor Bawana."

Conrad hands me a beer and asks, "Kevin, are you old enough to drink beer?"

"I don't know."

"Better not risk it then." Conrad stands over me. "Next time I come, I'll bring my camera. I'm sure you'll want some memories of this experience."

"You're killing me, Conrad."

Conrad sits in the chair, finishes his beer, takes out another.

"Why don't you sit over here?" I pat the seat of the couch.

"Why would I want to do that?"

"So, I can give a good reason for the doctor to heal thyself."

"I'll stay here." Conrad laughs.

I see no humor whatsoever. "Kevin, you can watch TV if you want."

Kevin pulls out the on/off button and cartoons pop onto the TV screen. I comment, "Oh for joy, Bob the Builder…again."

Conrad half-sits, half-lays in the big chair. "What a day. I had this lipo where I must have sucked out a farm silo's worth of fat out of this woman."

"Thank you for sharing."

"Should have charged her by the gallon."

"Do you want to hear about my day?" I ask.

"Not really."

I lift myself up onto the couch, making sure to emit enough groans to assure there is no question to the amount of pain to which I'm being subjected. "I don't know how much more of this I can take."

"Every person's constitution has a different threshold for pain and suffering."

"What great bedside manner you have, Conrad."

"Holding you hostage wasn't my idea."

"But you're condoning it."

"Let's merely say, I'm seeing it through."

"Conrad, this isn't funny."

"Actually, Jake, it is. You look like a hirsute, gay geisha in dire need of a full spa treatment." Conrad laughs at his own joke.

"Not funny."

"Yes, it is."

I wait, watch him sip the beer and speak slowly and distinctly, "Conrad, would you please get this off my leg?"

"I told you I don't have the combination."

I lift the lock so he can see. "You take the serial number of the lock, call the company, say you forgot the combination and they'll tell you over the phone."

"No can do."

"Why not?

"I don't have many minutes left on my cell phone plan this month. You wouldn't want me to go over my limit, would you?"

"Conrad..."

"Plus, there might be roaming charges."

"Then go to the hardware store, buy a hack saw and bring it back."

"I can't. I have to go soon. I have a date."

I put my hands over my eyes. I cannot believe this is happening. Kevin comes over and sits, leaning against me as he watches Bob build a shed.

"You two make a nice couple," Conrad says. "Gideon's coming over later."

"Can't wait."

"Said he was bringing reasons."

"Reasons for what?"

"Reasons for you not to marry Alyssa."

"Conrad, you are the smartest person I know. Don't you see this whole thing is utterly ridiculous?"

"I did at first, but you know Gideon does have some good points."

"Name one."

"Alyssa is a selfish, self-centered, mean-spirited bitch that will make you utterly miserable if you marry her."

Kevin's ears perk up at *bitch*.

"You're not allowed to swear around Kevin."

"Oh, sorry."

Doing my best to remain somewhat calm, I say, "Alyssa is nothing of the sort. She is a beautiful woman who will make an excellent wife."

"She's not a happy person."

"You barely know her, Conrad."

"She's cold, reserved and suspicious. You don't want to marry someone like that." Conrad changes positions in the chair, leaning forward with his elbows on his knees. "You love her more than she loves you, Jake. You are so busy trying to please her, you have totally forgotten what you need."

"That's not true."

"Yes, it is. You are so enamored by this woman, you can't see past her looks. She is not going to be beautiful forever."

"She will be to me."

"Jake, put your emotions aside for a minute and try to see it logically."

"I have."

"No, you haven't."

"Then it's my problem."

"Your problem is my problem, Jake. We're friends."

I sit up quickly and shout, "Well, how about the problem of me being chained up to a radiator, held against my will, developing jungle diseases on my leg? Is that our shared problem, too?"

"No," Conrad calmly says. "That problem is the result of previous problem. For example, remember when we got caught measuring the bust sizes of the girls in eighth grade and we tried to lie our way out of it by telling the nun we were solving a math problem, and she made us copy the entire catechism book as punishment? It's the same principle."

"Conrad…"

"If we solve the first problem, the resulting problems will disappear." Conrad rises from the chair, swallows the last of his beer. "Want another or should I put these in the fridge?"

I wave him off. "I'm good."

Conrad goes into the kitchen and comes right back out. "Got to go."

"And put an end to this swell time we're having?"

"Kevin, it was a pleasure."

Kevin is not sure what to say.

"I'll be back," Conrad says. "Can I bring you anything?"

"What do you think?"

"Jake, you know how I hate when you answer a question with a question." Conrad waves goodbye and exits.

Kevin remains seated at my side as Bob finishes the shed. It is six o'clock.

"I'm hungry."

"Your mom will be home soon with dinner."

"I'm still hungry."

"Anything in there to eat?"

Kevin runs into the kitchen, returning with an open bag of

Cheetos. In less than a few seconds, he is dusted from fingers to feet with Cheetos' dust. Predictably, one of the fingers enters his nose.

"That stuff is terrible for you."

"It's good."

"Let me try some." I reach in and take a handful. I'm hungry. "I'm only eating these because I'm in a weakened state of mind." I taste one, stale as cardboard. "I'm telling you, Kevin, this junk food can kill ya."

"It's good."

"But not good for you."

Public TV switches from kid to adult with a national news program. Kevin immediately runs to the dial and flips.

"Why can't we watch the news? It's good to stay current, even if you're homebound."

"It's dumb."

The dial goes around twice, neither time finding any animation. Kevin has to settle for an episode of *Jerry Springer*, where one girl, dressed out of the *Hee-Haw* clothing catalog, professes her love for her ex-UFC fighter boyfriend, who after a record of 0–12, has decided to give up his dream of glory in the octagon and return home to their doublewide.

"But, honey, I do love ya. I was jest tired last night," she tells her man.

The guy has lost so many teeth; he could eat corn through a picket fence, and is so jacked with head twitches, that he reminds me of a Mike Tyson bobble head. "I need my woman to be a woman when I need a woman," he tells her.

"It was a long bus ride from Tennessee."

"That don't matter."

"Plus, I'm havin' a visit from my meter reader."

"That don't matter, neither."

"You like this show?" I ask Kevin.

"Ewww!"

Jerry comes on the stage and announces, "Cindy Sue, Elwood has some show-and-tell for you."

"Really," the woman is thrilled at the idea. "I love show and tell."

"Welcome to the show," Jerry says. "Cindy Lee."

The woman who enters stage left is the identical twin of Cindy Sue with one exception. Cindy Lee is several months pregnant.

"She don't have no meter reader problems like you do," Elwood explains.

Kay comes home. Kevin jumps up to greet her. Kay appears exhausted. She carries plastic bags filled with Styrofoam boxes. "Whew," she says and sees Cindy Sue cold-cocking her pregnant twin with a knockout punch similar to the blows Elwood had endured. "What are you watching?"

"*Jerry Springer.*"

Kay turns off the TV. "You shouldn't let him watch that trash."

"I wanted to watch the news."

"And the TV dial switched to *Jerry Springer* by itself?"

"Sorry."

Kay collapses onto the couch next to me. Kevin climbs up next to her.

"Rough day?"

"You have no clue." Kay focuses on her son. "You must be starving."

"Cheetos," he tells her and shows her the empty bag.

"Oh, jeesh."

"Have you ever heard of fruit?" I ask.

"He won't eat it."

"He will if he's hungry enough and there's nothing else."

"You're not a parent, are you?"

"Not yet."

"Just wait."

Kevin pages through each piece of our crayon artworks and explains each in detail. His mother, much to her credit, heaps praise on each one.

As Kevin Scotchtapes each picture on the wall, Kay zaps the food she brought in the microwave, and the three of us eat pasta with chicken and artichoke hearts in a light cream sauce. Not bad. Kevin separates the ingredients and eats only the noodles. After dinner, Kay reads him a story and puts him to bed around eight o'clock. She comes back to the couch and plops down exactly as she did when she came home.

"Half of me feels like it's had a train driven through it," she says, sitting back and resting her hand over her privates.

"Sorry to hear that."

"I used enough lube to service a Chrysler and it still hurts."

"Brings a whole new aspect to a Jiffy Lube."

Kay moans. "I swear they hire the guys by the inch."

If I comment here, I can only lose.

"Whatever happened to the missionary position?" she asks rhetorically.

I move to sit facing her. "So, you don't like your chosen career?"

"No."

"Then why do you do it?"

"Money."

"Locked up in a pair of golden handcuffs, so to speak?"

I'm not sure she understands my reference. I heard it from one of the career counselors who never helped my career.

"My whole life is dependent on my pussy," she says in an exasperated tone. "Is that pathetic or what?"

"It could be worse."

"How?"

"I couldn't really say, since I don't have a vagina."

"You ain't missing much."

"Have you thought about a career change?"

"The positions I could list on my resume would not be the kind to impress many HR people."

"I wouldn't be too sure about that."

Kay chuckles, "I am pretty funny, aren't I?"

"You are," I tell her. "As long as you have a sense of humor, there's hope."

Kay smiles. I return one in kind.

"I'm glad to see you're still smiling, too," she says, nodding her head. "I'm not sure how I would feel if I were in your shoes."

She looks down at the fuzzy slippers I'm wearing. "Well, so to speak."

A knock comes on the door.

CHAPTER 26

Gideon, the Best Man

I figure I'm about half-way through my film's second act. It is referred to as the "point of no return" scene, when the actions of the characters push the story to a point, where it can only go forward to a logical, third act, conclusion. I know what I'm doing. Tonight will work, if it doesn't totally convince him, at least it will put him on the right track.

"I can't tell you how much I appreciate this," I say to my three new friends as we make our way to the second floor of the building.

"No problem," Smitty says. "I wish somebody would have done this for me."

I knock. The door opens. "Hi," Kay says.

We file into the apartment. "I heard Jailbait Jordan was back in fine form today," I tell her in complimentary tones.

"Yeah, bouncing around on pogo sticks."

Jake sits on the couch. If Alyssa could see him now, she might not want to marry him.

"How are you feeling there, buddy?"

"Fuck you, Gideon. Unlock me."

"Can't."

"Conrad said my ankle is getting gangrene."

"I just talked to him. He didn't mention anything to me." The three guys follow me into the room and immediately stare. "Kay, Jake, I want you to meet Larry, Bruce, and Smitty."

"Hi," Kay says, shaking their hands one by one.

One of the ways I got the boys to come was promising they'd meet Jailbait Jordan in person.

"Could I get your autograph?" Bruce asks.

"Sure," Kay responds with a total lack of enthusiasm.

"Jake, I thought it might be helpful if you heard a few actual testimonials."

The expression on his face says, *you have got to be kidding.*

"Larry, you go first."

The middle-aged guy, who is portly at best, scratches his psoriasis-filled arm before speaking. "I was once just like you, Jake—young, a real stud—and I met this woman who was a centerfold come to life. Not only did she have a body that could stop freeway traffic, but she could suck the bark off a redwood. She was everything I ever wanted out of a woman. Problem was, she wanted everything out of me. I married her and, in less than three years, she took my house, pickup, bass boat, dog, CD collection, and split with my best friend. The only thing she left me was eleven-thousand-dollars on my VISA card at twenty-four-and-a-half-percent interest. Jake, take it from a man like me, don't marry no beauty queen."

I clap my hands. "Let's give it up for Larry, everybody."

Bruce and I applaud. Everyone else stands, wondering whether they should laugh or cry.

"See what we're getting at here, Jake?" I ask.

"No." Jake says and asks with a snarl, "Who's next, Moe or Curly?"

"Bruce, your turn."

Bruce's tale of woe is pretty much along the same plot lines as Larry's, but Bruce adds a description of he and his beautiful ex-wife's sex life. "After we got married, a great night of sex for her was to watch *Beverly Hills 90210*, and a mediocre night of sex for her was to watch a rerun of *Beverly Hills 90210*." Bruce finishes his story by admitting, "After two years with her, I became bisexual. I could do it with either hand."

Jake sits with a totally blank expression on his face, like he's watched too many episodes of *Dancing with the Stars*. This is starting to feel like a bad *Saturday Night Live* skit.

"Smitty, you're up."

Smitty wears steel-toe boots, a pair of bib overalls, and has a neck bandana that's navy blue with splatters of fresh yellow mustard. On his forehead I can still see a crease from his hardhat. At first glance you'd suspect a redneck, but once he opens his mouth, it's obvious that he's both soft-spoken and sincere. You would never expect of a guy who rips up concrete all day to have such a sensitive side.

"Ever been through a contested divorce, Jake?" Smitty asks, but doesn't wait for an answer. "I have. From a woman who said she'd love, honor, and respect me 'till her dying day.' We were blessed with two kids, the most precious children you've ever seen. I love those kids more than life itself and, for four long years, she used that love to make my life a living hell.

"She wanted the divorce, but I had to leave the house I owned before we were married. That fair? I don't believe so. What was more unfair was her using our children as her main weapon against me. She wouldn't be home when I came to pick them up. She'd take them on vacations without telling me, enroll them in lessons or camp during my parenting time. Worst of all, she'd make comments that were not only lies, but past the point of being cruel. She'd curse me, call me every name in the book, paint me as the epitome of evil. She did everything in her power to turn the kids against me. Try to explain to a six- and a four-year-old that you had nothing to do with their dog dying.

"The funny thing about it, Jake, was that I knew marrying her was a mistake, but I was too stupid and too stubborn to admit it. All the signs were there. She came from a lousy family. Her mother was a tramp, her father a womanizer, she had a brother in and out of rehab, and a meth-addicted sister with two kids. She took, never gave. She talked, never listened. She spent, never saved. But I refused to see the obvious, because I was in love.

"She married me for my sperm and my paycheck, and I'm not sure even today which was more important. She had expensive tastes, wanted a lot more than I ever made and wouldn't settle for less, especially during the divorce. Yes, she was gorgeous, a prettier woman on the outside you will seldom see."

Smitty paces around the room slowly. "I never took the time or the effort to ask myself the following questions. Do I love her for what she is or what I want her to be? Would she love me if I didn't work two jobs, didn't buy her the BMW, or put a diamond on her finger that I couldn't afford? Did we value one another for who we are, what we believe, what we want? Did we respect each other? Are we best friends first and lovers later? Am I certain that she is the person, long after her beauty fades, who I want to be with the rest of my life? No, I didn't ask these questions, because I was in love with her outside, and didn't pay attention to what was inside."

Smitty pauses before continuing. "I have no idea who you are marrying, but do yourself a favor. Ask yourself the hard questions. Take your time, consider each carefully, bring each down to the lowest common denominator and answer honestly and fairly. It is easy to fool yourself, Jake, or to be charmed by a pretty face and voluptuous body. Relationships are built on respect and trust and, if you do not have those two functioning consistently, your marriage is doomed for failure just like mine."

Smitty sniffles into a dirty handkerchief. "I used to sit alone in my small apartment, tears falling from my eyes, wondering what I did to warrant such a fate. I was a faithful and loving husband, a great father, good provider. And what was my reward? Years of emotional stress, financial ruin, hours wasted in and out of courtrooms. My kids were scared, and looked at me like I was the devil. All I ever wanted was to be their daddy. It has taken me years to regain even a modicum of their love and respect.

"Trust me. If you have any doubt whatsoever, don't marry her. This is the biggest decision you will ever make. What you decide will affect you and everyone around you for the rest of your lives."

The room is as silent as an empty theater.

Kay takes a few steps forward and gently places her hand on Smitty's forearm. "I'm sorry," she says.

"So, am I."

"Don't worry," Kay says to him. "Kids are smart, they'll figure it out. It takes time."

"Time I will never be able to get back."

We finally got Jake's attention. He can't keep his eyes off Smitty as the man sniffles and wipes the moisture from his eyes. Even I'm a little misty at the end of the melodrama.

I pull out my wallet and hand Bruce a C-note. "Drinks are on me tonight, boys. Thanks for stopping by."

They are about to leave when Larry remembers and asks Kay, "Could I still get that autograph from you? I don't get to meet many movie stars."

Kay goes into kitchen and returns with three, eight-by-ten glossies and a felt pen. She personalizes the first two, but Smitty waves his off.

"No offense, I'm not much of a fan."

Kay smiles at Smitty and drops the last picture of her, with pigtails, dressed in micro-mini plaid skirt and tight, open, beige schoolgirl blouse on the coffee table. After the boys file out, Kay says, "I have an early call tomorrow, better get some sleep."

I thank her.

"Night," Jake says with a wave.

"Can you babysit again tomorrow?"

Jake asks me, "Are you going to set me free?"

"Only if you swear not to marry Alyssa."

"Although I won't be free, I can still babysit," he says to Kay while looking at me.

"I appreciate it and so does Kevin."

Kay makes a stop in the bathroom, before the bedroom.

"Well, Jake, pretty amazing stories, huh? There might be a movie in that last one."

"You want to tell me where you found those three?"

"And you think I go to strip clubs only to look at women."

Jake leans forward. "Gideon, what are you trying to prove?"

"That the waters in which you are about to dive are filled with problems, peril, and one big, man-eating piranha."

"All based on your personal opinion?"

"Not just me, Conrad's convinced, too."

"So, it's two votes to one?"

"In a manner of speaking."

"Doesn't it make sense that since this is my life, my vote should carry greater weight than yours and Conrad's?"

"When we were kids, if we couldn't agree on something, we'd vote and let the majority rule?"

"We're not kids anymore."

"What difference does that make?"

"Plenty."

"Jake, you have to admit to a lot of similarities between you and the boys tonight."

"No, I don't."

"Alyssa's selfish. Her mother's a nut case. She's not anywhere near as good a person as you are."

"So, now you're a relationship counselor, along with being a porn director and a kidnapper?" Jake takes a beat. "How do you ever manage to fit it all in?"

"Believe me, it's not easy." I take a beat. "Jake, if the shoe were on the other foot, I'd want you to do for me what I'm doing for you."

"And what is that?"

"Saving your life."

"Gideon, save someone else's life. Mine's just fine."

"You're going to thank me when this is all over." I glance at my watch. "It's getting late, I got to work tomorrow…"

"So do I."

"All I ask is for you to consider what they said, compare it to your situation and ask yourself the same questions Smitty never asked himself."

"Are you done?"

"For now." I make my way to the door.

Jake comes up off the couch, puts his hands together like he's ready to beg. "Gideon, please, you're killing me."

"I'll be back tomorrow night with another surprise. This one you're really gonna like."

CHAPTER 27

Alyssa, the Bride

I hate going to Walworth Recycling. The place reeks. Everyone here is foreign, black or Mexican. One step and my shoes are as good as ruined. Portia refuses to get out of the car. She makes me leave it running with the air conditioning on while I go inside.

"Is he here?"

"No."

"Did he call?"

"No."

"Have you heard anything?"

"No."

"Daddy…"

"What do you want me to do?"

"Find him."

Dad comes out from behind his desk. "One of my bachelor parties lasted all week. Don't worry about it."

"I can't help it."

"Did you call his friends?"

"Conrad's around, but won't call me back. The other asshole must have turned his phone off."

"You still have a few days. I wouldn't panic yet."

"Something's wrong, daddy."

"Alyssa, calm down."

"This is my wedding, the biggest day of my life. What's happening shouldn't be happening."

"Why don't you go get a pedicure or something, relax. Jake's probably in some Las Vegas hotel with a bad case of the Irish flu, and can't see straight enough to get to a phone."

"And that's a good thing?"

"Don't worry. When the music plays, Jake'll be there."

"Maybe I should call the police. Report him as a missing person."

"Don't be ridiculous."

"Daddy, please."

"Go, have a good time, do whatever you have to do. Jake will show up. He might be hung over, but he'll show up. Stop worrying."

"Daddy."

"Go, darlin', I'm busy. I have to go out and check the Green Cards of all the illegal aliens working here. I never had to do this with regular old black guys."

What am I supposed to do now? I walk down the aisle in less than seventy-two hours and I don't know where the groom is. Something is really awful, I can feel it.

Portia holds her nose as I open the door to get into the car. She was in the middle of playing with her fancy new phone. "What'd he say?"

"Not to worry."

"Why does he work here? It stinks."

"He owns it."

"He should sell, take the money and buy real estate."

I sit in the car. I could put it in gear and drive off, but I don't know where to go. I'm supposed to meet up with Bitzy, see the caterer and the florist today, but right now they don't seem so important.

"Why aren't we moving?" Portia asks.

"It's that bastard Gideon."

"Why don't you call him?"

"He won't take my call."

"Call him on my phone."

I find the number on my phone and recite it. It takes Portia a few times to dial it correctly. She waits for the connection and hands me her phone. "It's ringing."

Click.

"The party you have called is currently not taking calls, please leave a message at the beep."

I hand the phone back to Portia and she listens to the same

voice. "That's the same lady who answers my phone. She must be pretty busy."

I am not sure if that was a joke, with Portia it is hard to tell. After she breaks the connection, I ask, "You get Internet on that?"

"Yeah."

"Google Gideon Batch."

Portia's thumbs punch away at the tiny keypad.

"Not much on him. He has a P.O. Box instead of an address, but so do I." She pauses as she reads the small screen. "You know his parents are deacons in the Catholic Church. Is that like being altar boys?"

"How would I know?"

"And their son's a pornographer, that's great."

"What a slimeball."

Portia laughs. "What's his porn name?"

I have no clue what she is referring to. "What?"

"All porn people have porn names," Portia tries to explain. "It's like you take the street you live on and pair it with your pet to get your porn name."

"So you'd be Fifth Avenue Chihuahua?"

"Or," Portia says, "you can take your street, first name, and pet. So you would be Sunset Alice Chips."

"Alyssa."

"I know your name is really Alice," Portia informs me.

"And how do you know that, Portia?"

"I know a lot of things. People think I'm just a skinny, stupid twit, but actually I know a lot of stuff about a lot of people."

I put the car in drive and pull out. "And that gives you some sort of feeling of superiority?"

"Not really."

"I would appreciate it if you kept my real name to yourself."

"No problem."

Portia returns to playing with the touch screen on her phone. She doesn't look up when she asks, "How about your boob job, is that off limits, too?"

CHAPTER 28

Jake, the Groom

"How is your train station today?"
"Better, thanks for asking."

Kay is rushing around the apartment. Kevin is in front of the TV. I'm on the couch, where else would I be?

"Kevin, I want you to be a good boy today. Jake is in charge. You listen to what he tells you to do."

Kevin doesn't answer, too interested in what Big Bird has to say to the Cookie Monster.

"Where is your inhaler?"

Kevin doesn't know.

"It's over here," I show Kay.

Kay wears a pair of baggy jeans, a flannel shirt and no makeup, hardly the teenage sexpot. "It should wrap today, and I should be back late this afternoon. I wish you could take him outside."

"*You* wish."

Kay plops a bowl of Fruit Loops in front of Kevin, checks her purse, finds her keys. "I really appreciate you helping out. I hate taking him to daycare."

"I wouldn't tear myself away, even if I could."

"You're a sweetheart."

Kay gives Kevin a kiss, tells him she loves him, and hurries out the door.

While Kevin is enraptured by Bert and Ernie, I take a shower and get cleaned up. I wish I had an option for a style change. The kimono isn't doing it for me any longer. I check out my corduroy pants that lie on the floor, strung along the length of the chain. They are filthy and damp, as are the boxers I've been wearing. My stained shoes are in the corner. It will be a race to see which one grows algae first. I have no choice, another day of Japanese high fashion.

My ankle is killing me. I have a bright, red circle where the chain is wrapped. The washcloth has helped, but it can only do so much. It hurts every time I move.

"Let's play trucks." Kevin greets me as I come out of the bathroom.

"Let's play another game."

"No, let's play trucks."

"New game's going to be fun."

"Trucks are fun."

"Tell you what, we'll play my game first and trucks later."

"No."

"Trucks now, color trucks later."

"No."

"Yes!" Kevin throws a hissy fit, flailing his arms and repeatedly screaming "Yes."

"Knock it off, kid."

"No."

He's antsy, pent up, off-kilter. I give him a few seconds. "I'll make you a deal."

"No."

"Why not?"

He stops, stands, stares at me. "I got to poop."

"So that's the problem."

Kevin goes into the bathroom. About two minutes later, he calls out. "Help me wipe."

I don't remember signing on for this duty. "Didn't someone already instruct you in that area of expertise?"

"Help."

The activity is certainly a whole new experience for me, at least with a partner.

"Flush," he reminds me and pushes the lever down.

Feat accomplished, we are back in the front room after washing up. He brings over a truck.

"Tell you what, Kevin, you play my game with me now and I promise that I will give you an actual ride in the biggest truck you have ever seen."

"How big?"

"Huge."

"Today?"

"As you can see, I'm tied up today, but as soon as I'm free, I'll take you on the ride of your life."

The little wheels in his mind are turning. "Promise?"

"Promise." I raise my right hand.

"Mom come, too?"

"If she wants."

"Okay."

"Deal." We high-five on it. "Now, here's the game we're going to play."

He waits."

"I'm going to say an item and you're going to go around the apartment, find one and bring it back."

"Okay."

"You know what a file is?"

"No."

"The thing your mom uses on her fingernails.

Kevin runs off and returns with a nail clipper.

"Close, but no cigar, kid." I attempt to describe with the help of my hands. "Long, thin, metal, kinda rough with grooves in it."

Kevin fetches his Star Wars laser sword.

"No."

I go through an impromptu list: channel-locks, wire-cutters, snips, saw, pliers, wrench, sledgehammer and giant metal cutter?

"This game is dumb."

This kid needs a dad. The only tool he knew was a screwdriver, which didn't work on the keyhole on the back of the Master Lock.

I try filing down a link of the chain with the edge of a steak knife. It would have worked, but Kevin would be in high school by the time I was free.

What would MacGyver do in this situation? I never really liked that show, thought it was moronic. Who would ever find themselves in the situations he gets into?

I go over the chain link by link, and just my luck—a chain without a weak link.

The radiator isn't big and I could lift it, but I first need to unscrew it from the plumbing. My hands won't do the trick, without a wrench it's impossible. I try to file down a link against the radiator itself, a better idea than the steak knife. Kevin would only be in junior high when I was free.

By lunchtime, I briefly consider sawing my leg off at the knee with the steak knife like that guy on the mountain, but decide it would be too much to clean up.

In the afternoon, I draw Kevin a bad rendition of the dump-truck we'll ride in and his excitement grows. "Big truck," he keeps repeating.

Between cartoons, trucks, squiggling and during his nap, questions, comments, and thoughts revolve in my brain like goldfish in a feeding frenzy. Why was this happening? What did I do? I love Alyssa and she loves me. We are going to have the perfect family. I'm already good at wiping butts. How can my so-called friends even think that they could make such an important decision for me? I'm a man. I'm smart. I can think for myself, make my own decisions. Who the hell do they think they are? What do they think they know that I don't? I don't care what they do to me. I'm going to marry Alyssa, have a slew of kids and be the happiest guy on the block. I'll show them…if I ever get out of here.

Kay comes home at six. She isn't looking very well. Her left eye is red and swollen. She carries a large, plastic bag.

"You okay?"

She hands me the bag. It is soft and squishy. "I borrowed these from one of the lighting guys."

A pair of blue and gold sweat pants with *Lakers* stenciled up the side. "They're tear-aways," she says, "so you can get them on and off."

I hold them up against my lower body. They're about three sizes too big. "Thank you."

She takes the bag and removes a green tee-shirt. "I'm not sure if this will fit either."

On the front of the shirt, BonerZone.com.

"I really appreciate this," I tell her.

Kay chokes out, "The shirt you wore here is still in the hamper. I haven't had a chance to wash it. You must have thrown up on your shoes."

Kay is either weeping or both eyes are watering. I suspect the former.

"Sunday is my laundry day."

"Kay," I ask, "are you sure you're okay?"

"I have to go back tomorrow. I couldn't finish."

"What happened?"

"Right in the middle of the last scene, I got shot in the eye. I'm on my knees, can't see, thought I was going blind, and everybody is laughing. And they kept the camera rolling, the director's gonna use it as an *extra* on the DVD."

Kay falls against my chest and cries on my shoulder. "I hate my life," are the only words she can manage.

I hold her against me and tap her back as gently as a mom soothing a newborn.

CHAPTER 29

Conrad, the Groomsman

"Tell me about Alyssa."

"Why do you want to know?"

"Curious."

Farrin sips her martini, gives me an odd look. "You want to do her, too? Working through the family, are ya?"

"No."

"You wouldn't be the first guy who has tried."

"It's a simple question. I didn't ask it to make you angry."

Farrin takes a big swallow of vodka. I hear her gulp. "What do you want to know?"

"Is she a nice person?"

"No."

"Hardly a ringing endorsement from her sister."

"Stepsister."

It's five o'clock. We are the only couple in a WeHo restaurant. The owner should consider an early bird special for gay seniors.

"You don't share DNA, do you?"

"No."

Farrin finishes her cocktail. It is clear this conversation makes her feel like one of Cinderella's mean sisters. "We hated each other growing up. She was this gorgeous, popular chick. I was the punk sister, hanging around, needing a ride to the mall. I admit I didn't make it easy for her."

"Why?"

"Jealous."

"Pretty blunt."

"Alyssa got everything. If LaRue didn't give her what she wanted, she found some guy who would. She got good grades without trying, beautiful without makeup, a car at sixteen, and first pick of every male litter. Wouldn't you be jealous?"

"Maybe a bit."

Farrin signals the waiter for a refill. "I never figured Alyssa out until our parents divorced. She never got over her mother walking out on her and never will. So, she compensates by getting what she wants, when she wants it, and from whom she wants it. Can't say I blame her."

"You ever thought of becoming a shrink?"

"No, but it sure would save me a lot of money."

"All shrinks have shrinks, if you didn't know."

Her martini comes with a little umbrella on the top. She puts the pole end between her lips and twirls it around.

"What's this all about? Is Jake getting cold feet?"

"I wouldn't say that."

"Something's going on, isn't it?"

I watch two females, a fem and a dyke, being seated across from us. In a restaurant this big, you have to wonder why they put their only two pair of customers so close together.

"Come on, Conrad, fess up. Alyssa's freaking out."

"Nothing's going on."

"You're a lousy liar, Conrad."

"No, I'm not."

"She hasn't seen him, heard from him. He hasn't been at work."

"Women get nuts right before they get married, why can't a guy?"

"Is he getting second thoughts?"

"Not that I know of."

"Tell me."

I look over at the women, they make a nice couple.

Farrin leans forward, touches my hand. "Alyssa does love him, maybe only in her own way, but she does love Jake." She takes my hand into hers. "And we might not be the closest of step-sibs, but I don't want to see her hurt, especially on what she considers the most important day of her life."

I retrieve my hand, pick up the menu and change the subject. "Why don't we order, I have to see a patient at seven."

Farrin retreats, sits back in the booth. "Conrad, you're not a lousy liar, you're a terrible liar."

"No, I'm not, I'm an excellent liar."

Two hours later, as I walk up the stairs to Kay's apartment, a woman comes out of the apartment directly beneath. "What's going on up there?" she asks.

"Up where?"

"In the apartment of the whore."

"That's hardly a nice comment to make about someone."

"Are you a john?"

"No, I'm a Conrad."

"What's a Conrad?"

"Look it up." I continue up the stairs, leaving the crusty, peevish woman wondering. I knock on Kay's door.

"Oh, hi."

"What happened to your eye?"

"You don't want to know."

"I'm a doctor; yes, I do."

"No, you don't," Jake calls out.

I take a closer look at her eye and pull back. "I keep a bag in the car, I'll be right back."

I walk out, down the stairs to my car and retrieve my medical bag from the trunk. When I re-reach the stairs, the lower-level witch is waiting. I show her my bag. "I'm a doctor. House call."

"She's got one of the SUV diseases doesn't she?"

"No," I say. "She's got a four-door."

Inside, the kid is watching cartoons. Jake is on the couch sporting a new extremely colorful ensemble.

"I love the new look," I tell him. "Lakers in the Boner Zone defense."

He gives me a snarl.

Kay sits in the big chair, leans her head back so I can wash out her eye with a saline solution and apply a cream that should reduce the redness. Finished, she says, "Thanks."

"My turn," Jake says, lifting his leg my way. "Amputate, remove the chain, and sew my leg back on."

"Kay, do you have a big hunk of leather Jake can bite down on during the surgery?"

"No, I'm not into leather."

I hold his leg by the foot. There is a circular, red, inch-worth of tenderness where the chain rests. It looks painful.

I apply some cream. "This should help. Try not to put any undue stress on it."

"Stress?" Jake questions. "Why would I have any stress?"

"Don't know, you're just sitting around all day, aren't you?"

"No." Jake raises his voice, "Conrad, I'm pissed. You have no idea how pissed. "

"Could you wait until we leave before you start swearing?" Kay asks, putting her hands over Kevin's ears.

"Sorry," Jake says.

The door slams open and Gideon barges into the apartment, carrying a stack of DVDs, followed by a squirrely, middle-aged guy in a bad sport coat, Dockers, and beret on his head. "I brought you some movies Jake: *Basic Instinct, Fatal Attraction, Double Indemnity, Who's Afraid of Virginia Woolf.*"

"Go to hell, Gideon."

"Jake!"

"I can't help it, Kay."

"Come on, Kevin, we're leaving."

"I want you to watch these with an open mind," Gideon tells Jake, "in your spare time."

"Might be difficult to do," I say pointing to where the TV rests on its stand.

Gideon sees a VCR under the old TV. "Haven't seen one of those in a while, I thought they were extinct."

"Doesn't work anyway," Kay says, as she ushers Kevin towards the bathroom. "Go potty before we leave."

The funny, little guy in the beret stands and takes it all in, as if he's making a mental recording of the situation for later use. Gideon's pumped up, as if he is back on the set, ready to shout out "action."

"We're going to get serious tonight, folks," he announces.

Kevin comes out of the bathroom, then returns to flush.

Gideon gives Kay money.

"Thanks," Kay says. "We could use a night out."

"So, could I," Jake says.

"Jake," Gideon says, "you're going to get something tonight money can't buy."

"My freedom?"

"Not quite."

"Gideon, unlock this chain."

"Not yet."

"I'm not kidding, Gideon." Jake waits for Kay and Kevin to exit, then picks up the tempo of his argument. "Get me the fuck out of this."

"Jake, Jake, Jake, calm down. We have a special guest."

"I swear, I will wrap my hands around your throat and choke the fucking combination out of you, if I have to."

Gideon wisely backs up out of range. I follow his lead. Jake's moving side-to-side, like a chained tiger about to pounce.

"Okay, let's get started."

I don't know what to expect. Gideon hasn't filled me in. Our guest brings a chair from the kitchen and places it a few feet away from the couch. He puts on a pair of heavy, black glasses and takes out a small notebook and pen.

Gideon says, "Jake, meet Doctor Lou."

Jake peers down on the man's outstretched hand. "You sure you want to shake my hand, Doc?"

"Of course."

Jake leans forward, positioning himself carefully. "I could be contagious. Touch me and you could die a slow, painful death."

"What?" the man asks.

"My leg," Jake pulls up his pant leg, reveals his red, swollen ankle and thrusts it towards the man's face. "Gangrene, it's ready to fall off."

The Doc backs up quickly and turns to me. "Could that really happen?"

"Highly unlikely," I tell him.

"You're a doctor—make your own diagnosis," Jake shouts back.

"I'm a PhD, not an MD."

"He's here to give you a second opinion," Gideon says.

"On what?" Jake asks.

"Marriage," Gideon answers. "You and Alyssa go to her shrink, so I want to give you a view from the other side of the fence."

Oh, this should be good.

Doctor Lou sits, opens his notepad, and clicks his ballpoint open. "Jake," he says, "let's talk about love."

"Let's not and say we did."

"We fall in love for many reasons, Jake, but we stay in love for only one. Do you know what that reason may be?"

Jake answers in a sing-song manner, "*My baby's got me locked up in chains?*"

"No," the doc says in his best Freudian tone. "Vulnerabilities. We stay in love because our vulnerabilities are being compensated for. Now you and your intended…" He pauses.

"Alyssa," Gideon fills in.

"Do you feel vulnerable around Alyssa?"

"I feel vulnerable right now," Jake says.

"Because of Alyssa?"

"No," Jake says and raises his voice to finish, "because I'm chained to a goddamned radiator."

"I see that."

"Do you suspect, Doc, this might have something to do with my feeling a bit on the vulnerable side?" Jake asks in the same volume.

"I'm the doctor. I'll ask the questions."

Where does Gideon find these people?

"The true nature of a successful relationship is one person making accommodations and efforts in the areas where the partner is weak, and vice versa."

"I'll tell you where I'm weak, Doc," Jake says with as much sincerity as he can muster. "I'm weak, because I have two former friends who are holding me hostage so they can make a major decision in my life. Why don't you turn your attention to the two of them? They're the psychopaths. I'm the only sane one in this room."

"Jake, I feel your pain."

"You want to feel pain? Try having a Master Lock banging into your ankle all day long," Jake shouts.

Jake's overtly angry response doesn't seem to faze Doctor Lou. He sits with one leg crossed over the other, Clark Kent glasses perched on his nose, making notes on the small pad.

"Why are you so sure Alyssa is the right woman for you?" Doc asks.

"This is fucking ridiculous," Jake says, catching his breath to answer. "And it's none of your goddamn business."

"Does she ever lie to you?"

"No."

"If she did, what would you do?"

"She doesn't."

"Relationships can only exist in an atmosphere of absolute honesty."

"Gideon, would you get this pseudo Sigmund Freud out of my face?"

"Listen to him, Jake." Gideon adds, "Doc's an expert."

"Do you listen to one another? Have you two learned to communicate, fight, make up, and have your differences resolved in a positive manner?"

Jake doesn't answer. He leans back onto the couch and closes his eyes.

"Alyssa is gorgeous, isn't she?"

Jake continues his silence.

Doctor Lou asks a series of questions. To some, Jake mumbles answers. Mostly he just ignores them. As I watch Jake squirm on the couch, I begin to see a change. Although still angry, he's beginning to soften. He moves slower, massages his eyes and head. At one point he leans back, and then forward placing his elbows on his knees and head in his hands to rest. His anger seems to be dissipating, and I have a sense that he's starting to feel something, rather than just think logically. It is hard for me to believe, but Gideon's plan might be working.

"How have her looks affected your consideration of her as your wife?" Doc asks.

"What?"

"Jake?"

"What?"

"Answer the question. How has Alyssa's outward appearance affected your consideration of her as a wife?"

Jake's outward calm suddenly explodes into an anger I've never before seen in him. He jumps off the couch, lifts Doctor Lou up by his armpits and screams, "I'm going to marry Alyssa, Doc, if I have to chew this chain off my leg. I'm going to be at the church on Saturday and marry her, no matter what you, Gideon, or Conrad have to say."

Jake plops the so-called doctor back into his chair. The doc wipes spittle from his face with his sleeve. He slowly cleans his glasses with his shirt-tail.

"Even if you realize she is the wrong woman for you?" Doctor Lou asks, looking up over the rim of his specs at his suddenly aggressive patient.

Jake's answer is louder than his last. "Hell, I'd marry her now just to piss all you guys off."

Maybe I was a bit premature in my last assessment of Jake's current state of mind.

Doctor Lou flips his notepad closed and removes his glasses, stands. "I'm done."

"Really?" Gideon asks.

"He's much too angry to continue."

"Moi?" Jake asks.

"Sorry," Doctor Lou says. "I'm much better counseling actresses who don't have their clothes on."

It takes a few minutes for Doctor Lou to pack up. As Gideon shows him out the door, they are met by the shrew from the downstairs apartment.

"What's going on in there?" she asks, poking her head into the doorway.

Gideon blocks her entrance into the apartment. "Nothing's going on."

"There's all kinds of screaming. I can hear it downstairs over the TV," she says, trying to peer inside.

"Don't worry, lady," Gideon says. "We're rehearsing for a play." He closes the door, shutting her out and comes back into the room.

"Where do you come up with these people?" Jake asks a question I would have also asked.

"Doc is the shrink to the stars in the porn biz. He shows up when chicks get drugged out, flip out, or opt out in the middle of a shoot."

"Jesus Christ, this isn't fucking happening," Jake says.

I go into the kitchen, find three beers, pop 'em open, come back and pass 'em out.

"This one loaded?" Jake asks.

"Nope," Gideon answers.

We sit and sip for a few moments. We need a time out.

I say, "I had a patient not too long ago, an older guy, who came to me wanting a facelift. I asked why and he told me he wanted to look more hip for his younger lover. I examined him and realized it wasn't his first nip and tuck. I told him he could only go to the well so many times and his facial nerves were already stretched to the max. He didn't care. He wanted to look good strolling arm in arm with his lover through West Hollywood."

"And the moral of your fairy tale is?" Jake asks.

"I refused to do it. So he went to another surgeon, who performed the procedure, and three days later, the man lost the nerves on one side of his face. Now he sags like a suspension bridge."

"So, you think if I marry Alyssa, my profile will be ruined?"

"Not your profile, dumbass, your life," Gideon tells him.

Jake shakes his head side to side, closes his eyes, then says, "Gideon, remember coming out of film school and wanting to make movies so bad you didn't care what kind of movies you made?"

Gideon is caught a bit off guard. "What does that have to do with anything?"

"And remember us trying to talk you out of it?"

"Kinda."

I remember it well.

Jake continues, "Conrad and I didn't want you to go into that den of iniquity. It was beneath you, beneath your talents and beneath any accepted moral standard of decency. We talked until we were blue in the face about you going into porn, but you wouldn't listen."

"It was the only directing gig I could get."

"That's not the point. The point is you didn't listen."

"Hey, I can leave the porn business anytime I want," Gideon argues. "You can't do that if you're married."

"It's the same principle," Jake says, "except the roles are reversed."

"My going into porn was a business decision, not an emotional one."

"It's exactly the same," Jake says. "I want a beautiful woman to give me beautiful kids so I can live behind a white picket fence, coach the soccer team, and drive a minivan. That's what I want. That's what Alyssa wants. And that's the way it's going to play out."

"Except she is a miserable, calculating, dishonest, spoiled rotten, fucking bitch."

Jake doesn't react to Gideon's rather vile summation of his future bride.

"I deserve the same freedom to screw up my life as you did with yours."

"We won't let you."

"It's over Gideon. The only thing left for you to do is unlock the lock and let me be."

"I can't do that."

"Why the fuck not?"

"Because I know in my heart, marrying her is the wrong thing for you to do."

"That's not your decision to make."

"I'm your friend."

"Not right now, you're not," Jake says.

"Jake," Gideon says, "you're not thinking clearly yet. You need to consider what the boys said the other night and what the doc said tonight. You need to process it all. If you do, I swear, you'll see what we're saying is right."

I'm amazed Jake remains calm. Even I would be going nuts after all this.

"If I swear to you, right now," Jake says, "that I will not marry Alyssa, will you unhinge me?"

"No," Gideon answers.

"Then what the hell do you want me to do?"

"You'd have to call her on the phone and tell her you've decided not to go through with the marriage."

"You're serious?"

"And then I would talk to Alyssa to verify the exchange."

"Why don't you just monitor the call for quality assurance?" Jake asks.

"Good idea," I throw in for good measure.

"You know," Gideon says, "after this is all over, I should write this as a screenplay. I would do it as a romantic comedy in reverse."

"Could we please return to the topic of releasing me?" Jake says.

"Sure, call her."

"I'm not going to call Alyssa."

"Would you at least open your mind to the thought of it?"

"Why should I?"

"Because," Gideon says, "she's not a nice person."

"I could say that about you and Conrad," Jake says.

"But we don't want to marry you, we're your friends," Gideon says.

"And what would you do if you didn't have friends like us?" I ask.

"Get up and walk the hell out of here."

We all hear the key go in, the door open, and Kay and Kevin return.

"Hi."

Kevin runs to the bathroom. We hear that, too.

"How was the movie?"

"I can't believe I cried at the end of *Shrek*," Kay says.

Gideon says, "Don't feel silly. I cry every time I see *Home Alone*."

"The scene when the old man sees his granddaughter?" Kay asks.

"Yep," Gideon says. "Gets me every time."

Kevin shuffles out of the bathroom. He appears ready to pass out.

"We should be going, Gideon," I say.

"Wait," Jake says.

"Don't worry," Gideon says. "We'll be back tomorrow."

"And what happens after that? Saturday comes and I still refuse to capitulate to your absurd demands, what are you going to do then?"

"We're not sure."

"You have no backup plan?"

"I don't think we're going to need one," Gideon says. "Tomorrow night we're putting on the full court press. You'll see the light."

Jake pushes himself further back into the couch, totally defeated.

Kay sees Kevin yawn. "Get ready for bed, honey."

"Tomorrow's Friday, Jake, and don't worry, we can stay up all night tomorrow if we have to."

"Rub this on in the morning and try to keep your foot elevated," I tell my patient, leaving the salve for his use.

"If I ever get out of here," Jake says, "the first thing I'm going to do is find another doctor. Second thing I'm going to do is find new friends."

Kay gives Kevin a gentle nudge into the bedroom and follows us out of the apartment. "Wait."

Gideon and I stop as she closes the door behind her. "Are you sure this is still a good idea?"

"Yes," Gideon says without hesitation.

"Why do you ask?" I ask.

"I worry about him."

"Is he sick?"

"Not physically."

"If you knew Alyssa, Kay, you'd think differently," Gideon tells her. "She makes Cruella D'Ville look like Snow White."

"She can't be that bad," Kay says. "No guy that good could fall for a woman that bad."

"Trust us," Gideon says. "It happens every day."

CHAPTER 30

Alyssa, the Bride

"The ceremony is less than thirty-six hours away and I can't find my husband!"

"Calm down."

"He didn't show up for work again."

"What did your dad say?"

"Said he hates Mexicans."

Portia doesn't understand.

"What the hell am I going to do?"

"Let's go," Portia says and takes my keys.

I haven't slept in two nights. My skin feels like leather. How am I going to look in the wedding pictures? Every shot will have to be Photoshopped. I can't eat, which probably isn't a bad thing, but I can't sit still, either. I'm in constant motion, a strung-out Energizer Bunny. I'm achy, irritable, bloating up like a whale. Bitzy calls every thirty seconds. My mother is all over me. Guests from out of town want to party tonight. What am I supposed to say? *Jake's indisposed.* Makeup starts at eight. Pictures at ten. Three hundred people are going to be sitting in the church at noon. The Beverly Wilshire at one. My God, if Jake fucks up and ruins everything I've worked for in the last six months, I will kill the son of a bitch.

"This is nicer than the doctor I go to," Portia says, stepping off the elevator. "My guy's in a Brooklyn walk-up."

One step onto the plush carpet, and my eyes almost fall out of my head. "What the hell are you doing here?"

Farrin sits in Conrad's waiting room on a Mies Van der Roh chair, with two brown paper bags. "I brought breakfast."

"Breakfast?"

"Conrad and I have been dating," Farrin says.

"Good for you," Portia says.

"You're sleeping with him?" I can't believe this.

"So?"

"Good for you," Portia says. "Quicker you get 'em in bed, the quicker you can start collecting."

"Jesus Christ!" I'm furious. "When did all this start?"

The other three waiting patients drop their reading material to listen.

"We've been seeing each other since the rehearsal dinner."

"That's way too much time to wait," Portia says. "I would have jumped his bones much sooner."

"Why didn't you tell me?"

"Why should I?"

"Because I'm your sister."

"That's not a reason."

"Excuse me," the receptionist calls out, "could I be of some assistance?"

Barbie, or whatever her name is, is saying what she has been told to say when she doesn't know what to say.

"I'm here to see Conrad," I tell the vapid airhead.

"Doctor Blaine?"

"You have another Conrad working here?"

"Not that I know of."

"Tell him Alyssa Walworth is here."

"Are you a patient?"

"No."

"If you're not a patient, you'll have to fill out a form."

The idiot pulls out a clipboard with a Tiffany pen attached and brings it over.

Farrin asks, "What's this all about, Alyssa?"

"Jake's gone."

"Where did he go?"

"How the hell would I know?"

I can't tell if Farrin is bullshitting or telling the truth. It is tough when she's wearing all her face metal.

"Conrad know where Jake is?"

"I don't know."

"Did he tell you what they did at the bachelor party?"

"The only thing he said was Arty, Simon, and this minister

showed up, got shitfaced, so they left them at some strip club in the Valley."

"They didn't go to Vegas?"

"Conrad didn't."

Portia picks up a magazine off the teak table, opens to a full-page ad, holds it up for the women waiting, and says, "That's me." She pages further through, stops at another ad, "That's me, too."

The receptionist, holding the clipboard, clears her throat quite loudly.

Like I could give a shit. "Just get the damn doctor," I order.

The nitwit waddles off like a scolded child.

"I haven't seen Jake all week and I'll bet Conrad and that asshole Gideon know exactly where he is."

"Well, I don't. So, why the hell are you screaming at me?" Farrin fires back.

I'm losing it. I know it, but can't help it. "My wedding is Saturday and I can't find my fiancé."

My face must be bright red. My hands won't quit shaking. My feet hurt. I feel like I'm going to wet myself. I see the other women's mouths dropped open as they stare at me like I'm underdressed at a formal.

"Don't you think the timing is a little odd to be sleeping with the enemy?" I ask, getting more irate with every breath.

Farrin stands up, raises her voice. "Why the hell should you care?"

"The maid of honor is not supposed to be screwing the groomsman." We're face to face.

"What? I should be screwing the best man?"

The door to the offices open and Conrad is hustled out and over to us by the receptionist.

"Hey," Farrin says with a big, after-sex, smile. "I brought breakfast."

"What is going on?" Conrad asks. "You people can't fight in my waiting room."

Portia puts out her hand to Conrad. "Hi, we met at the rehearsal dinner. I'm Portia. I have a prescription for Oxycontin, but I left it at home, could you help tide me over?"

Farrin slides between the two, as if to protect her man-turf.

"What is going on?" Conrad asks again.

"Where's Jake?" I scream.

"Calm down."

"No, where's Jake? You got him somewhere. I know you do. Where is he?"

Conrad eyes dart to me, to Farrin, and back to me.

"I don't know," he says.

"You're lying."

"No, I'm not."

"Yes, you are, you lying sack of shit." I've never been this hot and I'm getting hotter. "You probably drugged, kidnapped, and are holding him somewhere."

"Would you please calm down?" Conrad pleads.

"Tell me."

"I don't know."

"Gideon got him?"

"I said, I don't know."

"That's it. It's that fuck-head Gideon. He's got him somewhere, doesn't he?" I'm shaking, I'm so mad.

Conrad takes a sec, and then speaks as if to reassure me. "Maybe Jake needs a little personal time on his own."

I rear back and throw the first bitch slap of my life. Unfortunately it misses Conrad, but scores a knockout punch to his latte and bagel, which fly across the room and hit the opposite, taupe wall.

"Get her out of here," Conrad says to Barbie.

Before I can throw another punch, Farrin grabs my waist and pulls me back. I stumble off balance and almost fall onto a couch.

Barbie isn't sure what to do. "Why don't you call and make an appointment?"

"Where's that asshole Gideon?" I scream as my stepsister drags me towards the elevator.

"At work, I would guess," Conrad answers.

"Where?"

"Hell, if I know."

"Do you know his porn name?" Portia asks him.

Farrin pushes the elevator call button, but doesn't let go of my waist. I feel actual beads of sweat fall down the side of my face, disgusting.

"He's my husband, you have to tell me," I scream at the top of my lungs at Conrad who stands in his embroidered lab coat and Abboud rep tie.

"Not yet, he isn't," the bastard replies.

I try to squirm out of Farrin's hold, but can't get any traction. Never wear Manolo Blahniks to a physical altercation.

Portia is slowly making her way toward us as Conrad faces his other patients and explains, "I assure you, this isn't about any procedure she's had."

"She's getting married Saturday," Portia announces to the crowd. "She's a little uptight."

The elevator doors open. Farrin drags me inside. Portia enters and pushes a button. Farrin doesn't let me go until the doors close.

"That was a hell of a morning after," Portia says to Farrin.

I collapse into the corner of the elevator and break into tears.

Next thing I know, I'm in my car, still crying, my silk blouse soaked. That bitch Farrin is probably off buying another bagel for that dickhead doctor. Portia starts up the car, but before pulling out, says, "Oh darn, I forgot to get the parking ticket validated."

I cry, shriek, and tremble at the same exact time.

"That was a joke," she says.

I can't stop weeping.

"We'll find him," she tells me.

"How?"

"Hire somebody."

"Who?"

"Don't worry," she says. "I've had plenty of practice. Just because guys look like they have money, doesn't always mean they do."

Portia punches her phone until the screen lights up. "Where's Robertson Drive?" she asks.

I manage to point.

"Good."

As I sit in the car, I wonder if Jake could be having second thoughts. This thought has never entered my mind until this second. It sends an actual chill up my spine. I've never been rejected, dumped, pushed out, or left for another woman. I've always done the deed, or at least beat him to the punch. It can't happen now. I won't allow it. Jake wants me. I know he does, because he wants what I want. We have a perfect life ahead of us.

He knows that, so why the hell would he have any doubts? I have to find him, talk to him. I will do or say anything to make it all happen. I will not be humiliated tomorrow, the most important day of my life.

The fix I attempt on my face doesn't do the job. I continue to dab cheeks, pencil eyes, and paint my lips as we wait in the reception area of one of those tacky, shared office suites.

Thank God, we don't have to wait long.

A big man, ill-fitting suit and rubber soles on his shoes, lumbers to where we sit and puts out his beefy hand to shake. "I'm Randolph."

Portia does the talking. "We need to find someone right away."

"If this is a felony, you should call the police," he says, his eyes on me.

"No, it is a private matter."

We follow Randolph to a small, corner, one-room office. It has a desk, two chairs, file cabinet and a computer with a huge screen on the pull-out credenza. We sit, he sits.

"We need to find him today," Portia says.

"I can't promise anything."

"His name is Jake Dombrowski," I say.

"I'll need a retainer before I begin."

I hand over a credit card, which he reads. "This yours?"

"My dad's company."

He runs it though his machine and copies down the number on a slip of paper. "Five hundred is standard. When that runs out I'll call you. Additional charges will also be placed on this card."

"Fine."

After a small slip of paper comes out, he rips it off, hands it to me, I sign. He hands me my dad's American Express card and says, "Spell the name for me."

I have to think, but recite the letters correctly.

"Relation?"

"As of tomorrow, he'll be her husband," Portia explains.

"Disappeared?"

"So to speak," Portia helps out again.

"I think his friend Gideon Batch has something to do with it," I tell him.

"Why?"

"Because the guy's a real shithead."

Randolph types his name into the computer. "You want me to look for him, too?"

"Find one, you'll find the other," Portia says.

Randolph peers at the screen. "Nothing much here. What does he do?"

"He's in porn," Portia says.

"You know his porn name?"

"No."

"What do you want me to do if I locate either of them?"

"Call me right away."

I give him my cell phone number.

"Does Jake have any close friends or business associates you could give me?"

"He works for my dad and I'm his best friend."

Portia gives me an odd stare.

"You know anyone this Gideon works with?"

"No," I say. "I don't know porn people."

"Wait," Portia says. "How about the girl he brought to the rehearsal dinner?"

"Kay something," I hesitate. "Kay Cameron."

Randolph types her name into the computer. "Jailbait Jordan?"

"Who?"

"Kay's porn name is Jailbait Jordan."

"That's a good name for a porn star," Portia says.

"Just find my husband," I say. "And please hurry up."

"Don't worry, little Miss," the man says, standing up. "Randolph Investigations always gets his man."

CHAPTER 31

Jake, the Groom

I got to get out of here.

I've tried rubbing two links of chain together, smashing links with the leg of the couch, dialing hundreds of combinations into the lock, picking the keyhole with paperclips. I even attempted to pull the chain apart with my bare hands. Hercules, I'm not.

Kevin helps, but does little good. When I get tired or run out of ideas, we read, play with his trucks or color.

"When do we get to go ride in the big truck?" he asks for about the fiftieth time that morning.

"As soon as I get out of here," I tell him.

"You promised."

"Yeah, I know."

At eleven-thirty, Kevin starts to wheeze.

"What's the matter?"

"Asth....ma," he says and wheezes louder.

I take his inhaler off the coffee table and examine it. Seems pretty straightforward how it works.

"Not yet," he is able to say.

"Why not?"

"Expensive, mom says…" He is unable to finish his sentence.

I grab him, pull him to me, position the inhaler in his mouth. "Ready?"

He nods. I depress the sideways plunger on the device.

Poof.

Kevin's eyes fill with tears. He bounces a bit in my arms, becomes still, takes a normal breath and sighs.

"That was quick," I tell him. "Maybe we should try it on my ankle?"

I'm as relieved as he is. I'd hate to have anything go wrong on my watch. It would ruin my budding babysitting career.

We play trucks until the door opens and Kay walks in an hour later.

"Kevin had an attack."

Kay immediately takes Kevin into her arms and holds him. "Are you okay?"

Kevin breathes deeply. Kay hugs and kisses him. "Thank God." She finds the inhaler and checks it. All is quiet and peaceful for a few minutes.

"He's fine," I say.

Kay seems reserved, removed, depressed.

"Something I said?" I ask.

"I hate my life."

"Don't say that."

"I do," she says. "I'm nothing more than a plaything, specially designed to give some horny loser a hard-on."

"That's not true."

"The only thing I've ever done with my life is increase the usage of Kleenex."

She releases Kevin who seems to know this is the time to turn on cartoons. *Scooby Doo* it is.

"You know how many guys I had to do this week?"

"No."

"I don't either. I don't count. It's disgusting."

"You know," I say, pointing to the TV, "at least when we were kids, we watched great animation, Bugs and Mickey and Elmer Fudd. Now all the stuff kids watch is so cheesy."

Kay doesn't look at *Scooby Doo*. My attempt to change the subject was an absolute failure.

"Not as cheesy as me."

"If you hate it so much, why don't you quit?"

"What else can I do?" she asks. "It's not like I can go out and start a hedge fund."

"Can you take shorthand?"

"Nobody takes shorthand anymore. Everyone uses computers."

"Can you do that?"

"No."

"The only thing I'm good at is having sex with guys I don't like in front of a camera."

"Don't demean yourself."

"I make my living demeaning myself."

"Kay…"

"I had to leave home at seventeen and first I made pretty good money as a stripper. Then some guy offers me even more money to pose nude, and when I got pregnant the first time, I needed even more money, so I blew some guy on camera while wearing knee socks and Jailbait Jordan gets born."

The tears begin, as I knew they would.

I choose not to dwell on her phrase "pregnant the first time." I pat her gently on her shoulder and she leans against me. The BonerZone.com shirt absorbs tears quite well. "You must have done pretty well being famous?"

"It's tough getting health insurance if you're a porn performer with an asthmatic son."

"Did you try an HMO?"

She sobs. "My life is a fucking disaster."

"You're not allowed to swear in front of Kevin," I tell her.

Kay doesn't apologize for breaking her own rule. She's busy crying and being miserable.

"Doesn't Kevin make it worthwhile?"

She sniffles, blows her nose. "He's not going to get better anytime soon. Doctor says asthma can last for years. I can't play Jailbait forever. What am I going to do? I don't want to end up homeless."

I'm at a loss for applicable career advice. "Maybe you should do a prison porn movie, your fans might consider it a logical step in your career; ya know, go from jailbait to prison mama?"

"I hate movies. I hate videos, and I hate sex."

"Nobody hates sex."

"I don't even know if I would even know how to have sex with a guy I liked."

"I wouldn't worry about that. Once you get back on the right horse, riding will be no problem."

Kay sobs on my shoulder.

I watch an entire *Scooby Doo* episode before I say, "Kay, you have to let me out of here."

"I can't."

"Why not?"

"I need the five hundred dollars."

"I'll pay you double, triple, whatever."

"What about Gideon?"

"What about him? He drugged me, kidnapped me, and is holding me against my will."

"But I promised him."

"And I promised someone I'd marry her...tomorrow."

"And I feel bad about that," Kay chokes out. "But I can't do that to Gideon."

"Why not?"

"He's the one who pays for Kevin's asthma medication."

Goddamned Gideon, he's Mother Theresa to Kay and the Ayatollah to me.

"Kevin's really enjoyed having you around," she says as her tears take a break. "He needs a dad."

"Well, dads aren't always what they're cracked up to be."

"You would be."

"I overcompensate when it comes to family."

"I wish I could," Kay says as she moves her head to a dry spot on the shirt. "But I can't."

"Yeah, but you try really hard. Kevin knows that."

We sit for a few minutes.

"You know, when my mom first started to get wacky, I looked around for a caretaker and couldn't find one. You're real nice, patient, a good mom. Maybe you could take care of old, demented, Alzheimer patients?"

"Wouldn't you have to have a license?"

"Yeah, but you could get one from one of those tacky colleges that advertise on daytime TV."

"I never thought of that."

"I've always considered myself an idea man."

"Really."

"My latest multi-million-dollar venture is to capture millions of cow farts and turn them into energy."

"Really?"

"I'm trying to raise funds to build a pilot plant. I'm thinking of calling it GTI — GasTroIntestinal Energy"

"Really."

"It sounds crazy, but I know it will work. Forty percent of the methane gas released into the California atmosphere is from cattle. Each cow farts hundreds of times every day."

"I didn't know that."

"The average person doesn't either, that's why it has been so difficult getting people to grasp the concept."

Kay's head comes off my chest. She sits facing me. "You're really nice. The girl you're going to marry is lucky to be getting you."

"You might consider mentioning that to Gideon."

"I will."

"You're very nice, too, but you should get out of porn."

"I know."

"It is wreaking havoc on your psyche."

"I know."

"Got to think of Kevin, he'll be in school soon and, you know...kids can be cruel."

CHAPTER 32

Alyssa, the Bride

Portia is having a salad with no dressing. I'm having my second glass of Rothschild Chardonnay '08. It's not yet noon. I stare at my cell phone, wanting, willing, and waiting for it to ring. The only person who called was Farrin, leaving a message to apologize. Bitch.

"You think Doctor Conrad would write me a prescription for Oxycontin?" Portia asks between bites. "I want to be at my best for the wedding."

"There might not be a wedding."

"Oh, sure there will."

"Why are you so sure?"

"Men don't walk away from women like us. We're their drug of choice. They stare at our pictures in magazines, buy us drinks in clubs, lie to their friends about knowing us, dream about fucking us, or imagine fucking us when they're doing themselves." Portia dabs at her perfect lips with the cloth napkin. "A guy came up to me in a club last year and offered to take me to Rio before he even knew my name."

"Vegas' Rio?"

"No."

"What did you do?"

"Carnivále."

I clutch my tummy, I feel awful. "It's hard to consider partying right now."

"Don't worry, Jake will be there."

My phone rings. I pick it up without seeing who is calling.

"Randolph," the male voice says.

"You find Jake?"

"Not yet."

My mood slips another two notches.

"But I got a 'where' on Dick Snatchly."

"Who?"

"Gideon's porn name is Dick Snatchly."

"Bastard."

"I went to Jake's apartment," Randolph continues his report. "I'm sure he got 'napped, nobody leaves for a week without packing. I checked out where his mother lives, nobody there has seen him. And that girl, Jailbait…"

"Yes…"

"I got a hold of the management company where she lives, and they tell me there has been a number of complaints about weird noises coming from her apartment.

"I sent out an email to my motel list, describing Jake. So far, two replies, that could be a long shot," Randolph says. "Batch has an editing studio in a garage in Chatsworth, I'm going there next. There is a warehouse in Sylmar where they mail out the DVDs and I'm in the process of getting his home address."

"I'll go see Gideon."

"You sure you want to do that?"

"I know he knows."

I copy down the address on a napkin.

"I'm through the first five hundred," he says. "Do I have the authorization for another five hundred."

"Yes."

"You sure you don't want to call the police?"

"Would they do an APB on him?"

"Maybe if you didn't mention *bachelor party*."

I think it over. "No, I don't want to risk that news getting out and reaching any of my friends someday."

"I'll be in touch."

I hang up, look over at Portia who has listened to every word.

"Aren't you supposed to say, 'Ten-four, over and out?'" she asks.

You would have to be in one sorry state of mortgage arrears to sink so low to allow your house to be used as a porn set. The driveway is filled with crummy cars. A truck is parked on the front lawn with cables running from it, along the walk and into the house.

Two mattresses are leaning up against a fence, you can see the stains. Stuffed laundry bags lie on the front porch. I can only imagine the festering filth lurking inside. The security guard, who is half-asleep, doesn't ask who we are, but gives us a disgusting, lascivious grin as we enter though the front door.

Garbage everywhere. Camera stuff is stacked in corners, duct tape secures wires onto the walls, which when removed will take the paint right off. Underneath the mess is black, lacquered, shiny furniture that was supposed to have died along with disco. I'm surprised there is not a black velvet picture of Elvis on the living room wall.

The first people we pass are two guys wearing dirty tee-shirts and thick gloves. They leer at us as if we are new meat for the fuck-buffet. "Where's Gideon?" I ask.

"Who?"

"Dick Snatchly," Portia says.

"Out back," the creep says, "doing pool shots."

"You can get undressed in there," the other idiot says, pointing to a bedroom down a hallway.

We ignore his directions and walk through the living room to the den, where there isn't an inch of wall space not covered by some pennant, picture, or memorabilia of the USC Trojans. There are millions of these obsessed jerks in Los Angeles. The loser who owns this place is no doubt the head of his own fan club.

With each step my anger is mounting. I somewhat rehearse what I'm going to say; but as I am ready to step outside, Portia grabs my arm and says, "Wait."

We stand and survey the pool-side situation. There is one guy with a camera on his shoulder, another guy with a small handheld moving around, and a cameraman seated in a chair on a riser, taking overhead shots. The subjects of their photography are five women with chests bigger than birthday balloons, and a number of guys I can't count, because they are so intertwined with the women. This is absolutely revolting.

"Wow," Portia says, her eyes riveted on the scene. "This is so hot."

I can hear Gideon, but can't see him. He's shouting out directions. "Face the camera, Susie. Cover up that spot on her butt, Ralph. Come on, keep fucking, everybody. Grab that cock!"

Gideon is off to the left, behind three monitors on a table. I step out the door towards him, but Portia holds me back. "We can't stop this now," she says. "The guys will lose their wood."

"How the hell would you know that?"

"Don't ask," she says. "I just do."

I am subjected to this debauchery for another ten minutes until finally I hear, "Cut."

The performers unclench, uncouple, and un-mouth. "Stay in your positions for close-ups," some kid, holding a clipboard, yells.

I break away from Portia and rush to Gideon. On my way, one guy tells me, "You are one smokin'-hot bitch." One girl gives me a dirty stare, and one of the camera guys whirls around to shoot me. "Smile, honey."

"You turn that camera off or I'll shove it up your ass."

"Alyssa?"

"Gideon." I look at the name on his chair. "Or whatever your name is. Where the hell is Jake?"

"How'd you find me?"

"It doesn't matter, Where the hell is my fiancé?"

He shrugs his shoulders.

"You bastard, you got him—I *know* you do."

"*Moi?*"

"Don't lie to me. Tell me!"

"Why should I?"

"We're getting married tomorrow."

"You hope."

"Where is he?"

"I'm not sure," he says in a smug, nasty tone. "Maybe he's reconsidering."

"Listen, you son of a bitch." I'm right in his face, my finger an inch from his nose. "You tell me what you've done with him."

"I'm the best man. I'm in charge of looking out for the groom. If he wants a little time to contemplate his future, weigh the pluses and minuses of marriage, I'm certainly not going to stop him."

"He wouldn't do that."

"You sure?"

I see Portia speaking to some woman as the performers and workers set up for the next shots. They act like they know each other.

"There is no reason in hell he would ever reconsider getting married."

Gideon's smugness spreads across his face like one of his stained mattresses. "Then you'll see him at the church."

"I need to talk to him."

Gideon pauses as if contemplating his answer. "I'm not sure he's taking calls."

"He'll take mine."

"Just because you want to talk doesn't mean he does."

The bastard is staying calm, which pisses me off all the more.

"Why the hell has this become your fight?" Portia asks, who returns, holding something in the fist of her hand. "Are you afraid of losing him to a better friend?"

"Jake doesn't have a better friend," Gideon tells her.

"I am," I say.

"I beg to disagree."

I can barely speak, all I can manage is, "But I love him."

"And so do I," Gideon says. "And I owe him one."

"Ruining his marriage," Portia says, "is hardly the way most people repay debts."

"To each his own."

That's it. I'm not taking any more shit. I scream for all to hear. "Listen, you fucking asshole, I don't know who the hell you think you are, but if you think you are going to destroy my wedding, you're out of your fucking mind."

"'*My* wedding,' doesn't that phrase say it all?" Gideon yells back. "You don't give a shit about Jake. He's just another prop that has to look perfect, be in place, and follow directions from Bitzy."

"That's not true. Jake wants exactly what I want."

"You don't love him. You love what you can do to him, how you can remake him."

"He'll never do better than me and he knows it."

"He couldn't do any worse."

"He loves me."

"Only because he doesn't see you as you are, but what he wants you to be. Jake's a dreamer."

"That's not true."

"It is and you know it is."

Gideon stands straight, staring into my eyes. The cast and

crew, dressed and undressed, have frozen in place, watching our own scene unfold, wondering what comes next.

"I have to talk to him."

"It'll have to wait until tomorrow."

"No."

"If you're so sure he loves you, he'll be there waiting at the altar as you walk up the aisle."

"I need to speak to him now."

Gideon returns to his smug attitude. "Don't forget, you're not supposed to see or speak to each other the twenty-four hours before the ceremony."

"I have something I have to tell him," I scream at the top of my lungs.

"What?"

"I'm pregnant."

CHAPTER 33

Conrad, the Groomsman

3pm Friday Afternoon

I feel guilty.

"Gideon, maybe we've taken this too far."

"No way."

"He's been chained up for four days now."

"One more night," Gideon says. "We have to make him see the light."

We are in my car, on the 134, about five minutes from Van Nuys and Kay's apartment. Friday afternoon traffic is terrible. "How did she find you?" I ask.

"I haven't the faintest idea."

"She call the cops?"

"And say what? 'My fiancé, who didn't come home from his bachelor party, is now AWOL.' Yeah, I'm sure the LAPD will put that up on freeway alert signs."

I'm not sure if I've ever seen Gideon like this before. He's on a precipice, ready to explode, his skin pale, muscles taut, sitting ramrod straight. He could use a mild sedative, but I'm not offering.

"What happens if we're wrong?" I argue. "Maybe Jake marrying Alyssa isn't such a bad deal? Maybe his father-in-law will front him the money for his cow manure business?"

"And they move to Bakersfield where Jake makes Alyssa, vice president of Fart and Flatulence. Oh, yeah," Gideon says, "that's going to happen."

"Just the same, he's marrying into a shitload of money."

"And all the time paying for it with his self-respect."

"They get divorced, he gets half, and he's sitting pretty."

"She made him sign a pre-nup."

"He didn't tell me that."

"Jake wouldn't get a dime."

I turn off the freeway. It's only a couple more streets to Kay's.

"What happens if we can't convince him, he marries her, and ends up never speaking to either of us again?"

"Why do you have to ask so many questions, Conrad?"

"Don't answer a question with a question."

"That's not going to happen," Gideon says. "I can feel it, Jake is this close to blowing the bitch away."

I shake my head in disagreement as I drive into the parking lot of Kay's complex.

"Stop the car," Gideon orders. "Back up."

"Why?"

"So, she doesn't see us."

"Who?"

"Stop the damn car."

"Why?"

"Alyssa."

I slam on the brakes, throw the Jag into reverse.

"That's her."

I see ahead, in the corner of the lot, Alyssa, Kay, and Kevin standing between a Mercedes and a bruised Toyota.

"Move, dumbshit, move," Gideon yells at me.

I swing the Jag around two rows down, off to the side and pull into a spot, where we can see them and hopefully they don't see us.

Alyssa looks pissed. She's chasing Kay around the car like a parent in a pediatrician's office.

"Stay in the car, get down if she drives this way."

We wait, scrunched down. I keep my eyes on the rear-view mirrors. A few minutes that seem like hours pass and Kay's Toyota shoots by, heads for the street, turns left onto Moorpark and disappears.

Gideon pulls out his cell, dials, waits. "Shit, she's got her phone off."

I'm waiting for the Mercedes. "You think Alyssa will check out the apartment?"

"If she does we'll have to shoot her and bury the body in the desert. I hope you brought a shovel." Gideon sounds serious.

The Mercedes retraces the Toyota's path, but turns the opposite direction on the busy street and I quickly lose sight of her.

"I bet they had an interesting chat," I say with tempered relief.

"Kay wouldn't say anything."

"Sure?"

"If she did, Alyssa wouldn't have driven off."

Gideon hops out of the car and heads for the building. I retrieve the two pizza boxes, beer, and follow. As I get to the stairway, the woman from the apartment underneath comes out and eyes me warily. "Making a house call," I tell her.

"She's not home. I saw her leave," she says.

"I'm checking for germs," I tell her. "You might want to move from where you're standing, flesh-eating viruses spread like wildfire. Go inside and try not to breathe."

The woman scurries back into her apartment, slamming the door. I hear the deadbolt, then the windows banging shut.

Stepping inside Kay's apartment, I see Jake. He sits on the couch, slumped as if all his muscles have atrophied. His chin rests on his chest, he hasn't shaved in days, and his hair looks like a frenzy of garden weeds. The green tee-shirt and Laker sweats he's wearing are wrinkled beyond any iron's capability.

"Jake..."

Nothing.

"Jake," I say louder.

He doesn't move.

I freeze, put my hand out to stop Gideon, and listen for the sound of Jake's breath.

Silence.

CHAPTER 34

Portia, the Bridesmaid

3pm Friday Afternoon

"**A**re you really knocked up?"

"Just drive the fucking car, Portia."

Every wedding I've ever been in was pretty much a fucking bore, costing me a shitload of money, but not this one. This is fun. We're racing through LA like Batman and Robin in Gotham City.

People think I'm stupid. And I am when I'm loaded, which is a lot of the time. Everybody sees me as some empty-headed, shallow, dumb-shit chick, and "the only thing she can do" is dress in clothes no one in the world wears, put on a pouty face and "fuck the camera" as we say in the model biz. This is all perfectly fine with me. Being thought of as stupid has its benefits. I never have to apologize for my actions, never get asked to volunteer, and if someone wants a loan, there is no better defense than being incapable of writing a check. And favors? Really, you have got to be kidding.

Let them think I'm dumb, I know better. I'm smart enough to realize this model gig won't last forever. I sock away every dime I make and every dime guys are dumb enough to give me. Hell, I don't spend nothing on food. If I could cut out the Oxy, the Xanax, the weed, and the booze, I'd be really rich. But a girl needs something to get her through the day.

To be honest, I can't figure out why Alyssa is putting herself through all this marriage bullshit. Shit, she sure doesn't need the money; and I'm even more sure she could find a better lay than Jake. If she wants someone to be around only when she wants him to be around, why the hell get married to get that? People I hang with, even if they have kids, don't bother getting married, that is so 1980s.

We're in the car, on the freeway, looking for the exit Randolph told us to take.

"What's the big, fucking deal with getting married, anyway?" I ask.

"You don't want to get married, Portia?" she asks, breaking a long silence.

"No. What's the point?"

"I'm thirty years old and I'm tired of being Ms. Superfuck."

"Why would you have a problem with that?"

"Every guy I've met in the past ten years has wanted to hang me on his arm in public and fuck the hell out of me in private. It has all gotten a little old."

"Why? That's just guys.

"It is all bullshit. I'm tired of it. I want a life."

"Then at least find some guy who is loaded, who you can clean up on when you get divorced." I pause. "No offense, but you can do a lot better than Jake." I say as we exit off the freeway.

"I don't want to do better than Jake. He is exactly what I want and exactly what I need. There is nothing he wouldn't do to make me happy. How many guys do you know like that, Portia?"

"Plenty."

"Well, I guess we have different tastes in men."

"I don't think so," I say to her as we wait at a red light. "Mister Goodie Two Shoes is going to bore you to death, Alyssa, and then what are you going to have?"

"A family."

We find the address of the apartment complex and drive around back.

"Look, there she is." I spot the chick first.

Kay, the porn star, is standing in the parking lot with a kid. I hit the brakes. Alyssa runs out of the Mercedes to stop her before they get into a crummy Toyota. I'm about to follow, but some jerk in a Land Rover is behind me wanting to park, so I pull back and around to let him by. I have to watch Alyssa and Kay from the car. Shit!

It is hard to believe Kay has a kid two or three years old. She looks about seventeen. I had a boyfriend who used to bring over porno for us to watch in bed, and he'd quit me when Jailbait Jordan came on the screen. I dumped the bastard after taking his credit card to the limit at Saks.

I'd love to ask her what it's like to "do it" on camera. I've shown my fair share of skin, but to spread 'em wide for some guy to bang away, while a cameraman is playing video gynecologist, that's a whole other scene. I wonder if she gets turned on and has real orgasms. I wonder if she knows who the father of the kid is.

The passenger-side window is rolled up and I can't hear the conversation, but I can see Alyssa starting to tremble, her fists are clenched. Not good. She stays on Kay's ass, as the porn teen queen puts the kid in the car seat and fastens him in. It's obvious Alyssa isn't hearing what she wants to hear, because Alyssa's trembles turn into shakes, and she's waving her arms in the air. She chases Kay around the car and must be getting one-word answers, because she doesn't seem to quit talking.

Kay gets into the car and slams the door. Alyssa's face is half into the open driver's-side window. She is shouting. Kay looks frightened. Alyssa's even scaring me. I am about to run out when the cell phone on the seat rings. On its screen is Randolph Investigations.

"Hello."

I listen, but watch as Alyssa's hands push down on the window going up. The Toyota is moving forward.

Out of the car, my head barely over the roof line, I yell, "Randolph's on the phone."

Alyssa hears me, releases the window before she loses her fingers. The Toyota peels out of the space and into the parking lane, spinning Alyssa into a non-ice, double-axle.

Running up to her, I hand her the phone.

"What?"

She's breathing hard as she listens to Randolph.

"Don't wait. Just do it." She pauses one second. "Goddammit, just do it." She hears what she doesn't want to hear and says, "Okay, okay." She hangs up. "Get in the car," she yells at me. "He thinks he's found Jake."

I only follow directions when I want to, or when I'm with a crazy person.

The only words Alyssa says in the next five minutes are, "Get back on the freeway."

The freeway is packed, too many cars for too little road. We inch along like a snail on a cement tree branch. LA on a Friday.

"Get off at Cahuenga and take it over the hill," she orders.

I see the off-ramp, get off, and aim for higher elevation.

"What did the porn chick say?"

"She says she hasn't seen Jake, hasn't seen Gideon, knows nothing," Alyssa says. "She's playing dumb."

"How can you tell?"

"She is. I know it."

"To play dumb you have to be smart enough to play dumb," I try to reason with Alyssa. "The woman blows guys on camera for a living, how smart can she be?"

"Those porn people stick together."

The mental image I get is quite colorful.

Passing a sign which directs drivers to the Hollywood Bowl, I ask, "Alyssa, where are we going?"

"To break into Gideon's place."

God, this is fun.

Randolph is leaning against his Chrysler Mafia car, waiting. We're in Hollywood and not the good part. The only Hollywood signs I see are covered with graffiti.

Gideon's apartment is a converted garage. You would think a successful porn director would live better than a college student.

"You think he's in there?" Alyssa asks, jumping out of the Mercedes.

"I can only hope," Randolph says.

"I don't see why you couldn't do this yourself?" Alyssa snaps at Randolph.

"If I'm going down on a B and E, I ain't going down alone."

"How did you find the place?" I ask.

"I paid off a guy at the DMV." Randolph retrieves a black case from the truck of his car. "Come on," he says and walks calmly up the driveway, past the "Beware of Dog" sign and through the cheap, chain-link gate. "Nobody's home and there is no dog."

"You sure?"

"It's cheaper to buy a sign than to feed a dog."

"You positive Jake's in there?" Alyssa asks as we approach the mini-house.

"No, but I wouldn't be a bit surprised if he was."

I am looking at the burglar bars on all the windows and wondering how we are planning on getting in. Randolph opens the case and removes what resembles a large, black gun. "You going to blast your way in?" I ask.

"No." He screws into the gun's short barrel a silver, cylindrical piece, aims the weapon at me.

I almost lose my cookies when he pulls the trigger.

The silver piece spins around and around. "Haven't you ever seen a cordless drill before, girl?"

"I live in a condo, I hire people."

In a matter of five minutes, Randolph has unscrewed the burglar bars and jimmied the window open. "You're the smallest one," he says to me. "You do the honors."

"Jake, are you in there?" Alyssa screams.

"Shhhh," Randolph admonishes her. "We're breaking-in, remember?"

Alyssa steps back, she's still shaking like a meth addict going cold turkey.

To make sure, I "woof" before entering, then climb inside, find a light, see no one, and unlock the front door. First time I've ever broken into a guy's place. Wait, make that the second time. I left a pair of six-hundred-dollar earrings at a one-night stand once.

"Damn," Alyssa says, entering with Randolph after I open the front door.

Gideon's home is one-room, not counting the bathroom. There is a kitchenette, a closet, a heater in the wall and a big, flat-screen TV. One side of the place has those cheap DIY shelves you buy at IKEA. I hate that store. The shelves are filled with books on film, filmmaking, screenwriting, directing, editing; the collection would put any library to shame. He has hundreds of brad-bound scripts both on the shelves and stacked in piles on the floor. He must sleep on the couch, because the desk takes up most of the room. He has three dry-erase boards on the wall, filled with scribbling. One is titled *Scenes*. One is titled *Arcs*. The third, *To Do*. His handwriting is atrocious.

"He hasn't been here," Randolph tells Alyssa.

"Sure?"

"He must have him stashed somewhere else." Randolph is

being careful to search, but not disturb.

"What should we be looking for?" Alyssa asks.

Randolph boots up Gideon's desktop. "Receipts, notes, phone numbers, anything from a motel or place he's visited."

Alyssa tears through the place like Katrina did New Orleans. She rips apart the desk, reading what she can and throwing the rest on the floor. She empties drawers, knocks over piles of stuff, and then goes to work on the bookshelves. If a Richter Scale 8.0 had hit on this exact spot, it wouldn't do the damage Alyssa is doing.

"Find anything interesting?" I ask the one-woman wrecking crew.

She pants. "Not yet."

Randolph concentrates on the computer. "I can't get in without a password," he admits.

"Try 'pussy,'" I suggest.

"Nope." Randolph types away. "Cunt, cock, fellatio, and blowjob didn't work, either."

"Try Fucking Asshole," Alyssa says as she rips out the clothes in the small closet, checks the pockets in each one and tosses them away like bad style choices.

A siren is heard in the distance.

Randolph gives up. "We better get out of here."

I turn to survey Alyssa's disaster. "Having fun?" I ask her.

"No."

"I am. This is a kick."

CHAPTER 35

Gideon, the Best Man

Friday, the Night before the Wedding

Conrad stops dead in his tracks seeing Jake on the couch. He drops the pizza and the beer. He puts his hand out to quiet me, listens, and rushes to our friend.

Jake isn't moving.

It's just the three of us in the apartment.

I stand, not moving a muscle as Conrad leans into Jake's face, to feel for any exhales coming from his mouth or nose. He straightens up, places two fingers on Jake's neck, finds the pulse, checks his watch and counts to himself.

"Is he all right?" I ask coming closer.

"His pulse is normal."

Conrad and I exchange a glance. He says, "Go get my bag in the car."

In the instant I turn away, Jake springs from the couch like a cobra. He grips a yards' worth of chain between his hands and flings it over my head, the metal catching right under my chin. He pulls back. I'm gasping for breath, as he garrotes me like a prison guard in a breakout movie. Grabbing the chain, I manage to get my finger underneath the links, pull forward and give myself some breathing room.

"I warned you," Jake cries out.

Pushing my entire body backwards, we crash into the couch, go down hard. I look up to see Conrad standing over the two of us, laughing, as we flop around like two fish out of water.

"Get this whack-job off of me," I manage to speak before my windpipe is crushed.

Conrad leans over in a fit of laughter, puts his thumb and forefingers together and pinches a spot between Jake's neck and shoulder.

"Ouch."

Jake breaks the hold. I scramble out from underneath the choke chain, as Conrad explains, "Pressure point."

I half-run, half-crawl to the safety of the chair on the other side of the room.

Conrad says to Jake, "Aren't we in a foul mood this evening?"

Jake's panting, "I swear to God, Gideon, I will kill you, if you don't unlock me."

Rubbing my now sore neck, I respond, "Not yet."

"You can't do this to me."

"We already have."

"I'm not kidding, I'm calling the police. You'll be arrested, put in prison and become Big Bubba's bitch. You'll be directing the ramming of your own ass."

I give him a minute, he needs it. "Jake," I tell him, "I promise, if we can't convince you that you're making a mistake, you'll be set free and can be at the church in plenty of time to get married to that witch."

"Untie me."

"Don't be silly."

"Now."

"Talk now, untie later."

"Gideon…"

"Listen, talk to us, have an open mind."

"How can you expect me to have an open mind after sitting on this couch for four days, watching *SpongeBob Squarepants*, chained to a radiator, with my leg ready to fall off?"

"Did I ever say this was going to be easy? No."

"I can't take any more of this."

"Think of this as a movie."

"*Escape from Alcatraz*?"

"No," I say, "more like an adventure film." I explain, "Conceptually, Jake, you're the hero. The hero has a problem, but he finds a mentor (that's me) who teaches him to see the error of his ways, so he will be able to overcome his problem and achieve his goal."

"Gideon, this is absurd, and you're still an asshole. Let me go."

"We've come this far, we've got to see it through. Stopping

now would be like walking out before the climax of the film. And if there is one thing I know something about, it's climaxes."

"I hate this movie, I want my money back and I want to go home."

"Jake, sit back, relax."

"Want some pizza?" Conrad asks, opening the box.

"No."

Conrad helps himself to a slice. "You know that pizza contains all four main food groups, meat, vegetables, grains, and dairy."

"Like I give a shit right now," Jake says flopping back onto the couch.

"There's no anchovies on it, Jake."

Conrad brings a kitchen chair over, sits across from Jake, and says, "Jake remember at St. Theresa's when we got caught selling *Playboy*s?"

"No."

"Of course you do."

"No," Jake answers. "My memory's shot."

"Remember," Conrad says, "you wanted to come clean and confess, lay the whole thing out for Sister Superior and beg for leniency."

Jake sits up, which is a good sign. "If Gideon wouldn't have sold them to the sixth graders, instead of only seventh and eighth graders like I said, we would have never been caught."

"Be that as it may, the point here is that we wouldn't let you confess, because we had already decided to stick to the story Gideon had made up."

Jake leans forward. "Yeah, I remember... Telling the nun that we were only selling the magazines to raise enough money so we could attend the weekend prayer retreat with Father Celcius."

"That was our story and we agreed to stick to it."

Jake gets animated, throws his arms into the air. "You actually think anyone believed that we'd pay to go off to some mountain cabin with a pedophile?"

"It worked. None of us ended up getting expelled."

"Because my mother begged Sister Superior to give us another chance."

"The point is," Conrad pauses, "you listened to us and realized we were right."

"You said you'd beat the crap out of me if I spoke up."

"We just said that to get your attention."

"What Conrad is trying is say is," as I enter the discussion, "the majority always knows best. And the majority tonight believes that you'll be a hell of a lot better off not marrying Alyssa."

"Majority?" Jake asks. "A majority of Germans elected Hitler. The Silent Majority put us into Vietnam. The Moral Majority got George Bush elected."

"Those were bad majorities. We're a good one, much smaller and more manageable."

"Jesus Christ, I'm arguing with fools."

"And we don't want you to argue," I say. "We want to discuss this as rational human beings and have you come to your own conclusion. Come on, just talk to us."

Jake takes an exasperated breath, as if to say, *Go ahead, assholes, have at me.*

"Okay," I say. "Let's go back to sex. Do you and Alyssa have an equal sex drive?"

Jake sits back down, but doesn't answer.

"Come on, Jake, is she willing to put out when you got to have it? Does she ever initiate the action? Has she ever surprised you in another room of the house?"

"Yes, on the kitchen counter," Jake explodes.

"Name another place."

Silence.

"If you were ever in prison, and it was your turn for a conjugal visit," I say, "Alyssa would show up with a headache."

"What business of yours is our sex life?"

"We know what makes you happy, Jake," Conrad concludes.

"You marry Alyssa, you're going to be horny the rest of your life." I try to put a period to the end of this topic, one point on the board in favor of dumping the bitch.

Jake's not buying it.

"Even if you had a great sex life," Conrad adds, "do you know the one aspect that all guys who marry beautiful women share?"

"No."

Conrad sounds professorial, "Show me a guy who has a beautiful wife and I'll show you a guy who is bored having sex with her."

"And where the hell did you pick up that indisputable factoid of knowledge?" Jake asks.

"*Maxim* magazine."

"Oh, of course, *Maxim*, the end-all, be-all, qualified expert on all subjects sexual."

"I would have preferred the *New England Journal of Medicine*, but *Maxim* took the survey."

"How much more of this shit do I have to take?"

"Jake," Conrad says, "I have it from a very good authority that Alyssa isn't a nice person."

"And your source on that statement is... *Hustler* magazine?"

"Farrin."

"Farrin says Alyssa isn't a nice person?"

"Yes, her own sister."

"Stepsister."

"She told me."

"And why the hell would she tell you that?"

"I asked her."

"When?"

"The other night at dinner."

"You're dating Farrin?"

"Didn't Alyssa tell you?"

"No," Jake says, "we've haven't had a lot of time to chat since I've been grounded with my phone privileges revoked."

"Farrin said that after her mom walked out on her as a kid, Alyssa grew a chip on her shoulder no surgeon could ever remove."

Jake puts his head down, pretending not to listen.

"She's damaged goods, Jake. She has trust issues."

"She trusts me."

"Then why did you have to sign a pre-nup?"

Jake doesn't answer. Put another point on the board for our side.

"I know you don't like her mother," I add. "How about her old man?"

"LaRue is all right."

"You have to say that," Conrad interjects. "He's your boss."

"Probably not anymore, since I haven't shown up for work all week."

"It's also a fact that the way daughters treat their fathers is the way they'll treat their husbands," Conrad says.

"Do you really want to become nothing more than an ATM machine?" I keep the pressure on. "And that stepfather-in-law you're going to get, what a piece of work that guy is. Did you see him on stage at the strip club?"

Jake shakes his head back and forth.

"There is an old saying," I tell him, "marry a woman who knows how to be married."

"And where did you pick that one up, *Juggs* magazine?"

"My mother told me."

"Your mother tell you to get into the porn business, too?"

"I'm quitting the porn business."

Conrad turns in my direction. "What?"

"I got enough money saved to last me three years and to start my documentary. No more jobs directing blow jobs."

"I'm happy to hear that," Conrad says.

"I don't believe you," Jake says.

"Remember both you guys told me I was making a mistake? Well, I'm finally hearing you." I pause to let the news sink in. "We're working on the exact same principle here. Listen to what we have to say, Jake."

"I promise I won't go into pornography—now unlock me and let me go home!"

"Maybe later."

For the next few hours the discussion goes around and around and around. We repeat the points we made and introduce new ones. Jake fights us at every twist and turn. The pizza's finished, the beer is gone. At 1:00 A.M. Jake asks, "Where are Kay and Kevin?"

"We put them up in a hotel for the night."

"Is there room for one more?"

"No."

We talk about Alyssa's handling of the wedding, her lack of humor at her shower, how she manipulates her dad into buying her anything she wants, her lack of a career, her weird pill-popping friend Portia, and what it will be like living in her house, with her stuff, under her rules.

Conrad and I establish certain unarguable facts: You come

from different social and economic backgrounds. You are a Type-A, she's a Type-Z. Her father, your boss, is going to own you like a Civil War sharecropper.

I sense Jake is weakening, tired or maybe just giving up, not sure which, maybe it doesn't matter.

It is going on 5 A.M. Conrad is yawning, but not me.

"Consider your mom," I tell him.

"What does she have to do with this?"

"A lot."

"Alyssa wants nothing to do with your mother, does she?"

Jake doesn't respond.

"Does she ever go with you when you visit?"

"No," I answer my own question.

"Does she ever call her or send a card or do anything to make her life a little better?"

"No." I answer the question again.

"My mother wouldn't know one way or the other," Jake finally speaks.

"That's not the point," Conrad joins in.

"Alyssa wants to ship her off to Santa Barbara, doesn't she?"

"It would be a much better treatment," Jake argues back.

"You really believe that?" Conrad asks.

"Look at the way Alyssa treats her own mother," I say.

"Brady deserves to be treated like shit."

"Does your mom?"

"No," I answer my own question for the third time.

"Alyssa at least acknowledges Brady. She pretends your mother doesn't exist. All she is doing is waiting for your mom to die." I lay it on as thick as I can.

"No, she's not," Jake says with little catch in his voice. I can tell he does not believe his own argument.

"She didn't send her an invitation to the wedding, did she?"

Jake avoids eye contact with us.

"She refuses to allow your mother to see her only son get married."

Conrad and I sit absolutely still, allowing the comment to sink into Jake's psyche.

Jake lays back, closes his eyes.

"Don't marry Alyssa, Jake. Don't do it."

We sit in silence. Sometimes we look at one another, most times not. No one wants to be the next person to speak.

Jake asks, "What the hell do you want me to do?"

"Don't show up."

"I can't do that."

"Then call Alyssa, apologize, tell her it's a mistake, the both of you are just too different, that it would never work."

"No."

"You know it is true."

"I can't do that to her."

"You have to."

"No," Jake says. "No one deserves that kind of hurt."

Conrad yawns again. I sit and stare at Jake. He knows it is wrong to marry Alyssa, I can see it in his eyes.

Jake leans back, lets his head rest on the arm of the couch. No one speaks. The room is quiet. Jake falls asleep, clearly exhausted.

I carefully move to the couch, ready if he's faking it. I jiggle him gently. He snores. I rustle him harder. He snores even louder.

"Leave him alone," Conrad says.

I go back to the chair. Conrad, who is about ready to drop too, stands to stretch. "What are we going to do?" he asks.

"He's as good as agreed with us."

"No, he hasn't," Conrad says.

"You heard him. He just doesn't know how to tell her."

"I didn't hear him say he wasn't going to marry her."

"He asked for directions on what he should do."

"So?"

"That means he's seen the light."

"Bullshit."

"When he wakes up, he'll call her."

"No, he won't."

"I'm positive he will."

"The wedding is six hours away," Conrad says.

"So, we don't have long to wait."

"Gideon, you promised if he didn't agree with us by morning that you'd let him go."

I hesitate. Now I have to convince Conrad too?

"I could see it in his eyes. He doesn't want to marry her."

"Eyes don't count."

"Conrad…"

"He didn't make the call, and that was the deal."

I need time. I sit back, review the scene in my head, rewrite the script, try to think it all through to the end.

Conrad says, "You have to let him do what he wants. You promised."

I don't make a sound.

"Gideon…"

"What?"

"We have to unlock him, get him up, cleaned up, and dressed for his own wedding."

"You're right," I tell Conrad, "you're absolutely right."

Conrad makes a move toward the couch. He's as exhausted as Jake. Conrad has never been good without sleep.

"Wait," I tell him, "we have some time."

"Not much."

"You go home, grab some z's. I'll let Jake sleep, while I go get his stuff, and bring it back here."

"When are you going to get dressed?"

"Don't worry about me, I'll make it."

"You sure, Gideon?"

"Yeah."

"You're going to wake him up, let him go and get him married?"

"Yes."

I put my elbows on my knees, rest my chin on my hands and let out a big sigh and repeat, "Yes."

"You're doing the right thing," Conrad says his hand touching my shoulder.

"I'm not so sure about that."

"It's over, Gideon, we tried."

"I sure would have liked to have seen the look on Alyssa's face when he left her standing at the altar."

"That's cruel."

"I know."

Conrad rises out of his chair. "It is his life, Gideon."

"Jake's our best friend."

"That's why you have to do what you promised."

"I know."

"I'll see you at church."

Conrad leaves quietly. I cover Jake with a Bert and Ernie blanket. His leg looks bad, I should have thought of a better constraining device. I go into the bedroom.

I'm as dog-tired, as I've ever been.

I lay down, but I can't fall asleep. One thought keeps me from passing out: *Alyssa sure didn't look pregnant to me.*

CHAPTER 36

Kay, the Porn Star Mom

10am Saturday Morning

Kevin loved the hotel, especially a TV inside an armoire on a handy swivel, with a working remote control. The minibar was stocked like a Seven-Eleven, and the bed so big he wouldn't stop jumping.

I couldn't sleep.

We get home a little before 10:00 A.M. The place is deathly quiet. At first step I think they are gone; but Jake is asleep on the couch. Gideon is in our room, passed out on the bed.

"Gideon, get up."

He doesn't stir.

I shake. "Gideon…"

I'm not sure if Gideon's still asleep, hung over, or stoned. I shake him harder.

He comes to, groggily hoisting himself up on one elbow. "I'm awake."

"Gideon, what's going on?"

"What time is it?"

"Ten."

"I fell asleep."

"What happened with Jake?"

"He fell asleep, too." Gideon rubs his eyes.

"What did he say when you told him Alyssa was pregnant?"

He snaps to attention. "How the hell did you know that?"

"Alyssa was here, yesterday. You told Jake, didn't you?"

"No."

"Why not?"

"She was lying."

"How would you know?" I sit on the bed, close to him.

"Alyssa would say anything to save her precious wedding day."

"Gideon, you don't lie about being pregnant."

"Alyssa would."

"You have to tell Jake."

"He's going to call her to tell her the wedding's off."

"Before he finds out he's a father?"

Gideon takes hold of my shoulder with his right hand. "If I tell him now, he'd make his decision based on her being pregnant, and not whether she was the right woman for him."

"Gideon, you have to tell him."

"No, I don't." Gideon climbs off the bed and hurries to shut the bedroom door. "I can't do it, Kay," he paces across the room. "I can't let him marry that woman. She's evil. He'll stay married and be miserable just to be around his kid and that's no life for one of my best friends. I owe him that much."

"You have to tell him the truth."

"What if she's just late? What if she loses the baby? And he gets stuck married to her?"

"Jake has a right to know he's having a child."

Gideon stops, stares into my eyes. "You got a lot of balls making that statement."

His words hit me like a punch to the stomach.

Gideon stomps around the room. "And you're not going to tell him, either," he says pointing his finger at me. "You owe me. You owe me a lot. You are not going to say a word."

I'm speechless. Close to tears.

He moves closer, leans into my face, "Are you, Kay?"

A knock comes on the door.

"Mommy?"

"Come in, Kevin," I manage to say.

Kevin opens the door, looks at me as if I'm some absurd character in an adult cartoon. "Mommy, are you okay?"

"Mommy's fine. Go out and see if SpongeBob is on TV."

Kevin exits. Gideon moves from the opposite side of the room to reclose the door. "Just remember who has been there for you, Kay. It's your turn to pay back."

"Gideon, you can't do this. You have to tell him, let him make his own decision. Let him do what he wants."

"I'm the best man, I have to do what's best."

"Quit playing God, Gideon."

He straightens himself up, moves toward the door, but turns back to me. "I'm trusting you."

"Where are you going? You can't go."

"I have to."

"No."

"You don't understand, Kay." Gideon runs out of the room.

A few seconds tick off the clock. I hear the front door open, then close.

I sit back on the bed, fold my hands in my lap, and stare at nothing, then at everything. A thousand thoughts go through my brain, but I can't make sense of even one. I try to pray, but forget the words to the Our Father...something, something. My body feels stiff and sore, my head starts to ache. I am not sure how long I sit, but the sound of the ankle chain being yanked taut snaps me out of it.

I hurry off the bed and into the front room to wait on the couch until Jake returns from the bathroom.

"Hey."

"Hey."

"How was the night's stay in the hotel?" he asks.

"Kevin loved it."

"I hope you two drank the minibar dry." Jake sits. "Where's Gideon?"

"I'm not sure."

I sit, nothing more than a bump on a log. These are times I wish I was smart and knew what to say.

Jake watches the cartoon on the TV, but talks to me. "I'm not going to marry Alyssa."

I can barely speak, "Why not?"

"Lots of reasons."

"Name one."

"I don't think my mom would like her."

"Really?"

Jake says, "Maybe I'm not in love, but in lust." His eyes stay glued to the TV as he continues to convince himself. "We are from different worlds. I'm not only marrying her, but marrying her lifestyle. Maybe I won't be able to do what I want to do with my life."

"Like the cow fart thing?"

Jake nods his head. "And she really isn't the nicest person I've ever met. She's not as nice as you."

It's difficult, but I manage a smile.

"She said she didn't want my mother at the wedding because it wouldn't be fair to Mom, but that isn't the reason. Alyssa doesn't want her there, because she doesn't want to take the chance of Mom going gaga, and ruining the biggest day of her life."

I get up, turn up the TV, which surprises Kevin, and sit back down, closer to Jake. I speak softly, so only he can hear.

"The first time I got pregnant, Jake..."

He looks away from the TV and into my eyes.

"I let the guy talk me into an abortion."

Jake's expression tells me to continue.

"It was awful. I have never felt so empty. I couldn't eat or sleep for days. It felt that I had lost a part of me, which I would never be able to get back."

"Okay..."

"I hated myself for it."

"Why are you telling me this?"

I continue as if not hearing his question. "The next time it happened, there was no way I wasn't going to have my child."

Jake is about to comment, but I speak quickly. "The father never knew, I never told him and I never will. I don't want Kevin to know who he is, how it happened or why." I stop, take a breath. "I thought that would work, but it didn't. I found myself under a whole new mountain of guilt, almost as bad as what I experienced before. Holding the information inside me made me feel cold, cruel, and miserable. It still does."

Jake's eyes never leave mine.

I swallow hard, check to make sure Kevin isn't listening. "I ask myself each and every day if I'm cheating my son out of a real home and a father?"

Jake doesn't move.

"What I've done, what I'm doing, and what I keep doing, is it fair to him? Is it me being selfish? Does Kevin have a right to know? What happens ten years from now when he asks me about his daddy?"

Jake waits for my next shoe to drop.

"Kevin hasn't stopped talking about you and squiggles, and the big truck he's going to get a ride in."

"No matter what happens, the truck ride is still on."

I take his hand into mine, hold it firmly, sniffle back the tears which are ready to fall and say, "There is something you have to know, Jake, and I have to be the one to tell you, because I can't handle anymore guilt in my life."

"What?"

"Alyssa's pregnant."

"What?"

"She was here yesterday, she told me."

Jake recoils back into the couch cushions as if hit by a thunderbolt.

"I'm going to be a dad?"

"Congratulations."

Jake's hands grip onto my shoulders and pull me toward him. "You're sure?"

"That's what she told me."

He sits, takes it in for several seconds and jumps up. "I have to get out of here. I have to get to the church."

He reaches down, pulls me up, and shakes me. "Help me. You have to help me. You have to find a way to get me out of here."

"How?"

"I don't know," he says.

"Me neither."

Jake lets me loose, he's frantic. "There has to be something you can do."

I think as hard as I've ever thought.

"Please."

It is as if one of those cartoon light bulbs pops on inside my brain. "You wait here." I tell him.

"Wait? I can't wait."

I run towards the door. "I'm not sure if this will work, but it's worth a try."

"Whatever…Hurry."

I rush out of the apartment, hearing Jake's voice, "Did you hear that Kevin? I'm going to be a daddy."

Five minutes later I return with my neighbor, Arnold, who

takes one glance at a man in *Laker* sweats and a BonerZone.com tee-shirt, with a leg shackled to a radiator, and says, "Should I bother asking?"

"Please don't," I plead.

Arnold examines the lock around Jake's ankle and traces the chain to the radiator. "I can't get the locks off. And my snips won't cut these links."

"I have to get out of here. I'm getting married at noon," Jake informs him.

Arnold stops and looks to me.

"Again," I say, "don't ask."

"I have to go to my truck."

"Truck," Kevin perks up.

"Not now, Kevin."

The clock hits eleven when Arnold returns with a wrench set, iron plugs, and a small dolly. "I can get you free, but you'll have to invite the radiator to the wedding."

"Just hurry, please," Jake begs. "I'll pay you double, triple, quadruple; just get me to the church on time."

Arnold shuts off the water, plugs the line, removes the radiator and loads it onto a dolly for easier transport. He tells me to go out and pull my car around to the base of the stairs.

I'm standing on the ground watching Kevin laugh as Arnold thumps the radiator down one stair at a time and Jake follows with the chain wrapped around his neck like a scarf. The lady who lives in the apartment beneath comes out.

"Hello, Mrs. Frobisher." Not only is she a loon, she is a loon that hates me.

"Is he chained up so he can't get away and infect the rest of Van Nuys?" she asks.

"I'd love to stay and chat, Mrs. Frobisher, but Jake has to get to his wedding."

"Who is the bride, Typhoid Mary?"

It takes some doing to get Kevin, the radiator, and the dolly into the backseat. With so much weight, the Toyota resembles a Tijuana low rider.

"Let me drive," Jake says.

I hand him the keys and hop in the front seat next to him. Jake fires it up, floors the Toyota, and it stalls. "Sorry, my NASCAR racer is in the shop."

Jake restarts and pulls out of the parking area.

"Do you have your phone?"

I take out my cell as he takes a turn way too fast. "Slow down."

"Call this number." Jake recites the number and I punch it into small keyboard.

"It's not working."

Jake passes a slow moving truck, using the bike lane on the right.

"Jake, be careful."

"Try this one." Jake gives me different digits.

I wait. The connection is made.

"Hello."

I hand Jake the phone, then put my hand on the wheel to help steer. If we get pulled over, we'll both get a ticket.

"LaRue," Jake yells into the phone.

The car swerves, another driver blows his horn.

"LaRue, it's me, Jake."

"You're not supposed to talk on the phone when you're driving," Kevin says from his seat in the back.

Jake swerves wildly around a Ford and drops the phone. A near miss.

"Slow down!"

I pick the phone off the floor. He tries to grab it, but I hold it back.

"You drive, I'll talk, but not until you slow down."

"Tell him, all wedding systems are a go. I'm on my way."

As I put the phone to my ear I hear a man screaming obscenities. I interrupt. "Jake wants you to know he's on his way to the church right now. He might not exactly look the part of the groom, but he can't wait to get married. He'll be there with bells on, sorta."

"Who the hell are you?"

"Someone who is low on cell minutes this month, so I better hang up." I pause. "And congratulations."

"What did he say?" Jake asks as I flip the phone closed.

"Welcome to the family."

CHAPTER 37

Farrin, the Maid of Honor, Stepsister

Saturday, the Wedding Day

Alyssa is a basket case.

Pudgy bags the size of soup spoons under her eyes, skin blotchy and even a couple of new wrinkles—she looks like she hasn't slept in days, probably because she hasn't.

We are at LaRue's house. It is a little after ten, the morning of all mornings.

The bridesmaids don't know what to say. Portia, the airhead, floats around the room. If Conrad was the one who gave her the Oxycontin, I'll rip his short hairs out. My mother and her mother lip-lash each other on what Alyssa should be doing. Brady says "prepare for the service," as if nothing is the matter. Doris yammers to send out a search party, find Jake, and bring him in by force if necessary. Arty and Simon, who were uninvited to the boys', before-wedding dress-up, sit in LaRue's kitchen in their tuxedos and don't say much except, "Top me off over here, would ya?"

I've been to funerals with a better vibe than what's going on here. The mood is so somber, you'd expect a dirge, regret lilies, and the smell of incense to fill the room.

The photographer, Sergio, hired to take pictures before, during, and after the wedding, flutters all over the place like a deranged butterfly, recording the wedding party's depression for posterity. He must wonder if this is an arranged marriage where the couple already hates each other and each other's parents. He's a little guy, no wedding ring, may be gay, but no ring on his right hand's fourth finger either; he's dressed totally in black, which makes him eligible for the reward of "most appropriately attired" for the occasion. You never see him come in or out of a room. He's just all of sudden there, on the floor, behind a chair, crouched over, to catch the light or to get the perfect angle. Like I said, a deranged butterfly. Makes me want to swat him. One camera hangs on his chest and another is on a strap over his shoulder. He wears aviator glasses, which is slightly odd, but I can't ever remember a photographer wearing glasses at all. Each time he takes a picture, he has to remove his specs; it must be exhausting.

With Alyssa, I have no clue what to do, say, or how to act. She never formally accepted my apology. We currently exist in a kind of truce or verbal ceasefire.

I've asked Conrad a hundred times, but all he says is, "Jake's thinking it over." I want to believe him, but I don't. I called him last night and I've called him today. He's not answering his phone. Gideon has been absent since Alyssa and Portia showed up at his porn shoot. I would have loved to have been a fly on the wall during that scene.

LaRue is livid. There are more flowers here than at a state funeral. The limos are bigger than my first apartment, and the stack of invoices Bitzy carries around is as thick as the Old Testament. Not to mention that cash is being spent hand-over-fist. Drivers, caterers, waitresses, bartenders, limo drivers all have their hands out, causing the wad of twenties in LaRue's hand to disappear like cash at a rigged Blackjack game. And this is before the wedding and the reception even begin. All for his one and only daughter, who, as I look at her again, is totally miserable.

Alyssa's in what we used to call the family room, but is now referred to as the great room. It's not too great today. She sits in front of a three-sided makeup mirror brought in by Babs the beautician, who I suspect is some distant relative of Bitzy. They have that same "I like to be around weddings, because I've never had one of my own" look about them. Alyssa has placed a framed picture of Princess Di on the table.

The rest of the female contingent including myself, are in the living room, where our dresses, shoes, veils, and whatever are laid out before us. When Shannon finds out that Alyssa subtracted one size off her gown, and gave her no choice but to squeeze in, she is going to be pissed.

I have drastically changed my appearance for the event; but stepsister doesn't mention my missing purple streaks, nose rings, and piercings.

Alyssa sits in the makeup chair, wrapped in a terrycloth robe while Babs attempts to do what I never thought I'd see—make Alyssa look good.

"You have to be positive," I tell Alyssa.

"How?"

"Think good thoughts."

"What happens if he doesn't show up?"

"We'll find a replacement."

"Short notice, don't you think?" she hollers at me.

"It was a joke."

Babs holds Alyssa's head up to re-apply blush.

"Why is this happening to me?" Alyssa cries out.

"Please," the makeup lady says, "try not to tear up again. You'll wash away your base."

"He's going to show up. He's going to be there. Don't worry."

"Call him again."

I call Conrad and, as usual, no one answers the phone.

"They're probably out, getting oiled up before the ceremony," I tell Alyssa, supposing the best scenario I can imagine.

"What, now they're gay?" Alyssa imagines a worse fate.

"Alyssa, you have to calm down and have faith."

"I don't want faith, I want my wedding day to be perfect."

Babs the beautician is ready to quit. "If you don't keep still, you're going to end up looking like Morticia from *The Addams Family*."

Portia, dressed only in push-up bra and thong, comes to us. "Anybody got a Xanax? I might have gone a little too heavy on the Oxy."

"No, I'm sorry," I tell her. "The pharmacy is closed."

"Damn."

"There might be one in my purse," Alyssa tells her.

"If there's two, I could use one," Babs says as Portia sashays to Alyssa's purse on the table.

Now, I know I could lose a few pounds here and there, but to be as thin as Portia is a crime against nature. The woman's body is like a broomstick with boobs. It's hard to figure out where the doctors found enough body to hang those two silicone sisters. Portia is past emaciated. Ribs are countable, long spindly legs are stilt-like, her neck is giraffe-narrow and her veins remind me of a river system on a Google map.

Portia empties the purse on the table, sorts the contents. "Somebody in this house has got to be holding," she says, disappointed.

"If Sly's coming to the wedding, maybe he'll have some," I say, mostly to get rid of her.

"I dumped his ass," Portia says.

"Wasn't the man of your dreams, huh?"

"You can't spend stock options."

Alyssa is flitting around in the chair. "What time is it?" she asks.

"Don't tell her," Babs says, pointing the business end of a blush brush at me. "She'll start ballin' and I'll have to start over."

"Time to get ready for the big day," I tell her.

Alyssa holds back tears. I stay by her side, holding and patting her hand.

Champagne corks pop in the other room. No amount of mimosa will calm this group, but the waitress passes them out anyway. Portia downs two, evidently her search for a Xanax was unsuccessful. I pass. I'm going to need all my wits about me during the next few hours.

Bitzy pulls me aside to re-review the plan for the umpteenth time. "You and the bridesmaids take the first limo at 11:40, and be sure that everyone has their bouquets in hand. Alyssa and LaRue will wait ten minutes and follow. The ride is exactly sixteen minutes. When you arrive at the church, meet the boys in the vestibule, don't step on the runner, wait for me. I'll start the music. The petal-toss will quiet the crowd, then you'll make your way up the aisle. Got it?"

"I not only got it, Bitzy, I got it memorized."

"Don't worry about Alyssa, she won't come out of the car until you are lined up and waiting at the altar."

"One question," I speak in hushed tones. "Is there a backup plan if the groom doesn't show?"

"In my entire career that has only happened once."

"What happened?"

"It took a while, but I got over him."

Bitzy leaves the room and house. The dressing room madness, now fueled by the slow burn of alcohol, continues. The two bridesmaids, mother, Brady, and ex-stepmother, Doris, sit at a long table, staring into mirrors, applying eye liner, lipstick, rouge, and blush. Anything to make them look just a tad better. Portia flits around, sipping her drink, smoking a cigarette. She will not allow Sergio to shoot her, and, if he tries, she sticks out her tongue, puts her hands over the lens, or flips him the bird. And this is how she makes her living?

Alyssa's face is taking longer than a Rubens painting.

"Could you smile maybe just once?" the photographer asks her, aiming his camera for a close-up.

And that does it.

Alyssa lets loose with a scream to wake the dead. "Goddammit. This isn't fair. Shit like this doesn't happen to people like me."

My stepsister erupts from the chair, grabs her cell phone, and slings it across the room, shattering into worthless electronics as it hits the wall. She rips off her plastic bib, tears it in two, and sails the pieces in my direction. "Fuck, this is MY wedding day."

Alyssa next launches a crystal vase filled with roses. That rocket hits the far wall with a major thud, but doesn't shatter, just dents the wall. It must be Waterford. "I'm supposed to be happy," she screams.

The bridesmaids, in robes and slippers, except for Portia who remains almost nude, run into the middle of the ruckus, only to back off quickly as Alyssa picks up brushes, combs, makeup, eye-liner, a bottle of astringent, assorted beauty knickknacks and a large ashtray shaped like an oak leaf; and begins slinging the items in every direction as she whirls like a crazed dervish, swearing up a storm. She's a human hurricane of anger, smacking her fists into the dresser, pulling paintings off the wall, knocking over lamps.

"Fuck, fuck, and double fuck."

I see Portia hit the deck and am not sure if she's been hit by wedding shrapnel or she's merely a coward. The photographer snaps away, darting about to get the best angles. I fear for Shannon, Babs, Brady and Doris, who cower like war victims in the corner behind a high-back chair. Someone could take a direct projectile hit and suffer permanent damage.

I have no choice. This has to end. I put my head down, push my shoulder out and lunge forward directly into the midsection of my stepsibling and spear her like an NFL linebacker. This is as close as I will ever get to playing football; and it is way too close for me.

We're on the floor. I'm holding on for dear life as Alyssa's arms flail like a spastic windmill. No one is helping. I'm on my own. I scream for her to stop, but she is a demon of destruction. My football tackle has turned into a wrestling match; all we're missing is the mud. She is kicking, hitting, and stomping, trying to get free of my grip. Unfortunately, I'm about as good at wrestling as I am at football. All I can do is hold on, keep my head down and take the punishment she's dishing out. And it hurts, it hurts bad.

She's screaming, I'm screaming, the crowd is screaming. We're rolling around the floor, tables toppling, and furniture crashing, glass breaking, as our arms and legs take out everything in reach.

"What the hell is going on?" LaRue's booming voice foghorns into the room loud enough to take the paint off the walls.

Alyssa comes to a complete stop. She is on her back. I'm facing forward pushed against her. We're both pushed against a couch, which somehow got turned over and now rested against the back wall. I feel sets of hands on my back, lifting me away from Alyssa's now-limp body. It is Arty and Simon doing the lifting.

"Wow," Arty says. "That was awesome."

"Totally hot," adds Simon.

I shake free of the two idiot step-daddies, and face Alyssa. Her hair is a tangled mess, face fire-red, mascara running down her cheeks, a demonic current of black tears. She could be the "before" picture for a discount exorcism advertisement. I take Alyssa in my arms and hold her. She weeps.

"I want to have the perfect wedding," she blubbers through her tears. "Is that all that bad?"

"I know, I know," I try to console. "It's all going to be okay."

I feel rather than see LaRue standing over the two of us, panting. When he catches his breath, he says, "I just talked to Jake…"

The room falls as silent as in the first seconds of a ceasefire.

"…he's on his way to the church."

There is a slight moment for the news to sink in, then a resounding cheer.

"He can't wait to get married," LaRue tops off the good news.

Alyssa pops up off the floor like a jack-in-the-box, uprights the makeup chair, sits back down, and pulls Babs off the floor and to her side. "Hurry."

"I'm telling you right now, I'm putting in for hazard pay for this job," the beautician says, finding a hairbrush amidst the rubble.

"Just do me," Alyssa says, "and do me quick. I'm getting married."

LaRue comes to his daughter, places his hands on her shoulders. 'Everything is going to be just fine, darlin''

"Why didn't you let me talk to him?" Alyssa asks her dad.

"You were too busy throwing things," he says.

"Plus, you're not supposed to," I say for some unknown reason. "It's tradition."

"Tell me, daddy," Alyssa pleads. "What did he say?"

"He said he'd meet you at the church."

"Did he say where the hell he's been?"

"No."

"Did he say it had something to do with those two assholes he calls friends?"

"No, dear."

"You didn't ask him?"

"Somebody else was doing the talking."

"Who?"

"I'm not sure. It was a woman," LaRue says.

"A woman?"

"Probably the limo driver," LaRue says. "What difference does it make? He's on his way to marry my lovely daughter."

"Well," Babs yells, "she's not going to be too lovely if she doesn't sit still."

From that point on, it is mass chaos; although it was pretty much chaos before, just a different brand of chaos now. The women bump heads as they lean over to check stockings for runs, horn-stretch shoes to fit, fix chipped nails, paint lips, and press lashes. Dresses are ironed one last time, yanked over heads, the zipping sounds like an angry hive of bees. Shannon "can't believe" she's put on that much weight since yesterday. The dress is so tight, she'll have no room for food at the reception. Portia gets dressed in about thirty seconds, it's nothing more than a runway change for her. She uses her extra time for another mimosa.

I do pretty much of a slapdash. Throw it on, smooth it out, hope for the best. No one is going to be looking at me anyway. What else is new? I can feel places where Alyssa whacked me and can only hope the black-and-blue marks hold off until after the ceremony. My attention is on Alyssa, who is making a miraculous transformation from belle of the brawl to belle of the ball. I admit it makes me angry that she can look so good, so easily, but it is her day and finally it is coming around, although not exactly as she had planned.

Removing her dress from the plastic, I'm stunned. Princess Di updated. The same shade of puff-ball meringue, the oval shaping, a train as long as a living room. I search in the bag for a crown or diamond-studded tiara, the only missing piece.

At 11:40, I herd the bridesmaids into the waiting limo. I take what must be Portia's fifth mimosa out of her hand before she climbs inside. "No drinking and driving."

"That's how I lost my license," she confesses.

"Go," I order the driver, before my butt hits the seat.

The limo pulls away and a wave of relief comes over me. I take a few moments, as do the others. It is as if we all need a respite, before the bell sounds for the next round.

I break the silence a few minutes before we arrive. "We all have to swear."

Shannon gives me an odd look.

I continue. "What went on in the dressing room stays in the dressing room," I pause. "Agreed?"

"Agreed," Shannon says.

"Fuck, yes," Portia says.

My eyes roll back as I shake my head at the model buffoon.

"You said we were supposed to swear."

Some idiot who can't read, refuses to read, or is too stupid to read, has parked in the reserved spot in front of the church. Then I notice it is Simon's car. Traffic sucks. The church parking lot is a tangled mess. Our limo has to go around the block, pull up on the side-street, find an opening, pull close, and stop traffic. Horns blare. Shannon and I get out, but Portia waits for the limo driver to open her door. The three of us have to walk about twenty yards to the front of the church, where the boys wait.

Conrad, in a tux, is rape-worthy. God, does he look good. "Bitzy said not to step on the carpet runner," he warns us as we approach.

Portia walks right over it to Gideon, who is also just arriving. "Hey, dude," she says.

"Hi," he says, sees her eyes and says, "or should I say really high?"

"Are you the one who gave her the Oxycontin?" I ask Conrad.

"No."

Shannon sees her husband Gary and daughter, and runs off to gush over how good Margo looks as the flower girl.

"I got to go to the potty, Mommy."

Shannon disappears with the child.

"And the groom?" I ask.

Gideon shrugs his shoulders.

"You didn't get dressed with him?"

"No."

"Is he here?"

"Should be," Conrad says.

"If he was right here, you wouldn't be asking, because you could see him," Portia says.

"He called LaRue, said he was on his way," I inform the pair.

Surprise hits Gideon's face. "He did?"

"Are you ever going to tell me what the hell is going on?" I ask Conrad.

"Probably not." Conrad checks me out closely, "You know I've never seen you un-punked. You look good, really good."

"Thank you."

A few late guests file into the already-packed church.

Bitzy comes out of nowhere. "Where the hell is Shannon?"

"She took her kid to the can," Portia says.

"Where the hell is the groom?" I ask.

"Somebody said he just showed up in the back," Bitzy answers.

"He did?" Gideon asks.

Conrad gives Gideon a very odd look.

Bitzy's cell phone buzzes. She reads the text. "We're doing this people."

Shannon and Margo return. Bitzy grabs the kid, shoves a basket of rose petals into her hands, and sends her up the aisle to sow the red runner. The instant Margo makes her first toss, the organ pipes up. The crowd quiets, turns, and tries not to get hit by falling petals aimed at their heads. It suddenly dawns on me why Alyssa had Shannon in her wedding, she wanted the perfect flower girl.

From behind me, car horns explode as Alyssa's limo stops traffic. I see LaRue get out, flip off the honkers, and help Alyssa out of the backdoor. It takes another sixty seconds before the train is all the way out of the car.

"Next," Bitzy orders.

Conrad takes Shannon by the arm and leads her up the aisle.

"You two," Bitzy says, interlacing Gideon and Portia's arms, "try not to screw this up."

I notice Gideon turn toward the approaching Alyssa. The two exchange a hate-filled, piercing glance.

"Go," Bitzy sends them on her way.

"You look beautiful," I mouth the words to Alyssa on her way up the walkway, and I'm not lying. She looks gorgeous.

Bitzy pulls me onto the carpet, fluffs my hair, straightens my dress, and adjusts the flowers in my hands. The music changes to Pachelbel's "Canon in D Major." She gives me a slight push, and I begin my trek up the center aisle.

I smile for the videographer recording the event, and Sergio, who juggles his glasses while rifling off shots faster than Billy the Kid. When I do look up, my first revelation is the absence of a groom waiting at the altar. I search left, right, and who do I see in the very last pew, just behind a pillar… is that Johnny "Buck" Vierra?

What the hell is that slime ball doing here? What is he planning on doing, rapping on the glass with his fists, yelling "Alyssa, Alyssa" from the choir loft?

Up the aisle I go. The guests all smile, some say "hello," a couple women have tears in their eyes. I am halfway to the altar and still no groom. This is not good.

I pass by the second pew where the mothers stand. Their respective husbands sway like tipsy trees in a breeze.

As I reach the altar rail, the organ music stops.

I stand with the girls on the left, the boys on the right. Minister Francis O'Grady comes out the side door, walks to us, and stands between me and Gideon.

"Still missing someone, are we not?" I whisper to the pastor.

"Oh, he's here, all right. He's definitely here."

A trumpet wails. The *Trumpet Voluntary* melodically fills the airspace. So traditional. So Alyssa. Every eye turns to the back of the church as our very own princess steps up and into the aisle. She is on her way to becoming queen. Her arm is interlaced with LaRue's. They make an impressive pair. Each guest is staring in awe of her beauty and grace. I can see her smile through her thin veil. Alyssa was made for this moment.

Alyssa and LaRue are about halfway up the aisle, when a commotion is heard off to the side. From the same door from which the minister emerged comes Jake limping out, barefoot, wearing a blue and gold pair of silky sweats with *LAKERS* going up the side. On his upper body he wears a black sport coat at least three sizes too small, over a Kelly green, tee-shirt, which has BonerZone.com scrawled across the front. His hair is a greasy mess, and his face is like dirty Astroturf; but what is most noticeable is the chain attached to his leg, with several links wrapped around his neck like a dog collar. If this sight isn't enough of a shock, what follows is enough to create imagery overload. A woman and a young boy are walking behind Jake. The woman maneuvers a dolly with a three-foot hunk of iron, which appears, but can't possibly be… a radiator?" The small boy helps hoist the chain, though he struggles with its weight. The whole thing is surreal, like a prison gang packing a different kind of heavy heat.

Due to the angle and the flabbergast of guests standing, oohing and aahing, Alyssa doesn't see Jake. She walks with her head down for that pious effect, but when the trumpet stops mid-note and LaRue booms out, "What the hell?" Alyssa's eyes rise to see her future husband looking like Jesus on a chain gang. She freezes along with the rest of the congregation, except Portia who asks, "Cool outfit. Is it European?"

Alyssa lets out a shriek which, I swear, shakes the stained glass windows. Under her veil, I can see her face contort into a grimace of rage. She shakes violently, and, I swear again, I can hear her knees knocking under layers of meringue.

All that can stop Alyssa is Jake coming down the aisle, hands raised, making a loud plea, "Don't Alyssa, not in your condition."

Guests' eyes rivet back and forth between the intended like they are fans at a tennis match. LaRue has gone slack-jawed. I've never seen him at a loss for words. Brady and Doris fan themselves to keep from fainting. Bitzy collapses in a back pew and no one in the entire church could care less. It is a moment of absolute shock and awe.

Breaking the mood is Arty's question to Simon. "I thought the chains go on after the ceremony?"

Jake struggles down the center aisle, stops, and announces to the crowd, "I had a little trouble arriving, but I'm here and I'm here to get married. So, let's do this."

No one argues. In fact, no one says a word. Now I know the true meaning of "stunned."

Jake continues down the aisle, leading his radiator entourage, and stands in front of Alyssa and LaRue. "Sorry for my appearance, but I made it." He shakes LaRue's hand. "I promise I'll take good care of her and our family." He pulls Alyssa's veil back.

Alyssa's face is a mask of frightened disbelief. One touch and it would shatter into a million tears. She's fallen into a state of somnambulistic shock. Her brain must be completely boggled to take in all this on top of the last several days.

Jake puts his hand on her tummy. "You are making me the happiest person on the face of the earth." I hear him tell her.

Jake takes her by the hand and leads her up to where O'Grady waits. "Go ahead, Father, marry us."

I recognize the dolly lady is Kay from the rehearsal dinner, who parallel parks the radiator close to the altar rail. As Jake passes by her, she stops him, removes the chain necklace from around his neck and lays it on the floor next to where he is going to stand. "You can take it from here," she says. "Congratulations."

"Thank you," Jake tells her and says to the boy, "I'll be in touch about the truck ride."

"You promised," the kid responds.

Kay takes the boy by the hand and exits out the door they entered.

"Dearly beloved, we are gathered together…"

"Wait," Jake interrupts the pastor. "Get over here," he says to Gideon and points to his ankle.

Gideon kneels down and spins the dial on Jake's leg. The tumblers click, the lock opens and Jake is no longer a member of the chain gang.

Gideon rises to come face to face with Jake, "I'm sorry," he says.

"No, you're not," Jake tells him.

The activity seems to snap Alyssa out of her trance. She takes one step back and one step to the side. "Gideon," she says, causing him to turn his body and attention to her.

"What?"

Alyssa shifts her bouquet from right to left hand, makes a fist and, not making her previous bitch-slap mistake, throws an Olympic worthy, uppercut smack into Gideon's crotch.

Gideon collapses into a fetal heap of misery, holding his bruised and swelling jewels, moaning in absolute pain and suffering.

Alyssa calmly moves back into position, and smiles up at Jake.

"Thanks," Jake says, smiling back. "He needed that."

The guests, wedding party, even Portia, are beyond incredulous. We all stand motionless, mouths as wide as airplane hangars, muscles droopy, and all eyes riveted on the takedown of Alyssa's low blow TKO.

"Okay, Padre, let's get this party started," Jake orders.

Minister O'Grady clears his throat, opens his prayer book and re-begins. "Dearly beloved, we are gathered together to join Jake and Alice in holy matrimony."

"Alice?" Jake pipes up. "Who's Alice?"

"I had to use my real name to make it official," Alyssa explains.

Portia slaps Shannon on her arm and says, "I knew that."

"You've never told me your real name?" Jake asks, clearly surprised.

"I was going to get it legally changed."

"Why?"

"I hate the name Alice."

"No, why didn't you tell me?"

"Because I hate the name Alice."

"Go ahead," Jake says.

"To join Jake and Alice, slash Alyssa, in holy matrimony."

Jake can't keep his eyes off Alyssa. He seems to be searching her face, eyes and neck as if he's searching for a blemish. She has a hard time looking directly at him; and I can't say I blame her. His scruffy beard is going to carve furrows in Babs' foundation work. His breath is awful. I can smell his sweat from here. His sweats and tee-shirt combo is atrocious. The sleeves of the jacket only go half way down his wrists. Homeless people dress better. Actually, much better. If the video ever makes the Internet, Jake and Alice/Alyssa will be a You Tube sensation.

"Marriage is the most sacred rite in the eyes of the Lord. It is based on trust, honesty, fidelity, and love. These fundamentals must form into unbreakable bonds for the marriage to prosper and succeed."

Jake interrupts, "Could you skip all the hyperbole and get this over with? I want to get cleaned up before the reception."

"No problem."

Evidently, the minister can't wait, either.

"Rings, please."

Gideon's one hand leaves his squashed lemons, he reaches into a pocket and lifts two small cases upward to the minister, groaning with the long stretch.

"Please face each other."

Alyssa and Jake turn and look into each other's eyes.

"Do you Alice and-or Alyssa take Jake to be your lawfully wedded husband?"

"I do," she says, sliding the wedding band onto Jake's finger.

"And do you, Jake…"

Jake takes her hand into his. He is close enough to kiss her.

"…, take Alice/Alyssa as your lawfully wedded wife?"

Jake pauses, as if he is seeing something for the first time. He backs off just a bit. "Is that a rash?"

"What?" Alyssa says.

"Is that a rash?" Jake repeats.

"What are you talking about?" Alyssa asks.

"On your neck, your skin looks funny."

Awkward pause would be an understatement, even during this

ceremony.

O'Grady harrumphs. "There is a question on the table, do you take…"

Jake turns to his groomsman. "Conrad, look at this."

Conrad, who has remained totally cool and collected through the entire debacle, shifts over, takes one look at Alyssa, nods to Jake. "Yep, Aunt Scarlett's making her monthly visit."

Jake takes a step back. "You're not pregnant are you?" he asks Alyssa, loud enough for the entire congregation to hear.

Alyssa pauses, swallows hard, jerks a bit and says, "No."

"Did you say you were pregnant just to get me here?"

Alyssa's eyes leave Jake's and peer down, as low as she can look. "I didn't know what else to do."

Jake takes another step back and glances at his best man writhing on the floor, then at Conrad, and finally back to the minister. "The answer to your question, sir, is, No, I don't."

O'Grady slaps his prayer book closed. "Well, that wraps this up." He signals the choir loft and the organist pipes up the Wedding March. "You can kiss, if you want. Me, I need a doobie."

Jake limps slowly to the side door and exits. Alyssa does a 180 to see the horrified looks on the faces of the three hundred guests. She waits about a nanosecond and then takes off running down the center aisle, as if a gun went off to start the hundred-yard dash.

I take chase, but slip on a clump of rose petals near the back set of pews. As I struggle to get to my feet, I see Alyssa leaping into the limo followed by Buck Vierra, who jumps in behind her and slams the door. The limo takes off with about fifteen feet of train flapping in the wind.

I rise, turn back around. All eyes are on me. Some guests are standing on their pews to get a better view. Some have moved into the aisle to see around others. Some faces are pasty white, others heart-failure red. No one is laughing or crying or talking. The music has stopped. A few rows up, two feet protrude onto the runner, like the wicked witch of the east in the Oz story. The female torso attached to the legs is scrunched on the floor of the pew. I recognize the sensible shoes and know its Bitzy. The body is jerking a bit, so she is either dead with post-mortem muscle-twitches, or suffering a well-deserved nervous breakdown. Her spasms are about the only human movement in the congregation.

I reach down and pick up the bouquet Alyssa dropped on her mad dash down the aisle. I bunch it in two hands, then fling it skyward, as if I were the bride tossing the bouquet. A hot, young girl I have never seen before leaps up to catch it, then falls into the arms of her sugar-daddy boyfriend. She plants a kiss on his lips. If Bitzy revives soon enough, she should give the couple her business card.

At the altar, the entire wedding party is on the steps, sitting around Gideon, who is finally breathing a little easier, though still holding onto his marbles. The group resembles a formal dance band on break. I make my way slowly towards them, but stop at LaRue, who sits, elbows on knees, his head in his hands, like it's some great weight. Marge is next to him. She gives me a happy face and a wave. What an idiot! I tap LaRue on the shoulder, he peers up. "It would have been a very beautiful service," I say softly. "But, ya know, LaRue, shit happens."

He nods in agreement.

My mother comes out of her pew, "You looked lovely, dear, so feminine without those nose rings."

"Gee, thanks, Mom, hearing that from you, means so much to me."

I step inside the communion rail. "Anybody want a drink?"

Three hands rise. I turn back around and walk straight to step daddy and Simon. "I know one of you has got some, so hand it over."

Arty reaches into his back pocket and produces a half pint. "Salud!"

Back with the wedding party, we swig and share, except Shannon, who takes off toward her kid and husband. "I can't wait to get out of this dress," she says.

Portia pulls out a joint from her bra. "Anybody got a light?"

The guests are filing out. I hear their comments: "She was exquisite." "Didn't know Jake was such a big *Laker* fan?" and "I'm surprised she could run so fast in that dress."

Portia uses one of the altar candles to light the joint, she inhales twice, passes it around once; then she and Minister O'Grady bogart the remainder. "I thought it was totally rad," is her summation of the event.

"This could make a great movie," Gideon manages to say

through his pain.

"No one would believe it," Conrad answers.

"Me," I say, watching Sergio take one last shot, "I can't wait to see the wedding album."

CHAPTER 38

Jake

The only person I told was my mother.

She didn't have much to say, although she did have some questions: "Who are you?" "What's the matter with the name Alice?" "Wasn't the radiator hot?" And one comment, "I never pay more than one-fifty-nine for asparagus."

I got lucky after leaving my wedding. I stepped out into the street without looking both ways and almost got run over by a garbage truck. How ironic. Next, a yellow cab skidded to a stop not less than an inch from my bruised leg, and instead of screaming at the driver who was screaming at me, I got in the back and gave him my address.

At home, the first things I did were to shower, shave, and soak my sore ankle. It immediately started to feel better. I wish the rest of me could have followed suit. After I cleaned up, I cried and cursed, ate cheap pizza, wasted hours on the Internet, slept most of the day, and watched horrible TV and movies all night. Being dead to the world seemed fitting.

I deleted all emails before reading, didn't open my snail mail, and after days not answering my phone, it finally quit ringing. People came and knocked on the door, but I wouldn't answer, no matter what they said, how much they pleaded, or how long they stayed. You can wait out anybody if you have enough patience.

In the mornings I was mad as hell at Gideon and Conrad for what they did. By the afternoons, I was thankful. It is not that I didn't want to talk to them or wouldn't talk to them, or that I never wanted to talk to them again; I simply couldn't come up with what I wanted to say. Confused to the max, I hated and loved them at the same time, wanted to high-five with my right hand and strangle them with my left, make them feel terrible for ruining my life, but thank them for saving it.

Time is a funny thing when you're miserable. It creeps by second by second, moving slower than a sick sea slug, but in retrospect, time zips by faster than a shark on a lunch run. All I knew is that I needed time, the "how much" was the mystery.

I thought about my mom, LaRue, his wives, their husbands. I couldn't picture Conrad and Farrin being an item, obviously a knee-jerk reaction to his non-acceptance of Alyssa and me. I considered writing Gideon a note congratulating him on his decision to leave porn and chase his dream to become a real filmmaker; but rejected the idea due to an absence of a postage stamp.

The person I didn't think of much was Alyssa. How strange. Like the minister's book slapping shut in church, her chapter in my life was now closed, and I saw no real reason to open it up. At times I felt bad, because I didn't feel badly about her. I didn't feel anything. I certainly should have, the biggest day of her life was an unmitigated disaster. Her dream turned into a living nightmare, though not as tragic as Princess Diana's. Life goes on.

I thought a lot about Kay and Kevin. Was Kay still doing guys on camera? Was Kevin sitting by the telephone, waiting to hear the date and time of his big truck ride? Did she get her radiator returned? Did Gideon and Conrad pay for her stint as a jailer? Would she claim the money on her income taxes?

I like Kay. She is the epitome of the pure woman in an impure world.

Mostly my brain turned on the topic of Jake Dombrowski. The unmarried, unemployed, almost broke, miserable Jake Dombrowski. I felt bipolar, although I have no clue or understanding of what a bipolar existence would be like. On one extreme, I was glad it happened. Alyssa wasn't the woman for me. Yeah, it would have been an ego trip having her hanging on my arm, the envy of every guy at the party; but that would have faded quickly. Her understanding and definition of marriage is so far from mine, but we would have made a disastrous couple, which probably wouldn't have bothered her in the least. Alyssa would be perfectly satisfied to live a life where she could buy what she desired, live in her perfect house, drive her new Mercedes, have her kids, pick her friends and do whatever captured her fancy for the day. A husband to Alyssa would be merely another item on the shelf, an acquisition taken down when she needed it, and ignored when she didn't. Alyssa will forget me quickly, but the memory of the event will take years to recede into her past. I don't hate her, or myself for that matter.

I miss my job. Garbage and I worked well together. I long for trying to communicate with the Mexicans, the sound of aluminum cans being crushed, and glass being shattered. There is a consistency to trash, because no matter what happens in our lives, what successes or disasters befall us, there will always be trash left for someone to come along and pick up.

One afternoon, weeks into my odyssey of idleness, I awaken and decide it is time to make good on my promise. I make the call. The next day, Kay follows in her Toyota as a very excited Kevin and I lead the way in the Volvo.

"Truck, big truck," he must repeat it a hundred times.

The empty garbage trucks were coming back into the yard as we pull in. A number of workers come over and greet me, take off their gloves to shake my hand. I hope they're saying how much they miss me, but I'm not sure.

LaRue must have heard the ruckus from inside his office and comes out into the yard. As he approaches the three of us, I toss him the keys to the Volvo.

"I figured you wouldn't want to see me, but you'd want the car back."

"You finally got something right," he says.

"You remember Kay from the rehearsal dinner?"

LaRue nods, "Of course."

"This is her son, Kevin."

LaRue reaches down to shake the small hand. "Nice to meet you."

We stand around a few seconds, wait for the each other to start speaking.

This is uncomfortable.

"You hear the whole story?" I finally ask him.

"You cost me a shitload of money," he answers.

"Don't swear around Kevin, LaRue."

"Sorry."

"You know, LaRue," I say, at least trying to make him feel better, "you're lucky I didn't take the Dombrowski money in advance. You'd be out a heck of a lot more."

LaRue tries to give me a dirty look, but can't. Best he can do is shake his head back and forth. He'll never admit it, but LaRue likes me.

"Alyssa's in Paris," he says, as if I deserve or should know.

"A honeymoon minus the groom."

"She went with some guy I used to hate."

"Oh."

Kevin tugs at my hand, pulls me to him and whispers in my ear.

"Before I disappear forever, LaRue, I have a favor to ask."

"I don't have any more money," he says.

I tell him my wish and nod my head toward Kevin.

He points. "Take number nineteen. It has a full cab."

I smile. LaRue is a pretty good guy.

Kevin almost jumps out of his own skin, as I point to Walworth #19.

"Thanks," Kay says to LaRue. "You have no idea what this means to him."

"Enjoy," LaRue says to Kevin. "Good luck," he says to me.

LaRue and I shake hands for the last time.

I drive, Kay rides shotgun, Kevin between us. We go around the block six times, stop in a vacant lot, get out, and I teach Kevin to pull the lever for the scoop to go up and back.

He's thrilled. If only everything in life could be this easy, exciting, and rewarding.

After another few trips around the block, my Disney Garbageland ride is over and I drive back into the yard. I park the truck in the wash line, turn off the engine, and help Kay, then Kevin, out of the cab. Kevin wraps his arms around my neck and won't let go, his way of saying thanks.

Kevin falls asleep in the Toyota on the way back to my place, sensory overload, no doubt.

"What are you going to do?" Kay asks.

"Right now?"

"Yeah."

"Go inside my apartment, eat cold pizza, and feel sorry for myself."

"Really?"

"I'm quite good at it. I've had plenty of practice."

"How about with the rest of your life?"

"I'm not sure." I pause. "How about you?"

"I'm not sure either, but I'm no longer doing what I used to do."

I smile and wink, my subtle manner of applauding her decision. "What's your next career move?" I ask.

"Cleaning houses."

"Good for you."

We travel a few more miles in silence.

"I wouldn't mind staying in garbage," I tell her as I point to my apartment building up on the left. "I like trash."

"That's nice."

She stops the Toyota in front of my building. We sit in the car with the engine running. Kay keeps her hands on the steering wheel and her eyes forward, as if we're still in traffic.

My fingers find the door handle, but don't pull.

Kevin stirs in the backseat.

"My place is really filthy," I confess. "I could use a cleaning lady."

"Can you afford one?"

"No, but that doesn't mean I don't want one."

There is an awkward silence.

"I have some cold pizza," I say, "if you'd like to come in for dinner."

"What's on it?" she asks.

"Everything, except anchovies."

"Good," Kay says. "I hate anchovies."

"Me, too."

THE END

WHUPPED TOO has arrived!

Jake, Gideon, Alyssa, Farrin, and all the whupped ones from WHUPPED are back in action, as their stories continue to collide in unpredictable hilarity and heartfelt emotion in the sequel to the first book.

Get a taste of what's coming in the following "WHUPPED TOO" chapters.

CHAPTER 1

Farrin, Ex Maid of Honor

Every woman in this place is gorgeous. I feel like a Big Mac at a vegan buffet.

They're looking at me wondering when I'll be called up to the stage and introduced as the winner of the grand prize drawing for *The Complete New You*, which includes a new set of breasts, liposuction for life, and thigh gap therapy.

"Oh, thank you so much, The Southern California Plastic Surgeons Society, for making all my dreams come true." I'll gush my appreciation to the five-hundred assembled guests. "I can't wait to look like all the rest of the women in this room— perfect!" Then I'll shed a few tears, blow my nose into my hand, and wipe the snot with a hunk of my dirty, tangled hair.

Oh, God, gag me before I gag myself.

What as Conrad thinking when he invited me to this opulent, self-congratulatory, medical celebrity, wing ding? Does he want all his contemporaries to see, in person, the *before* picture of his greatest challenge? He could be seated next to a babe with perfect set of *C* cups, a twenty-two-inch waist, long blond tresses, whiter than white teeth, and a butt so tight you could bounce a quarter off it, but he invites me. What was he thinking?

I glance around the room. There are enough diamonds sparkling in the crowd to rival the Aurora Borealis. The unwrinkled women wearing these diamonds, whether they are married, single, divorced, or digging for gold, all share a similar beauty. Their hair is perfect, smooth skin radiant, eyes clear, breasts firm, and bodies taught. The adoring looks upon their faces, as they watch Conrad's every move, tell me they also share one distinct feeling and desire concerning my date for this evening: "I'd fuck this guy in a New York minute."

And I'm here, seated at the #1 table? I should be at the tucked away table in the back of the room with the other pudgies, saggers, and muffin toppers, who sit stretching their ugly necks to glimpse the beautiful people in front of them. But lo and behold, I'm right next to Conrad, who wears a perfectly fitted tuxedo, and looks even better than he did at Alyssa's wedding, when he looked fabulous. This should be my Cinderella evening, but I feel more like the uglier of her two ugly stepsisters. Even a pair of Jimmy Choo glass slippers wouldn't help my cause.

I won't let myself believe Conrad loves me, but he must feel something or he wouldn't have brought me here tonight. On the reverse side of that coin, I'm hopelessly in love with the guy. At first I was merely totally infatuated, but now I can't get him out of my head. I think about him constantly. When I'm trying to work, the thought of his touch comes into my brain and I either drop the brush or spill my palette. In the shower, I have to relieve myself when I picture his naked body. The only way I can get to sleep (alone) is to clutch an oversized pillow between my knees and arms. The last time I felt like this I was seventeen and in love with bad boy Danny Therhume, but in retrospect, those feelings could've been the result of the constant cloud of marijuana smoke, which acted as the glue in our relationship.

How did I ever get to be the lucky one?

Besides being smart, rich, accomplished, handsome, and rock hard, Conrad exists on a plane above all others. Nothing seems to faze the guy. At Alyssa's wedding when my bridezilla step-sister uppercuts best man, Gideon, in his family jewels, and lays him out like a flopping out-of-water flounder, Conrad hardly batted an eyelash. And when Jake, at the altar looking like Jesus on a bad hair day, right before he's supposed to say "I do," asks Conrad if Alyssa is on her period; he merely says, "Yep, Aunt Scarlet's reading her meter right now."

No wonder Conrad's getting the award tonight.

"Ladies and gentlemen, welcome to the SCPSS's Annual Nip and Tuck Ball."

The chattering ceases, the event begins.

"I'm Dr. Lionel Scapaletta and a funny thing happened to me on my way to the Beverly Hills Hotel..."

Doctors are rarely trained in the art of public speaking and this guy is no exception. He tries a few jokes that don't work, segues into all the do-gooder stuff the association is doing, which is pretty much self-serving bullshit, and finally gets to the important matter at hand.

"Tonight, it gives me great pleasure to announce this year's Plastic Surgeon of the Year award."

Applause.

Conrad doesn't break a smile.

"Never has a surgeon come so far so fast in our field of medicine. He has rocketed his way to the forefront of stem cell tummy tucking, has pioneered new techniques for labiaplasty, and is blazing new ground in bingo wing brachioplasty surgery."

Applause, applause.

"A surgeon so sure with his hands, he could perform a left and right eyelid transplant simultaneously."

Applause, applause, applause.

"Ladies and gentlemen, I give you the Southern California Plastic Surgeon of the Year, Dr. Conrad Blaine."

Standing ovation.

Conrad rises from his chair, and his tuxedo magically un-wrinkles as he pushes away from the table. He smiles to the applauding attendees, gives them a nod, and makes his way onto the stage. As he approaches the podium the emcee hands Conrad the Gold Sculpture Award, a solid gold scalpel encased in clear liquid plastic, mounted on a tiny operating table. The inscription reads: *A Cut Above the Rest.*

Conrad, holding his trophy in his right hand, speaks slowly and assuredly into the microphone. "I am humbled and flattered to be accepting this award. Thank you very much."

Short, sweet, and to the point. No one could have said it better.

When the final ovation dies down and the guests sit, the emcee ends the evening with a reminder for all to pay their yearly dues. The house lights come up. The older doctors with older wives head for the exits. The older docs with younger wives, the ugly doctors with the good-looking wives, and the rest of the crowd head for the bar to offer their personal congratulations to the man of the evening. The crowd hovers around Conrad. Beautiful women form the first circle, gushing their good wishes as if he just won the Super Bowl. Not only could Conrad go to Disneyworld, but he could take all these women with him.

I try to hold my ground somewhere near my date, but that proves more difficult than playing solitaire in a windstorm. I feel like a pinball being simultaneously bumped by every bumper on its way to thirty-seven free games, as I'm jostled in the crowd of adoring maidens to their god. The women all want to touch him, and not just lay a hand on his sleeve. They're tapping his cheek, rubbing the back of his neck, or sliding a breast or two up his arm or torso. Fellow docs are slapping his back, and medical salesmen push their business cards into Conrad's hand as if they were tips to parking lot valets.

And Conrad takes this all like a politician amongst his most ardent supporters. He's gentle to the women, humble to his contemporaries, and cordial to the salesmen. The smile never leaves his face. He's as calm, cool, and collected as a guru in the midst of meditation.

How could any woman not fall in love with this guy?

"Congratulations, Conrad," I say as we start home riding in his new Maserati. "You should be very proud."

"I guess I've come a long way from a wiseass kid in St. Theresa Grammar School."

"Yes, I'd say so."

"If I didn't say it before," he says, "you look very nice this evening, Farrin."

I'm no idiot. What he's saying is, "Thanks for leaving the piercings and nose ring out, going easy on the black eye makeup, and adding only one streak of purple to your hair."

"Thank you, Conrad," I tell him.

There is a short pause as we head down Sunset towards the ocean. "Conrad, I have to ask you one question."

"Go ahead."

"What the hell are you doing with me?"

"What do you mean, Farrin?" He's being polite.

"I don't hold a candle to any of those women. I don't even hold a matchstick to them. They're all gorgeous. They're perfect. They're the reason Darwin came up with his theory."

"You're being too hard on yourself."

"I'm being honest."

"And that's one thing I like about you, Farrin."

"Oh come on, Conrad. You can't tell me you aren't attracted to these women?"

Conrad chuckles; he's enjoying this conversation. "Those women are for sex, Farrin, not conversation." He pauses. "Unless it's a conversation about sex."

"And where does that leave me?"

"In the challenge category."

"What? You want to climb me like Everest? See how long you can hold your breath? Try for the Guinness record for being mismatched?"

"You have qualities I admire, Farrin. Although often hidden behind your punk façade, you have diamonds waiting to be polished."

I pause before speaking. "I'm not sure if that's a compliment."

"I assure you it is."

"Do you love me?" I ask.

"Like a summer's day." He quotes Shakespeare. Could this guy be any more perfect?

I spend the night in his penthouse condo.

It is mind-boggling to believe, but sex with Conrad keeps getting better and better.

I'm whupped.

CHAPTER 2

Jake, Unemployed ex-Groom

Living in LA without a car is cruel and unusual punishment. I walk three blocks and have to wait fifteen minutes for the bus. Once aboard, I go twelve minutes and get off at the train station. I take the Expo-line downtown, where I wait another ten minutes to transfer to the Purple Line, which gets me to Union Station, where I have to walk across a mile of terra cotta floor, and wait to transfer to the Gold Line, which will take me to the San Gabriel Valley, where I finally get off, exit the elevated station, and stand at another bus stop to wait for the bus to get me three blocks away from Sunset City.

All this to go see my mother, who won't have a clue about who I am when I finally arrive.

"Hi, Mom. How you feeling?"

"You're not from the gas company, are you?"

"No, Mom, I'm your son. Remember, you birthed me twenty-eight years ago?"

"I think there is a problem with my meter," she tells me.

Actually, she's pretty good today. No mismatched shoes, her hair is somewhat brushed, and her fingernails don't look like they let her play in the litter box again.

"Did you get to go on the field trip yesterday, Mom?"

Each week the Sunset City staff herds the Alzheimer's patients together, jams them onto the company bus, which takes off to visit a local garden, museum, historical venue, or other point of interest. In the Sunset brochure, they make a big deal out of these weekly excursions, but the reality is, the bus never stops. It just rides out one way for an hour, gets to its destination, turns around, and rides back. Nobody ever gets off, goes anywhere, or visits anyplace. Oddly enough, none of the patients seem to mind. They must love it because they stay calm as they peer out the window at places and things they have seen a million times before, but seeing them now as if it's the first time.

"I can't remember," Mom says, an understatement in its finest form.

Back when I drove a company car, I would pile Mom in and get her out of the place. We'd go visit some of our old haunts, drive by the house we used to rent, past my grammar school, and to the graveyard where my Dad waited for her to join him.

Every-so-often on these memory flogger sojourns, she comes out with a comment that is not only lucid, but also touching.

"I always knew you would make good, Jake. You could always feel what other people were feeling."

"Thanks, Mom."

She then she goes on to talk about the price of asparagus.

Now during my weekly visits, we're left to sit outside on the patio, by the pool, in the depressing day room, or in her room, which she shares with another woman, who also doesn't know if it is six o'clock or Wednesday.

Today, we're outside. I tell her I never did get married. Instead, I was hijacked by my two ex-best friends, who thought they knew my future wife better than I knew her. I also tell her I'm unemployed, broke, lost my car, and have been eating spaghetti and hot dogs to stay alive. I leave out the part about me becoming pretty much a miserable recluse.

Mom tells me, "Dan Quail will make a great president."

"I'm sure he will, Mom, I'm sure he will."

I can only take about two hours of this. If I was feeling depressed before I got here, I'm pretty much suicidal as I get up to leave.

"Excuse me, Mr. Dombrowski."

Ah, oh. It's Mrs. Futtz, the accountant, comptroller, and Simon Legree trained collector of past due bills.

"Mrs. Futtz, how nice to see you."

"There seems to be a slowdown in your monthly payments."

"Really?"

"And it seems to be getting slower day by day."

This conversation always begins in the absurd; and this isn't the first time the topic has been discussed.

"I have to be honest with you, Mrs. Futtz." I'm lying and she knows I'm lying. "I am in the process of re-assembling my assets, so I can reap the maximum tax benefits before I liquidate."

"And when can I expect payment for your mother's care from this liquidation?"

"I'll ask my financial advisor the next time we meet."

"And when will that be?"

"Soon."

She gives me the same hard stare she gives me at the end of all these conversations. It's a stare that could melt eyeballs.

I'm not sure she knows that I know the way this all works. In California there is a law, which states that once admitted to a facility such as Sunset City, a patient can't be kicked out for non-payment. The facility can take her Social Security, any pension and assets she might have, and convert those into cash, but they can't throw her out into the street. Sunset already gets her Social Security, which is the only asset she has, but it's obviously not enough.

What Mrs. Futtz wants is the extra money I pay to give my Mom the next level of care. If I quit paying the overage, Mom will be back wearing two different shoes and sitting in a wet Depend all day. I'm stalling, trying to keep Mom dry until I can get another job or sell my bovine gas idea to a venture capital firm.

"How about if I give you a partial payment to show my goodwill in this matter, Mrs. Futtz?"

Before she can ask me for the amount, I pull out my wallet, find the one folded up check I keep for emergencies, take her pen from her clipboard, and start writing.

She waits.

I hand her the check with the brightest smile I can muster.

"Fifty bucks?" she says with her cold stare morphing into disgusted disbelief.

"From the little acorn grew the mighty oak."

***

The biggest event of my day is the arrival of the mailman. Is this pathetic or what?

In this age of the computer no one sends letters, cards, or first class mail anymore; that's why email was invented. Today, our mailboxes are filled with circulars, ads, come-ons, subscription offers, cable and phone deals, and coupons for stuff you can't afford or never need. The majority of the mailers are addressed to Resident, Homeowner, or Poor Schmuck. The only other mail you receive are bills or letters from the government.

So, what do I do every day when I see the mailman coming up the walk to my apartment building? I take off down the stairs like Ursain Bolt. I am waiting and praying for two pieces of government correspondence. The second is a notice to appear for jury duty, which would be a great reason to get out of this apartment for a few days. The first is a check from the Unemployment Office with a corresponding letter, granting me full benefits, which aren't full enough to pay even half my bills. When I went and applied for unemployment, I filled out the form, took it to the window, where the bored-to-death clerk checked my checked boxes, then re-asked me if I was laid off or quit. "I was fired," I answered without hesitation. She then stamped some stamp on the form, put it in her out box, and announced, "Next."

I've been waiting weeks for my first check.

Today, the envelope arrives. I take it out of the mailman's hands before he slips it into my cubbyhole, and tear it open.

No check.

It's a letter stating: *Upon contacting ex-employer, La Rue Walworth from the Walworth Recycling Company, the reason for leaving listed was a failure to report to work for an extended period of time, and not a firing or lay-off. Your request for full benefits has been denied and you should re-report to the nearest office to refile your claim.*

What? This can't be. I need that money. My rent's due. I'm so broke I can't afford tap water.

What the hell is he telling these people? LaRue knows I got kidnapped. It wasn't my fault I couldn't get to work. I was chained to a radiator for a week. I'm a victim of circumstances, not a guy trying to scam the Unemployment Office. There's no way I can live on the second-tier payments. The amount of money is a hell of a lot less for a guy who quits, compared to a guy who gets canned. What am I going to do?

After all the poverty I've been through in my life, you'd think I'd be good at this.

Thank you for reading *Whupped*. I certainly hope you enjoyed my novel, and if you did, please let others know of your good reading fortune. The easiest way being through cyberspace, via social media networks, such as Amazon, Facebook, Linkedin, Goodreads.com and Twitter. Please put out a good review to your friends and contacts, it will be greatly appreciated.

About Jim Stevens

Jim Stevens was born in the East, grew up in the West, schooled in the Northwest, and spent twenty-three winters in the Midwest. He has been an advertising copywriter, playwright, filmmaker, stand-up comedian, and television producer.

Contact him at JimStevensWriter@gmail.com

By Jim Stevens

WHUPPED

WHUPPED TOO

HELL NO, WE WON'T GO, A Novel of Peace, Love, War, and Football

Also by Jim Stevens

(The Richard Sherlock Whodunit Series)

The Case of the NOT-SO-FAIR-TRADER

The Case of MOOMAH'S MOOLAH

The Case of TIFFANY'S EPIPHANY

The Case of MR. WONDERFUL

The Case of the WOEBEGONE WIDOW

The Case of the MISSING MILK MONEY

And Coming Soon

Bundle of Joy

www.ingramcontent.com/pod-product-compliance
Lightning Source LLC
Chambersburg PA
CBHW030036180626
46810CB00001B/394